MW00942570

I'll Die For You

By

Joseph A. Sheppard

Disclaimer

This is a work of fiction. The events described here are imaginary. The settings and characters are fictitious. They are not intended to represent specific places, businesses, events or persons even when a real name may be used or events actually occurred. The publisher does not have any control over and does not assume any responsibility for author or third-part websites or their contents.

ISBN-13 978-1511641791

ISBN-10 1511641797

Table of Contents

Author's Introduction

Afterwards

Author's Introduction

It was the summer of 1989, when my brother and his wife moved into a little brick home in South Carolina on the outskirts of Gibson, North Carolina. I looked across a field behind my brother's newly acquired residence and saw a huge structure. Trees, bushes, and vines had grown up all around it, causing it to be obscured from plain site.

Being the curious boy I was, I proceeded to jump the ditch and eagerly made my way to the building. My imagination went wild. I stumbled upon a cotton gin, perhaps from the 1800's. My curiosity grew as I saw another structure off to my right. I went over to investigate. The building appeared to be a slave house or possibly a smoke house for curing meat. I explored a bit further and saw the remnants of a house that had been burned down. Within the rubble, there was a large fireplace and brick steps that at one time may have led to a grand front porch. I thought to myself, 'I bet this was a magnificent old home.' It was probably similar to the mansion portrayed in the movie "Gone with the Wind", a favorite of my mom and sister. I was only 5 years old when I first watched the film, but I remember it well. My mind's eye recollected the plantation. I visualized the ground I was standing upon as the homestead in the movie. I've used this occasion and several other memories from my youth as resources for this book.

One childhood memory in particular came from a conversation with a dear friend, Beacham McDougald. Mr. McDougald took me to a church outside the small community of Sneads Grove, North Carolina. While there, he shared some information about Sherman's March. He told me the church was used by Sherman's soldiers and out toward the city of Laurel Hill, NC, there were machine shops that were most likely used to create weapons for the Confederacy and then destroyed during the war. Today, there's a sign along Interstate 74 in Laurel Hill identifying the location as part of the historical sight of Sherman's March. I included interesting tidbits I've heard throughout the years about Sherman's March to perchance make this fictitious story a little more entertaining.

It's my hope that you enjoy this slight glimpse into my imagination!

2

Chapter 1

Tobacco to Market

The sun hadn't broken the horizon when the elderly lady's voice called out through the bedroom door. "Get up child, 'for your pa gets back in here and takes that leather strap to your hide."

"I'm up Grandma," uttered the cranky boy, sounding as if he had a frog in his throat. It was the voice of fifteen year old Elijah, who had not yet completed puberty. "I thought Rock's crowing woulda woke me up," he called back, "I musta been sleeping really hard."

"No child, Rock's still asleep his self. The sun ain't stirred him up yet, so don't go blamin' him." She called out again, "Come on now, I got yer plate waitin' for ya." "Get movin', you got to hurry." This morning his grandmother had cooked a breakfast of grits, sausage, eggs, biscuits and molasses.

Elijah pulled up his pants and slipped on his boots. He walked across the room, picked up the demijohn and urinated in it. Once he relieved himself, he sat it down and hurried out of his room. He then rushed to the back porch and quickly dipped his hands in the basin, which all the family used for washing up with lye soap.

As he crossed the threshold into the kitchen, he found his grandfather Moses and grandmother Ester sitting at the table sipping coffee. "Morning old rooster head" his grandfather called out with a smile.

Elijah looked over and spoke "Morning Grandpa. Why'd you call me rooster head?"

"Cause that hair of yours is standing up on your head higher than Rock's comb. You better be careful he might want to fight you, thinking you're another rooster comin' to take over his territory," chuckled, the old man. Elijah started rubbing and patting his head in an unsuccessful attempt to flatten out his hair.

"Moses, let that child be, he needs to eat. Anyway, when you crawled out from under the covers this mornin', your hair was sticking up too." Ester exclaimed, coming to Elijah's defense.

"Oh hush Ester, that boy knows I'm only punnin' him, don't you Lijah?"

Elijah had his mouth full, enjoying his sausage and egg biscuit while trying to pretend he wasn't paying any attention to the comments. He did, however, look up and give Moses a half smile as he continued chewing. After gulping down a sip of milk, he finally answered "Yes sir, I know Grandpa."

The sound of boots stomping on the back porch interrupted the conversation. Elijah's father, John, entered. He strolled over to the fat boy stove, picked up the coffee pot and poured himself a cup. "It's gonna be another hot one today," he commented, then walked over and joined the others sitting at the table.

He glanced over to his son, "Well now, good morning Mr. Porcupine," he said while reaching over and giving Elijah's hair a ruffle. Elijah quickly moved his head beyond his reach.

Moses gave a smirk. Ester broke in, "John, leave that boy alone. You and Moses need to stop worrying that youngin about his hair."

"Baby as soon as you eat, go comb your hair so your foolish pa and grandpa will leave you alone."

At that very moment, Rock, the rooster, crowed causing Moses to burst out in laughter. "Oh Lijah boy, he's out there getting ready for ya." He looked over at John and said, "Son, we gonna see us an ole cock fight between Lijah and Rock. I told him just this morning his head looked like a rooster," Moses added.

The boy's father continued the joshing. "I'll put 25 cents on my boy". "Make it 50 cents and I'll take Rock. You know that old rooster done lost one eye from fighting" Moses shot back grinning.

Elijah just smiled while finishing off his biscuit. He got up, pushed his chair under the table and headed off to his bedroom without a word. Laughter was heard all throughout the old farm house.

Elijah reappeared with his hair all slicked down. Only Ester remained in the kitchen. He had the demijohn jug in his hand when she yelled, "Get that thing out of here, before I smack you. Don't forget to take your grandpa's and mine down to the outhouse too."

Elijah went to the back porch and saw Moses' urine jug and Ester's bucket, which they occasionally used during the night when nature called.

Tobacco to Market

He quickly stepped off the screened porch into the yard. Looking around and noticing the sun cresting the horizon, he headed down the path to the outhouse.

Elijah stood six feet tall. He was as tall as any man, but, his slim wiry frame let everyone know he was still a boy. His black hair shimmered in the morning sun. The deep purple and blue hues in his locks looked like a raven's feathers in the bright sunlight. His blue eyes sparkled and gleamed with the vibrancy of youth.

Leaving the outhouse, he glanced toward the barn. Holding his hand up to shade his eyes from the bright rising sun, he noticed three of his cousins and their father coming down the dirt path to join Moses and John who were gathered at the wagons. Scurrying along with the containers, he placed them on the back porch and quickly ran over to meet his kin. "Hey ya'll," he called out.

The three dirty faced boys yelled back, "Hey Lijah."

Danny, Dewey and Little Dale, were his first cousins. Their father, Dale, was Elijah's Uncle, his mother's brother. Elijah's mother died of yellow fever the year before, leaving John alone to raise their son. John didn't want to live in the home where his wife had died. So, at his parents' insistence, he and Elijah returned to his childhood home to live with them. John felt Elijah needed a mother figure in his life, and who better could fill that role than his own mother. The farm needed John and Elijah's strong hands, and the elderly couple needed them for so much more.

The men and boys gathered around the rigged up wagons. John and Dale had modified the two wagons to haul the loads of tobacco. Days prior, the men had stood eight foot poles up in the bed of the wagons. Four for the corners, and four for the sides. After the poles were nailed down, chicken wire was placed around three of the sides. The back section was left open for loading and unloading the tobacco. The wagons looked like two raised chicken coops on wheels. The contraption would be used to haul at least a ton or more of the golden leaf known as Carolina Gold over to Laurel Hill.

The demand for tobacco was especially high in the Northern States and Europe. This caused Southern farmers' production to double in recent years. It was the fear of the Southern States secession that sparked the demand. Rumor had it the Southerners were planning to stop selling the products so many people enjoyed. Crops like peaches, cotton, peanuts, oranges, strawberries, potatoes and especially tobacco.

Tobacco to Market

Tobacco was the commodity that kept John and his family's necessities stocked. And at the present, they were happy to oblige those seeking it.

John much appreciated Dale for all his help. His deceased wife's brother was both a comfort and a great support during trying times, especially for his son Elijah.

While waiting to start work for the day, the boys talked among themselves. "Give me a chew," said Dewey to his older brother Danny. Danny pulled out a plug of tobacco that was wrapped in old greasy, crumpled up, brown paper with tobacco twine tied around it. He passed it over to Dewey, who tore off a chunk. Dewey then tossed it over to Elijah for him to take a chew.

"Nah, I don't like chewing much, it makes me gag. But I like smoking my pipe ever now and then," admitted Elijah.

Dewey spit out a stream of brown tobacco juice near Rock who had been suspiciously eyeing them. The rooster walked over and pecked at the spit then quickly left the scene. "It musta not been his favorite flavor," said Dewey. The boys roared with laughter.

"You oughta go ahead and try my plug, Lijah. It's my own personal blend and it tastes mighty good," bragged Danny.

"I tell yah, he made it up right this time," commented Dewey while chewing away.

"You made it yourself?" asked Elijah.

"Yep, sure did. I'm gonna be rich one day like them Virginians and them big backer companies they got in North Carolina," answered Danny. Elijah thought he better find out what all the fuss was about, so he tore him off a thumb size piece, put it in his jaw and began chewing.

The family dog, Red, came out from underneath the porch and wandered over to where the boys stood. He looked up at Elijah chewing away on something and waited around for him to give him a bite. After chewing a while, Elijah spit out a blob of tobacco spit on the ground. Red took a lick of it, then hurried over to his water bucket for a drink. After he drank some water, he crawled back under the porch to lie down.

The boys once again laughed, "Don't seem like that old ridgeback nor that rooster like my blend," chuckled Danny.

Elijah spit again and remarked "It's not bad. Got a good taste to it. Bout the first time I ain't gagged from chewing backer. When you sell it and get rich don't forget about us poor folks. Remember your kin," said Elijah.

"I won't forget cuz," Danny said with a smile.

"I hear you boys a laughing and cutting up back there, that must mean ya'll ready to work," called out Dale to his three sons. Moses threw his two cents worth in on Elijah, "Yes sir Lijah cheated us out of a good fight this morning with Ole Rock, so we need to work him extra hard."

Moses began sharing with Dale, how he teased Elijah about his hair at breakfast earlier that morning. Dale laughed, "Well his hair looks slicker than a new born calf, if you ask me.

Lord, I almost forgot, you youngins take them water buckets over yonder to the pump and fill um up."

Dale added, looking over at Elijah "Take yours and do the same and when you boys finish, we'll be ready to head to the barns."

The three boys proceeded to fill their buckets, while little Dale, the youngest, sat on the wagon buck board seat and watched. He was only eight years old, but he too had a job. It was his job to keep water supplied to the working crew and pick up any tobacco leaves that had fallen to the ground. Once the water buckets were loaded, Ester appeared with a basket of food she had prepared and shooed them on their way.

The two wagons headed toward the tobacco shed that was closest to the farm house.

It didn't take long before everyone was working at a frantic pace. They pulled the tobacco from the barn and stacked it carefully in the first wagon.

It was break time when little Dale brought a worm riddled tobacco leaf to his father. "Here you go Pa, dis the last one I saw. Dale looked at the youngster and smiled.

"You done good little Dale, now take it to your brother Danny, and tell him, I told you to give it to him." The kid disappeared and went to find his brother.

Moses, John and Dale were resting in the shade under a chinaberry tree. The boys decided to lie underneath the one wagon that was empty.

"Now we worked like men on that barn," Dewey said.

"Well, in that case we need to work like ten men on the last one over yonder," exclaimed Danny.

Danny was fourteen which was a year younger than Elijah. Dewey was thirteen. Elijah and his cousins lived five miles apart. Elijah's family lived in South Carolina on the outskirts of a town named Gibson, while Dale and his family lived near the town of Laurel Hill in North Carolina. Laurel Hill was the town where the tobacco was hauled to. Then it was railed to Wilmington, North Carolina. Once it arrived in Wilmington the tobacco was processed and shipped on to Durham, Winston Salem, Greensboro or out across the Atlantic to European shores.

Danny yelled out, "I wanna go swimming! You reckon we'll finish by 5 today?"

"I don't see why not, if we hurry up and get the work done," said Dale.

Danny yelled, "Come on fellers, let's get going." At that moment, he took a huge bite out of his tobacco plug and offered some to Elijah, but Elijah declined.

"Gimme a chew," Dewey called out to his brother.

"Look now," Danny told him, "You need to start making your own plug. Why don't you take this leaf, chew on it some," suggested Danny as he flung the worm riddled leaf, over to his brother. Dewey caught it and stuck the leaf inside his pocket.

He was quick to point out to Danny, "You just remember I gave you some of my maple syrup to help you make that batch."

"Shhh, hush boy, don't be givin out the secret recipe. Lijah might steal it and get rich," complained Danny as he handed the plug over to Dewey.

Elijah was quick to add "Not me cuz, I got my own dreams. One day, I'm gonna own me a big house like them McCloud's house down the road. I'll get some land, marry me a beautiful wife, and have a pile of youngins. I ain't got time to be messing with backer. I'm wantin' me a general store too," he added.

"Sounds good to me," Danny said, "Then you can sell my backer in your general store."

Elijah decided to change the subject, so he said, "Grandma makes some good fried honey biscuits, don't she? I believe that's why Grandpa loves her so. Now, I'll tell you, she's tough too, she keeps Grandpa and Pa straight, when they go to pickin' on me."

9

"Breaks over, let's move out," yelled John.

The boys began beating the dust off their clothes, as they crawled out from underneath the wagon.

Moses was up on the buck board of the loaded tobacco wagon, shouting out to the mules, "Yah Joe, Yah Jim." The big burly sure footed mules heeded his command. They seemed eager to hit the trail up to Laurel Hill to drop off the heavy load.

As the mules headed down the dirt road, Elijah ran up to the wagon calling out to Moses, "Bring me back some jaw breakers, please, please."

"Ain't you too big to be begging for candy?" replied Moses.

Sheepishly, Elijah said, "I reckon I am, Grandpa." He stopped, turned and walked back over to where the others were. He could hear Moses singing a tune, as the mules made their way down the dirt road. The other two men, John and Dale headed back toward the second barn. The boys were exhausted, but they knew the work had to get done.

Dale yelled out "Let's get those sticks down in a hurry boys, before the hottest part of the day is upon us." It was already a scorching hot 105 degrees inside the barn.

Little Dale was busy picking up the leaves, while the boys passed the sticks along to each other for piling. John was stacking the tobacco in a corner as each pile was handed to him. Dale and the others were in the top of the barn handing down the tobacco. John didn't notice Little Dale picking up the leaves behind him, and as he turned, bumping into him, he knocked him over. Little Dale tried to get up, but began to wobble.

Immediately, John lifted the child into his arms and quickly ran out of the barn. He feared little Dale might be suffering from the heat. John was familiar with the signs, as he had seen plenty field hands pass out from heat stroke. He placed the child under a shaded area of the shed then pulled out his handkerchief and dipped it several times in a nearby water bucket. He began squeezing the water out over the top of the boy's head.

He continued pouring the water over his little body to help cool him down. Minutes later, the lad took a deep breath and looked up at John. Dale and the other boys appeared just as John was giving him a drink of cool water.

"Ah," said Little Dale as he looked up still dazed and confused. The lad told his father, he saw lightening bugs flashing before his eyes.

Dale was so happy to hear the child talking. He comforted the boy with a hug and said, "It was just you having a heat stroke boy, are you ok, do you feel alright?"

"I spec so," answered Little Dale who was struggling hard to get up.

"No, you sit it out for a while and rest, just breath nice and easy. We can handle this," said Dale, who kept a watchful eye on his son afterwards.

Around that time John pulled his pocket watch out and noticed it was 1:48 p.m. they were right on schedule with the workload. Finally at 2:57 p.m., he yelled out, "We did it! We've finished."

Elijah was looking around for the water bucket for a cool drink. He was mighty thirsty. It felt like his tongue was coated in a couple layers of dust.

He didn't want to bother Little Dale. When he reached the bucket, he dipped the dipper into it for a cool drink. After taking a big swallow, he yelled out to his father, "Somethin's wrong with this water. It taste like backer mixed with dirt."

John called out with a loud voice "Oh boy, get you some water out of your Uncle Dale's bucket. I washed my handkerchief in that water bucket."

Elijah tried everything to get the nasty taste out of his mouth. Realizing what he had done, everyone was standing around laughing at Elijah.

Little Dale, being the little trooper he was, was back on the job. He went inside the barn to look for more leaves. He spotted a few leaves. He quickly gathered them up and carried them over to his uncle John. "Here Uncle John, this is all of em."

John looked at the leaves in Little Dale's hands, and noticed they had been trampled on and were laced with dirt. "You stand over there and give em a good shakin'," advised John. So, the child slapped em round a bit, trying to shake the dirt off, but the dust was embedded deep inside the nicotine gum of the leaves.

Little Dale thought of another idea, he would just rinse them off in the water pail. He walked over to the bucket and gave them a good dip. He was happy because some of the dust came off so he put them on the ground to dry out.

Meanwhile, Danny was thinking about making his next plug. So, he said to his uncle, "Dem there leaves, drying out over yonder, do you want them or can I have em, Uncle John?" "Well, I was gonna give them to Lijah, he grinned.

You know how he likes to smoke some tobacco in that corn cob pipe his grandpa gave him. But you can have some, and get you a few more leaves off the wagon."

At that point Dale cut in, "Boy, don't be begging folks for their mess, you hear?"

Oh Dale, John said, "I offered him them ole leaves. Let him have em."

Dale was a share cropper. He didn't like asking anyone for handouts. He believed in hard work and had his pride. John wasn't aware how deep rooted Dale's feelings were. Dale harbored resentment toward people who owned land and property. Owning land was out of his reach, or so he thought, since he was a share cropper for a wealthy family named the Tates.

The Tates owned most of the acreage near Laurel Hill and Old Hundred. They owned the general store, restaurant, bank, machine shop, blacksmith shop and numerous farm houses, including Dale's house.

Dale's brother-in-law, John, and his family had somehow beaten all odds. He owned his land outright. His tobacco fields and barns belonged to him.

Dale thought, at least he owned the make shift wagons that John used to transport his tobacco. John had been gracious enough to split the money from the tobacco sale with Dale for both his help and the use of his wagons. Dale appreciated his deceased sister's husband giving him a helping hand and not a hand out.

After tossing the water from the buckets, John and Dale climbed up on the buck board. Dale pulled little Dale up beside him. His other sons gathered near the front area of the wagon to climb aboard. "Look you two, just follow along, ya'll gonna have to walk. Myrtle and Harry can't pull us all.

At that point, Dale's boys began snickering and laughing. John asked, "What's gotten into them?"

"Ah, they're laughing about the name I call the female mule when the wife's not around. Myrtle is her mama's name. The boys laughed again. "When her mama is around, I call the mule Maggie. You see my mother-in-law is pretty rough on me. She's always talking about what other folks got. I know what she's doing. She's rubbing my nose in it, cause I'm a share cropper and ain't got my own place. So I get even by calling the mule Myrtle, a little revenge never hurt anybody, huh?"

"Well Dale, I feel for you, brother. I didn't have to go through that. Anyway, your Ma and Pa, they're some of the best folks I know. And they ain't ever treated me out of the way."

"That's cause you wuz taking sis off their hands, doing them a favor," Dale said with a smile.

Dale began sharing with John, "My daddy use to be a rough character. He'd get drunk and whip me just cause I'd look at him wrong. "We seem to be alright now that he's got old, but times back, it was hard." Dale had never been this upfront with John before.

John sat quietly listening. "Giddy up" Dale shouted, flipping the reins on the mules to get them on their way. The mules slowly plodded along carrying the heavy load. The boys kept steady pace with the wagon. Elijah, reminded his father and uncle about going swimming since they finished the workload before 5 p.m.

"Yeah," Dewey and Danny, began pleading. "Can we go, daddy? Please."

Dale looked at his youngest son sitting beside him and asked "You want to go too"?

"No", replied Little Dale, "I'm gonna stay with you and go to Laurel Hill." The boy knew if he went with his pa, there might be a treat in it for him. But he also knew, if he goes swimming with his brothers, they would horse around and dunk him in the cold dark water.

"Well, I was going to tell you youngins to take Little Dale with you, but since he wants to tag along with me, I guess it's ok. Just be back to the house before dark, or I'll skin your rumps," Dale threatened.

"Yes sir," they called out. The boys trailed behind the wagon for a short distance.

Elijah then said to his cousins "Let's go to the Bayfield hole."

"No," said Dewey, "We gonna go to Ida Mill Bridge, they got a rope tied up in a tree. We can swing on it and jump in the water. It's fun."

"Sometimes other folks hang around the swimming hole too," chimed in Danny.

"Alright then, it is closer, so we going to the bridge," said Elijah. They started running and soon passed the wagon hauling John, Dale and little Dale with the load of tobacco.

Chapter 2

Rachel

When Elijah, Danny and Dewey finally reached Ida Mill Bridge, beads of sweat were streaming down their backs. Their clothes stuck to them, and their faces were red from the run and the day's labor of hard work. They couldn't wait to dip their bodies into the cold flowing water.

Danny and Dewey stood on the bridge's railing, waiting for Elijah to take his shoes off. As Elijah climbed onto the railing, he nervously exclaimed, "I ain't divin. That's too high; I'll break my neck."

"Ah, go on down the path yonder and jump in with your scared ass," said Danny.

"Ah, I'm gonna tell daddy you cussing," said Dewey. Oh yeah, well ass is a donkey. If you tell, I'll throw you off this bridge and won't give you any more of my backer," warned Danny.

Dewey didn't have to think twice about that, so he quickly exclaimed, "I ain't gonna tell. I wuz just pickin'. I cuss too."

Elijah looked down into the dark, black, murky water, closing his eyes praying there were no snakes in it. He knew the others were watching, so he took a deep breath and bravely took the plunge. He was glad it was the deepest part of the river, otherwise several feet to the left or right, he would have landed with his head on the bottom. The water felt really refreshing to his tired soul. After cooling down, he decided to show off a bit, he yelled, "Watch this ya'll." Elijah leaped again doing a forward flip into the water. After a moment under the water, he came up spitting and sputtering, feeling proud of himself.

Danny wasn't going to be out done, so he yelled back "You watch this cuz; you ain't got nothing on me." Danny with his back turned toward the river, hesitating at first, did a backwards flip and landed in the river feet first.

"Not bad, show off!" Elijah exclaimed.

Dewey was too busy sneaking a plug of his brother's backer, so he didn't see a thing. But he told Elijah and Danny they both did good. Danny and Elijah were playfully floating on their backs, waving their arms and kicking their legs, when Dewey decided to join in with the fun.

Rachel

"Just watch," he called out, "I'm gonna dive off the bridge, but, I ain't doing that flipping mess like ya'll." He told them. Danny yelled back, "Dive in then, you chicken."

"I ain't no chicken, so shut up and just watch." Dewey jumped off the bridge; it was not a pretty sight when he hit the water doing a belly flop. He cried out "Ohhhhh," as he came to the surface.

Danny and Elijah couldn't contain their laughter. Dewey blinked back the tears, "Stop laughing, it ain't funny," he complained.

Dewey not only had swallowed tobacco, but his belly hurt like crazy. He didn't want the guys to see him cry, nor did he tell them about the backer. So, he pretended that he swallowed some water and something had gotten into his eyes. As he headed for the bank, Elijah and Danny trailed behind him making their way back to the top of the bridge. They all decided to lie down on the railing of the bridge to dry off and bask in the sun.

Meanwhile, Rachel Ann McCloud was quietly sitting in the buggy with her house servant named Sarah. James, the family's butler, held the reins to the carriage as he drove the stallion down the dirt road. "Miss Rachel, child, it sho is terribly hot out chere," said Sarah.

"It is smothering, if I do say so myself," Rachel sarcastically remarked, "My father sure picked a fine time to travel up north to Massachusetts and New York. He knew it would be cooler for him."

She went on to tell Sarah, "He has promised to bring me back some of those nice lady things I've been looking at in the catalogs. You know, them things ladies are fond of wearing. I told him, I want me some fancy hats, gloves and some make-up. He also promised me, some novels to read too, especially the ones with all that royal scandal in them."

Rachel was still rambling on when Sarah interrupted, "Miss Rachel, look up yonder, dim trashy boys on that bridge, laying around stretched out like ole snakes." She figured it could mean nothing more than trouble and mischief.

As the carriage was nearing the bridge, Rachel called out to James "Could you please stop, I want to cool myself."

"Yessum, Miss Rachel. I sho nuff will," replied James. James felt it his duty to warn Miss Rachel, so he said "Child you needs to mind yo self, the likes of dim fellers can be some ruffians out to rob or kill us." Rachel smiled, "I think you perhaps might be mistaken.

Rachel

They are just country bumpkins out for a swim. I can't say I blame them on a hot steamy day like this. Wow, would you look at that," she smiled as she pointed to the lad with the beautiful black hair. Such a gorgeous man, she thought. She just couldn't take her eyes off Elijah.

The buggy rolled to a stop on the bridge. All three boys looked up at the strangers with curiosity. "Good day to you gents," spoke Rachel. "Is the water cool?" Dewey was waiting for the others to say something. Since they didn't, he took the lead, "Yes ma'am, it's really cold and deep."

Sarah and James sat silently in the buggy, hoping Rachel would not talk to the boys any longer. Both Sarah and James had been taught not to speak to white folks unless they were spoken to first. And they were never to look whites in the eyes. Rachel knew this rule, and she knew James and Sarah would keep her secrets. "James, go to the edge of the river and wet my hankie, so I may cool myself off. This heat is unbearable."

As James was reaching down to take hold of the hankie from Rachel's hand, Elijah jumped off the railing and quickly grabbed the hankie. He said "I'll wet it for you, Miss Lady."

James would not let go of the hankie, although Elijah kept tugging at it. Rachel was amused, "James, allow this young gentleman to do me the honor." Reluctantly, James let go of the hankie. Elijah was over the railing with a splash, soaking himself and the hankie in the cold water.

Surprisingly, Danny looked at Sarah, and said "Do you have a handkerchief you want me to wet for you, Miss Lady?"

Sarah didn't know what to say, so she just stared at him. Rachel said, in a stern manner, "Let the boy wet your towel for you." Sarah passed it over to him and like Elijah he went over the rail with a splash.

Dewey, who was watching all this, was not about to be left out of the fun. Noticing the red handkerchief in James' pocket, he walked over to him and said pointing to the hankie, "Hey Mister, let me wet that one for you." James wasn't going to have any of this nonsense. But the lad pleaded with him saying, "I see the sweat rolling down your face, surely a cool wet hankie would feel good."

James glanced over at Rachel, who was still smiling, "Oh go ahead, James, allow the young gent to bring you some relief from this torturous heat." James had never heard of such. He thought it was wrong for white people to serve slaves, but he did as Rachel asked.

Dripping wet, Elijah walked up to the side of the buggy and presented Rachel the soaked hankie. She smiled, as she accepted it and thanked him kindly. After wringing out the hankie, she dabbed her forehead, exclaiming "Ah this is indeed refreshing, just the cooling down I needed."

"What's your name?" Elijah was blushing, as he replied, "Clark's my name, Elijah John Clark." He held out his hand to Rachel. She hesitated. He thought to himself, what a fool. Then, she extended her hand to him in a friendly gesture. Elijah couldn't help but notice his hard calloused hand next to her soft and dainty hand.

Rachel noticed how gentle his handshake was, despite the roughness of his hands. He was indeed nice to look at. His eyes, his smile, his gentleness were all mesmerizing. She smiled, "Well Mr. Elijah John Clark, that is a real fine sounding name. I recall a prophet whose name was Elijah, and he could call down rain from the sky. Can you call us some rain out of the heavens today?"

"I wish I could, just for you Miss."

"Oh, forgive me, my name is Rachel Ann McCloud and it's so nice to make your acquaintance," extending her hand to him once again.

Elijah said, "I know some McClouds, well I don't know um, but there is a McCloud family with a big plantation over in South Carolina. It's on the other side of Gibson, across the state line. It's a big grand house, mind you. My daddy's met the man a time or two. Do you know them McClouds, Miss Rachel?"

Rachel said, with a smirking smile, "Why, yes I do know them, Elijah, I live there. That's my father's home."

She had such a sense of pride in telling him this. But, it soon changed when she sensed a difference in the young man's demeanor. "Well, I better be letting ya'll go to wherever you're going," said Elijah stepping back from the buggy.

"Yes, we best be heading back, and thanks for dampening my hankie, you are such a darling. Bye now!" She turned to James and said "Let's go." James popped the reins and the stallion took off in a gait.

"Cuz, I saw you trying to put the moves on that pretty gal," said Danny.

Dewey teased, "Kiss, kiss, hug, hug; look at Mr. Lovebird."

Elijah said, "Shoot, that gal's a McCloud! I ain't got the upbringing to be seen with the likes of them folks." Elijah smiled as he expressed "Lord knows she's pretty, got the most beautiful green eyes I've ever seen.

And did you see dem freckles on her face across her nose? I would kiss dem right off her nose."

"Yuck!" said Dewey, "What you gonna do if she blows a booger on your lips while you kissing her?"

"Shut up," said Danny, "You got no room to talk, you were holding Mr. James' snot rag."

Dewey looked down at his hand, and began rubbing them on his pants leg. He shouted, "No, that was his handkerchief, he uses it to wipe his sweat. Anyway, you had a black lady's snot rag."

Danny grabbed hold of his brother, and they began wrestling. "I'm gonna chunk your ass in that water boy." They tussled with each other, while Elijah watched. He would stop them if it got too serious.

Just then, out of nowhere, Elijah heard the sound of chatter. He looked down the path and saw some young men coming toward the water. "Hold up ya'll, somebody's comin'," said Elijah.

Both boys stopped, looked up and down the dirt road and didn't see anyone either way. They then turned to look at Elijah and noticed the direction he was looking. Sure enough, up the path walked four boys. They had not seen them around before. The odd looking guys all wore shorts, not the usual tattered worn overalls.

As they approached the bridge, they began taking their smokes and matches out of their pockets. They laid them out next to a tree.

Elijah kept eyeing their smokes. One of the boys walked up to Elijah and asked, "Hey fella is the water cold?"

"It felt pretty good to us," Elijah replied. So they all took the plunge. Elijah was thinking what a strange looking bunch. He was trying to figure out what race they were. One looked white, the other looked tan, one of them had a reddish color, and the younger fellow was dark. He thought maybe they were them high yellows he had heard the folks talk about. Elijah kept watching as they swam about in the cold water.

The boys felt at home in the water, like fish. When they decided to walk back up to the bridge, the oldest of the crew asked "Ya'll from around here?"

Elijah, Danny and Dewey all spoke out at once, telling them where they were from. The other boys laughed. Then Danny said, "Me and this un is from Laurel Hill up near Old Hundred." Elijah reluctantly said, "I'm from the outskirts of Gibson." The oldest of the four remarked, "Well me and my brothers, we from Sneads Grove.

Rachel

We came to town with Grandpa to bring his backer up." We figured we would go swimming to get some of this dirt off of us. We followed the river all the way down here, well almost, we swam some too. My name's Jimbo. Dem's my brothers. He's Phil, this one is Sandy and the ole baby boy is Chad."

To Elijah, Jimbo was a mixture of them all, Phil looked white, Sandy looked tan, and Chad was the darkest of the group. Such a mixture of colors to be brothers, Elijah thought. Dewey plainly came out and asked "What kind of people ya'll? Ya'll darker than us."

"Boy, shut your face" said Danny. Phil spoke up bravely, "We people like you little man. We Cheraw and Irish."

"Huh? What's a Cheraw?" asked Dewey.

"That's an Indian tribe, that's what it is," Phil answered. The four boys went over to gather up their tobacco pouches and began rolling out a smoke. They each had what looked like a corn husk in which they rolled their tobacco.

They were puffing away, when Danny decided he would go and get his chewing plug. He offered a piece to Elijah and Dewey. Dewey pounced on it, while Elijah declined. Elijah said "I'd love to have me a smoke," as he eyed the four brothers puffing away. He walked over to Jimbo and remarked "I saw you rolling up your smoke in a corn husk, I ain't never had me a smoke like that before. I like my backer in a corn cob pipe," admitted Elijah.

Jimbo grinned and offered the cigarette to Elijah. "Here, take you a puff and if you like it, roll you one."

Elijah took a puff, then remarked "I'll smoke one, if you let me." Jimbo handed the pouch along with the husk to him. Elijah rolled one up, and then asked Jimbo, if he could borrow his matches. Jimbo lit the cigarette for him. "Thanks man," said Elijah

The group sat around telling each other about different games they love to play.

Jimbo, Phil, Sandy and Chad talked about their favorite game, "cock fighting" especially the Bantam Roosters. They also love sling shots, hunting, and carving with their pocket knives.

Dewey and Danny told them about how much they enjoyed fishing, playing marbles and rolling around inside big drum barrels. They explained how they would take their father's wagon, jump inside, then roll it down the hill while standing up on it. Those were memorable and fun times for them.

19

Rachel

They were laughing and enjoying themselves when Danny remembered what his father had told them, 'be home before dark.' So they quickly said their goodbyes and made their departure from the four Indian boys.

Elijah headed toward his home. After he had walked three miles of his five mile hike, Elijah noticed two wagons approaching from behind. He stepped off the dirt road to let them pass. While glancing back at one of the wagons, he noticed it was the buggy he had seen earlier. It was Rachel and Sarah was driving. "Where is Mr. James," he called out to Rachel as they rolled to a halt.

"Are you blind," she asked? "Why he's up there, in the wagon that just passed you." Indeed, Mr. James had come to a stop sitting on the buck board of the wagon ahead. He looked back at Elijah with a smile.

Rachel asked, "Where are you headed?" Elijah told her "I'm heading home, but I've got a couple more miles yet."

"Well, would you like a lift, at least for a mile, since we are headed in that direction?"

"Mr. James, Wait up," Elijah called out.

Elijah was getting ready to jump into the wagon beside James, when Rachel called out, "Come back here with me." He noticed she was good at giving orders, but never the less, he walked back to her buggy with a big grin on his face. "Can you drive a buggy, she asked?"

Elijah looked offended. "Yes, I can drive a buggy," he said. "Well, Sarah, you go ride with James and Elijah, you take the reins for me." Sarah looked at Rachel with a disapproving glare and reluctantly handed the reins over to Elijah. Elijah helped Sarah down. She walked toward the waiting wagon and noticed Mr. James rolling his eyes while smiling.

When Elijah hopped into the wagon beside Rachel, she remarked "You smell like smoke." Well, I had a cigarette down at the swimming hole after I seen you."

"It's after I saw you," she corrected. "You're in the company of a lady, so speak proper," she said jokingly.

Elijah gave her a big smile and replied "Yes Ma'am, when I saw you."

"Oh well, with a little work you'll get better. Shall we go?" asked Rachel.

"We shall go," he replied as he shook the reigns to start the horse moving.

Rachel

Both the wagon and the buggy continued down the beaten dirt road. Elijah was full of questions. He wanted to learn as much as he possibly could about Rachel in the short ride. Rachel didn't seem to mind, in fact, she seemed pleased to provide him with answers.

She first, shared her age with him. It turned out, she was nine months older than he was. She wanted to attend Catawba College to become a nurse, but her father wanted otherwise. She confessed, "Father says a girl like me doesn't need a trade, I just need to know how to entertain my husband's friends and business acquaintances. But I like helping folks."

Fascinating girl, he thought to himself. Not only pretty, but smart too.

Rachel was enjoying his company and was very curious about him as well. "Elijah, please tell your friends, they made my servants' James and Sarah feel really good today, they liked the attention."

She laughed, today was the first time I ever heard a white person address a black as Mister and Miss. "What a lovely bunch."

"Them's my cousins," answered Elijah.

She giggled, "They are my cousins," she corrected him again.

"Alright Miss Proper, I ain't educated, I got no time for school."

"What do you mean, you don't have time for school?"

This conversation was becoming very uncomfortable for Elijah, but he opened up and shared a few things with her. "I'm a farm boy, and I work hard on the farm with my Grandparents and Pa. Work has to come first, schooling second. I do go to school two months out of the year. The months, December and January, then the rest of the time, I'm working."

Rachel realized she had hurt his feelings. She didn't pity him, but a real compassion moved through her heart. "My, I didn't know." Now she understood why his hands were so calloused and rough. It all made sense.

"Well, you don't work at night do you?" she asked.

"No, I don't work at night, but after a hard day's work I'm worn out."

"Well if you got to spend some time with me on the front porch some nights, would you be too tired for that?"

He didn't know what she was getting at, so she spelled it out for him. "I can teach you to talk more proper, at night, after you finish your day's work. Would you like that?"

He gave her a strange look, "How you gonna teach me? You ain't no school teacher. Anyway, your daddy would shoot me for sure."

"I could shoot you for the way you butcher the language. You are supposed to butcher pigs and cows, not nouns and verbs," she joked. "You come over and we can sit on the porch together and I'll show you."

"I don't know about all that," he spoke quietly, as if dejected.

She chimed back, "Every good business man in the south has to be educated, and you are no exception."

The road forked, she looked over at Elijah, "Here we are, this is my turn off."

Elijah slowed the buggy, not wanting it to end, for he was so enjoying her company. "I'll drive you up to your house if that's ok," he told her.

"Be my guest," she chanted. Elijah turned into the roadway leading to the huge McCloud mansion. There were gigantic pecan trees that lined the driveway. Elijah had seen the mansion many times, but not from this view. As he got closer, he grew excited. The place was stunning. He had never seen such beauty in one setting. He felt a sense of pride swell up inside him, so he immediately sat up straighter in his seat.

Rachel took notice. Elijah followed the trail of the wagon James was driving, which was headed around the back of the house. "No," she said, "Pull up front." He kept looking at her, while heading the stallion up the path to the front porch.

He quickly jumped down to tie off the reins. Rachel waited, "Aren't you going to help a lady down Elijah?" "Oh yeah, I was heading in that direction to do just that." He extended his hand to Rachel, but at that very moment James appeared and said "I will help her down." Rachel was pleased Elijah had offered.

James was about to collect the buggy to drive it around back, when Elijah said, "I can drive it around back for you, Mr. James." Mr. James just shook his head and left leading the horse and carriage around the house.

"Elijah, you need to be careful around here how you address our servants, all that Mister and Miss nonsense. My father said it defeats the will we impose over them."

"Defeats the will? What will is that, Rachel?" asked Elijah.

"Well, when you show kindness, they become uppity. They start placing themselves on your level, and we can't allow that, can we?"

He didn't know what on earth she was talking about. The only help around his home place was his cousins, and he wasn't about to put himself above his kin folk.

22

He was a little perturbed at this point, so he told her his father and mother had always told him to respect his elders; so when he sees someone with white or grey hair, he does just that.

"Well, it's ok for you to be respectful, but around here, don't let any whites hear you saying such things."

At that moment the door opened. A well-dressed young man stepped out onto the porch. "Sarah said I would find you here. I've been waiting for you."

"Hello David," she said. "This is my friend, Elijah."

David replied in a sarcastic tone, "Oh a blessed Christian name."

Elijah replied, "As I recall, so is David." David chuckled, and went on to say "I'm William David McDonald" extending his hand. "And, I'm Elijah John Clark" politely shaking David's hand.

David noticed the roughness of the lad's hand and knew he must be field help. He couldn't quite understand how Rachel knew him.

So he asked Elijah, "I couldn't help noticing how tough your hands are. They're as rough as tree bark. You must be a lumber jack, no doubt," he said while chuckling. "What occupation are you in boy?" David rubbed his own hands.

Elijah was having a bad day, first to be insulted by the most beautiful girl in the county, and now this arrogant stranger trashing him. "I do man's work," he replied. "What do you do, fold silk? From the likes of dem soft hands, you must do woman's work."

Rachel giggled. David replied, "No offense young man, I've just never felt such calloused hands before. Even the nigra's hands aren't that ragged. But I meant no disrespect to you. You're a bit touchy, huh?"

"No, I ain't," said Elijah. "I just meant your hands were mighty soft, like a baby's bottom."

"Enough of this you two, shall we go inside?" asked Rachel. "Come on in Elijah, I'll have Sarah make us some tea." Elijah told Rachel "I had better be heading back to the house. Perhaps we could chat again another time."

"Nonsense," said David, "Stay awhile and shoot the breeze." He didn't want to sound rude, by bluntly asking why Elijah was there. So for now, he would just play along until he could find out.

"Say, I would love to hear your opinion on the Origin of Species, the theory that's sweeping the country side. Everybody is talking about it," said David." The what?" asked Elijah.

Rachel

David was out to make a point, to show just what a numskull this young man was. David had grown up around Rachel, and was passionately in love with her. He didn't think this common country boy would ever be a threat to him, but never the less, he was not going to take any chances.

Rachel, sensing how this was causing discomfort to Elijah, stepped in, "David, Elijah doesn't want to hear about how man descended from apes or crawled out of the sea. He has worked hard today and I'm certain, he would rather go home and get some rest, than to sit here for your amusement."

David ignored Rachel and looked Elijah directly in the eyes and point blank asked "Why are you here, Elijah?"

Before Elijah could say a word, Rachel quickly answered. "He's going to be our new driver, if you must know. Since Jeremiah died, we haven't found a replacement, and James has way too many other things to tend to around here, than to be driving us around."

David looked at Rachel disapprovingly. "I don't think it's a good idea for you to be discussing such matters with strangers. Your father would not approve I'm sure. And, besides, I'm sure Mr. Clark has other things to do with his time besides riding around in a buggy, don't you Elijah?"

"Yeah, I got plenty to do, real man's work. So ya'll excuse me." Elijah walked out. James opened the door for him, "Mr. Clark, Sir, you have a nice night, ya hear?" "You too Mr. James," said Elijah.

"You are the rudest person I know, David," screamed Rachel. She turned and ran up the huge marble stairs to her room. Slamming the door behind her, she quickly opened the window, hoping to get a glance of Elijah. She called out, "Good night Elijah." He turned and waved, as he said to himself, "good night Rachel."

Chapter 3

Monkey in the Morning

It was late afternoon, when Elijah walked quietly in the backdoor. He knew things had gone well at the tobacco market in Laurel Hill. There was a wonderful smell of chocolate cake in the air. Often on good market days, Ester would whip up a cake, knowing there would now be money to replenish her supplies. It was just her way of doing her share. She always knew how to reward her men folk. Ester had laid out a slice of chocolate cake on a plate covered up with a dish towel on the table for Elijah.

Moses and John were out in the barn celebrating. They had broken out a jug of whiskey. The farm was self-sustaining and supplied most of their needs. Moses had planted a surplus of fruit trees on the farm. There were apple trees, peach trees, a fig tree, and a number of pecan trees. Wild berries grew in the surrounding woods. Elijah would go in the woods picking huckleberries or blue berries as them rich folks called them. Elijah couldn't count the times he had gotten red bugs, searching the woods to find them huckleberries for his grandmother. There were grape vines too. Ester loved making her a jug of wine each year. "Wine was good for them stomach aches", she would proclaim with a smile.

Gardens were plowed and sown each year. Moses made sure enough was planted to keep them with a staple diet throughout the winter months. Sweet potatoes were Ester's favorite. In the winter, she would stick a few sweet potatoes in the ashes in the fire place. The aroma would travel everywhere throughout the house and the outside. Things the farm didn't produce, like sugar, flour and salt would be bought from the general store in Gibson or Laurel Hill. They would also haul their corn over to X-Way, near Laurel Hill, for grinding into corn meal.

The farm looked like a small village. It had a lot of out buildings. There was a smoke house where they stored cured meat. Other buildings included a dry shed for seed storage, a chicken coop, a canning shed for Ester's fruits and vegetables and the two-seater outhouse with a crescent moon carved in the door. There were many other make shift sheds with fences for the mules, cows, pigs, and goats.

There was so much hard work to do on the farm. Sometimes, even Dale would come over to help out, although he had his own work to tend to.

Elijah helped himself to the supper that was warming in the bread warmer over the stove. As he sat at the table, getting ready to enjoy his meal and cake, he thought about Rachel. Then, he closed his eyes and thanked God for the food, and offered up a special prayer for her. He was especially thankful this day.

After he finished his food, he quickly took his plate out to the back porch for cleaning. The wash basin still had the soap suds floating from Ester just finishing cleaning Moses' and John's plates. She was a stickler about cleanliness. Like most women of her time, her motto was 'Cleanliness is next to Godliness.'

As Elijah walked quietly around the farmhouse, he found his Grandmother sitting in her big cushioned rocker reading the Bible. Ester didn't use this room often, and very seldom was Elijah allowed in it. Ester called it her parlor, and only company was allowed in there. Next to her was a small stool, which she used as a table to put her hurricane lamp on. Elijah could hear her reading, slowly calling out each word loudly, as she meditated on the passages. "The Lord God is my strength, and he will make my feet like hinds feet and he will make me to walk upon thy high places, to the chief singer on my string instruments." She stopped and placed a piece of string between the pages then closed the Bible in her lap. She took off her glasses and wiped her eyes with a small white hankie.

"Hey Grandma, that meal was mighty good and I loved the cake."

He walked closer to her and sat down on the pinewood bench that ran along the wall. "What book you reading from tonight?" he asked. "Lord child, I wuz reading about one of them prophets, Habakkuk."

'That's a good one,' he thought. Ester made sure Elijah listened with both ears, when she read the Word to him each week.

"Grandma, that McCloud girl, up the dirt road tole me I don't know how to talk."

"What you mean child?"

"She said, "I don't use good English." Ester looked up at him without saying a word. "She tole me after I finished working the fields, if I want, she can teach me English. Somethin' bout knowing all them parts of speech."

Ester thought to herself, how time had flown. Here, her little Elijah was becoming a man right before her eyes.

"Honey, you need to stay shy of dem folks. Ain't nothing good gonna come to people who hold other people in bondage. The Lord's gonna punish them for their wicked ways. Look how he did that Pharaoh in Egypt." Sadness swelled up in his mind as he remembered the story.

Before his mother passed away, she would read the Bible to him every night as he was going to sleep. He loved hearing about Moses parting the Red Sea.

Elijah thought he could read and thought he could talk ok. It was only today, he realized how uneducated he really was. "Rachel kept correcting me," he told his grandmother. His grandmother couldn't help but chuckle. "What's so funny," he asked?

"Well baby boy, you speaking English right now, ain't ya? Just hold on." She opened the front cover of the Bible.

"Where is it?" she asked while eyeballing the inside cover. "Oh, here we go. Translated out of the original Greek by his majesty's special command into English 'The King James Version,' there you go right there. This good book is English. Not that nonsense that McCloud gal wants to teach you." Looking up at him, "Ya sure she's got learning on her mind, or is something else cooking up?"

Elijah's face turned red, he looked up at her and said, "She's pretty, Grandma. And I do wanna learn stuff, and she's so smart. She's gonna go to college and be a nurse, you know, one of them doctor's helpers in medicine."

"Ole hush boy, women folks place is in the home, I never heard of such nonsense. But, if it's to your liking, you do what you may. It's your time and nobody else's. But don't do it cause she's wantin' you to. The Lord gonna look after you regardless."

"I know, I know Grandma," he smiled adding, "And he protects me too." It was Ester's favorite saying.

"I'm off to bed child." "You know your Pa and Grandpa still out yonder in that barn drinking moonshine? They been at it since they got them a belly full of cooking. Oh, I almost forgot, your Grandpa left you a bag of hard candy there in your room. I think your Pa was in your room earlier. I don't know what he was up to. He mighta snuck off with some of your candy to put in his jug of moonshine. He says it makes it taste good. Ya know he's been known to do that.

I've sipped some wine in my time, but Lord knows that hard stuff they drink ain't for me. Moses talked me into trying some of it, and it burnt all the way down. Never had a hankering for that mess, sides, I call it the devil's brew. Now wine is a different story."

"Yeah," said Elijah, "That's the Lord's Brew. The Lord turned the water into wine, and everybody said it was the best."

Ester laughed, "Child, you know the Word, you just keep it in your heart and you'll be blessed." She stood up holding the book, walked over and kissed him on the forehead and patted his cheek. "Just be mindful of them folks I tell you bout, Lijah. You can't trust nobody but the Lord, right?"

"Spec so," he answered.

With that being said, the elderly woman shuffled off to her bedroom. She sleeps in a separate bed from Moses. She often tells of his snoring and he teases her about her hot flashes, kicking the covers off and putting them back on. So they manage to keep peace by sleeping in separate beds.

Elijah, thinking about the candy Ester mentioned, decided to go to his room. He walked over and lit the lamp. The light was burning brighter than usual. He lowered the wick in the oil to dim it. He was in a dim mood, and so he felt he didn't want the glow from the light to outshine him.

He looked inside the bag, hoping the sight of candy would perk him up, and it did. There were several jaw breakers, cinnamon sticks, lemon drops and licorice. From the likes of all that candy, Moses really had a good day from the sale. Elijah decided on the lemon drops. He popped one in his mouth, laid back on his bed and began to think of Rachel.

Before long, he had dozed off to sleep. He dreamed he was riding the stallion that pulled Rachel in her buggy. He rode by Rachel's home on the stallion and smiled while waving at her. But all of a sudden, Rachel got a disturbed look on her face. "Get up child. Get up!" He could see her plainly saying the words, yet it was his Grandmother's voice he was hearing. "Get up," she repeated. Rachel was shaking him. Then the dream burst into a soft light as he awakened. "Huh? What?" He said in a groggy voice.

He sat up in bed, as he saw Ester's face hovering over him. "Child, they out yonder fussing. Somethin's going on. I heard the voice of strangers. I wuz gonna go out and check on it myself, but Moses might put his hand to me for interfering in men folks stuff.

Get out yonder and see who's out there. Your Grandpa's liable to do anything, when he's had him a drink."

It didn't take Elijah long to get going since he still had his clothes on. "What did I tell you bout your shoes in the bed, child? You know better, but I ain't got time to worry about that now. Get yourself out and see what in the devils happenin'.'"

He hurried out the door. In the moonlight, as he got closer, he could make out some horses tied outside of the barn. Red stood near the barn door. "What is it boy?" He asked, as he was reaching for the door handle. He pulled it open and Red followed. Red began growling at the strangers.

Elijah grew frightened as he saw Moses with a double barrel shot gun pointed at the two men. John looked at Elijah and yelled, "Git over here boy, this concerns you."

As he walked closer, he noticed David and an older man about his father's age just standing there. "Pa, what in the name of heavens is Grandpa doing?" he asked. John snapped back, "These two good for nothin' fellows, Sam McDonald and his pup, come down here running their mouth bout you. Talk about you slipping round that McCloud house, where you got no business. Is that so boy, or they lying on you?"

Before Elijah could say a word, Moses yelled out, "They say they ah wantin' you to stay away, or Sam's gonna teach you a lesson. Well, I ain't standin' for none of this...I'll be the one teachin' the lesson."

Sam was a big man. His neck was as thick as Elijah's thigh. Rumor had it Sam had beaten many slaves to death with his bare hands, and had even hung a few, just for the pleasure of it.

Sam spoke to John, "I don't want no trouble from you, nor your Pa, but Mr. McCloud don't take kind to boys fraternizing with his daughter. And, since he's up north, he left me in charge. I don't want your boy romping up there causing problems for me. So, it's best if you keep him away."

David stood quietly by his father staring at Moses' red eyes while nervously peeking at the shot gun. "Damn it, you listen here. You ain't comin' on my property actin' like we some nigra around here, we white folks. I've known you all my life Sam. You wuz a bully when we wuz young, and you still a bully. But, you ain't never tried to bully me, cause you know what's good for you. You know I'd gut your tail if you ever think about putting your hands on my grandson."

John spoke up and added, "Ain't no nigras here for you to be whipping on or driving. You been working up there on that plantation so long you done forgot who you are. You just a white man's nigra yourself, Samuel McDonald."

"Elijah," John called out.

"Yes sir?" answered Elijah terrified.

"I don't know if you been up there or not, or what you done, but you stay the hell away from that McCloud place, or somebody's gonna get hurt."

"But, Pa I ain't been up there without being invited. Rachel asked me on their land."

"Who the hell is Rachel?" asked Moses.

"That's Mr. McCloud's daughter," Elijah answered.

"Well now," said Moses. "Seems like if the man's own child let my grandson come up there, you ain't got no say in nothin'. She's got more right to say who comes and goes on her land than either of you two. I say I'll shoot the two of you right now and say you tried to come here starting trouble and attacked us." The old man cocked the shot gun.

"Please hold up Grandpa," begged Elijah. Both Samuel and David's eyes got as big as case quarters, hearing what the old man threatened. Elijah knew there wouldn't be such an uproar if they had not been drinking. "Before somebody gets hurt, please, put down that shot gun and settle down," pleaded Elijah.

The boy made sense. John thought for a moment then said, "Tell you what Samuel, you and your boy go ahead and take your leave. Send Rachel or get Henry to come tell my boy to stay away, and he'll stay away. But until then, both of you get the hell away from here and don't set foot on our land again without being invited. Now git!"

Moses pointed at the barn door with the shot gun. Samuel and David moved out. Once they mounted their horses, they quickly vanished down the dirt road. Just as a warning, John fired off a barrel into the night sky. He was glad with all that commotion going on he didn't have to pull out his colt pistol he carried in his pocket, especially since his father didn't know about it. Moses had taken care of it all without his help.

Moses laughed as the men's horses darted off with fright from the gun blast. "We showed em, didn't we? Come on back in the barn," he waved to John.

"Moses, Moses…Ester called out. She was at the back steps of the house. What's going on?" she yelled.

"Oh Ester we just having fun, we got rid of a couple of snakes. Now you carry your tail back to bed, ever things alright."

Without saying another word, Ester went back inside. Eljah started to follow her, when his father called out, "Hold up Lijah. Git back here, we gonna have a word with you."

John stood propping the barn door open with his back up against it. Red walked in with his tail tucked between his legs ahead of Elijah. He too looked scared. John put his arm around Elijah's shoulder. Elijah could smell the strong rotten corn and alcohol odor on his Pa's breath. "Boy, you been up there at that McCloud house trying to get you some pinkeye?" he said laughing.

Moses joined in as he uncorked the jug he was holding. "Yes sir, that boy of yours is after him some rich leg. His balls ain't even dropped yet and he's running around sniffing behind women folk already," he chuckled. Elijah felt like melting.

John walked over and placed the shotgun against the mule stall gate post and took him a swig of the devil's brew. "Ah…that's some mighty good stuff." He pulled his pocket watch out and flipped the cover open "Hell its only 10 o'clock." He walked over and sat down on the bale of hay. "Son, I don't know what you've done to get under Samuel's skin, but you need to stay shy of him."

"I know what he's done" said Moses.

"This is how I see it and you can tell me if I'm wrong, Lijah. You done caught that McCloud girl's fancy. I believe that Sam's boy told his daddy they's a new stud in town wanting to mount the McCloud's mare and he's jealous."

"Grandpa, please" Elijah knew Moses had way too much to drink, and he didn't want him to say anything more.

"Now hold on child, let ya Grandpa finish," said John.

"Now ole Sam is hoping his boy can tie tails with that McCloud gal, so he can be in the money his self. He sees Lijah here as a wall in the road he is climbing up. He wants to be somebody big round there. He knows he's common white trash. Eating out of McCloud's hands and riding around whippin' slaves and abusing people. He ain't wantin' Lijah to mess things up for him, that's what. How bout dem apples?"

31

Elijah thought for a couple of seconds and decided he would have to think on it for a moment. "Well," he told the men, "David did seem a little jealous of me. He seen me ridin' up on that buggy with Rachel," Elijah said with a grin.

"Ridin' in a buggy?" both Moses and John echoed at the same time. "You better tell us all bout it."

So Elijah told them about the two encounters he had with Rachel that day. Then he went on to tell them about the confrontation with David. As he was telling them about David's soft hands, he was smiling. He related how David had tried his best to shame him with worldly talk.

"Worldly talk," they asked?

"Yeah, he wuz askin' me about a Charles Drawing or Species, somethin' like that … I don't know, it just sounded to me like some uppity mess, I reckon."

Moses spoke up. I know what he wuz talking bout. "That boy wuz talking about Charles Darwin's, '*Origin of Species*'. It's a book that just came out this year. Some ol' British science man claims all kinds of hog wash. If you ask me, it's things that aren't worth Ole Red pissing on."

"Things like what Grandpa?" Elijah asked.

"Well, for one, I believe it was said, he is tellin' only the fittest survive. Or more like the strongest survive and the weak die off. Shit, that ain't so, cause you look at them Red Savages here in the good old U.S. My daddy said, them there wuz some big strong built people. Said, they had muscles on top of muscles strong. Now where'd they all go? Story has it there's still a mess of em in Robeson County. That's about the only place around here in this state and maybe some Cherokees up in the mountains. Now had they been so strong, why didn't they survive, hum? That's one thing the man claims, then he goes on to say we came from monkeys."

John then said, "Oh hush, you ain't ever seen a monkey with the hair people got. And if people comes from monkeys, how come monkeys still around, seems like they would all turned into humans by now. So that British fellow is a fool and should keep that fool talk to himself. If anybody believes that mess, they fools too."

"Shoot Grandpa, you smart," said Elijah. "I just took the cotton out of my ears and put it in my mouth, so I'd listen more and talk less. That's how you learn stuff child."

32

"Well, now Mr. Teacher, you want some more of this rot gut?" said John offering another drink to Moses.

Moses took a swig... "good stuff, ahhh burns good. Lijah you growing to be a man now. John, you reckon we can give your boy a taste of this?"

"Heck no, that boys foolish enough." John grabbed the bottle back from Moses.

Elijah said "I don't want none anyhow." He knew Ester would wear him out, if she smelled the devil's brew on his breath.

John then laughing said to Moses, "You say that Darwin feller thinks we come from monkeys? Maybe humans can turn into animals. Didn't you see them two jackasses that was in here a while ago? I believe Sam's boy messed in his pants," roared John. "I did smell stench." They all laughed.

The night wore on as the three of them talked about everything from war to women. Elijah grew sleepy and finally told John and Moses good night.

"Good night boy," Moses said. "Good night son, and don't let us find you turned into a monkey in the morning," added John. They laughed, as Elijah headed out.

Chapter 4

Mark My Word

"You g'won now, and get on up out of that bed Miss Rachel, it's way past sun up, and here's yo breakfast I say now," said Sarah.

Rachel sat up in her four post canopy bed. She yawned, and muttered, "Well, it smells good."

Sarah was standing holding a silver tray, with the silverware, crystal glass and porcelain cup all laid out on it. The bone china dinnerware was decorated with roses. The tray was filled with smoked ham, toast, eggs sunny side up and a bowl of hasty pudding.

"Set it down, Sarah," Rachel snarled.

"Yes em," Sarah answered as she placed the food tray on the night table beside the bed. She walked over to the drapes and pulled them opened to let the morning sun in. The sunlight's rays burst into the room, filling it with brightness. Sarah thought she better try and cheer up Rachel..."I say it's gonna be blazing hot again today, Miss Rachel."

Rachel was enjoying her breakfast. "I declare Sarah, you must think I'm a field hand with all this food, but it is mighty tasty."

She loved the hasty pudding which was made from sweetened brown corn meal. The butter made it even tastier. Her father didn't like it, he always said, 'Corn was fodder for the animals and slaves.' But Sarah gave Rachel some hasty pudding when she was small and she loved it. So her father didn't complain too much about it after that.

Rachel and her father had a close relationship since her mother had died. Her mother had died of bee stings. While she was sitting in her rose garden, a swarm of bees had attacked her. Before the doctor could reach the McCloud plantation, she suffocated from an allergic reaction. Rachel was an infant, still in the crib at sixteen months of age. Her father Henry never remarried. Rachel was Henry's world. He had spoiled her rotten. Rachel had no memories of her mother and remembers her father as being her only parent. Through the years Sarah had become somewhat of a mother figure to Rachel.

"I had a dream about Elijah, she shared with Sarah. He was sitting out on the porch down stairs laughing.

Then he ran and jumped off the porch into the water. I dreamed our house was surrounded by water, and Elijah was swimming around like a fish. I do declare, that boy knows how to make me laugh." She went on to say, "The dream seemed so real."

"Well none of that, Miss Rachel, it's time for you to git dressed. I needs to make dis bed," called out Sarah. Rachel gobbled down the last tid bit of her breakfast. Just thinking of Elijah had given her an appetite.

Rachel sat down at the huge dresser. There was an oval mirror mounted to the back of it. Looking into it, she brushed her long golden blonde hair with highlights of orange glimmering through it. Sarah thought she was striking. On top of the dresser, lay her mother's precious jewelry box. The box had been designed just for her; it was twelve inches across, seven inches wide and four inches deep. In it she kept her bracelets, rings, necklaces, and earrings. The right side of the jewelry box contained her silver jewelry, while the left side housed her gold and diamond jewelry. A beautiful pearl necklace was kept in a drawer all to itself. She loved looking at the diamonds as they sparkled. Rachel found a medallion necklace that had been carved by one of the finest artist in New York. It was a cameo. The lady was said to have been her mother. On the wall was a portrait of her mother. The cameo did indeed resemble her. She decided to wear it today and called out to Sarah, "Fasten this one for me please."

"Yes em," Sarah stopped what she was doing and went over and placed the necklace around Rachel's neck. She secured the clasp tightly. "There you go child, ain't nothin' prettier. Miss Rachel, you beautiful. I's almost finished cleaning up in chere", said Sarah as she walked over to pick up the silver tray. "Now you goes head and put yo clothes on, and come on down. I's gonna be in the kitchen, ya hear?"

Rachel got up and disappeared into her closet looking around at the dresses. She called out to Sarah, "Wait, wait Sarah." She held in her hands, a pink laced dress and a light blue dress. "Which one shall I wear today?" she asked.

Sarah eyed Rachel suspiciously, for she had never asked her opinion on what she should wear before, so she didn't rightly know how to answer her. "Miss Rachel, child, you look good in all dem clothes, blue or pink."

Rachel gave a devious grin, "Well, which one do you think a boy might like to see me in?"

"Oh child, I sees now, you's thinking bout that Elijah boy. Look here child, that boys nothing but troubles to you. That old cracker, I mean Massa Samuel done been down to them folks place and told him not to comes round her no mo. So you needs to don't mind youself wid him. I heard that dim men folks pulled guns on Massa Samuel and Massa David. They come back here all red faced and want to go back down but David talked his Pa out of it. So you just don't bother yo self with that Elijah boy." Rachel was outraged at hearing the news. "I can't believe that Samuel would do such a thing. Are you sure you got your story straight? You know how all the gossip around the slave quarters goes."

"I sho as the the sun is shining out there. I did see em leave on two horses and they turned down that way that boy walked yesterdee."

Rachel was infuriated. She went and placed the dresses back into the closet. She then dressed in a more summery casual outfit.

"Is that it, Miss Rachel?" asked Sarah.

"Yes, Sarah it is. I'll see you later." Rachel stormed out of the house. She went around to the back of the mansion where the stable barn was. To the left of the barn was the huge cotton gin. As she walked she saw two little slave kids wrestling in the dirt. James was laughing and rooting for both to get the other. "James," she yelled. James quickly stood up from the stump, he was sitting on.

"Yessum Miss Rachel?" he asked.

"Have you seen Samuel or David today?"

"Yessum, Massa Samuel and Massa David over yonder at the gin, Miss Rachel," he nervously answered.

She looked in that direction. At that moment it didn't sit well with her as it dawned on her how the slaves addressed Samuel. "You listen to me, James, you do not call Mr. Samuel Master no more, he's not your Master. My father is. Go now and prepare me a horse, I'm going to the gin to see Samuel this instant."

"You'll wantin' me to hitch the buggy?" James asked.

"Yes," she answered in a stern voice.

James darted out to the barn. "You children stop that nonsense," Rachel yelled. They grew frightened and stopped in their tracks, as they looked around for James, but he was gone.

"He's in the stables," remarked Rachel. They both took off running as if a ghost were behind them. James returned leading the black stallion and buggy out of the barn. The two children followed closely.

"You wants me to drive you Miss Rachel?" asked James.

"No, I'll drive myself," She answered. She climbed up into the buggy as James passed the reins to her. She struck the horse with the whip. The stallion took off, causing the buggy to shake her to and fro. She pulled at the reins, to settle him down. As she thought to herself, 'I won't take the whip to him again'. She drove up to the cotton gin, and tied him off under the shade of chinaberry trees. She stormed inside and looked around the dark area. The smell of cotton and dust over came her breathing. She stepped back and decided not to go further into the building. She held her hands to her mouth and yelled. "Samuel McDonald!" She yelled again louder, "Samuel McDonald!"

Samuel emerged with gloves and a whip in his hands. "Yes ma'am Miss Rachel, what can I do for you?" he asked innocently.

"What may you do for me?" she screamed. "For one, leave my friends alone. And another you need to stop having my father's slaves call you Master, because you don't own a soul around here. You are hired as an overseer. You oversee the work details at our plantation. You are hired help only!!! And trust me, my father will hear of you meddling with my friends. I was informed you paid Mr. Elijah Clark a visit last night. It was told to me you warned him to stay off this property. Might I remind you, you don't own this property."

"Well, Miss Rachel," Samuel said quietly, "Your daddy told me to look after things and to make sure you're protected. I am only trying to keep order while he's away."

"Samuel, I am not a little girl, and if I was viewed as such, my father would have taken me with him. You see my father knows I'm quite capable of taking care of his house as well as myself." She then pulled out a small pistol from her bosom. Waving it around, she said "With this, I fear no man. My father taught me how to protect myself. You need not worry; you just take care of your own business and don't concern yourself with any of my company or friends who venture here. In fact, if I hear tell of you harassing any of my friends, your job here will be terminated. I'm sure my father will agree with my recommendations. Is that clear Mr. Samuel?"

"Yes ma'am, it is Miss Rachel, I meant no harm." For his sake, he pretended to be humble. Rachel was taken aback by his demeanor for a second. She expected at least some back talk. But Samuel knew the score. She almost felt sorry for the way she had spoken to him. Tongue lashing was not her style. "Well wonderful Mr. Samuel." She then proceeded to climb back into the buggy and headed off.

David came out and said "Daddy, was that Rachel I heard?" "Yes, that little snooty spoiled brat was here." "Hey now" said David, "Come on now, why you saying them things?" Samuel turned to his son with fury in his eyes. "She's that, 'cause I said so, she coming up here running her mouth bout us going down to John's house to tell his son to stay from here. Don't bother her friends or be in her business, she said. I tell you what Mr. McCloud needed to do, is put her tail over his knee when he was rearing her. Then she'd be more respectful, the little hussy. And you David, you need to be more of a man and catch her fancy again."

"Let's go!" They went back into the hot gin to oversee the slaves processing the cotton. The slaves had to make sure the cotton had no cotton bows, cockle burrs or other trash in it.

Rachel drove by the house and headed down the dirt road toward Elijah's home, hoping he was there.

Elijah had eaten his breakfast and had gone out to do his daily chores of taking care of the animals. His had to feed the chickens, hogs, cows, mules and the goats. He couldn't forget about Red, who was following him round with a hungry look on his face.

Elijah next gathered up the fruit that had fallen from the trees. He picked them up and stored them in their assigned baskets. His grandmother had a basket for each type of fruit. It was his job to turn the fruit over to make sure there were no rotten ones in the bunch.

The temperature outside was beginning to rise. He walked over to the water pump to get him a cool drink of water. The chinaberry trees shaded the pump area and kept the water really cool. He placed a peach on the table where the water pail was kept. He decided he would eat it later.

The table had been built around the pump to hold the buckets as water was pumped into them. Just then, Red let out a loud bark, and kept barking like he was getting ready to go on a rabbit hunt.

Elijah looked in the direction the dog was barking, and in the distance he saw a buggy coming up the dirt road.

His heart stopped beating. He knew immediately who it was. He quickly stuck his hands in the pail of water and splashed the water all over his face and head. Then, he began rubbing his hair, nervously hoping it would not be sticking up. He hadn't bothered to check to see what he looked like this morning because his father and grandfather were still in bed and he didn't want to disturb them. As he headed toward the house, Red started howling. "Shut up Red," he shouted.

The buggy pulled up. "Hey Gal" he said with a smile.

"Well hello to you. Don't tell me you've been swimming already?" beamed Rachel.

"Not yet," he said, as he patted Red's head. Not being used to strangers Red growled at Rachel. "Shut up boy, get back under the house."

"Is that a Rhodesian Ridgeback breed?" Rachel asked.

Elijah looked down at his dog, as he was cowering toward the porch. "I don't know nothin' bout that name you threw in there."

Rachel laughed. "Well that's what he looks like to me. My father has a book on different breeds of dogs. There are thousands of pages of beautiful painted illustrations which describes in detail all the different types of breeds. In fact, my Father's library has two thousand plus books. Every time he travels, he returns with two or more volumes to add to his collection."

"So he enjoys collecting books?" asked Elijah. Then he asked "What do you enjoy collecting?" Rachel blinked her big green eyes at him and smiled.

She then went on to say, "The reason I'm here is, I want to apologize for our disrespectful hired help, Samuel McDonald. He was totally out of place to come and announce to you to stay away from our property. You are always welcomed at our home. I want you to know that. I guess he is just protective of me, since my father is away. But, mind you I gave him an earful before I left the house." She began looking around, "This is a beautiful quaint little place your folks have, Elijah."

Elijah spread out his arms and said, "Well, welcome to the Clark's homestead." He was beaming. Rachel's heart melted. "Do you?" he began and she interrupted, "Do I what, Elijah?"

"Do you want to walk around, you know, take a better look at the place?"

"Well I don't see why not. Be a gentleman and help me down."

He quickly walked over to the buggy and gave her his hand. "Hey, let's pull your buggy around in the shade, so your horse can stay cool."

"Of course, I know General would like that."

Elijah led the horse over to the chinaberry tree and tied him to the leg of the pump table.

General soon spotted Elijah's peach laying on the table. The horse started going for the peach. "Hey feller, that's my peach." Elijah protested. But he was too late. General had the peach in his mouth chomping it. The pit didn't seem to bother him a bit. "That's some horse." said Elijah.

Rachel laughed as she said to General, "Bad horse. You must not take what doesn't belong to you."

"Aw, it's all right," Elijah said. "There's plenty where that came from."

They walked around and ventured out to the pond. She pointed and asked, "Do you swim in there?"

"Sometimes, but ain't no water like running water, the creeks for me. This water is mostly for the animals." He pointed to the milk cow, "That's ole Milly over yonder. Grandpa use to have a mess of cows, but when my Pa left, he sold them all off, except Milly."

As they walked further, they came upon the fruit orchards. He pulled a peach from the peach tree and held it out "See I told you, they's plenty. You want one?" Elijah took a bite of the peach. Its moist juices coated his lips, giving them a glossy appearance. Noticing his lips, for a second Rachel had trouble catching her breath. She wished they were kissing hers.

She said, "No thanks. I like apples much better."

Elijah began telling her how his grandmother made good peach cobbler from the peaches on the farm.

She replied, "My father loves peaches too."

As they passed a fig tree, she looked up at its fruit and saw the figs were ripened, so she asked "May I eat a fig?"

"Go ahead, you sho can."

She took a bite of the fruit. "Mmmm that's good."

"Yeah they is good," he answered.

Rachel started to correct his grammar, but then thought better of it. "Do you read the Bible?" he asked Rachel.

"Well, I do have my Mother's Bible. I can't say I read it a lot, but I do read it sometimes." She began to tell him about her mother and how she died when she was a baby. She pointed to the cameo around her neck, then took it off and handed it to him for him to take a closer look.

"She's beautiful, just like you. I now know where you get them good looks from." Elijah couldn't believe he was saying those things to her.

He became very uncomfortable and starting telling her all about his mother. He told her about how her skin had turned yellow, and how he had to wear a soaked alcohol handkerchief around his mouth for fear of catching the dreadful disease that had claimed her life. Both stood silent looking off into the distance.

A breeze blew through as if it was a sign. A dust devil appeared and pulled up some fallen leaves taking them for a swirl in the air before dropping them back down. Rachel knew the pain he was experiencing. They both had lost the most important person to each of them in their very short lives.

She broke the silence. "I would like another fig," she said as she walked around the tree looking for a larger one. She plucked another one from the tree. As she held it in her hand, she thought, I'll take this one with me.

"O yeah, back to what I was talking bout when I asked you if you read the Bible. Do you know about the forbidden fruit in the Garden of Eden? Some folks say it was a pear and others think it was an apple. But as for me, I think it was a fig."

"Why on earth would you think it was a fig?" she asked.

"Well, listen up. In the Bible it says after both of em ate the forbidden fruit, they saw, they was naked. Then they put fig leaves over their privates," he said blushing. "And it goes on to say, their eyes was open and if that's so, what's the first thing they seen...must have been a fig tree."

She laughed. "Hold on, hold on, now", he said. "Look, eating fruit from that tree caused mankind to fall from grace. That's what's been told from the beginning in the Old Testament."

"Let's see I can't remember which one, but in one of dem gospels it says Jesus done an went to a fig tree and cursed it.

Mark My Word

Now to me that was God's own youngin destroying the tree that caused people to fall from grace. It's simple. People talking bout the Bible hard to understand, it's like opposites. In the beginning we moved away from God, then in the end we go back to God. See in the beginning Adam lived and then died in the end, they say you got to die to live. Just like Jesus died, then he come back to life to live again."

When he finished speaking, she stared at him in amusement. "Where do you get this from? Are you some kind of a preacher man?"

"Shucks, I don't know bout all that gal." Elijah's mother and grandmother had always instilled in him a faith in God. Elijah didn't know what to talk about with Rachel, so he told her stuff he thought she wouldn't know about, so as to make him appear smarter.

They continued their walk circling back to the yard. Rock was pecking at the peach pit General had spit out.

Rachel took a look at the rooster and said "Now that looks like a Plymouth Rock, with its beautiful speckled plumage."

"With it's what?" asked Elijah.

"Speckled plumage," she answered.

Elijah said "The plums is back yonder, and he ain't got no plums on him."

Rachel couldn't help but giggle. "I said plumage, which are feathers, you crazy boy, giving him a slap on his arm."

Elijah just smiled.

"I tell you Elijah, you just need to come over to our house and I'll let you look through Father's books. Especially the encyclopedias, you would love them."

"What's an en, what did you call that book?" he asked.

"En-cy-clo-pe-dia," she said slowly pronouncing each syllable.

"What's that? Sound like them hurricanes my Grandpa told me bout."

"How should I put this...it is a collection of books from A to Z. The book describes things in detail, what it means, the origin and a lot of other different facts. They are so fascinating. Trust me, you would enjoy them. We can look at them together if you like."

At that moment, John came out on the porch and stepped slowly down the steps. He looked up at the morning sun.

Moses came moseying out behind him. They both shuffled over to the water table. "The pump's lost its prime again." Moses called out, "Prime that pump." So John began pouring water out of the bucket into the top of the hand pump. He kept pumping until the pump caught its prime and water began streaming out. John cupped one of his hands under the water and brought it to his lips as he continued to pump. Moses then stuck his hand out to take him a drink. "Boy, that's some good water," He said to John. John poured water all over his father's head. Moses said, "That feels good too." He then tossed the water from the bucket out across the yard, just missing Rock. John filled the bucket back up with water for the next priming. Their little drinking escapade had made them thirsty this morning. They couldn't get enough water. John noticed the buggy and asked "Whose horse and buggy is this?"

Elijah and Rachel walked over to the men. Moses chimed in, "How do you do, young lady?"

Smiling at Elijah, he said, "You got to be the McCloud gal," as he held out his hand.

As she took his hand, she was reminded of the roughness of Elijah's hand. She remarked "You got to be Elijah's Grandfather, right?" I came down to talk to Elijah and you."

"Excuse me, Miss, you'll have to talk to John, 'cause I got to go."

Moses quickly walked toward the outhouse. Elijah was shaking his head and said "When nature calls, you got to answer."

John stepped up and took her hand and said while pointing to Elijah, "This young lad is my boy. So you're the cause for all that fuss from Samuel and his boy. I can now see why they would want Elijah to stay away. Keeping you all to themselves, huh?"

"Well I don't know if I would say all that," commented Rachel.

"Well I did, and you're a beautiful young lady if you don't mind me saying so. You are almost as pretty as Lijah's Ma."

Rachel was blushing, so she walked over to General, pretending to straighten out his bridle. Elijah couldn't do or say anything, so he smiled.

After she regained her composure, she walked back over to Elijah's side. "Sir, I do apologize for my father's hired help."

"Oh, don't you fret none, Miss Rachel. Samuel's an ass, if ever I seen one." Elijah and Rachel broke out in a laugh at the donkey humor.

He looked in the direction of the mules, "Joe and Jim I didn't mean to cuss ya'lls kin like that." John yelled.

Elijah laughed again, while Rachel wondered who on earth was Joe and Jim? "Oh, them's the names of our two mules," he told her.

Rachel got the joke, seeing him compare Samuel to an ass, and the mule's father being a donkey. She laughed. "I do say Mr. Clark, you are one humorous man. You do a sad heart good. I can see where Elijah gets his humor."

She loved being around Elijah for that very reason, he made her laugh. She hadn't had much laughter in her life except when she was little and would sneak around and play with the slave girls without her father's knowledge. Now as a young woman, life was all a joke to her but without the laughter.

"Well I must be getting back," she said. "I've taken up enough of your time. I have enjoyed meeting you and enjoyed my visit here at your homestead, Mr. Clark, the place is striking."

"Hold up, hold up," called out Elijah, "You gonna meet my Grandma. Come on." He led her by the hand and she followed along like a little child. As they entered the house, Elijah yelled out, "Grandma."

"In here child, and hush that hollering for I take a stick to you." He looked over at Rachel and raised his eye brows, smiling, he said, "Come on." As they entered the company room, they found Ester reading her Bible.

"Grandma, this here is Rachel."

The elderly lady looked up and said "Howdy child, you that McCloud girl?"

"Yes ma'am, I am," she nervously answered. She wasn't sure about the expression on his grandmother's face so she didn't know what to expect next.

"What you doin' here with my grandson?" she asked.

The question took her aback, "Why, I'm only befriending him, that's all."

"Listen child, I don't mean to sound cruel with my question. But I can see trouble behind you taking up with Lijah. He's not ready for your kind of people. He never will be, regardless of what kind of schooling you think he needs." Rachel knew Elijah had discussed what she had told him yesterday about helping him with his English. It let her know just how close he must be to his grandmother.

"Grandma," said Elijah.

"Hush up boy, some things need saying." Looking toward Rachel, "You probably pity him, or got some kind of lust in your heart for my grandson. If I was your age, I'd want him chasing after my dress too. But honey, I ain't your age, I'm seventy years old and I done seen a lot in this old world. Your kind and our kind don't mix. Yeah, it's true we white folks and such. But we different and people around these parts want to keep it that way. They murder and kill to do just that. Dim men that come here last night, come to do Lijah harm. His Grandpa and Pa would die for that child standin' next to you. Lijah knows, I myself would lay down my old good for nothing bones for him, if need be. What I'm tryin' to tell you is we don't want Lijah hurt. Now, I know that your heart is good, and I know you never known the love of a man whom you loved in return. You a virgin, the kind of woman I want to love my grandchild. I also know you would love him with everything in you. But, that's not the question here, the question is what I asked you earlier, 'what are you doin' with my grandson?' The life you come from ain't his. He wouldn't know the first thing about ruling no plantation. The child is in the 5th grade at the age of fifteen. He's missed more days of school than you probably attended. You must fancy yourself on schooling. You gonna go on with your education to be a nurse. Well home is where I say a woman's place is. Maybe I'm old fashion, maybe I believe in the word of God so much it lives in me. The only thing I know is if that boy takes up with you, they's trouble. And I know you won't want to be the one who brings it upon him. Dim men who come here last night or, please forgive me, even your daddy may bring it on him. I don't know when or where, but mark my word it will happen. You don't want this heartache, but never the less you gonna be the cause of it. You need to stay clear of each other."

Ester continued, "Now I've had my say and I don't want you leaving here with no hard feelings, because you shouldn't. What I done said was the truth, and sweetheart the truth should never cause you hurt if you love it. The truth should be welcomed and cherished like a brother, sister or mother. You don't have to say you befriend Lijah, cause he don't need friends, he needs the truth. They's comin' a bad day across this land.

Because people holdin' people in bondage. It ain't right to enslave people, and the Lord knows the hurt, pain and sorrow of all people.

45

Mark My Word

Dark skin people in Egypt held them Hebrews in bondage for hundreds of years. Now look, today those dark skin people are the one who's a slave.

It can't last and will not last, you mark my word. God heard them people, I've heard them, riding by fields they work in around your place. What goes around, gonna come around."

Having said her mind, Ester then told Rachel goodbye. She added, "I will pray for you and your family." Rachel walked quietly out the door. Elijah followed closely.

"Elijah," she said sadly, "You have so much of your Grandma and Grandpa in you. One is funny and the other is religious. You are sandwiched between them." Elijah could sense she was upset, as he helped her up on the buggy. He told her, "Don't pay no mind to my Grandma." But Rachel took the reins and left without saying goodbye.

Chapter 5

Truth Hurts

As Rachel was driving the buggy down the dirt road, all she could hear were the sounds of General's hooves striking the hard trampled dirt. She had left the Clark's place dumbfounded. Elijah jogged alongside the buggy for a short distance, calling out to her. She stared straight ahead, not hearing him at all.

He stopped at the end of the drive. Rachel continued traveling ahead, leaving a cloud of dust between them.

Rachel was put out and stunned. She had never had anyone speak to her in the manner Elijah's grandmother had. It was as if the old woman had read her like a book. Ester knew Rachel was a virgin, but yet she knew she had a stirring inside for Elijah. She had spoken so true about how Rachel felt and wanted to feel. The profound truth however, had left Rachel overwhelmed. All Rachel knew was, she wanted to put some distance between her and the elderly woman. She couldn't help but think, what if, just what if, what she said about them bad things could be true, bad days coming, and all that about bondage.

What did she mean about Elijah being hurt because of her? Rachel's mind raced. Would Samuel, David or her Father hurt Elijah? She would never believe her loving Father could cause the young man harm. So many questions kept popping in and out of her mind. She drove right past the road of the McCloud's plantation.

Rachel realized the horse was running at nearly full speed, she shouted, "Whoa, whoa," as she pulled tight on the reins. General slowed and finally came to a halt. White foam was dripping from his mouth. She steered him back onto the road in the direction of the plantation. As she pulled into the front of her home, a young yard hand saw her and quickly went over to take the reins. She climbed down without speaking and rushed inside. She raced up to her room and collapsed on her bed where she began to weep. She couldn't hold back the tears any longer.

Sarah was inside the kitchen helping to prepare food for all the servants. She had to prepare twenty-six helpings of food, which included herself. She was overseeing most of the work.

Truth Hurts

Sarah was still young enough to get around well, plus she was as tough as nails, as James would say. She was forty-eight years old with a few silver hairs streaking her temples. She wore a scarf tied around her hair, while she did the domestic work. Her forearms were as muscular as any man's. Her body was thick, not fat or flabby, just thick. She had picked cotton for twenty-three years in the blazing sun, ever since she was seven years old. She was Rachel's grandfather's slave hand. Sarah had worked in the main quarters for twenty years, four years before Rachel was born. Among all the slaves, there were three under the age of five (two boys and one girl).

As Sarah hurried to finish up her kitchen work, a young girl age four, named Delilah, walked up to the back porch and knocked on the screen door. "Who's that a knockin'," called out Sarah.

"Moola, Moola," the voice cried out calling Sarah by her African name. Sarah rushed to the door, "Child you better hush callin' me that, I's take a switch to yo boomcum. I says, what's you doing out cherr a hollerin' for?"

"That cracker man done whoopin' up on Uncle Mandoh, the African name for James.

"Child I'm tolds you bout sayin' them kinds of thangs round dis house. I'm Sarah and he's James, you best never let that man hear you calls him no cracker. Who's you says he a whoopin'?"

"James, Massa Samuel whoopin' him." Delilah was shaking with tears in her eyes.

"Lowd, I's don't know what I can do bout that."

Delilah's mother, Mary, was one of the aids helping out in the kitchen, she cried out "Git in this house." The little girl ducked under Sarah's arm.

"You better shut that child's mouth up, Lowd knows she's gonna get us all whooped. She say that Samuel done gone to whoopin' up James. Lord, I wish Rachel wuz here."

Delilah had seen Rachel's buggy come into the stables, so she darted up the stairs before anyone could stop her, she was running as if her life was in danger. She banged on Rachel's door. "Come in, it's open." Delilah peeped inside.

"Miss Rachel, Moola, I mean Miss Sarah needs you please, please come down now, hurry. Massa Samuel done whoopin' Massa James."

Rachel quickly rose from her bed, "Delilah," she called out, but the child had already gone.

Rachel opened the door and saw her at the bottom of the stairs heading for the kitchen. That child's going to break her neck if she keeps racing around like that, thought Rachel.

Rachel made her way into the kitchen. "Mary, please stop Delilah from running in the house for she could hurt someone or herself."

Sarah marched over to Rachel and began to tell her what Delilah wanted. "Lowd, Miss Rachel, that child say Massa Samuel is whooped up on James."

Delilah burst out in tears because her mother had popped her hand. Rachel and Sarah's eyes met, they could see Mary was disciplining the child, but didn't say anything.

Rachel hurriedly made her way to the back porch. "Should I's come witcha Miss Rachel?" asked Sarah.

"No, stay here."

She opened the screen door and saw Delilah standing there, "Where are they Delilah?" she asked. Delilah was still sobbing and pointed to the horse barn. "The stables?" She rushed out as fast as she could, heading toward the stables.

"Now I know you done got word to Miss McCloud, you nosey nigra, a running around here telling everything that's none of your business." "I's ain't says nothing, Massa Samuel," he cried out through the pain. James was tied to a horse stall gate on his knees. Samuel and Vernon Smith another white man who was hired to oversee the McCloud's gin, were standing there when Rachel marched into the stable. She screamed, "What's the meaning of this, Mr. McDonald?"

Samuel and Vernon turned in surprise to see Rachel. Rachel was furious. "Umm Miss Rachel," said Vernon. "We believe this one is trying to start a slave uprising like that nigra Turner up in Verginnie." The mere sight of Samuel beating the old house butler was too much to bare.

She yelled, "Get out, the both of you! You leave here now, and leave James alone, I tell you!" She rushed over to James' side, and began loosening his bonds.

"But, Miss Rachel," Samuel said.

Rage was in her eyes, "Don't you Miss Rachel me, my father will deal with you when he gets back, damn you! Leave here and do not touch another servant with your whip. You are disgusting!"

Vernon walked over to help with the untying of James' other arm. She screamed, "You leave here this instant, I said! You're a party to this too. You're just as guilty as Samuel McDonald, to sit back and witness this abuse."

He stood there for a second. She freed James' left hand and went to his other side, "Get out of my way and leave now Vernon. I will inform my father of the part you played in this. How you neglected your responsibilities at our gin. Who's running it now?"

"Sam's boy David, David is running it ma'am. Well, you were hired to do the job, not David." Vernon walked out and didn't say another word. He headed straight to the gin.

Samuel was there waiting. "Vern, that Rachel is gotten to be a real bitch lately. She's done run off at the mouth to me two days back to back. I know that nigra I whipped told her about me and my boy going down to them Clark's house. What he's done, is tell one of them uppity nigra whores in that house and they done told her. Seems like she siding with dim nigras over a white man. "Don't touch another servant with a whip," he said in a loud voice mocking Rachel.

"Pretty soon them nigras gone be lying up in that house telling them white men what to do. Shoot, over my dead body they will. I'll put holes in as many of ums' hinds as I can with my revolver."

He pulled his pistol from his holster and gave the bullet chamber a spin. "Six shots, six dead, the way I see it." He was pointing his revolver in the direction of a slave who was dumping a sack full of cotton into a bin.

"Hey, you heard bout that book one of them scientist wrote about saying we come from monkeys?" said Vernon.

"Man I ain't come from no damn monkey, these black coons round here might have, but I ain't," said Samuel. "My boy was talking about that book. I told him, if he believed a white man came from an ape, he ain't no damn son of mine. He shut the hell up real quick like. If he believes that mess, then he needs to take his tail up to them northern states where he can see all the free monkeys he wants. Up there, they free as a white man, walking around, gitting educated, and they probably sleeping with them white women too. That's disgusting to me, you hear?"

Vernon couldn't help but laugh. "Now it's different with them nigra gals. It's ok the other way around. They ain't nothing no way. We superior to them, if not, we'd be the slaves."

Samuel bragged, "I'm just sharing my superiority status with them nigra gals. Now a white woman laying down with them, ain't getting nothing superior. They are just getting the lowest end of the bargain."

Vernon said, "What you saying don't make much sense to me. I looked up Egypt, you know that Africa place, where them blacks come from. The way I see it, they had white people for slaves too, them Jews white huh?"

Samuel barked back, "Ain't you got to run this gin or something. Your boy doing a good job in yonder Samuel, he can handle it. My boy ain't none of your damn slave Vernon, get your tail in there and do what I say, git."

Vernon left laughing. He was the only one who Old Samuel allowed to get the best of him.

Samuel saw a slave resting; he yelled and cracked his whip. "Don't make me come over and crack this across your back, boy. Get to unloading them sacks," he shouted.

Rachel had gotten James out of the ropes, when she heard some whimpering coming from inside the stall. Two small boys were inside. They were twins, named Mark and Matthew. James was down on his hands and knees, his wounds laid open. Rachel couldn't contain herself. Tears began to flow at the sight of James' pain. He looked up at her, then closed his eyes, it was more painful for him to see her grieve. She called out to the boys, "Children, go and get Sarah, tell her to come quickly."

"I's here," she said walking into the barn. "I seent that old Massa Samuel leave with that Misser Vernon. I thought it be safe fo me to come on out cher." She carried a pail of water and tore off her apron for a towel. "Lowd I say, he's whooped you somethin' terrible James."

Sarah dipped the cloth in the water and wrung it out over James' back. The water cascaded down into the open wounds. James gritted his teeth, trying to bare the pain. Rachel looked on, as the water flushed over his back exposing his pink ripped up flesh. She turned and quickly rushed to the doorway.

A blood hound pup came around sniffing the air. "Get away from here, Frog." She screamed.

She had named the puppy Frog, because the first time she heard him bark, he sounded like a croaking bull frog. The dog was startled and hurried away. Rachel turned and said, "Help him Sarah, please."

As she walked back to the mansion and up to her room, she noticed Mary standing there with her dinner on the tray. Once again, a feast had been prepared just to her liking...pork chops, collards, corn bread, potatoes and corn. She didn't touch the dinner, but told Mary perhaps at supper she would feel like eating.

Rachel asked Mary to fill the large claw foot tub with hot water, hoping to soak away the events of the day. She felt like she was in a nightmare and couldn't wake up. While Rachel waited, Delilah came creeping at the door. Rachel called out to her "come in."

The child was carrying a serving tray with a piece of mail on top. "Moo, I means Sarah, want me bring you dis. I sorry for running in de house, Miss Rachel," said Delilah. Rachel noticed the sincerity of the child and felt real compassion for her. "Child I'm sorry you got disciplined today by your ma." Delilah looked up at Rachel, but quickly remembered she wasn't supposed to look at white folks in the eyes. She dropped her eyes and asked "What's discipline?"

Rachel remembered nigras were forbidden to learn to read or write, so she told the child it was a spanking or whipping for doing something wrong. "But Uncle James got whooped, wuz he disciplined?"

Rachel was not sure how to answer her, so she just said, "Child, I better read this letter, we'll chat later." Rachel opened the letter, it was from her father. She was thrilled, so much had happened, especially in the last few days. She eagerly opened the letter and began reading:

"Dear Lilly, my sweet flower,

I have so missed you and our home something terrible. I must say however, I'm disgusted with these Yankee folk. They're always trying to cheat, swindle, deceive and dupe us old boys from south of the Dixie Line. You know your father's not having any of it.

I have a special gift for you for being the responsible young lady you are in taking care of the house. Do give my best wishes to Samuel, David and Vernon and yes James and Sarah too for taking good care of my sweet flower since I've been away. I will return on September 11th. Sending my love to you my child.

Your Father, Henry McCloud

52

Truth Hurts

Rachel jumped up with a shout. She excitingly picked up Delilah. She looked in the child's face and announced, "Father is coming home soon." Oh my goodness, what's today?" She quickly put the child down, ran over to her night stand and rummaged through all the junk to find her calendar. She looked at the calendar and started counting off the days. "Tomorrow, Father will be home tomorrow."

At that moment it dawned on her, she had never picked up a servant's child. She touched the child's cheek and told her "you've brought me joy today." She went back to the nightstand and retrieved a piece of candy. "Here take this," she said. "It's a jaw breaker". The child eyed it suspiciously. "Oh, it won't break your jaw," she laughed. Rachel took the candy over to the fireplace and used the brass handle of the poker to smash it into pieces. She scooped it up and told the child to open her hands "Don't swallow it, just suck on it." Delilah placed a piece in her mouth. Rachel asked, "You like it?" Delilah nodded her head up and down. She told Delilah to "Run along and play", then immediately replaced it with "No, walk along and play. Don't run in the house."

Mary came in and announced "Yo water ready, Miss Rachel." Rachel sank into the warm refreshing water trying to relax. Her mind reflected back on the day's events and how chaotic and frightening it had been. She wanted to see Elijah again. But, his grandmother had been a rude awakening for her. She saw only the reality of her harsh words. The truth was spelled out, "Oppression, hurt and shame." That day she completely understood, the truth hurts.

Chapter 6

Smile for Me

Rachel's father, Henry Harrison McCloud, stepped down off the platform of the train depot in Laurel Hill. He looked around taking a deep breath while stretching and massaging his lower back. He stood 5ft 11in tall and weighed over 200 lbs. His belly overlapped his belt. He ran his fingers through his blonde mane which was thinning a little on top. He wore the Vandyke style beard, a style fashioned into a V shape and worn by many gents of the day. He pressed over his mustache and beard, pulling the tip tight. As he turned, he looked up toward the box car at his travelling companion.

Out stepped a young man in his twenties. He had broad shoulders, blonde soft wavy hair and sparkling green eyes. His complexion was a slight bit lighter than olive. His dress was impeccable. He indeed was a stately man. "I thought you'd got lost in there Michael," called out Henry.

The young man's name was Michael Joseph McHeir. He was known to be Henry's first cousin's son. Michael had been raised in an orphanage where he had been given special attention over the other children. When he was older he learned why he had received this preferential treatment. He was told some generous benefactor had given charity under his name. This charity was ongoing until he reached 17 and had completed his high school education. Then the orphanage school master informed him of a $3,000 trust fund which was to be used to assist him with furthering his education. He attended Harvard University in Massachusetts to study law. It was now, after completing his studies, he found himself down south in a forsaken place called Laurel Hill.

A huge man dressed in all white with a yellow handkerchief protruding out of his coat's breast pocket stepped out onto the platform. He wore a wide brim hat. "Well if it isn't the King of Laurel Hill himself," said Henry to the man who stood behind him. The man was being attended by four black slaves.

"How you been Zack?" asked Henry, walking toward him and extending his hand. He was Zachariah Tate one of the wealthiest land owners within twenty miles. He owned Laurel Hill, and his cronies, the Blues, the McHeirs and the Gibsons owned the other parts of the district.

The McHeirs believed in spreading their wealth around and settled up the road a way along with the McArthurs, McLeans, and McLaurins who were just a few of the other Scottish wealthy in the area at that time.

He looked at Michael and held out his hand, pardon my manners, my name's Zachariah Tate, people just call me Zack for short."

"I'm Michael Joseph McHeir."

Hearing Michael's last name, Zack raised an eyebrow and remarked, "You related to the McHeirs down in Laurinburg?"

Henry readily spoke up, "They're a different set of McHeirs. Michael's from up north, he's from Massachusetts."

"You boys get the gentlemen's luggage, and pick up their other items." The slaves went over quickly and started gathering up the trunks, suitcases and a briefcase.

Michael called out, "Hold up there Sir, I'll take that." The slave pulled back his hand. Michael picked up his brief case and nodded to the man. Zachariah overheard Michael speaking politely to the servant. He looked over at Henry and gave him a disapproving look.

They walked across the street behind the depot to Tates' Plates, a restaurant owned by Zack. They went inside the dimly lit diner. A few hurricane coal filled lamps were placed on walls to provide light. The men made their way to the back of the restaurant where a table was awaiting them. It was the one farthest from the door. This particular table was always reserved for Zack and his company. The chairs surrounding the table had deep comfortable cushions.

Shortly after, a waitress appeared at Zack's side. "Would you and your friends care for a cup of coffee Mr. Tate?" she asked.

Looking over at the others, he asked "You fellers hungry or thirsty?"

"I'll take a cup of coffee Pearl," said Henry.

"I'll take a cup of tea, please," remarked Michael.

"Young man, you a mighty respectful fellow. You sound like one of those real cultured gents," said Zack. "We could use someone of your caliber in my bank across the street. You'd do better here than most anywhere."

"Hey," cut in Henry. "Michael went to school to be a lawyer and practice law is what he'll do. The family needs a good lawyer, so people like you can't cheat poor folks like me." said Henry laughing.

"Oh, I know better than to cheat you, Henry. We make some good money together."

"You know I'm joshing with you, Zack." "Speaking of money, how is my money doing over there in your bank?"

"It's growing like cotton on a hot and rainy summer day," he smiled. Pearl brought their coffee and tea. Zack called her next to him and whispered into her ear. She stood up and went to the backroom. Soon after, she came out carrying a whiskey flask and Zack's briefcase. Mr. Tate smiled gratefully as she presented both to him. He opened the case, reached in and took out several pouches. Inside the pouches were coins of gold and silver.

He passed them over. "Is it all there?" asked Henry. "To the last eagle," answered Zack. He looked over at Michael and said, "I bet your case don't have what my briefcase contains. Now does it son?"

Michael was taking it all in with interest. "No Sir, I can't say it does, Mr. Tate. But if you like, we could trade." They all laughed.

"The lad has a good sense of humor," said Zack, as he handed the case back to Pearl.

"Well, the company's been good, but I got to be going. Rachel Ann will be walking on coals awaiting my arrival." Turning toward Michael, he said, "Let's leave this old geezer to his money, shall we?"

Michael stood up and extended his hand to Zack. "It was a pleasure to make your acquaintance Sir, and any time you want to trade our briefcases, just let me know, he said smiling."

"Tell you what son, if you find you don't enjoy working with all that uppity law mess, you come see me. I'll put you to work and put some real money in that briefcase of yours." "Oh yes, I almost forgot, Henry, some fellers are coming over from Rockingham Friday to play studs, can I count you in?" asked Zack.

"I'll pass," said Henry."

"Well it's at the Lodge, if you find a hankering to part with some of those coins you robbed me of," he shot back with a grin.

Zack, pulled a cigar out from his inner coat pocket, lit it and began to take a puff.

"You fellers want a smoke?" he asked.

"Sure," said Michael. "Thank you kindly. Umm I do savor the flavor."

"Nothing better than a good smoke and a good stiff drink." Zack said while handing the cigar to Michael. "Care for one?" he asked Henry.

Henry took the cigar and pocketed it for another time.

"What brand of cigar is this?" Michael asked.

"I get them specially made by an Indian feller out of a place called Shoe Hill. This feller told me a strange story, swore that it was true."

"The story was his great, great Grandpappy fought in the 1710 uprising of them Tuscaroras. Said his ancestors were captured and sold out to the West Indies, Cuba or someplace off the coast of Florida. Then he told me that he learned how to make cigars down there. After years of exile, he was told, him and his two sons would be given passage up to New Bern. Well as the story goes, he then headed up to the Neuse River to find his people but they were all gone. Said some of them went north up to New York, I believe, while others went south to a place called Drowning Creek where them Tuscarora and Cheraw Indians live today. I came through Shoe Hill where the train stopped and I got off to stretch my legs. I spotted him at the depot, selling cigars, leather belts, hats and some other pottery junk. Hell, I bought me one of them cigars and enjoyed it so much, I bought the whole lot from him, all seventy-two. That's when he began to tell me the story. It was a hell of a story. Don't know if it's true, but these are some mighty damn good cigars son."

Michael struck a match and lit his cigar, then remarked, "Yes indeed, Mr. Tate, this is a mighty fine smoke." He puffed some more and blew a smoke ring.

"I aint never been able to get the hang of that," said Zack. "You'll have to show me how you do it, one of these days."

"Well, today's not the day," Henry complained, "Come on son, we got to be heading out. Good bye Zack and thanks for lending us the carriage and driver."

Henry and Michael stepped into the carriage. They road along in silence, this was the first chance Henry had to talk to Michael in private. Michael learned it was Henry who had taken care of him by sending money to the orphanage and to fund his college. Henry spoke about Michael's parents' untimely death in a fire. He shared with him how he had wanted to come and get him.

But he learned he had already been placed in an orphanage. So Henry arranged for them to take special care of him. Henry added he wanted Michael to achieve big things and knew if Michael lived down South, he would never have gone to Harvard. He hoped Michael understood.

Michael shared with Henry that he had wanted to visit his parents' grave, but was not able to locate the grave in Boston. After diligently searching for other family members, Michael happened upon many families with the name McHeir, who said they may have been his kin folk, yet they acted as if they could care less. Henry told Michael that he was his family. So, Michael decided to take Henry up on his offer to come down south with him.

Rachel woke early this morning. She had gone through another restless night, but excitedly anticipated her father's arrival. As she looked down the road out across the fields, she thought she saw Elijah with his dog. They were walking in the distance, heading toward Gibson. She wanted to rush out and meet him and tell him she loved him. Then, she thought to herself, how silly.

She pondered for a few minutes the concept of love. Yes, she loved her father and she loved Sarah. They both protected her, brought her comfort, and both were devoted and loyal to her. But her feelings for Elijah were different. She felt a bond between them, both emotionally and physically. She found herself wanting to be held by Elijah. She began daydreaming about him. She recalled how he looked shirtless as he swam. She vividly remembers the water dripping off his hair and gliding down his body. His body was different from David and Samuels. No other white men had ever been shirtless around her.

She thought Elijah's body looked like the Greek statues of men she had seen in her father's books. His black hair and blue eyes had pierced her soul. Inside, she felt a desire for him. A magnetic pull, she couldn't explain. Elijah had made her feel secure when he spoke those religious things to her. It was the same feeling she felt when the Presbyterian Pastor talked to her. Both he and Elijah made her feel God loved her. All she wanted was Elijah to love her too.

Elijah was going for a swim, and had taken Red along for company. He felt really bad about his grandmother sharing what she did with Rachel. He felt a bit embarrassed walking past her plantation.

He couldn't explain or understand why, but it wasn't the first nor would be the last time Ester would speak so openly with people. The folks around said she had the "Eye" they called it. She could see stuff and do things that frightened a lot of people. But some of the people would come from miles around to question her. She was like a seer of the future.

It stopped years before Elijah and John moved in. Word had it, that Moses had gotten drunk one day when a couple dropped by to see if she would tell them what she saw in their future. So, she did her ritual of looking them in the eyes. Then she offered up a prayer to her Maker, asking him to let them see what was good for them or see what evil was lurking. Afterwards, she would sit down and hold the Bible tightly shut. Then she would utter a word three times... "Prophesy, prophesy, prophesy."

After speaking the words, she would open the Bible, and then would began reading the pages of whatever passage the book opened to. She would tell the people what it meant in their lives.

Moses had repeatedly told her she needed to collect some money for what she was doing. Well, as the couple was standing before her, Moses stumbled into the room. He started cursing. He told the couple, his wife was not a fortune teller, and if they wanted their future told, they better hand over some coins or get the hell out. Moses was waving his revolver wildly so the couple left in a hurry.

Ester emphatically told him, she would never charge anyone for a free gift she had received from God Himself. In his drunken state, he slapped her around and told her to never let him catch another soul in his house looking for their fortune to be told. "If I do, I'm gonna tell you your future old woman," and threatened to rip up her Bible.

"No Moses, No Moses," she pleaded, "I ain't gonna help no body, no more, please don't tear up the Good Book." It was a very sad day for Ester.

Moses went out to the barn and never spoke of the incident again. John had caught rumor of the story. He didn't know if it was true or not, and he couldn't imagine Moses doing such. But he did vow to himself, he would never allow his father to ever put his hands on his mother to hurt her.

Elijah was walking along and talking to Red with a sour weed stuck in his mouth. As he chewed on it he told Red, "I hate Grandma done run off Rachel. She's the only friend I had that lived round here. Them other youngins, who lived back yonder toward Cedar Church done moved away.

They don't nobody live in that house now. I wish somebody would move in it and they had a youngin bout my age. We'd run in the woods, go fishing and do all kinds of mess. You never know they might have a gal dog just for you Red."

The dog just kept walking lazily beside him with his tail wagging like he understood. "Boy what would you do about a gal friend?"

At that moment Red growled and was about to bark, when Elijah looked up. He saw a wagon heading toward him. The carriage contained a black man and two well-dressed white men. As they got closer he could tell that one was a young fella, and the other an older man. "Stop boy," Elijah said to the dog who was growling and ready to protect his family.

"Hey Ya'll," Elijah called out.

"Hello yourself young man," The younger one called out. The older man just waved, as they rode on by. Elijah kept watching to see which way they were heading. There was so much open field, he could see over a mile down the dirt road. He saw them head toward the McCloud Plantation. The buggy then turned to go up to the McClouds' house.

"Well, they ain't going to our house, that's for sure. Come on boy let's go." Elijah stuck the sour weed back into his mouth and took off running toward Bayfield Beach. Red ran off ahead of him.

Rachel was standing on the porch when Henry and the young stranger arrived. She dashed down the steps and ran to her father. He picked her up and gave her a big hug and kiss. "Oh Lilly, you're going to hurt my back," he complained. "You've put on some weight, I do believe." He pinched at her waist and laughed. "Where's James, I need him and the others to collect our things. Oh yes, Michael, I want you to meet the flower in my life, my precious daughter, Rachel Ann McCloud. And Rachel this is Michael Joseph McHeir, he's your 2nd cousin from up North."

Rachel extended her hand to him, and he remarked "Your hands are so tender and soft." She smiled thinking to herself how Elijah would have described his hands as woman's hands no doubt. "Well Mr. Michael, welcome to our home," she went on to comment, "I see you've got our family's green eyes." "That's Scot Irish Clan blood." bragged Henry.

Sarah was out on the porch smiling, "It's so good to have you home Missa McCloud," she said. She never addressed him as Master like the other servants. Henry had told her they go too far back for that.

Henry said, "Come on you two," pulling both Michael and Rachel's hands leading them up the steps. "Where's James, I asked?"

It was Sarah who spoke up.... "Lowd, James is in a awful way. He's done got himself a whooping a mule couldn't stand up to, I says."

Henry turned quickly to Rachel with a raised brow, "What the devil is she talking about? What do you mean Sarah?"

Rachel said, "Father please let's go in and not ruin this moment, we will talk about it soon enough. Sarah get someone to get father's and Cousin Michael's things. And bring us some tea."

Sarah walked around back. Shortly after, four young men came and gathered up the luggage along with the boxes and trunks. "Bring them into the parlor," Henry called out.

"Come sit down father and tell me all about your ventures in the northern states, and how you came about bringing a dear relative home with you."

"Well I told you I was bringing you a gift. He's your gift. Remember, I mentioned it in the letter; You did get it?"

"Oh yes, father," she smiled.

The four young men placed the items on the parlor floor. "Where's my brief case?" Michael asked. He jumped up and hurried out the door. The carriage was already making its way down the driveway.

Michael yelled, "Stop!" But the driver continued down the dirt trail with the horses at a gait.

Michael pulled off his shoes and struck out after the carriage. He saw he would not be able to overtake it down the road, so he cut across the field to his left. He leaped over the cotton rows, as if he was a frog leaping to and fro on lily pads. Finally, he got ahead of the buggy. He stepped out in front of the carriage one hand up, the other hand on his knee. He was slightly bent over and breathing hard.

The carriage came to a halt. The horses were chomping at the bits breathing just as hard as Michael was. Michael looked up and took a deep breath and gulped as if he was swallowing something. "You've got my brief case in your carriage sir." He walked over and pulled it from underneath the seat.

The driver cried out, "I's so sorry for dat Massa."

"Oh that's quite alright sir. I'm sorry to hold you up from your journey," said Michael. The man looked at Michael as if he was insane. Michael said "Sir, why are you looking at me in such an odd manner?"

"No reason, sir, no reason at toll. I'm sorry sir." The driver thought to himself he ain't never had no white folk say nothing like that to him before.

"What is your name, may I ask?" inquired Michael.

"Joshua, Massa."

"Well then, Joshua I want you to tell your Master, I am truly sorry for holding you up. You take care of yourself and have a safe journey back, God bless you."

Joshua took off. "Getty up Horses" he yelled out while thinking to himself, 'I ain't telling my Massa nothin'. He skin me live for even talkin' to dem white folks.'

Michael headed back toward the plantation. As he walked up on the porch, he noticed his shoes were gone. Henry was standing there. "Lord, son, you shot off across that field like a fox running from a pack of blood thirsty hounds. You can run, I'm telling you. I came outside and was gonna whistle and stop the carriage, but before I could take in some air, you bolted out. I tried yelling but neither you nor the driver could hear me. I guess we don't know what good a whistle would of done." Henry stuck his two middle fingers in his mouth and blew.

Michael dropped the brief case and covered his ears. Once Henry had finished whistling, Michael said "My, that was the loudest whistle I have ever heard, it was louder than a train whistle."

Henry laughed, "Come on inside son." "Someone seems to have picked up my shoes," he said sheepishly. "Nah, I gave them to Mary. She took them up to your room. Let's go." They went inside.

There was Rachel beaming like a candle in the dark. Rachel got up and hugged her father. "Thank you for my goodies and my gift."

"Yesser, I thanks you too for mys beautiful dress and my bottle of sweets Mr. Henry," said Sarah. Sarah had a mason jar filled with chocolates, while Rachel had four jars filled with all different sorts of candy. There was a little box all wrapped up with pretty paper. Inside the box lay a beautiful necklace with a matching ring.

"Wow!!" she said, "Just for me."

"Just for you Lily," said her father.

Smile for Me

Sarah noticed twenty-four extra mason jars, but they were all empty. "Now what dem jars for Mr. Henry?" she asked. Henry told her "They are to be used to put preserves and jellies in. It's a good invention. You can turn the metal on top and press it down for an air tight seal." Michael chimed in, "Why yes, that's the latest invention from a man named John L. Mason. He put those out last year. I guess not many people down here in the south have them yet."

Michael went on to inquire, "Where are my sleeping quarters, if I may ask?"

Rachel yelled for Mary. Mary immediately appeared at the top of the stairs. "Yes Miss Rachel?" "Show cousin Michael his room."

Michael hurried up the stairs two steps at a time following behind Mary who seemed to float ahead of him. She stopped in front of a door and pushed it open. "I put yo shoes next to the bottom of yo bed. I put yo clothes away for you too."

Michael walked into the large lavishly decorated room. There was an oversized bed that would hold all the orphanage kids at once, he thought to himself. The size of the chest of drawers could house a general clothing store's clothes. The room was lovely indeed. It even had a fireplace, which was a nice addition. He loved to sit by the fire and read a good book.

He turned and looked at Mary, who immediately dropped her gaze to the floor. "Lady Mary, I do thank you for your kind hospitality."

"I fluffed yo pillars and pulled yo covers back fo you too. Is theys anything else you a needing Massa Michael?"

"No, thank you. Oh yes there is one small thing I need from you. I need you to smile for me." Mary quickly backed out of the room. Michael called out, "Thanks."

Mary thought to herself, I ain't smilin' for no white man and I ain't gonna be no nigra gal for white men.

She hurried back to the kitchen area. Sarah caught a glimpse of Mary smiling as she sang.

"Lowdy child, what done got into yo, smilin' like a old possum eatin' persimmons?"

"That Massa Michael axed me to smile for him," explained Mary.

"Lowd, Mary that feller done gone and jinxed all the women folk around here. You better watch yoself round the likes of that feller." Sarah cautioned.

Chapter 7

A Special Someone

Red crawled into the creek lapping up water as he wadded. It was crowded around the swimming hole today. Elijah spotted two of his cousins sitting on a log with two giggly girls waving their legs back and forth in the water. The water came up to their knees.

Elijah went to the water's edge and gradually slipped in. It was colder than usual. All along the river bank was white sand. Some years past, folks in the neighborhood had gotten together and brought in wagon loads of sand. Some folks claim it was as beautiful as the ocean sand.

Bayfield was a small close knit, white folk community. The primary residents included folks that worked at the cotton gin, the saw mill, the feed mill and the slaughter house. The workers often came down for a swim, but today, there were a lot of young folks swimming too.

Elijah decided he would cross over the river to the rope swing tied up in a tree. He dove in and fought the current until he finally made it. Once he climbed up the tree, he swung out on the rope and dropped in the water like a hook and sinker.

The current carried him down stream. As he floated under the bridge he noticed a dirt dauber nest. They were busy making a clay nest on the support columns of the bridge. He decided to stick around for a moment to watch. It was cool under the bridge. The shade was a welcomed relief from the sun.

As Elijah was getting out of the water, he heard a woman's voice screaming. "Larry, Larry," Where's my boy?" She kept yelling. "Please God where is my child?" She was running around hysterically pleading.

The woman's voice got his attention as the water amplified her frantic pleas across the river. Everyone began searching the water near the woods.

Elijah yelled out, "I see something, I see him." A small white body floated near the bridge about to be swept under the water by the current.

Elijah wasted no time jumping in. He grabbed hold of the child's limp body and pulled him along as he swam to the embankment. Once he got him out of the water, he saw a frightening sight.

A Special Someone

A four foot black cotton mouth snake was latched onto the child's leg. Without thinking, Elijah immediately grabbed hold of the snake and pried it loose from the child. The snake whipped its head around and bit into his wrist. Elijah beat it against the bridge, killing it. Knowing he needed to get the venom out of his body quick, he began sucking the bite area frantically, drawing the venom out then spiting it into the water.

The mother grabbed her child in her arms, crying out "Larry, Larry, oh God please, don't let my child die!" She kept holding him tight crying out "Baby, wake up!"

Elijah then tried to suck the venom from the child's calf. His mother didn't want to let him go, making it almost impossible for Elijah to help. "He's dead, he's dead," she was crying out.

"Woman!" yelled Elijah, "Give me that youngin." Elijah saw the blood oozing out of the wound from the snake bite. Wasting no more time, he yanked the child from his mother's grip. As she got down on her knees to pray, she fainted.

Elijah sucked the venom from the child's leg. He then blew seven strong breaths into the child's mouth. As he placed the boy on his back, he began banging on his chest, just hard enough to cause it to move up and down. Finally, as he turned the boy over water began gushing out. The boy coughed, Elijah held onto him with a firm grip. The child was crying. Elijah hugged him tightly for a moment. He patted his back as if he were an infant being burped.

As Elijah looked around, he noticed the boy's mother was dazed. She murmured "Where's my boy?"

Danny and Dewey pushed their way through the crowd, helping the boy's mother up. "It's ok, it's ok," they replied to her.

Elijah gave the boy to his mother. Then he started heaving over the side of the bridge, vomiting into the dark waters.

Danny and Dewey raced to his side. Red walked up behind them and starting barking. Elijah noticed Red was barking at the snake. "Hush boy, it's dead."

Elijah grabbed it up and swung it out into the murky swamp. "Hey, I could of skint that rascal," said Danny. "Had me some real snake hide."

"Well go git him, you seen where he was flung," answered Elijah.

"Run down yonder and get that snake for me Dewey," said Danny.

Dewey just laughed. "Alright, forget it," smirked Danny.

Elijah said he wasn't feeling well and that he was heading home. The crowd was still in shock at what had just happened.

After walking down the road a while, Elijah began to feel better. He heard his name being called out and as he turned to look, he saw his cousins running toward him. "Good God, man you can walk fast," said Danny.

"Don't use the name of God unless you bout to pray or you talking bout the Bible, cuz."

"What's gotten into you? You know I just said good God, and God is good ain't he?" snapped Danny.

"All the time," said Dewey grinning.

"Boy you bout foolish," was all Elijah said to him and began walking again.

"Man you should of heard them people. Me and Dewey went back to tell Pam and Paula bye, and looked round and you wuz gone. Lijah you sure should of heard em talkin' bout you. They said you wuz a healer, and somebody said you know magic." Elijah and Danny couldn't help but laugh.

The woman put her child in some folk's wagon to take him to the doctor. She was a crying and yelling, "Thank you Jesus, thank you God for sending that boy to save my child's life. He was an angel and I know it."

"People kept asking where you live, said you had some kind of power, and so me and Dewey just took off a running, and here we is with you." They tried to cheer up Elijah. They started telling him about the two girls, Pam and Paula. Pam was the oldest at age 14, while Paula was 12. "They want us to go together."

"I ain't wantin' no part of Paula, she's nasty, said Dewey.

"Don't worry, Danny laughed, she ain't gonna want you neither, when she gets to know you."

"Shut up, butt face," said Dewey. Dewey was getting pretty upset, so he decided they better start talking about other stuff.

Elijah told them he wished they could live in that sharecropper's house near his house.

"That wouldn't work," said Danny, "Daddy wants to kill the man now he works for, so I don't reckon he wants to live in another sharecropper house. But we would love to live down yonder. Daddy said, it would take two growing seasons for us to start to get him out from under dem Tates. If dem crops fail, it would put Daddy into a world of debt.

A Special Someone

I heard him say to mama, just the other day he owes Tates General Store eight hundred dollars. That's some money, I'm tellin' you. Well, here's our turnoff, it was scary watching you blow on that youngin like that. Seemed like you were blowing life into him. Daddy said your Grandma got a seeing third eye, says she can see the future. Maybe you got that in you too. You reckon that's the case?" asked Danny

"Aw, it won't nothin'. You member how we use to swaller air and make ourselves burp to see who could burp the longest and loudest? Well, that day you beat me at the family reunion, I decided I didn't want to lose no more. So when I was a workin' by myself around the house I was practicing for you. One day when it was blazin' hot, I drunk me a heap of water and burped out loud. So I started practicin' more. Before I knew what was happenin', I burped up water, started coughin' and snottin' water out of my nose. I quit practicin' then. But when I seen that youngin in the water and knowed he'd done swallered a bunch of water. I knew right then and there I would try to make him burp it all up. That's all it was, ain't nothin' special."

"I knew what to do about the poison because one day Grandma said she didn't see one of her hens. She said she heard it clucking under the house and she sent me underneath the house to find her. So I crawled under the house thinking I was just getting some eggs. I found the hen a setting on a mess of eggs. I tried to get um and she went crazy. She was trying to spur me, and started fluttering her wings and shuffling her feet. She pecked at me too. I nearly fell over. I reached up to grab one of them joist under there and a black widow bit me twix my fingers. I slapped it dead as a doornail. I quickly got out from under that house and starting sucking on my finger. I would spit it out and after a while, it didn't hurt no more. It swelled up a little, where it bit me. Bout the size of one of them bumps on your face you get sometimes."

After they heard Elijah's stories, they didn't think there was anything special about him after all. They looked down at Elijah's bite marks and could barely see a bite. "It looks like a small strawberry you get fallin' and scrapin' your knee. Or where Grandma mighta pinched you in church," they laughed.

Danny rubbed Red's head and the boys said their goodbyes. Elijah walked down the roadway, looking up at the McCloud's house, longing to see Rachel. He felt as if someone was watching him.

A Special Someone

He looked toward the house at the window, where he had last seen Rachel, but he didn't see anyone, so he continued walking.

Rachel had been watching as she sat near her window, enjoying the candies her father had brought her. She peeked out occasionally hoping that perhaps the young man who came into her life would come around once again.

She wanted him to meet her father and cousin Michael. But she especially wished things were different for them. She felt in her heart that Elijah would not go against his grandmother's wishes, and then something popped into her head. She ran down the stairs searching for her father. She searched but could not find him. She went into the kitchen to inquire, but found only Mary there. "Have you seen Father?" she asked.

"Yessum, he outback, checking on James."

Rachel left the house and sped over to James' cabin just down the path out back. James had the largest servant's quarters on the property. She went to the doorway and saw everyone gathered around James' bed. She got a big whiff of the smell of blood. Her stomach began to churn.

She called out "Father."

"Don't come in Lilly, it's too hot inside. I'll be out to speak with you." She heard the sound of a harmonica playing and James thanking Father.

Michael walked out. He had an angry countenance on his face. "It should be illegal for a human to be subjected to such cruelty. Animals aren't treated like this. I've heard of this but could not fathom how it is possible. But today, Lord, I beheld with my own eyes, I witnessed it. Whoever did this, needs to pay for this crime."

Rachel said, "Look, this isn't the northern country cousin, this is the South. And it's a hard life down here. I too wanted to shoot Samuel upon seeing this abuse. But I'm a woman and I haven't any say. Samuel is a tyrant and he has caused me to lose a dear friend. I don't want him around any longer," She confessed.

Michael could see the sadness in her eyes. "Cousin Rachel, it'll be ok, we'll set matters straight. Tell me, who is this friend of yours you claim you have lost on account of this low life Samuel?"

"He's walking down the road, he and his dog. He's a special someone," she answered while watching Elijah and Red off in the distance.

Chapter 8

My People

Samuel and his son David rode up on their horses and tied them off where they tied them every morning as they reported for work at the McCloud's plantation.

Samuel strutted up to the back porch and called out to Sarah.

"Sarah, me and David are ready for our coffee."

Sarah hurriedly took the tray that held a small craft of coffee and two cups out to them. This was the routine when the men arrived each morning.

Also, on the tray were a couple of buttermilk biscuits with butter and apple jelly. "Now that's a good girl, mocked Samuel," as he sat down in the swing on the back porch.

She set the tray down before them and turned to leave. "Good morning to you Sarah."

"Good morning Massa Samuel."

She quickly walked back into the dining room, where Henry, Rachel and Michael were sitting eating their breakfast.

"Mister Henry, that Samuel and his son are out back on the porch."

"Sarah this is a lovely breakfast that you have prepared, and I fully intend to enjoy it," said Henry.

"Samuel will be tended to later."

Rachel interrupted, "What are your plans Father?"

"Lilly, this is men's business, Michael and I will tend to matters. You don't worry that pretty little head of yours. Don't you fret. You should have never had to witness that ugly sight in the first place." Henry replied as he finished off the last mouthful of breakfast.

Michael had a toothpick in his mouth, still savoring the last morsel. "Uncle Henry, that was a gourmet meal for breakfast, I don't know if my waistline can handle too many breakfasts like that. I must say those hominy grits were a new novelty. Back home, the best we folks from Massachusetts can hope for is cream of wheat, oatmeal or porridge."

On that note, Henry stood up tossing his napkin on the table. He wore his colt revolver pistol in its holster on his side. "Let's go, shall we?"

Michael rose and they started off to the back of the house, as Mary and Sarah watched ever so closely.

Henry walked to the back of the porch, only to find the tray with coffee cups sitting on it. "They seem to have already left to start their day of work," he said to Michael.

"Yeah, you old gossiping nigra, you better be glad that gal come when she did. I aimed to break you in right, you wantin' to run and tell my business," Samuel whispered to James.

"You leave Pap be," called out Mark, one of the twin children.

"Hush now child, please!" begged James. The child then sat on the floor with his brother with both eyes glued to Samuel.

"Why you little cuss, how dare you to speak to a white man and try to tell me what to do. You little nappy headed nigra. I'll teach you!" He uncoiled his whip and cracked it across the floor.

"David, get hold of that little bastard and take him out of here," demanded Samuel.

David went to grab the child by his arm, when the boy began crying in protest, "Let me be."

"Get your hands off that child," a voiced echoed.

Both Samuel and David turned to see Henry standing in the door way. David released the child who immediately ran over to James' side.

"Ah, Mr. Henry Sir, when did you get back?" asked Samuel. "We shore glad to have you back," he stammered out quickly.

"I didn't get back soon enough I see. You've overstepped your authority here Samuel McDonald," announced Henry.

James told the children to go outside and play. The twins darted out of the cabin. Henry moved to the side to let them pass. "Let me make myself perfectly clear in the name of justice. You were hired as an overseer over my servants in the capacity of a foreman. I expected you to make sure they put in a good day's work. I even turned my back when you had to strike some of the rebellious ones to keep order around here. But when you took it upon yourself to strike my personal butler, James, you crossed the line and there's no uncrossing it for you. Your service here is no longer needed."

Henry pulled out a coin pouch and jiggled it, then threw it at Samuel striking him in the chest. Samuel caught it and began pleading, "But Mr. McCloud I...'

"Don't but me Samuel, leave my property and take that damn whip with you."

Samuel tried pleading once again, to no avail. He realized that his bread and butter were being snatched from him. He rolled the whip up slowly, then tied it to his side. He walked closer as if he was going to challenge Henry.

"What about my boy, David? He's not abused nobody round here. You gonna fire him too?"

Samuel was hoping for the right answer. He knew they needed some regular money to get by.

"The way I see it," remarked Henry, "He was about to abuse little Mark, so he must go too."

Samuel knew it was too late to plant crops. So he uttered, "Now wait a damn minute here! I gave you eight years of my loyalty and done all you've asked of me. Mr. McCloud Sir, I ain't got no crops to reap to feed my family. Please," he begged, "Give me another chance. I'll do better you'll see."

Henry quickly replied, "My decision's been made. End of discussion." Henry stepped outside the cabin as Samuel and David walked out behind him. Samuel decided on one last plea.

To which Henry replied, "Do I have to spell it out? Rachel told me how you threatened the neighbors and acted like this was your plantation. I'm home now, and I don't need you around any longer. If you vacate now, this will be the end of the matter."

They noticed Michael leaning against a pecan tree. Samuel was outraged, he retorted, "You gonna regret this. You nigra loving son of a bitch!"

"You better hold your tongue talking to my Uncle in such a manner."

Michael walked closer, rolling up his sleeves. David was watching closely with hatred in his eyes. "And who might you be?"

"I don't have to answer to the likes of you, but if you must know I'm kin. So do as my Uncle has told you, or should we get the law involved? As of now, you are trespassing, which is a violation of the law. You broke it the moment he asked you to leave and you didn't."

"Why you uppity Yankee, thinking you well educated, quoting the law around these parts. We don't need no law, we take care of matters ourselves, just ask old James?" He mockingly said.

As Samuel walked away, he spat at Henry's feet, "To hell with you and that Yankee nigra lover." He shoved past Henry calling back to his son.

"Let's go David, this ain't no place for a decent white man to be no way."

They both mounted their horses and galloped off. Samuel called out, "This ain't the end of this McCloud, you ungrateful bastard!"

McCloud pulled out his revolver and shot in the air.

They were at the end of the dirt road, when Samuel spoke up. "Don't that beat all? That white son of a bitch, all I done for him. It's all cause of that little snotty nose brat of his. She's why all this trouble come down on our heads. Her and that damn Clark boy".

"Yeah, Pa, he's the start of it, coming around here not knowing his place," agreed David.

"Shut up boy, you wuz supposed to tame her, but evidently you wasn't man a nough. This ain't the end of it. Did you hear that damn Yankee, 'get the law'. They'll pay. They'll get what's coming."

Rachel and Sarah came out of the house as soon as they heard the blast from the gun shot. Both were expecting the worst. Surprisingly, they saw only Michael and Henry standing about talking. The other servants came running out of the house with worried looks on their faces too.

As Michael gazed around in wonder, he said "Oh yes, there's going to be a change this morning," as if making an announcement to all of Henry's servants. "Mr. Samuel McDonald will not over see your labors any longer."

He went on to explain, "I know you're glad," as he chuckled, "The old cracker is gone. You need not worry."

They looked around at each other in bewilderment, as if to say "What does he mean?"

They didn't know if they should celebrate or be fearful. At that point, Henry spoke up and said to Michael, "What do you mean by what you said old cracker?"

The servants listened intently. "Well Uncle Henry, I've heard that expression used by some of the servants. Yesterday afternoon after we arrived, I was riding the land and decided to leave the buggy. As I began walking, I passed a group of slaves in a field. They were singing and not really paying attention to the wood line. I saw them glance over at the gin area as they were working, and one of the fellers yelled out 'cracker coming', then another one passed the word, 'here comes a cracker'. I heard another mocking, 'here comes that damn cracker always cracking his whip. I'd love to crack him over the head.'

72

My People

At hearing this, I thought it best, I make my presence known. I cleared my throat loudly. He jumped and started working twice as fast as he was previously. He didn't know I had found his comments humorous, especially about calling Samuel a cracker. Bestowing such a name on an abusive man was only fitting."

Henry shared with Michael, "I knew there was something, but I couldn't quite put my hands on it. A couple of times previously, I had to reprimand Samuel for the harshness of his treatment to my servants. Once a young man let me know Samuel had beaten one of the servants and he escaped. Samuel never mentioned this to me, so I let it be."

"On another occasion, I heard there was a tiff over a female servant. Samuel tried to have his way with her, and a young feller stood up to him. Samuel struck him on the back several times. I did let Samuel know that I was disappointed and informed him to find a better way in dealing with the servants. I never realized it would come down to Samuel putting his hands on old James. James wouldn't try to stir up any rebellion against me, you see when my father died, James had been his personal butler. I offered James his freedom, and even told him I would set him up with a place up North. James refused. He went on to tell me that he was home. He knew no other life, and he didn't want to be any other place than here."

Anyway, I freed him long ago. He chooses to stay here on the plantation and work. I offered to pay him, but he refused, stating that he has all he needs, a home, food, and friends. So, I've put his money away for him. It's wages for ten years of servitude. I can't put a monetary value on his services to me and my daughter, but he does have three thousand dollars put away."

Michael exclaimed, "Why you Old Cracker," and smiled.

"Now, I have the task of finding Samuel's replacement. How about you Michael? Good food, excellent living quarters, and wonderful company. Never a dull moment."

"Me?" Michael asked.

"Yes, you, dear boy."

Michael, without any reservation, said "I'm not qualified. I don't know the first thing about the workings of this system you Southerners have in place here. No sir, I'm not interested." "Well wait, hear me out. I'm not saying something on a permanent basis, just lend me a hand until I can find someone else to take Samuel's charge."

"Look, I'm against this system. I see it as an injustice to another human being. Uncle Henry, to be perfectly honest with you, I come from a state that abolished slavery in 1783 and here it is 1860 and the practice of cruel and unusual oppression is the norm around these parts. I'm sorry Uncle Henry, but my answer is a resounding no. I wouldn't drive, beat nor rule over anyone working under my leadership."

"Michael, no one is asking you to abuse anyone. Just think of yourself as a foreman or overseer over the family enterprise. You don't whip or even touch any one of the workers or I'll fire you. So, please, what do you say, come on and help out a family member in need."

Michael remarked, "I didn't come down here for this."

Vernon rode up as they were talking. Vernon climbed down from his horse and hurried over to Henry. "Mr. McCloud sir, I've missed you, glad to have you back. If you got a moment, I need to speak with you concerning something of great importance."

"If it's about Samuel, I've already taken care of that, you don't need to concern yourself. I've dismissed him and he is no longer part of the McCloud's enterprise. Vernon, I'd like for you to meet Mr. Michael McHeir. Hopefully, he'll be our new labor supervisor."

Michael and Vernon shook hands. Then Michael said, looking at Vernon, "Excuse me sir, I need to speak further with my Uncle before he makes any formal statements."

Michael looked at Henry for a moment, "Look I've already given you my answer, you are asking me to do something that is unethical in my eyes and I feel it's morally wrong. I just don't agree with slavery, Uncle Henry and that's the bottom line."

After a moment of silence between the two, Henry said, "Michael, ever since my father died, I have wanted to put an end to this business. But, Lord knows, I'm just too greedy. I don't need the money. I've made enough money for me and Lilly to live comfortable for the rest of our lives, which includes supporting James and Sarah. But, I just can't turn these people free. If I did, I would be killed that same day. The white folks around here who own slaves would come and burn down this place. They would either kill everyone I freed or capture and enslave them once again. There would be no inheritance for my grandchildren, or anything to pass on. It was my father's father that handed down this plantation and the wealth it reaps.

I do agree that it's morally wrong, and I know it's hard for you to grasp the enormity of this slavery issue. And if I made a stand and told all my servants, they were free, where would they go, how would they manage? The first sighting of a black person walking through the community without a white person, would only mean their capture or possibly their death."

Henry continued explaining, "Think about it Michael, these people are all depending on me for food, clothing, shelter and even their small pleasures. There's not a great amount of work for them to do in the winter months, this gives them a chance to be with their family and reflect on their lives. They are not starving or dying off like those Indians who were hunted down and killed or forced to leave their home lands to go west of the Mississippi just twenty years ago. I want to see them free, but I'd be dirt poor and they would be even poorer. I know this sounds like a sermon, but please let me continue.

There are white people who were ruined because of droughts that destroyed their crops. They had no food and have had to hire themselves out like slaves. That is how Samuel came to work for my family. He too had crop failures on his farm and on top of that, the locust came and finished the crops off. We survived because of store houses and the canal system we put in place for our crops. Everyone doesn't have that."

Henry continued, "Even in the Bible up to Jesus' day they spoke about servants, Michael."

Michael interrupted, "Please don't give me a theologian speech. I'm quite aware of what the Good Book says. Plus, may I add Uncle, that was over eighteen hundred years ago, when Christ was here on earth."

Henry began again, "You're sharp, I'll give you that, now if you'll just give me a little more of your time. Tell you what, just hear me out. You don't have to actually work. All you have to do is just take a horse and ride by the fields' daily. Heck you can mosey around and socialize all day if you like. You'd be like a scare crow in a field. The images the crows see aren't a real man, but they think it is because of the way it's dressed up and presented. The way I see it, you riding around looking all sharp and eyeballing the area, they would think of you as an overseer. I just need an image. They work, and you get paid and everything is calm as a pond on a hot summer day without a breeze."

My People

Henry smiled and pulled out the last ace he had hidden. "Besides, boy, this way of life is what paid for all that fancy schooling. What do you say, help out old Uncle Henry?"

Michael looked as if he had lost the war that he hadn't even been conscripted for. "I'll help but under these conditions: First, you must promise me, in the future when circumstances present themselves, you will try to end this miserable injustice of slavery. Second, the servants will be treated like human beings with feelings, none of this Master crap. Third, I don't know how to ride a horse, so someone will have to teach me to ride. And lastly, I'll make the hideous scare crow appearance daily, but you must give me free rein to your library."

Henry cocked his brow, "Now hold on, just a minute boy. My library? I don't think so, that's my favorite escape the world spot. And now you want part of it? I'll pay your wages in coins, but not free rein of my library."

Shaking his head, Michael remarked back, "Nope nothing doing, all stipulations met or I'm out."

Henry knew he had been beat. "Hum, you drive a hard bargain, but I need you, you're family, plus we could always use a good lawyer."

Henry held out his hand to Michael, "Got a Deal?" They shook on it.

As they were heading back into the house, Michael said, "By the way, that was a crock of bull you handed me. I want you to know if you were a lawyer, your arguments were weak. You offered convincing evidence as to why you were holding onto slavery, but not convincing enough, at least to me. So I ask you, why don't any of these folks you see around your place have the same equal chance as you, to earn a better living and build a future for their grandchildren? No doubt, they would like to live in grand homes that have twelve bedrooms like yours. Why do you have so many bedrooms when it's just you and Rachel here?"

"It's not just us. When my father died, Sarah moved in, then I let her talk me into letting Mary move in. Mary was pregnant and the child's father had run off, you know the one I told you about Samuel whipping. So now, there are five. I asked James to move in, but he refused and told me he wanted to stay out back with his people."

Chapter 9

At Any Cost

Rock crowed, signaling Elijah it was time to meet the day. He dressed, ate breakfast, went outside and greeted the world. He said, "Hello sunshine. Good morning to you clouds, grass, trees and especially you,dirt. Elijah felt a kinship to his family's land. "Good morning to you too Rock."

The rooster flapped his wings and crowed several more times. "Alright, alright, I'm going, I know it's feeding time." He walked inside the barn looking for Red. Red was getting old and the barn brought him more security than the cold ground underneath the porch.

He didn't see Red, but noticed Milly was waiting to be milked and fed. He fed her then noticed the mules weren't there. He grabbed a handful of ground corn, walked outside and tossed it to Rock who began pecking away.

Elijah then entered the chicken pen with two buckets of whole and ground corn. He fed the ground corn to the hens and the whole corn to the pigs. Elijah laughed as he listened to the pigs eating. They were slurping, crunching and smacking their mouths while simultaneously oinking.

He repeated the process for watering the farm animals. Once he completed the feeding and watering, he walked through the orchard gathering up the fruit that had fallen. It was 10 o'clock when he finally finished.

"It's cooling off some, fall's a comin'," Ester said while carrying the milk pail. "Lord, knows, it's been a scorcher, this summer." When they got back to the porch, his grandfather was sitting there cutting his fingernails with his pocket knife.

He began talking about the weather too. Old folks love talking about the weather, it was their favorite past time, and the old man was no exception. "Ester, you know," said Moses, "It's not as hot as it use to be. 'Member that year I brought you out here. You remember? You complained every day how hot it wuz. We would hit that pond back yonder like two ducks. I believe that's where we made your daddy, boy. And maybe that's why you love swimming like you do, yo daddy did too, when he was your age."

"Moses, you need to hush your mouth, with that kind of talk around that youngin. Don't mind him Lijah child, he's got that old timers disease saying foolish stuff." Ester was blushing.

"Now Ester that boys nearly grown, he knows he ain't come from no chicken egg, don't you youngin?"

Elijah laughed at them both and answered his grandfather with a yeah. "Where's Pa," he then asked.

"Oh he's gone over to Gibson to get some coffee and other things I asked him to get," replied Moses.

"Well, I sure hope it ain't no more of that corn liquor that makes ya'll foolish," said Ester.

"I don't know Ester, John's a grown man, and can do as he pleases," he said with a wink at Elijah.

"Well, just 'member to keep from around me with that brew. I ain't got no need for it."

"Speaking of corn, it's time to get that corn in out of dem fields, ain't it?" She asked.

"Yeah, Dale and his crew said they'd be over Satdy to help knock it out."

They sat there a while, when Ester asked, "Now I wonder what's taking John so long? He's usually back by now. Well speak of the devil," she looked up the road, "Here he comes now."

John got out of the buggy and walked up the steps. As he reached the top step, he fell over onto the porch.

"Boy, you done got into that jug 'for you got back here?" Moses yelled.

John rolled over clutching his ribs. Moses and Elijah rushed over to him. His face was bloody. His right eye was swollen shut. He moaned, "Git me my shot gun. I'm gonna kill Samuel McDonald, his boy and that Allen Johnson. Help me up from here."

Elijah grabbed his father and began pulling on him, while Moses tried to help. John was groaning as he strained to get up.

"What the tarnation happened boy? Can you tell me," asked Moses?

They helped John inside to the table. "Oh Lord," Ester said rushing over to her son. "You look somethin' terrible." She quickly went over and got a wet cloth. She came back dabbing it around his eye and face. "God Almighty, tell us what happen'd John?"

"That damn Samuel McDonald and his crew." "Watch your tongue or I'm gonna pop you in your already bloody mouth."

"I'm sorry Ma, but they jumped me and ole Red."

"Red?" Elijah asked.

"Yeah, he's out yonder in the wagon. I believe they done broke him up somethin' bad. Go check on him boy and help him," John called out to his son.

Elijah went running to the wagon in fear. He found Red lying there with the saddest look he ever saw on his friend's face.

First things first, he thought. The mules were chomping at their bits. So he grabbed their reins and drove them to the back of the barn. He unhitched them and pulled the wagon under the shelter. Elijah was afraid, his father and Moses would rush out and seek vengeance, before thinking things through. So if the mules were not hitched up, it might buy some valuable time. He led the mules and put them in the stalls.

He hastily returned to the wagon to take care of Red. "Come here boy," he called. The dog crawled over to him whimpering. Elijah jumped into the wagon and saw his dog's head swollen on one side, and his front leg was swollen too. He reached down to touch his leg, but Red let out a big yelp. Elijah just rubbed his head and said, "I know, I know. Good boy, I know you hurt."

The dog continued to make mournful sighs. Elijah took off his shirt and placed it under Red. He gently picked him up and carried him over to the water pump table.

He dipped his hands in the water pail and brought some water up to Red's mouth. "Drink up boy." Red lapped at it. Elijah gave him several handfuls.

Red looked up at his dear friend with pleading eyes as if to say thank you. "It's ok," Elijah kept repeating. "I might have to splint you up," he commented while checking out Red's body. He gently pressed on different areas of his body to determine what was causing him the most stress. When he touched one particular spot, Red moaned.

Elijah reached down under the pump where the pipe came up from the ground feeling around for clay dirt.

He felt the soft texture of clay and scooped up a hand full then gob it on the table's edge. He began smearing it on the places where Red seemed to hurt the worst.

After he applied the clay, he looked at his injured friend and summarized the situation. "Looks like a cracked jaw, broke front leg, two broken ribs and a messed up hip. Boy you took a real beating along with Pa, and it looks like you got the worst end of the bargain."

Elijah rubbed the top of Red's head and said, "You were a real help. Good boy."

Elijah went into the barn and came back with some pieces of thin wooden pallets and some old tow sacks. He took one of the slats and measured how long he'd need a splint for his dog's hip and leg. Once he knew how long a slat was needed, he snapped the thin board across his knee. He braced Red's leg between two slats and tied them together to keep it stabilized. Red growled a few times. But Elijah had to continue the procedure for Red's sake.

After Elijah looked at all the wooden splints, he stepped back and said, "Well, boy you look like a mess. We better get you in the barn and lay you down till you feel all better." He tenderly lifted him up, and then placed him onto some dry straw he gathered for bedding. Elijah then returned to the wagon for the coffee and other dry goods.

Moses came out and noticed Elijah standing there with the jug in his hand. His Grandpa told him to put it away like a good boy. Reluctantly, Elijah took the jug inside the barn.

As he walked back to the house, his father appeared at the doorway holding his shot gun. "Elijah, what the hell ya do with that wagon?" He asked while walking down the steps grimacing with each step.

Moses had disappeared into the house. He could hear his grandmother shouting something inside. Ester appeared in the doorway, she said "Child, you got to be a bigger man than your Pa and Grandpa, this day, hear?"

He wasn't sure what was happening, but Moses came out with two pistols strapped to his waist and waving a butcher knife in his right hand. "Go yonder and get that breech loader of yours, boy, we need all the firepower we can get. We gonna show em, they don't mess with no Clark and get away with it. Hitch them mules back up to that wagon," John yelled as he walked toward the barn.

"But Pa, you sick, why you don't wait a while, till you feeling better," pleaded Elijah. Ester called out, "Honey don't do it, ain't nothing good can come out of it. Let it be. Stop this foolishness for I lose one of ya'll. Cause if you live by the sword, you die by the sword. Please child, I beg you."

Poor Elijah felt as if Ester was on his left, John on his right, Moses in the middle and Red on his back. What's a feller to do?

Moses looked up at Elijah, "You comin' boy? You a man now."

Elijah walked back into the house and returned with his rifle in his hand. Ester was crying. "Grandma, I got to listen to Pa, you know you done told me time and time again, honor your mother and your father."

"Don't you quote the Good Book to me boy. This ain't bringing no honor, just disgrace."

He dropped his head and walked out the door toward the barn. He had never disobeyed his father, and he prayed he was right, in not doing so now.

Moses and John were there in the barn, sharing the whiskey jug. "Boy, get them mules out there now and hitch em up."

"Pa, you hurt and ain't in no condition to do no brawling."

"That's why I've got old buck here," John said, patting his double barrel shotgun. "As long as I got your grandpa and you, I'm fit enough to take on the likes of dem white trash."

He grabbed the whiskey jug for another swig. "That's good stuff, when it burns you going all the way down, you know you getting the real deal!"

Elijah was still trying to reason with him. "Pa, please tell me what happened, what caused all this?"

John looked at his son, calming down a bit at his pleading. "That damn Samuel come in Gibson's General store along with that back stabbing Allen Johnson, who I thought was my friend mind you. Anyhow, after I paid for the dry goods, I walked out to the wagon to put them in, when that feller followed me out."

"I'm finishing packing the dry goods in the wagon, when Samuel called out 'You and that boy of yourn and your half breed daddy done got me fired from McCloud's place."

I turned and looked at him straight in the eye and said "What you talkin' bout?"

He began muttering something bout McCloud finding out he had come out here to our place. And cause of that, McCloud fired him for threatening us. He said, "That no count boy of yours hangin' around the place with that gal."

"Rachel," Elijah announced, "Her name's Rachel."

"Yeah, anyway I tol him we ain't had nothin' to do with what McCloud done with him, he needs to take that up with McCloud. So he says, he will in due time, but that he was taking it up with me right now. He sarcastically remarked, you think you wuz a big man that night with a gun, shooting off at the mouth."

"So, I looked at Allen and told him to talk some sense into Samuel. That son of bitch tells me that Samuel's right, I owe him an apology and a week's wages of work cause of me and my family. I laughed and turned to get in the wagon, and then Samuel comes and blind sides me. He pops me good in the eye ball. I stumbled against Jim, but I caught my balance. I pulled up both my fists tight, to slug it out. I rushed toward Samuel and tackled him to the ground, and punched him with my fist, upside his jaw. Then that damn Allen hauls off and kicks me in my rib and blind sides me, hitting me right in my face twice. Red jumped off the wagon and latched onto Allen's arm. That boy of Sam's kicks Red side the head. Red rolls and tries to get up, when he kicked him a second time."

"Next thing I knew, Sam's a huffing and puffing ready to go at it again. Then we hear a gun shot. There's old Jimmy Gibson hollering break it up, break it up out here in front of my establishment. Well, we stopped, and I tell 'em that Samuel started it. He points his shot gun at Samuel and Allen and tells them to move on. Samuel starts to protest, when Jimmy pointed the gun at him again, telling him there's a female customer inside who said she saw them jump me like a pack of hounds on a coon."

"You should a seen it, Allen went running away and screaming like a little girl." John let out a laugh, then reached for his ribs. "I'm gonna kill that Allen for double crossing me. Boy, I'd a loved to had you and Dale wit me, I'd a creamed old Sam's ass and Dale could've whipped up old Allen." Looking at his son, "you coulda beat the snot out of Sam's brat."

Moses chimed in, "What about me, I could've whopped up on somebody's head."

"Pa, you know you too old to be brawling. You coulda watched, I suppose."

"Watch my ass. Hell, I woulda jumped on Jimmy Gibson's tail, he's round my age. Hand over that jug of whiskey."

John passed it on over to Moses, who turned it up and drank two healthy swigs. "Awww!" He hollered, "I'm ready to go now. You young dogs, remember, I'm leader of this Pack."

82

Elijah thought perhaps he could keep them talking for a bit longer, hoping they would keep drinking and the tonic would calm them down a bit. It seemed to be having that effect on John, but Moses was getting all riled up.

"Tell me what happened then Pa?" Elijah asked.

"Yeah, John, tell us what happened next?" Moses added.

"Well I told Samuel to bring his tail back to my place and we can finish this matter. So Jimmy whips the gun around in my face. He says to me, John, I don't reckon I know what these fellers got ginst you, but you'll have to move on. I hear Red whimpering underneath the wagon, laid out like a hide to dry in the sun. So, I give him a tug, and he yelps. By now Samuel and his crowd done moved on. I kept cussing them for hurting Red. The old colored man that works for Jimmy, come round and helped me put him in the wagon. I had to hold onto Red's mouth, cause he was trying to bite him."

"I thanked the man and gave him a penny. Jimmy had a fit, hollering, don't give his nigra no coin. That's his job to help customers. Jimmy tried to pocket the penny, then I told him to hand it over, if the feller couldn't have it, he wasn't gonna have it either."

"I made it up on the wagon. The bouncing up and down during the drive home bout killed me. Hell if dem mules hadn't brought me and Red in, I don't know how we'd got back." "Ya'll good boys, Jim and Joe. Elijah get over here and feed dem mules an ear of corn."

Elijah walked over and grabbed two ears of corn and held it out to the mules. Jim and Joe wasted no time gobbling them down. They looked like twins with the ears of corn protruding out of their mouths. Elijah couldn't help but laugh.

"What the hell's funny," asked John?

Moses then turned and looked at the mules and starting laughing. "Dem mules." "Well don't make me laugh, my side is done hurting 'nough," said John. "You know I think my ribs are broke."

Elijah could see John was in pain. He knew that a buggy ride would only add to his suffering.

"Pa, dem McDonalds and Allen will get what's coming to them for what they done to you and Red. Just don't go back over there today. They hurt you and Red, and I don't like it none that they called Grandpa a half breed either. But, we can take care of it later."

John put his hand on Elijah's shoulder to straighten himself back up. The pain was now getting unbearable. He said, "Son, I speck you right. I guess I best hit that jug again 'for yo Grandpa drinks it all. It helps ease the pain."

John looked toward the house, he could see Ester. The barn doors swung open and Moses was leading Jim out by his halter. "Go get Joe youngin. I'm ready to ride," announced Moses in a slurred voice. "They gonna pay for what they done to my boy."

"Hold up Pa," John said. He sucked on the cut on the inside of his mouth and spit blood on the ground. "I believe I might be bleeding on the inside. I need to sit down."

Elijah became frightened, he grabbed him up, and called out "Pa, you bleeding on the inside?"

John winked at Elijah. Elijah helped him back into the barn. He sat down on a bale of hay. Moses followed still leading Jim. "I know I'm gonna put some lead in them rascal's ass now. Got my boy bleeding on the inside," Moses was furious. His face was turning redder with each word he muttered.

"Hold on Pa," John said. "Let's hold off a while, I could be dying and you want to run off and fight. I ain't a lick of good to you nor to Elijah. Just settle down will ya, and where's that jug?"

"Here boy, put Jim up," Moses said as he walked over and picked up the jug from behind the bale of hay.

John moaned as he reached for the jug. Moses asked "What is it?"

"Hold it to my mouth for me Pa and let me get a swaller." Moses stepped up and pulled the cork out and placed it near John's mouth.

Moses was shaky and hit John's front teeth with the jug. "Ouch!" John called out. "Sit down Pa, you drunk. Let me get that jug."

"I thought you wuz hurt," said Moses. "I'm feeling better now that the pain jumped from my ribs to my mouth."

Elijah stood watching John and Moses. He said, "Ya'll don't need no guns since we ain't going nowhere. Let me put um up in the house for ya."

"Hold on now Elijah, them som bitches might get the nerve to come round, I'll keep my pistol, but you take your Pa's up to the house." "If they come, you can always get them back," said Elijah.

Moses handed the pistols to Elijah, who stuffed them in his waistband then carried his breech loader along with John's double barrel inside the house. Ester was busy kneading dough for biscuits. She looked over her shoulders and saw her grandson walk through with the guns. "You's a good youngin. God's gonna bless you child."

He sat at the table, and said to her, "They beat up Pa and Red pretty bad. Broke both of em's ribs. I believe Red got a broken hip, front leg and a cracked jawbone too. When I went out earlier this morning, I was wondering why I didn't see him."

Ester said, "He left here trotting off with ya Pa. I seen him following 'hind that wagon. Now I bet his rump wished he'd stayed under that porch. I feel bad badgering your Pa and Moses bout that coffee. I only had enough for two cups. I told em that. And had they not been drinking they'd remembered me telling em. I drank one cup, and by the time they got up, I was a drinking on the last cup. Lord, Moses was ill and wanting his coffee. John saw he was getting mad. So after he finished his breakfast he said he'd go to Gibson and get some and a few more things. I knew when your Grandpa got up and followed him out the door, he was a wantin' him to pick up some more of that old corn liquor. Now the damage is done. Is they gonna be alright?" she asked Elijah.

"I believe so, they been back in that jug, but I reckon it's calmed dem down. Plus Pa ain't feeling good enough to go and do nothing."

"Get you a piece of that fried tater bread over yonder."

Elijah loved his grandmother's sweet potato bread. He moved to the counter top, lifted the cloth, took a piece and bit into it. "Umm," he said. Then he heard what sounded like Red trying to bark. It was enough warning to have him walk out onto the porch to have a look around.

He saw two people coming down the dirt road. One was in a buggy while the other one was on a white horse. "They's somebody coming," Elijah called out. Elijah tossed the rest of the bread in his mouth and darted back toward the bedrooms. He reappeared carrying his father's shot gun. He went out the back door expecting Allen and Samuel. He recognized the buggy and General, and figured the visitors were not there to do harm, so he lowered his gun.

"Can I help you?" he called out.

"Perhaps you can, but we didn't come for trouble," the man on the horse said, looking at the shot gun in Elijah's hands.

"Oh sir, I'm sorry," he sat the gun down against a post on the porch. "You see we been having some problems. Some men roughed up my Pa and I thought maybe you was them."

"No, we haven't come to cause anyone harm. In fact we're here to offer a job to your father. He turned me down once 10 years ago, but maybe he'll reconsider and accept my offer today. I'm Henry McCloud, and this is Mr. Michael McHeir in the buggy back there."

Elijah walked over and shook hands with Rachel's father who noticed the roughness of the youth's hands. "I see son, you're a working man yourself." Elijah was walking over to the buggy to shake hands with Michael. As Michael shook his hand, he pressed a note into it and whispered "It's from Rachel. She asked me to give it to you."

Elijah quickly took the note and put it into his pocket as he walked from the buggy.

"Now, as I was saying, I'm looking for a replacement, someone to work my plantation as a Master Supervisor." He peered at Michael, knowing his discomfort with the issue of slavery. "Do you think your father may be interested in the job young man?"

"Well, I can't answer for my Pa, but seeing we got so much work 'round here to do, I can't see how Pa would want to take on more. So I reckon the answer would be no, Mr. McCloud."

"It's not a hard job, in fact, where is your father, so I might speak with him if?"

"I don't think Pa is in a speaking mood right now Mr. McCloud. You may want to come back tomorrow, he'd be in a better way then."

Moses stepped out of the barn and was heading off toward the outhouse. He stopped and looked at Henry and Michael. "Well I'll be, Henry McCloud, boy you look like your daddy as much as a youngin ever dared looked like a daddy. How ya doing?" Moses walked over to shake his hand. After which he remarked, "I'll speak with ya in a while, right now I got to go sit on my throne."

He made his way down the path to the outhouse, while shouting out to John, "We got company."

A moment later John appeared at the door holding the butcher knife that Moses carried earlier. He saw it was Henry and handed the knife to Eijah, "Here, take this in the house son."

He called out "How you doing Old Henry? You gonna have to overlook me not shaking hands with you, no disrespect but reaching causes my ribs to ache."

"Well, I'm doing alright, now that I'm back home. I must say, it appears I'm doing better than you, old friend."

"Yeah, I got into it with Samuel and Allen Johnson up there at old man Gibson's General store." John swayed a little.

"Do you see the kind of savage Samuel is, Michael? I can't believe I worked him all those years and didn't really see him for what he was, a real brute."

"That bastard said me and my boy, and Pa was the cause of him getting fired. Is that the reason you fired his ass Henry?"

Henry was taken aback and didn't fully know how to answer the question. "Well, certainly not. He abused James, who is my personal friend and butler. I couldn't tolerate that. I also mentioned I would not tolerate him threatening Rachel's friend, your boy Elijah. So if he got that in his head, that's where it came from."

"Well, he had me steaming. I was gonna kill him. But Allen Johnson jumped me. I was getting the best of him, til Allen hauled off and kicked me in my damn ribs."

"Sorry to hear about all that commotion. It was certainly not my intent to cause any fuss for you. I came here today to offer you his job, if you want it. It pays well and all you have to do is ride the horse and organize the work details for my acreage. You know, keep order," said Henry.

John looked at him and smiled. "You asked me some time back to do the same thing. Well I said no then and I'm gonna have to turn you down again. No thanks. There's way too much work around here that needs doing. But hey, I do believe you'd be a good boss man and anybody who'd work for ya would be in good hands."

"That's the problem, I can't find me a good man, one I can trust. I'm looking for someone who won't abuse my servants or think they own my plantation. I do wish you would reconsider or at the least give me some recommendations of who might fit the bill."

"Henry, I can't say I know anybody right off hand, I would of said Allen Johnson, but now, I wouldn't recommend that backstabber to wash a hog's ass ," said John angrily.

Elijah spoke up, "What about Uncle Dale, Pa? He could come down here and move in that house headed to McColl down the road there?"

"Boy you know Albert Tate ain't gonna let him out of that share cropping he's got him under."

"Say, he works for Zack Tate's brother?" asked Henry.

"Yelp," said John.

"This Dale, is he a decent man?" Henry inquired further.

John looked up at Henry, "He's as decent as any man I know, Henry."

"What you think, think he'll work for me?" asked Henry.

John didn't have to think, "Shoot yeah, I don't think you would have to twist his arm, if he can get out from under the debt he owes Albert."

"How much debt are we talking about," asked Henry?

"He owes Albert round eight hundred dollars."

"Oh boy, that's a mighty nice piece of money."

"Well, you see Mr. Henry, Dale got in debt with Albert during the drought."

"Tell you what John, when do you think I can meet this Dale feller?"

"Today," Elijah spoke up. "I'll go get him."

"Son, hold up now, hold them horses. He might be working now but soon as we can, we'll send him. It would be nice if he could get out from under Albert. And it would be nice to have him nearby.

Henry looked at Elijah and smiled. "Well, if you can, John, have Dale come see me at his earliest convenience."

Henry looked at Elijah, nodded then said, "It was nice to meet you, young feller. My little Lilly mentioned you. She didn't know I was coming over to also inspect you, he said smiling. I can tell you're a strong hard working young lad. I'll keep my eye on you. Take care gentlemen," with that, they headed off.

After they traveled down the road a bit, Henry said to Michael, "So we may have us another overseer soon enough. What do you think about that Elijah?"

Michael answered, "He seems like a strong willed young man. His hands felt as rough as rocks."

"Just curious, do you think my Lilly cares for his kind?" Henry asked.

"To be honest Uncle Henry, that lad seemed fearless out there with that shot gun in tow," he said laughing, "I know he sure would protect her at any cost." Henry turned and looked ahead. "Do you play cards Michael?"

Chapter 10

A Letter

Rachel approached her cousin Michael and grabbed his arm. "Did you give it to him? Please say you did."

"Yeah, Yeah, I passed it on to him as you requested." Rachel, please, there's no need to grab hold of my arm like that."

"Oh dear, I am sorry Michael, I do apologize, where are my manners?"

"It's quite alright, just relax," he said. "The young lad is handsome enough, but he is still quite rough around the edges. I mean literally rough. Take those hands of his. Talk about calloused hands. I don't think your Father's slave's hands are as abrasive as his."

Rachel said "Yeah, they are rough, but he's gentle. He has a heart of gold." She shared with Michael about the incident where he jumped into the river to wet her hankie, the morning they walked through the orchard, and how he had given her a piece of the forbidden fruit.

"Given you a piece of forbidden fruit, girl what are you talking about?"

She couldn't wait to share it with him, so she retrieved the family Bible and said "Let's read it together."

Michael laughed and said, "Now that's a revelation I'll have to ponder on. For such a simple feller, he could come up with some complex ideas."

Rachel said "I admit he's not well versed in the English language. No doubt you noticed, but his charm makes up for it."

"Hum," said Michael.

"Thanks for passing that note on to him, you're the best cousin a girl could have."

"Seems to me I'm the only cousin you have, so don't try to do a snow job on me," he said laughing.

"Oh no, we have other family members in Moore county. They visit at least once every spring. They are a real snooty bunch."

Michael said, "Well, I'm off to Uncle Henry's domain, that is, his library. I just want to browse around and discover some of his interest."

"Oh Michael, you'll find it to be marvelously stocked with some of the most extraordinary literature there is."

A Letter

Michael turned to Rachel and remarked "Rachel my dear, I've been to Philadelphia's library which is considered the first and foremost circulating library in the Union.

Benjamin Franklin founded it in 1731 and Harvard has a pretty extensive collection to boast too. So, we'll see what Uncle Henry's has to offer." They both entered the room.

Elijah went into his room, closing the door behind him. He lay on the bed, unfolded the note Michael had given him and read aloud.

"Dear Elijah,

I do hope you receive this letter. I really didn't know how or where to start. In fact I prayed before I picked up the pen. I miss you so, there I said it. I know that it sounds strange because we barely know each other, yet I feel like when you're around me your beautiful blue eyes look deeply into my soul. The moment I saw you my heart fluttered. I find myself wanting you near me.

I know your grandmother doesn't want you around me, and she has probably told you to stay away. I was overwhelmed by her frankness. She is correct, I know in so many ways, especially the way I feel about you. But, I know for the love of God, I would never want you to suffer or be hurt because of me.

My father too said it was in my best interest to stay away from you. At least until he has an ample time to give you a once over. Like you are some animal or slave he's going to purchase. That angered me inside, which I rarely feel toward my father.

I wish we could meet. I saw you with your dog walking along the dirt road. As I sat there looking out the window I was hoping you'd come up to our house, but you didn't. Please take care and know in your heart, I am your friend.

Sincerely,
Rachel McCloud."

Elijah folded the letter carefully and placed it in his pocket. He walked toward the parlor where he found his grandmother reading her Bible for the second time today.

A Letter

He sat down on the bench and kept silent for a moment while waiting. After about five minutes, she closed the book and looked up at him. "I know you in here wantin' to talk about that McCloud gal. I saw her pa and that feller in that wagon out yonder. What did her pa say? He didn't want you runnin' around with her neither did he?"

"No Grandma, he was looking around for somebody to work for him. He asked Pa, but Pa told him no."

"Good. They's too much work round here to do, and McCloud's got all dem slaves working for him, what's he needing somebody else fer?"

"He needs somebody to take that old Samuel's job, Samuel done got himself fired," Elijah told her.

"I can't see anybody in their right mind who would want to slave somebody out in a field and work um like a dog," said Ester.

Elijah told his grandmother, "I think he might hire Dale to come to work for him. I wish he would, they can live right down the road from us in that house going toward McColl." Elijah was excited at the very prospect of his cousins being so close.

"Lord child, I know you'd like that, you'd have Dale's youngins a rompin' round like a stampede of loose billy goats."

He just smiled at his grandmother. "Like I said you ain't come in here to talk bout no Dale and his boys. It's about that gal of McCloud's, ain't it? There's nothin' wrong with her, it's just they's somethin' wrong with the life style of dem people. You foolin' round with horror at that house, anythin' can happen. I done heard stories bout slaves uprisin' twenty somethin' years ago. They's one whose name was Nate, Nat or somethin'. He and dem people is said to have killed fifty-seven white folks. Now what would you do had dem people was to uprise? They'd kill you youngin."

"I'd run Grandma," he said.

"You mean to tell me you'd run off and leave that pretty gal behind?"

Elijah dropped his head. "No Grandma," he mumbled.

"Yes, that's what I thought. Child I know you a man and you want a woman, the good Lord done put it in your bones, it's a part of life. But, Lord, I wish you had an eye for another, one like us and not one who thinks they above us."

"She ain't like that Grandma, I promise."

"Honey, that youngin is spoiled. She's had dem slaves waitin' on her hand and foot.

She'd have to have all kinds of things to keep her happy, and the minute you couldn't give it to her, she'd make yo life a livin' hell; a naggin' and a cryin'. You'd be gray headed before you turned thirty. All that purty black hair would be whiter than mine," she said, as she brushed her hand through his hair.

"I was wantin' to see her again, if it don't make you mad."

"Lord Child, I ain't said you can't see that gal. Now, no I ain't wantin' you to, but I ain't told you not to or forbid you to. I ain't the one you should be worryin' bout, her pa catch you up there, he might have somethin' to say."

Elijah thought about that for a moment, he did recall her father did seem to put on a fake smile when he looked up at him. "Boy, you got your work cut out for you to try to keep that gal happy, that's tween you and the Lord. But, maybe you'll give me some great grandbabies 'for I see Paradise. I believe you and that purty little gal would make some beautiful little ones."

"Grandma, I love you," he said.

"Well, get yo tail up and give me a hug," she reached over and pulled his face down and kissed his cheek. "I love you boy. But I do wish you'd think bout what I dun an tol you."

"Oh, I will Grandma," he said, turning to walk out.

"I thought I might find you in here and you've got Lilly, the co-conspirator, with you," said Henry. Sarah was in tow. Michael was thumbing through a volume of old vintage poems, while Rachel had an encyclopedia reading about figs.

Henry walked over to his desk opening up a drawer. He took out a little wood box and sat it down on the table. He then turned to look at the study table off to the corner. "Let's remove that lamp and clear that table," he said. He went and placed the box on the table taking an inkwell pen holder off as the others collected the papers, the lamp and a group of dictionaries.

Michael peered inside the dictionary cover, "Wow a Noah Webster original 1828. This may be the most impressive volume here," he remarked.

"What do you have on your mind, Uncle Henry?"

"Cards, I'm gonna see if you really know how to play like you said you did or you using some kind of lawyer's bluff," Henry laughed. "I would have brought James up to play, but he's not up to it. He does seem to be doing better. He's out back carving with those set of knives we brought back.

A Letter

It's amazing what he can do with a pile of wood and a pocket knife. I've seen him make the smallest beads for necklaces." Henry kept chatting away. "Now, let's see, we need chairs. He went over and took his cushioned desk chair and placed it at one end of the table. "Grab those," pointing at two chairs that faced his desk. "And grab one from the hallway." Sarah said "I'll git it sir."

She walked out the door and reappeared with the chair, "Where'd ya like it set?" she asked.

"Place it across from me, Sarah," Henry spoke up.

She picked it up and sat it down across the table facing Henry. Giving the cushion a pat and said "Here ya go chil" as she called out to Michael.

"No," Henry said, "You take that seat." She stood there looking at him curiously. "Please be seated Sarah."

She quickly took her seat. Henry opened the box and withdrew two decks of cards, one blue and one red. He removed two stacks of chips, counting out ten and placing them in front of the other players. "The name of the game is five card draw." He announced.

"I don't know how to play that game," Rachel spoke up.

"Me neither, Missa Henry," said Sarah. "I knows how to play goes fishin', me and Rachel done play dat before."

"Yes, father can't we play that instead?" asked Rachel.

"Hold on now honey, tell you what, I'll be your partner. Sarah you can be Michael's partner."

Sarah looked over at the young man who was scooting his chair next to hers. She grinned and said, "Ya helps me chil and we can win."

"I'll do just that, Miss Sarah, we'll teach Uncle Henry and Rachel a lesson."

Henry scuffed and began shuffling the deck. He dealt out five cards to each player. In his possession, he had an ace, jack, 6, 4 and a 3. He decided to keep the ace and return the rest. "Now honey, let's see what you've got," he looked at Rachel."

Rachel had pulled a pair of kings, a 10, 4, and a 2. He whispered for her to keep the pair of kings and toss back the other three in the discard pile.

Michael had a pair of 7's, he discarded the other three. He peeked over at Sarah's hand who had 4, 5, 8, queen and a 10. "Tell you what, keep these two," pointing at the queen and 10.

A Letter

"All right now, here we go," said Henry. He passed each player the number of cards they needed to replace the ones discarded. Henry pulled an ace giving him pair. Rachel caught another King, giving her 3 of a kind.

Sarah drew an 8, 9 and Jack, giving her a straight.

Michael could get no help with his pair of 7s. "I fold," he announced. He laid his cards down.

Henry looked over at this daughter's hand and saw she had him beat, so he announced, "I also fold. You two go at it."

Once the cards were exposed, Henry declared "Sarah as the winner." She was grinning, and felt overjoyed as she clapped, while the other's smiled.

"We done good, Missa Michael."

"Aw that's just ladies luck, you and Rachel got them good hands. Now that you've caught on how to play, whoever makes the best hand will win. Come on Michael said, "Let's show them how to play a full house, three and four of a kind or a straight flush." He explained the different combinations and how to make the best hand. They started with three bets to open, one bet to stay and one bet on the last. They played the cards for hours.

At one point Michael was winning all the chips. Then they played seven card draw and Henry came out the winner.

Sarah got up in a panic, "Lord I suppose to help cook y'alls supper, Lord, look at da time."

Henry smiled, "Calm down little lady, it's ok that we've detained you."

Mary called out, "Supper's ready."

Michael, Henry and Rachel sat down and savored every morsel as if they had been at work all day. After supper, they went back into the library, where Henry and Michael enjoyed a few shots of fine liquor. Henry announced it was 8:30pm and there had not been an accounting of the servants. He promptly looked over at Rachel, and said, "Lilly, you go and make sure everyone is accounted for." Rachel asked Sarah to come along.

Henry began telling Michael what an excellent card player he was, "You know there's a game tomorrow, and it will be a great opportunity to take some of the big wigs' money. Zack and his brother Albert and the rest of the hot shot landowners around here will be playing up at the Lodge in the Sandhills tomorrow. The way I see it, now would be an excellent time to target Albert.

A Letter

John told me that Dale was a fine feller, and if I can have the opportunity to get old Albert in my pocket, then I can have Dale come work for me. Not sure if this plan will work, but we can give it a shot. How about it?"

Michael looked at Henry, feeling the effects of the alcohol. "Well I don't know if I have the full picture, but I'll trust your instincts and go along with you this time. Right now though, I'd love to have me a good smoke."

Henry walked over to his desk and pulled out a cigar box. He lifted one out, giving it a sniff. "Umm," he said as he handed one over to Michael. "Remember Michael, you're family and family sticks together, I'm with you until the end."

Elijah lay awake in his bed. He got up and walked over to the window. As he was staring out into the darkness illuminated by the light of a full moon, he lifted the window and jumped to the ground. He decided to check on Red. He sat for awhile talking to his friend, reassuring him, rubbing and petting him.

Feeling restless, Elijah couldn't get Rachel off his mind and before he knew it, he was walking down the road heading toward the McCloud plantation. He walked quietly up the dirt road. As he got nearer, he could see the house was dark inside. The only flicker of light was seen in a down stairs window.

He crept up and decided to peek inside. He saw Henry and Michael wrapped up in camaraderie. He looked up at the top floor, staring at Rachel's window. The window from which Rachel had called out to him the first time he visited the plantation. He pulled out several kernels of corn that he had stashed in his pocket. He threw several, striking the window pane. There was no response. He decided to throw the five kernels he had left all at once. Still no response.

As he walked slowly away, he turned to look back. He could now see a light glowing within Rachel's room. He noticed Rachel's silhouette appear behind drawn curtains. He ran back. Rachel pulled the curtains back and saw Elijah standing there. She quickly lifted the window and called out in a soft whisper "Well hello, stranger."

Answering her in a loud voice, "Hey yourself."

"Shhhh," she whispered. "Be quiet, don't let anyone hear you." Elijah could barely hear her.

He waved for her to come down. She shook her head no. "I can't", she said. "Father's awake".

Elijah placed his hands to his ears to try and hear what she was saying. He still couldn't hear, so he motioned for her to hold on. He walked around the side of the house where there was a stone chimney of smooth riverbed rocks. He thought, 'I can do this.' He was already in his bare feet, so he began placing the tips of his toes in the corner edges of the rocks.

He grabbed each rock slowly, having confidence it would take him to Rachel. In a matter of minutes he was on the roof. He crept around to Rachel's window. As he stuck his head in the window, Rachel almost let out a scream, but she placed both of her hands to her mouth. "Dear God, you nearly frightened me to death," she told him.

Elijah smiled, "Now we can talk."

Rachel began messing with her hair. She always tries to present her best and was very self-conscious about her appearance at that moment.

"Ain't you gonna let me in?" he asked.

She didn't know how to answer. Never before had a man come into her bedroom, not even Michael. She wanted him to come in, but she was at a loss with mixed emotions.

He asked again, "Can't I come in? Just let me in."

She moved to the side as he climbed in. She stared at his bare feet. His feet had dirt and debris all over them. "Hold up," she whispered. She went and got a cloth and water from the alabaster washbasin. She tossed the wet cloth to him, "Here clean up that mess and wipe your feet."

"Yes madam," he answered. He was so happy to be in her presence at that moment he would have danced a jig if she asked. As he was cleaning up, she went over and brushed her hair quickly.

Elijah held the towel outside the window and shook it off, and then he tried to give it back to Rachel. "No sir, you keep it," so he laid it out on the roof. "Now, tell me, what brings you creeping up here, like some thief in the night?" She didn't want him to know the real excitement she was feeling inside.

He looked up at Rachel and said, "Gal you're beautiful with your hair down."

Rachel blushed as she walked over to her candy collection. Elijah looked around the room, taking in every detail. The walls had flowers painted on them like they had been planted there.

Painted daisies and roses flowed throughout the room. The floor even reflected the lantern light. It shined like a mirror. A huge rug was under the large bed. The bed had a canopy over the top. There were four different styles of heirloom furniture. The dresser had a mirror attached to it. He was amazed at the sheer size of the room. One mirror was larger than all the mirrors in his house put together.

All of a sudden his thoughts turned to his grandmother. Her words began haunting him. 'Boy you got your work cut out for you to try and keep that gal happy.' It was at that moment he truly sensed the meaning and wisdom of her words.

Rachel held out the mason jar of candy, "Here have a treat."

He reached out to take a piece, when she pulled the candy back and coldly announced, "Your hands are soiled where you've been washing your dirty feet." Then she smiled, "Here, just tell me your preference and I'll put it into your mouth."

"The red one," he said.

"Oh, that's the strawberry cinnamon, good choice. Open your mouth," she popped one into his mouth and then licked her fingers, smiling all the while. "Would you like another?" she teased.

"Umm, yes, I'd like the orange." She started rubbing his lips with the orange candy. "There's another flavor you'd love I'm sure."

"No thanks, that's enough for now," Elijah replied.

As she carried the jar back to the dresser, she noticed him still looking around the room. She walked over to him and bragged, "Those candies came from the northern states. Father brought them back."

He ignored her, and then said, "That sure is a big mirror."

"Oh, that's a cheval glass. "Come," she took him by the arm and led him in front of it. He looked at himself, as he was standing there looking like a country bumkin next to a princess, dressed in a full length flowered night gown. As he turned to the side, she moved closer to him, "We make a nice couple, look at us," she said playfully.

He moved away from her feeling downtrodden. He looked at the bench with the elaborate upholstery. "This is a banquette," she proudly announced, "Come sit here beside me."

He walked over and sat down. "If you come here to sit, what's that over yonder?" he pointed.

A Letter

She got up and walked over, "It's a divan." She laid back on it. Elijah's mind was racing.

He was awestruck at the opulence. "I had no business coming here, I think I better go."

She stood and rushed over to his side. "No please. Come let me show you my favorite thing in the all whole wide world." She took his hand and guided him over to her dresser where she pulled out a jewelry box and opened it.

Elijah's eyes widened and he was rendered speechless for all the treasures he saw before him.

"Gal, you must be a princess."

Rachel giggled. "No silly boy, these are three generations of jewels. My father's mother, my mothers' and now mine." She fingered through the items and withdrew a ring. "This was my grandfather's. Here try it on."

Reluctantly, he slid the ring onto his finger and held it out for her to see. It had a large diamond in the center with cloves carved all around the band. It appeared to be a mixture of gold and silver. "Now you're the Prince, if I'm a Princess." Elijah's heart sank, as he pulled the ring off his finger.

"O yeah, I know what I come for." He took her letter out of his pocket and handed it to her. She felt thrilled, thinking it was a letter he had written her in return.

She graciously accepted only to realize it was in her own handwriting. "I don't understand," she said. "What? Don't you want my letter?"

Elijah could see the hurt on her face "No silly gal, I was hoping you would read it to me and let me hear you speak your thoughts. I liked the letter. It felt good to my heart to know you thought enough of me to write me. So now, please read it."

She looked at him smiling. "Gosh, you know how to make a girl feel awkward. Okay, let's sit down on the divan." She sat down holding the letter, as she patted the spot next to her for him to sit. "Come now I won't bite, I promise."

She cleared her throat, then looked at him, "Are you sure you want me to read this?" She hoped the answer would be no.

But he answered "Please, read it."

"Dear Elijah," As she read the letter, she kept glancing over at him as he looked up at the ceiling with a smile on his face. "Hey you," she rapped him across his thigh. "What?" he answered.

"You aren't paying any attention."

"Oh yes, I heard every word you said. It's just that sometimes I feel so dumb."

"Stop now!" she ordered, "You aren't dumb, yes maybe unlettered by some people's standards but not dumb. Even Michael was impressed with your logic and reasoning abilities. Michael talked about how wise a lad you are. And he has a doctorate degree in Law. Don't you know that our whole Union adopted its laws from the Bible? And you know the Bible, so you are far from being dumb. Now, I will thank you to never put yourself down like that in front of me again."

"I'm sorry," he answered. She began talking to him about virtue and chastity. He was blushing but listening.

He folded up the letter and kissed it, then placed it back in his pocket stating, "My first ever letter."

Rachel was so happy to have him all to herself in that moment. She asked him questions such as his favorite foods, favorite season of the year, favorite church hymns and favorite Bible characters. They sat enjoying each other's company way into the night.

Rachel asked, "Have you ever kissed a girl?"

Elijah jumped up and pointed, "Hey it's gonna be daylight soon, look out yonder to the east. I got to go!" He opened the window and scurried back down to the ground. As he turned to leave, he waved bye to Rachel.

Walking home, Elijah decided he would add the letter to his prized possessions. He used a tin can to hold things he held dear, like arrow heads, clay marbles, a gold coin and other significant things. Most importantly, it held his mother's wedding ring. The ring he intended to give to the woman he'd call his wife. Elijah's letter from Rachel would soon become his second most cherished item inside the can.

Chapter 11

Better Man

Henry and Michael hopped into the buggy and headed off to the Tates place for the Friday night card game. They met up with Zack Tate and his brother Albert.

"Henry, I thought you weren't coming to join us for the fun," said Zack.

"I changed my mind," replied Henry. "Wasn't anything better to do around the house and I thought this would give Michael a chance to meet the big wheels that roll around this area. Or should I say, the ones who rule the area?" Zack laughed then turned toward Michael and shook his hand.

"Son, your Uncle is taking you into the lion's den. Them fellers from Richmond County will take hold of your money before you get a chance to dump it in that briefcase I saw you carrying when we first met. If you get in a bind and need a loan, I'll give it to you. In return you can come and work at my bank? What do you say?"

"Alright Zack, that's enough trying to bait Michael to work in that bank of yours. We've come to take some money, we didn't come to give any up," explained Henry.

Albert spoke up. "Aw hell, Henry, we remember when you were green and lost your profits in three hands. Zack is just trying to look out for the young man."

"Well I've got my own eyes to look out for Michael. He's blood, and none of his blood is going to be spilt tonight. You boys are like them sharks down at Myrtle Beach, you think you smell blood, but all you smelling are them night crawlers. You give a new meaning to card sharks," Henry laughed. Michael added, "I'm ready to throw my lot in to better my knowledge of the game and increase my capital while doing it."

"Whoa." said Albert. "There may be something more to this champ. We just have to wait and see how well that top notch northern education of his will serve him. Here comes John now."

The carriage was a fancy stage coach. All four men climbed inside. Albert and Zack sat facing each other, while Michael and Henry did the same. Zack opened up a compartment and retrieved four glasses. Each glass was made of fine crystal with hollow openings, cut with diamond cubes.

He handed a glass to each gentleman, while he pulled out a finely crafted flagon filled with brown whiskey. "Here young man, this will calm your nerves. You look like you could use a good stiff drink."

He then poured Albert and Henry some. "Aren't you going to join us Zack?" Henry asked. Well sure, I am, but I'm having me some brandy. Brandy clears my head. That liquor you're drinking will make me feel like a cub in that lion's den I spoke of earlier."

Zack then made a toast, "Tonight we're gonna take all them Rockingham boy's money," he said smiling. They all said in unison, "Cheers!!! Cheers!!!"

"That's some nice smooth whiskey," said Henry.

Michael chimed in, "I don't normally drink brown whiskey."

"And why the hell not," asked Albert?

"Well, rumor up north has it, Southern gents use dirty muddy water in processing the whiskey, that's why it's brown."

"Bullshit," said Zack. "This whiskey comes from Jim Jack, a good clean Tennessean if there ever was one. The liquor is brewed and stored in barrels for years, which gives it that good smooth taste." He then hands Michael another drink.

"Ah," said Michael smacking his lips, "I've got no complaints, Mr. Tate."

The carriage was approaching the entrance to the lodge in a grove of massive long leaf pines. The driver dropped off the passengers, then pulled the horse around back where the stables were. A group of carriage drivers were mingling with each other, discussing which carriage was the most prestigious. It was a show of wealth, indeed.

Once inside, Michael looked around smiling as he gazed at all the deer heads that graced the walls. He noticed the bar lined with twelve stools in front of it. Women were sitting there with a few elderly men. The old men were caressing and snuggling up to the women, whispering in their ears. Four tables were arranged in the middle of the floor. Dealers sat at each table with chips and decks of cards.

Michael thought to himself, 'This is some pretty serious stuff. A nice set up indeed.' Then he noticed a man puffing away on a cigar and swaying somewhat. Michael knew he was tipsy.

He called over to Henry, "I'd like to try my luck at this table." Henry cautioned, "There's a $100 sitting fee, you know?"

Michael removed $150 from his money bag, placed it on the table and took a seat. Henry joined him, choosing a seat three chairs down.

The gent still puffing on his cigar spoke up "Good day gentleman, my names Bob Goodwin."

Michael and Henry introduced themselves.

After about five minutes, the dealer called out, "Table two is ready to roll."

Three other men walked up and settled into the empty chairs. They pulled coins from their bags and placed their money on the table.

The dealer announced the lodge rules. "Gentlemen the game will be seven card stud. Nothing's wild, bet in turn, low card must ante up to start each hand with a minimum $2 bid and $5 maximum. Only two raises allowed. If you fold your hand, no white faces will be shown. You will not be allowed to see what your next card is until the end of the hand. Keep your eyes on your own cards. This chip will keep the deal rotating. I'll place it in front of the man who is to receive the first card. As if each of you are taking turns dealing. If a hand is called at the end, the players will lay out their hands so the hand itself will determine who the winner is. There will be no arguing of any sort. We are respectable men and here at the lodge, we expect all to conduct themselves accordingly. Any questions gentlemen?"

No one spoke up. "Well now with that taken care of, to be fair, I'll spread these cards out and let you all pick to see who will receive the first card from the deck. Whoever pulls the highest will go first."

All the men pulled a card. Henry pulled the ace of hearts. He was given the first card from the deck when the dealing began.

After three hours of constant play, Henry and Michael were doing really well. Two men had already dropped out.

Zack came over and took a seat with a mound of chips. "I came to try my luck with you big boys. I've cleaned clocks over there." They all turned and saw a table vacant. The gamblers were at the bar chatting with some of the ladies.

Others had already left with only their pride still intact and a few hundred short of the assets they came with. Mr. Goodwin had sobered up some and was playing a bit more cautious.

Several hours later, after the dealer announced Henry had the winning hand, Mr. Goodwin said "I've dropped five and I think that's enough for one week. You Scotland fellows got the best of me this go round.

I'll try my hand next week." He patted Michael on the shoulder "You did well young man and you're a pleasure to be around, enjoyed the company unlike your old uncle here. He's a real scrooge, tight as a size ten shoe on a size twelve foot. Zack, you and Henry take care of this feller, perhaps he can be a new addition to our organization. He's mighty intelligent to be so young. Good night gentlemen, I will leave you with this thought, It's okay to run away, as you may have the opportunity to fight another day."

After the farewells, the card game continued. Two more hours passed and Michael and Henry were working on Zack's stash. "Break call," said Zack. "I need to stretch my legs and back a little, all this sitting is getting to me."

The dealer looked at his pocket watch and agreed, "15 minutes and we will continue gentlemen."

Everyone got up stretched and walked over to the bar. Glasses were filled and cigars and cigarettes were passed around. Conversations commenced concerning both their wins and losses.

Zack said to Henry. "If I didn't know any better, I'd say you and that nephew of yours was double teaming me. I should have carried my ass over to Al's table and pulled the stunt you two are working on me. Heck my luck was running so good, I felt like I couldn't be whipped. But you boys have gone and taken all my profit along with 20 more of my personal funds. I'm going to fight back though, can't let the new kid show me up."

After several minutes passed, Albert walked over to the bar and stood next to his brother. "I'm beating him down over there like a captured escaped negro."

After taking a swallow of his drink, Zack spoke up, "I'm glad you're doing something over there, as for me, these boys are whipping me like a hired out mule."

Albert looked around, "Who?" "Old Henry and his nephew, I believe they're double teaming me, ain't that right Henry?"

"No Zack," replied Henry. "You just been getting caught in the cross fire. I've been trying to teach Michael a lesson, but you keep getting in his way. So, no, I don't have my sights set on you. That boy done took me for a ride playing cards last night. So, ain't no friends at these tables. His money spends just as good as anyone elses."

Albert looked over at Michael, "Young buck, you and your uncle trying to take Brother Zack for a fast one?"

103

"It's like Uncle Henry said, "Ain't no friends at that table, Mr. Tate. In fact, I'd like to spend some of your money, if you'd like to donate to the cause."

Somehow, that didn't sit well with Albert, he got flushed around the ears with a touch of anger and hoped no one noticed. He looked at Michael and said "What cause would that be young buck?" Michael didn't care to be called 'Young buck.' This gave him added reason to dislike Albert. It was bad enough for Africans to be enslaved here in this country, but it detested him more for a white man to enslave another white man under a mocked up concept like 'share cropper' which was nothing more than slavery in his eyes.

"The cause is for my bank account," he grinned.

Albert was becoming unnerved, until he saw the smile on his brother's face.

"Well old brother," Zack said. "Sounds like a good cause to me."

Albert shot back at Michael. "Zack said he needed you in his bank to work for him, so I'll help put you behind a desk. I was playing cards while you were still wet in diapers. You boys excuse me." Albert went over to the table and said something to the dealer. They shook hands and he returned to the bar.

"Well, seems like, if your Uncle can't teach you a lesson, let me see if I can help out. I'll be joining you at your table now." He ordered a whiskey shot and downed it quickly. He looked around as he sat at the table and announced, "I don't want no hard feelings after this, I hope we all will remain in good graces with one another. Heck I'll even buy you a steak dinner next time you're over in Laurel Hill, just come on in to Tate's Plates.

"Tell you what, I'll come to the bank and buy you a meal every Friday if you whip me," shot back Henry.

"That's a tall order," said Albert. "So whenever you all are ready let's get at it."

The dealer was sipping his coffee. He put it down and began shuffling a deck of cards. After four shuffles, he picked up another deck and shuffled some more. By this time Zack, Michael, Henry and another gent made their way to the table.

"Stone, this ain't got nothing to do with you. You sit down here you'll leave a broke man," said Zack to the 5th player.

"Oh hell Zack, I'm out to get some money back from that brother of yours, he's taken 4 off me. I'm just looking for a change of scenery. Besides, yall's dealer looks better than the one at the far table. He's ugly like you Albert."

Albert looked up, "Stone, you are a sight for sore eyes yourself, looking like a possum crawled out of dead cow's ass." Everyone burst out laughing. Stone sat down at the vacant seat.

The men gambled, cursed, and became agitated. By 12 o'clock Albert called out, "This ain't going anywhere. Back and forth, back and forth like a damn rocking chair. I say we go 5,10 and sky's the limit on the end, unless you boys can't handle the raise."

Henry knew this was his chance to hurt Albert's pocket book. "I'm in," said Henry.

Zack said, "Count me in."

Then Michael smiled, "I wouldn't miss this, count me in, but first let me see, if I understand you correctly? Instead of the 2 and 5 bet you want to raise the bet to 5 and 10 and sky's the limit? I take that to be you can bet as much as you want on the last card?"

"Damn boy, that's exactly what I mean, young buck," retorted Albert. Mockingly, he said "You're a smart one. No wonder Zack wants you in his bank."

Michael paid no attention to his sarcastic remark, but looked at his stack and started counting. "You've got 18 hundred there," said Albert.

"Which I'll put with my 24 over here if you decide you want to play with the big dogs or you can be a pup and run on over to the fire and hang out with one of them fine ladies."

"Ha Ha Ha!" Albert laughed.

"Well, that does sound good, but those young ladies would lose their minds over a young stud like me after being with an old fart like you," Michael boldly replied.

At that moment, not only did Albert's ears turn cherry red, but his face and cheeks did too.

"I'm in", said Michael.

"I'm out," said Stone, "Getting a little too hot in here for me." He said his farewells and departed.

After twenty plus hands had been played, Albert was on top.

Better Man

Albert had won $600 of Michael's money, Henry had taken $1,000 from Zack and $200 from Michael. Michael thought to himself, 'damn $800 is what it cost to pay up that Dale feller's debt, and here it is I'm down with only $800 remaining. Is this the sign I need?'

Zack picked up in the game and Henry remained the same. Michael would call a hand if his first three cards were 3 of a kind, 2 or 3 cards of the same suit or a pair. He'd tried for an ace for two rounds hoping to catch another. If none of those landed in his hand he would fold. After a few good hands he was up to $2200.

Albert eyed the stack. "I see you're turning that ant hill into a mountain over there, young buck. I'm gonna have to go mining in that mountain, if I catch you out there in that pot."

"Good Luck," replied Michael.

The money changed hands around the table from one gambler to the other. Finally, Albert burst out cursing, "Damn it, this is a kiddy game and I say hell with the 5 to 10, let's go 10 to 20."

"Hold on now Mr. Tate," said the dealer. You can't bully players. That takes the sport out of the game, you know the house rules."

"What the hell you mean bullying?" Albert replied. "I mean you can toss 5 in, and any man may call, but you start tossing in 20's and a man with a winning hand maybe reluctant to toss his 20 in."

"Listen, are you tossing 20's out there Vernon?"

"Well, no I'm not," said the dealer.

"Alright then, shut your pie hole." The dealer shuffled the deck of cards, ignoring the remark.

"I'll tell you what, just forget 10, 20, make it sky's the limit on all bets. How's that sound?" said Henry.

"Now that's what I'm talking about McCloud, you are a true southern gentlemen that knows how to gamble. Let's do it," said Zack.

Michael chimed in, "I don't know about that," as he looked over to his Uncle. His uncle gave him a wink. "I need a drink," said Michael. He stood up and stretched.

"See if they've got some chicken feed while you're up?" bok, bok, bok, joked Albert.

All the rest got up and followed Michael to the bar. To Michael's surprise, Albert bought him a drink. One of the girls walked up and put her hand on Albert's back. "Hey big Al" she said.

"Oh, hell Barbara," he turned and gave her a hug. Albert pulled a coin from his pocket, here sweetheart, passing her the double gold eagle.

"Last week when I was down, I couldn't give you anything, but, I hope this will show you I do appreciate you, Barbara. You did good Sugar." She smiled and placed the coin inside her small pouch, which she kept stashed away inside her bra.

"We can get him now," Henry whispered to Michael.

"Uncle I don't know if I want to agree to that outrageous bet with no limit."

"Hell grow some balls Michael, we can take them. Remember, you're fighting for a man's freedom, isn't that what you want?"

"Yeah, don't remind me. Poor fellow, I'd hate to work for the likes of Albert. We'll make him turn that Dale fellow loose. If we can get 800 dollars from his pocket, Dale's free at no charge to us. It's win win, but you have to be in it to win."

"Got it!"

"Bartender you got some chicken feed back there stashed away?" asked Albert in a loud voice. It was then and there that Michael decided he would go all out to shut Albert's mouth. After a few laughs and jokes, Michael walked back to the table took his seat and waited for the other players. "What did the young buck decide?" asked Albert.

"I'm here, aren't I?" Michael said angrily.

"So he is and the sky's the limit," Henry reminded the others. They started playing cards with a seriousness that the dealer hadn't seen all night.

Albert bought a few hands with some high stakes betting. Henry fell victim to a couple of bad hands. Zachariah beat Albert out of one of the largest pots of the night $1,700. The night wore on as Michael and Albert played tit for tat. Then, the night's master of all pots was on the table. It was all or nothing. The bet went down to the final card. The dealer started with Zack. He dealt two cards down and one card up to each player. It was all on the line.

Zack's hand consisted of a Jack of diamonds and an 8 of diamonds in the hole, with a 9 of hearts turned up. Henry's hand was a Queen of hearts and a 7 of hearts in his hole with a 4 of hearts turned up. Albert's hand was a Pair of Kings in the hole, and a 6 of clubs turned up.

Better Man

Michael peeked at his two down cards and saw a King of spades and a Jack of spades with a 4 of diamonds turned up. He realized he was the low man, he wanted to fold, but realized he couldn't, so he placed a 20 dollar bet to see who would bite. He did like the two spades he had in the hole, particularly since he didn't see any other spades on the table. He hoped his five hand cards would be spades. Zack called him. Henry tossed in another 20 to raise. He had 3 hearts and his chances for a flush were good with only one other heart on the table.

Albert laughed. "I see you boys are growing a set of nuts. I'm gonna crack em for you, if you stay in this hand." He tossed in 60 to raise Henry. Albert was feeling pretty good about his King's being top dog.

Michael hoped Albert was trying to bluff, so he did some bluffing on his own, hoping no one would call. "I raise it to a straight 100," he said.

All eyes turned as they gazed upon Michael. Henry looked shocked, which everyone else took notice of. Zack looked at his cards again. He could have a straight or perhaps a flush developing, so he added 80 dollars and called. Henry threw his 60 in to protect Michael from being double teamed by the Tate brothers.

"Well I'll be damn, old young bucks' testicles have popped out and he's ready to do some mounting. But for sure it won't be on old Al here. "I call you" said Albert.

The dealer carefully flipped the cards out to the players. Zack received a 10 of diamonds. Henry, a Queen of clubs. Albert hit a King of clubs for which he jumped for joy inside at the prospect of winning. Michael smiled when the dealer flipped his card, the 10 of spades. He liked his odds even better now, but pretended to be disappointed. "I'll check," said Michael.

Zack already had an open end straight, he could get a 7 or Queen and have it made. "100 it was and 100 it is," he said, putting 100 into the pot.

Henry had 3 hearts and a pair of Queens, so he called. Zack laughed and said "Boys I appreciate you donating to the Tate foundation. I'll see your 100 and raise you 200 more."

Michael felt like he was bluffing because he had a King in his hand, so Albert couldn't possibly have a pair. He wanted to fold, but he looked around the table and then at the faces of the men. When his eyes landed on Henry, he noticed he had a smile from ear to ear. Michael then turned his attention to Albert.

Better Man

"Well, Mr. Tate you just might get them old nuts of yours cracked, if you're not careful. I'll call." The others followed suit. The pot had already grown to $1,600.

The dealer once again turned each card over slowly and decisively. Zack hit a deuce of hearts, he was hoping for 7 or a Queen. Henry received a 4 of spades, for which he was thrilled. His 2 pair is a good hand for the first 5 cards. He then looked on as Albert hit a 2 of spades.

Michael began to feel some discomfort, he needed spades for a flush and 2 of them were already drawn. He was dealt a 7 of clubs.

The dealer called out, "Mr. McCloud, you're the high man with a pair of 4's sir, you lead."

Henry looked around and decided he must have had the best hand. He tossed 300 into the pot.

Albert looked over at him and smiled. "Looks like you must have triple 4, betting a hundred on each one huh?"

Albert tossed out 600 dollars himself. Zack threw his 600 in and Henry placed his extra 300 on top of the pile and said, "Come to Papa you sweet pile." The pot was at 4,000 dollars.

The dealer announced final one up and began dealing. Zack received an ace of clubs; Henry was dealt an ace of hearts.

Albert received a 7 of diamonds. Michael was given a Queen of spades. His heart was relieved, out of six cards; he had only a hope of a spade flush. Now he had 4 spades, no pairs, no possible straight. He had the worst hand of them all. He didn't think he could win. He only hoped Henry would fare better. Henry was thrilled to receive 4 hearts and 2 pair. His chances looked better than the other player's hands, from what he could see of them.

Henry decided to go out on a limb. "I'll put 800 in a modest bet," he announced.

"Modest may ass, that's 8 months' pay to some folks," said Albert. "Let's go ahead and make it 1000 since you want to be so modest."

Michael was down to 1,200 dollars, he tossed it all in and said "1,200. I'm in."

"That a boy; give it all you got son," said Zack, who had to go into his money belt to retrieve an additional 400. Henry added 400 dollars to the pile. 4,800 dollars, the winner would be much wealthier by any standard. Albert looked at his pile and counted out all he had remaining.

109

550 dollars, he placed the 200 he owed and then pushed in 350 extra. He put the 350 down and said," I'm in."

Michael spoke up, "Fellers, I have exhausted my funds, and unfortunately I don't have any more to add."

"I'll cover you," Henry said, reaching down into his money belt. "Oh no Sir," said Albert, "You know the rules no passing money while a hands in session. Henry looked defeated but the rules were rules.

Zack threw in his 350 and Henry did the same. "The young buck can't see the last bets all."

"What's that?"

"1,050 put it to the side."

"Hold on" said Michael, "I've got a watch and this." He pulled his graduation ring off his finger.

Albert reached over for the ring, eyeing it admiringly. "That's a nice one, you sure you want to part with it young buck? Tell you what, I'll accept, if the two other ones will."

Zack held out his hand to take a closer look at the ring and watch. He turned it over as if he was appraising its value.

"I'll accept it, and if me or Albert wins, you've got to give me, let's see two weeks of work in the bank. How's that sound?"

Michael knew there wasn't too much he could do at this point. He was desperate, he needed a 9 of spades or an ace of spades for a straight flush, or any spade would give him a flush. He knew he had to hit at least one spade regardless. He recounted two on the board, four in his hand, possibly three in the others down cards that he couldn't see. That left four spades out of twenty-eight remaining cards. There was the number eight again.

"I'll give you two weeks Mr. Tate, if Uncle Henry or I lose this hand."
"You can keep the watch," said Zack.

"Oh, no sir," said Albert, "It goes in the pot also."

He placed the watch on the pile of money as Zack sat the ring on top of it.

"Deal them Vernon," said Henry. "This card is down and good luck gentlemen. May the best hand win."

Zack was dealt a Queen of diamonds, giving him a straight of 8, 9, 10, Jack, and Queen. Henry was dealt a 6 of heart, giving him a heart flush. Albert bleakly looked at his hand. He saw a 7 giving him a full house of 3 Kings and 2 Sevens. He leaned back in his chair and let out a sigh.

Zack spoke up "I got a straight."

"I got a flush," said Henry, he pulled up his fist.

"Both of you can fold, cause I got a full house. Kings over sevens," he turned his hand out and added, "Read em and weep boys."

Michael's heart sank, he hadn't even looked at his card yet. He gathered up the three down cards and placed the final card behind the others. He peeped at all his face down cards.

Albert spoke up "Come on young buck, you can go ahead and toss your cards in too. I'm the better man with the better hand tonight. I'm buying everyone a round!" He yelled to the bartender.

Michael saw a black Ace, then he saw the SPADE.

Albert shouted out again, "Let it go son, you fought hard." Michael laid his cards out carefully on the table for all to see, his hands were trembling.

Albert's mouth dropped open. "Well, I be damn, hold them drinks," he shouted at the bartender.

"Keep pouring," said Michael.

"Well, I'll be a rat's ass," said Zack. "I ain't seen one of them in about two years. I've seen a couple of little ones, but boy you got the royal one."

Henry pushed the pile of money toward Michael. Michael stood up smiling and raked in the dough. He placed the ring back on his finger. He then picked up a 100 and walked over placing it on the bar. "Compliments of Mr. Albert Tate", he announced.

Albert walked over and slapped him on the back. "Boy beginner's luck indeed. I just knew I had those winnings in my pocket and you pulled it off. I took you for at least a flush and damn you hit that royal. Well, I came here with $2,500 and Zack had $2,500. Don't know what your Uncle had. If I'm right, there was around 9,000 dollars and some change in that pot. The largest ever. Before tonight $7,400 was the record. I spect you're one happy man now. What are you gonna do with all that money? Or can't you share that with us old boys?"

"Thinking of buying some freedom for someone," said Michael. Well, hell, boy, I'll sale you some nigras if that's all you want. Henry walked up holding the bag with the winnings. "Got your money right here," said Henry smiling. He handed the bag over to Michael. Michael placed it on the floor. The crowd congratulated him for being the big winner of the night. The ladies all gathered around smiling, hoping for his companionship.

Michael dug through the bag and gave the ladies a coin each and thanked them for looking pretty. He looked at his uncle and passed the bag back to him knowing he would take care of it for him. He then walked out with a pretty little brunette. After about forty-five minutes he returned with a plastered grin on his face.

"Are we ready to go now?" asked Henry.

Albert, who was drunk, walked over to Michael. Zack wasn't far behind. "You were the better man tonight."

Chapter 12

Friend for Life

Several days later, Henry and Michael rode their horses to the Clark homestead. Elijah was in the loft of the barn. A slight breeze blew through the opened front and back doors. Red was down below barking. Elijah thought he best investigate, something could be wrong. Walking out, he saw Mr. McCloud. Quickly he ducked back inside the barn. He didn't know if they knew about his night visit, so he thought it best to stay out of sight.

Elijah listened as he heard the screen door slam. He peeked out and saw his Pa speaking with Mr. McCloud. "Elijah," his Pa shouted, looking out towards the groves and pond area. Then his eyes scanned toward the barn. "Elijah," he called as if he knew he was inside. "Elijah, come on down out of that loft and listen to what Mr. McCloud's got to say."

There it was, he thought, Mr. McCloud was going to order him to stay off his property and forbid him to see Rachel. Elijah called out, "I can hear him from here."

"No, you need to get your tail down here now."

Elijah jumped from the perch to the ground. He squatted on his landing, stinging his feet, but didn't let it show. Elijah darted up to where his father was standing. "How you doing Mr. McCloud?" asked Elijah. He then turned and looked at Michael.

Michael said, "That was some leap Elijah, you're in good shape."

"Thanks." Elijah said with a smile.

"Aw, he just wanted to play tough is all," said John.

"Well go ahead and tell him," John added. "Elijah, I'd like for you to go and see your uncle Dale, isn't that his name?" Henry began.

"Yeah Dale's his name," said John.

Henry continued. "I want to meet with him for consideration of the job I was telling you all about. I already acquired the house down the road there. It was Alfred Lucas's place. I purchased it at a decent price. And with a little fixing up I think it can be a fine place for his family. I was going to speak with Albert Tate concerning your uncle's debt, but then thought better of it."

He pulled out his leather money pouch. "You see, I have the money to cover his debt with Albert, if he'll accept the job." "Wow" said Elijah, "What cha need me for?" "I need for you to go and get Dale. I feel like having you all around will tip the scales in my favor. Will you fetch him for me?"

"Yeah, let me go hitch up one of the mules,"

Elijah turned to head toward the barn, when Michael called out "Hold up Elijah. You can ride Eagle over to his place; that is if you wish." Michael confessed, "I've recently begun riding and my legs are mighty sore."

Henry laughed, "Michael you'll get the hang of it."

"Elijah, you ride don't you boy?" he asked.

"Yeah, I had me a horse once, well, he was a pony. He ate a bunch of Hell born plants and died from it."

"Son, you must be talking about the hellebore plant. Was it large leafed and had greenish drooping flowers?"

"Yep, that was it, he'd eat anything green. Ole Brownie was what I called him, cause he was brown, he giggled."

"Well, you are more than welcome to ride Eagle," repeated Michael offering him the reins.

Elijah looked at Eagle and said "Ok, I will." He leaped onto the horse's back, and the horse let out a neigh. Elijah began patting his neck. The horse started trotting. Once he was out of sight of the others, he kicked Eagle's ribs and the horse began to gallop.

Elijah got excited from the rush of the wind in his hair and across his face. He had never traveled at such a fast speed. "Aw boy, you like to fly like them Eagles," he pulled back on the reins for the animal to slow down and come to a halt. Elijah realized he could have fallen to his death. He patted the horse's neck again then continued down the road at a much slower pace.

As he approached his uncle's home he saw Little Dale sitting in a swing underneath the big elm tree in front of the house. When he noticed the gigantic horse coming his way, Little Dale immediately ran inside.

Danny came out of the house and leaped off the porch holding a colt peace maker, single action, six shot revolver. After seeing it was only Elijah, he quickly yelled out, "It ain't nobody but Lijah, that's all. "Where you git that horse, Lijah, you steal him?" He asked with a devilish look in his eye.

"No, he's a McCloud horse. They sent me to fetch your daddy."

"What you want daddy for?" asked Danny, sticking his pistol in his pants.

"Look here, just go tell him Mr. McCloud is wantin' to see him."

"I ain't telling him nothing, till you tell me what for."

114

"He's wantin' him to go to work for him. All he has to do is ride around and look at them black folks."

"You mean a slave driver?" asked Danny.

"I reckon, plus he's got the house down the road all ready to put ya'll in, if you daddy wuz to come to work for him."

Dewey came up, "Where you got that horse from Lijah, he's a big'en."

"Ain't none of your business, squirt, he might of stole him," said Danny winking to Elijah.

"Where's ya'lls daddy?" Elijah asked again.

Uncle Dale stepped out onto the porch. "Lijah boy, whose horse you got?"

"Uncle Dale, he's a McCloud horse. Mr. McCloud dun sent me down here to ask you to come up to our house. He's a wantin' to talk to you."

"Now what in tarnation is he a wantin' me for?"

"Danny burst in "Daddy, he's wantin' you to go work for him. And watch over them slaves he's got. I could help you daddy. Danny whipped out his pistol, "I'll shoot um if they run."

"Boy, git in that house and take that thang with you, 'for I slap the hair off your head."

"Yeah, it ain't even loaded," said Dewey. Danny turned and slapped Dewey on the back and said, "Shut up."

"That's what he's wantin'?" asked Dale.

"Yes Sir. Said he's got money to pay off your debt to Mr. Tate and that house from down our way is ready for you."

Dale rubbed his stubbled chin. "Damn that sounds good. Hell, them slave drivers don't do nothin'. They a lazy pack. What happened to Sam McDonald? I thought he was his slave man."

"Mr. McCloud run him off, I heard." "Well, let's go see what this man is all bout."

Dewey turned and looked up "Daddy we gonna move?"

"I got to go talk to that feller first boy, just hold your horses. Speaking of horses, boy, that horse is foaming at the mouth, you been running him hard? Go git him some water."

Elijah climbed down off the horse and led him to the water well. He drew water up and poured it in the square trough. The horse apparently was mighty thirsty, he drank it dry.

Dale told Lijah, he'd be out in a minute. He left and went inside to speak to his wife. Danny came back out, "I'm hoping daddy will take that job. I don't like him working for dem Tates. He seems meaner since we lost the crops and all. Mama says we stuck with the Tates cause of all the money we owe em. Lord, we owe them for supplies and seed not to mention the mules and mess. We dun ate dem hogs, ain't got nothing left, but some chickens. And Daddy forbids us to eat out of the garden till the Tates get their share. Don't seem like we ain't never gonna have crap round her."

"Boy, go get Sour Weed," his father called to Danny. Sour Weed was a mustang brought from Texas as a colt at the end of the Mexican war. He got his name from eating sour weeds. Most animals avoided the sour shoots that sprouted up along dirt roads and fields, but not him, he loved them. The horse was nearly thirteen years old.

Once Sour Weed saw Eagle near the trough he began whinnying and pawing the ground. Eagle neighed and snorted. Danny kept a tight grip on Sour Weed. The mustang became uncontrollable trying to get at Eagle. Elijah had to pull Eagle back from Sour Weed's bite. Dale then struck Sour Weed across the rump with an open hand. That calmed him down.

Uncle Dale grabbed the reins from his son and flung himself onto the back of the mustang. As he was getting ready to leave, he called out, "Boy you round up them chickens, pull the wagon up to the back porch for your ma, and I'll be back after a while."

Danny took this as a sign, they would be moving, "Yes Sir" he answered and ran off toward the barn.

"Let's go Lijah," said Dale as he trotted Sour Weed down the dirt road. As they rode along, Dale called out to Elijah, "Boy that horse looks like one of them quarter horses. Let's see what he'll do."

"A quarter horse, what's that mean Uncle Dale?" asked Elijah. "Them's a race kind of horse, s'pose to be able to run good in quarter of a mile."

"Oh he's fast alright, Uncle Dale, I run him before I got to ya'll's house and he scared me running so fast."

"Whoa boy," Dale pulled back on the reins and stopped. "Well let me try him out while you ride Sour weed. "I don't know Uncle, they let me ride him, they might get mad at me if I let somebody else on him," said Elijah.

"Oh bullshit boy, I'm your uncle. Besides, I'm gonna be working for them people, I'm sure they won't mind and you can get him back after I done tested him out."

Elijah climbed down and reluctantly handed the reins over to his uncle. Dale in turn passed Sour Weeds reins over to his nephew. "You see that tree up yonder? I'm just gonna run him to there. I just wanna see what he's made of, I always heard they was fast."

Dale mounted Eagle, and struck him across his shoulder blade and gave him a kick in the ribs, "yah!" Dale yelled. The horse bolted off like a gun shot. He was running at a faster pace than when Elijah ran him. Dale was in awe of the powerful horse's speed. He kicked the ribs again with his heels, this time the horse was traveling at a speed that Dale had never experienced or witnessed.

At that very moment, a bee flew smack into Dale's forehead stinging him and leaving the stinger inside. Dale turned loose of the right rein leather strap to swat the insect while he was still trying to hold on with his left hand. Eagle suddenly took a left turn, which caused Dale to be flung out into the corn field.

Elijah quickly mounted Sour Weed and took off heading in the direction of his Uncle. Expecting the worst, he called out "Uncle Dale, Uncle Dale." He thought his uncle was hurt badly from the fall. As he walked over he saw Dale's body stretched out flat on his back. "Oh God, Uncle Dale, I'm sorry."

Elijah got down on his knees. He could see Dale trying to stir around. He had ripped up corn plant in his hair, dirt on his face and a huge red mark on his forehead. Dale sat up spitting, as he rubbed the area of his forehead where he had been stung.

"Yeah, I believe I'm okay, youngin. Damn that horse can run. I got stung by a bee or something." Dale stood up looking around, "Ah, shit," he said looking at his right hand. His pinky finger was disfigured. He grabbed and pulled on it trying to straighten it out. Elijah heard bones clicking. "Whoa shit, that hurts," said Dale. He held his hand up inspecting it. "Done went and broke my damn finger boy. You can't tell nobody bout this, you hear?"

"Uncle Dale, you scared me, I thought you was hurt bad."

Eagle had stopped as soon as Dale was flung from his back. So Elijah walked over and took hold of the reins to his bridle and walked him out onto the road.

As he looked around, true to his name, Sour Weed was chopping down on some sour weeds along the ditch bank. "It is amazing to watch him do this with the bit still in his mouth," Elijah laughed.

Dale gathered up the reins of Sour Weed and climbed on him. "Let's go Lijah," he said.

At first Lijah was uncomfortable riding Eagle, but he remembered what his father had told him. Never let a horse or any animal smell fear. So, he mounted Eagle with the confidence of a race horse jockey.

They made their way back to the Clark's homestead. Once they arrived safely, they were able to laugh about the incident. As they got off the horses, Elijah gave Eagle some water. Red appeared barking and raising havoc, because the horse was drinking from his water bucket. Elijah told him to quiet down. So he crawled back under the porch to enjoy the shade.

Elijah ran up to the porch to see where his father, Michael and Henry had gone. He found his Grandmother sitting there rocking in her chair with a fly swatter waiting on a fly to land. "Where's Pa?" he asked.

"Ain't no telling. I'm aggravated with this fly child. Ten times now I tried swatting him, but he always gits away. I'm gonna put him down tho, you just wait and see."

"Grandma, let him be, he's God's creation too." said Elijah.

"What'd I tell you boy, bout quoting the Good Book to me? Youngin that fly been aggravatin' your Grandma's eyeballs out."

At that very moment, Elijah spotted the fly buzzing around. He walked over and swiped him out of the air as quick as a cotton mouth strike. He caught the fly in his hand. He didn't have his hand fully clinched shut. He could feel the fly bouncing around trying to free himself. "I got him Grandma." "For real?" "Yes ma'am, he's in my hand." He then walked over and held his hand up to her ear.

Sure enough, she could hear the buzzing. "Well I'll be, you did git him, now you git him out of here."

Elijah opened the screen door laughing as he opened up his hand. The fly was crawling around in his hand, like he was disoriented. Elijah spoke to the fly, "Go buddy, go on git." He shook his hand and the fly flew up and landed on Elijah's nose. He then buzzed off and was soon out of sight.

Something caught Elijah's eye. He saw movement in the loft of the barn. He walked out and climbed up the ladder. Moses, Dale, Henry and Michael were all sitting on bales of hay.

As he guessed, in the middle, there sat the jug! Already Elijah could tell Henry, his father and Grandfather were feeling the effects of the potent brew.

Dale was taking a swig. "Ah, Lijah, there you are. What did you do to your Uncle Dale? Hit him in the head to git him over here?" John asked

Elijah smiled at his Uncle Dale, "No, Pa."

"Then tell me, how did he git that big bump on his head? He's telling us a wasp or bee stung him, is they any truth in that?"

"Had to be, 'cause when he left his house, he didn't have a bump on him," answered Elijah.

"Now I say Dale, I understand everything you said and here's what I propose. I give you this money to settle your account with Albert. I'll pay you 50 dollars a month, which is 50 over what Al is paying you, plus I'll sell you the house for let's say $950, which I'll...."

"Ahem" Michael said clearing his throat. Henry looked over at him.

"Alright, just give me $300 and you can have it."

Dale took a double swig, from the jug, he couldn't believe his ears. He could own his own place. His dream could come true. He readily held out his hand to Henry and said "You got a deal, Mr. McCloud.

Henry said, "Better go easy on that jug, before something bigger than a bee stings you," he laughed.

"Lord, how me and my family gonna ever thank you enough? I ain't never had nobody this generous to us. That's more than neighborly."

"Don't thank me, just yet." said Henry. "You really should be giving them thanks to Michael."

Michael gave him a look of bewilderment. "Uncle Henry," Michael said, "I asked you not to mention me."

"Aw shoot son, you the one who made it all possible, you paid off his debt, with Albert's own money, I might add." he said laughing. "And you bought the house you gonna give to him."

"Well, you still charged Dale $300 for it," said Michael. "No I didn't. Henry protested, that's to pay for that horse I sold him."

He looked over at Dale, Eagles yours and I figure if you owed me a little something, you would stay working for me. I need you. But, if you don't want the horse which I bought for $300, then you don't owe nothing."

Dale smiled, "Oh I'll take the horse." He placed the jug on the floor and got up to shake Michael's hand. When he finished shaking his hand, he grabbed him up in a hug and thanked him over and over again.

"Put me down," said Michael, "You're wrinkling my suit."

"I'm sorry Mr. Michael. Here let me take care of it," he started brushing Michael's suit.

"Somebody, get this man away from me," Michael said smiling. "You just do a good job for Uncle Henry."

"There's a few things that I need to get out of the way with you, so there's not ever going to be any misunderstanding between the two of us."

Dale was all ears at that point. "You are to never strike any of them. You can threaten all day long, but you can't carry it through. Dale looked him in the eye, "Mr. Michael, I don't agree with people being in slavery. I don't care what color folks is. I ain't never owned none, less you count my boys and I've worked the dog out of them, but thems my boys and they gonna be good strong men one day. You ain't ever got to worry 'bout me whipping them people. If there's a problem, I'll come to you and let you figure it out. Deal?"

"Deal," Michael agreed. "I don't agree with slavery, but I know those people at Uncle Henry's are like little lost sheep. I know they could be freed or sold off to somewhere else and their plight very well could be worse, if they were freed. I'm not sure they would know where to go or what to do. So, I've come to the conclusion they are sheep and today, you have become their shepherd."

"Alright! Alright! Please don't start with the preaching, the old lady preaches it enough as it is, plus we are drinking out here," complained Moses. Dale told both Michael and Henry, he wouldn't let them down.

It was settled, Dale would work for Henry McCloud. First he needed to settle up with Albert and move his family. "You don't have to mention where you got the money from," said Henry. "He'll find out soon enough."

"You're the boss, said Dale.

Henry smiled, "You've got two bosses, Michael and me. Dale, you'll see we are fair and just men."

Dale walked over to both men before they mounted the horses, "If you need anything I can give you, I'll give it. Ya'll just made youselves a friend for life."

Chapter 13

I'll Die for You

Dale and his family quickly settled into their new home. Within a couple of weeks, Elijah and his cousins had worn down a path from each other's houses. They fished, swam, hunted, trapped and worked together. Oftentimes, they would camp out in the family barns at night.

Elijah didn't realize how lonely he truly was until his cousins moved nearby. He was too occupied with boy things to worry about a girl. Although, Rachel played on his mind when Danny and Dewey mentioned Pam and Paula, the two girls they'd met at Bayfield Beach. They'd go courting when they didn't have work to do.

The days were getting cooler and fall was close. This was the season of the year famers plowed under the remnants of old stalks from crops that had been harvested. Burying the stalks would cause them to rot and give the land nutrients to make the soil ready for the next planting season.

After a day of hard work tilling the soil, Elijah lay down on the pump table, exhausted and breathing hard. He heard Red bark and looked up to see Dale riding up the driveway on Eagle. Young Dewey was on Sour Weed. Little Dale was perched up in front of his father.

Dale marched the horse right up to the well. "You're just the man we come to see."

"Hey Lijah," said Dewey.

Elijah asked, "Where's Danny? Ya'll leave him behind?"

"No, he's off with Pam coon dogging," said Dewey.

"Alright now, I'm gonna coon dog you," said Dale. "Well that's what you tell us when me and him want to go swimming, you says we wants to go coon dogging."

"Hey, you do as I say, not say as I say, you little coon dog. You just mad cause you ain't with Paula, so hush." Little Dale was laughing, as his father lowered him down from the horse.

"You shut up Little Dale, you got a little black girlfriend," said Dewey.

"I do not," yelled Little Dale.

"Yes you do. You love little Delilah. I done seen you and her playing at the McCloud's."

"She's my friend," Little Dale replied. "Yeah your little girlfriend," teased Dewey.

Dale said "Alright you two, that's enough, I'll take my belt to you both, if you don't hush that fuss."

Dewey turned Sour Weed in the direction of home. "Bye Lijah. Bye Dewey," Elijah called back.

Little Dale pulled a tied up handkerchief out of his pocket and handed it over to Elijah. It's for you, it come from Miss Rachel, she wanted me to give it to you. She gave me a piece of candy to bring it and I had to promise her I won't open it. I ain't opened it Lijah, but I believe she sent you some candy too."

Elijah untied the handkerchief and sure enough, there was some candy and a letter. He plucked two pieces of candy up and gave them to little Dale. "Thank you cousin, I 'preciate that."

"Let's go Mister Messenger, said Dale.

The little boy turned and walked back to the horse holding his arms out for the father to pull him up. "Bye Lijah," said little Dale.

"Take care son, and be careful", added Dale.

They left, and Elijah popped a piece of candy in his mouth and threw the other piece of candy to Red, who had walked over to investigate. Red lapped the candy up, but then spit it out. He then lapped it up again and swallowed it whole. He wagged his tail looking up at Elijah expecting more. Red had made a remarkable recovery from his run in with Allen and Samuel.

"I ain't got no more Red," he said as he patted his head. Red was sniffing at his hand, so he petted him some more and then told him to go, so he could read his letter. Elijah went to his room and closed the door. As he lay on his bed, he caught the odor of a nice fragrance. It was the letter, it had a sweet smell. He brought it closer to his nose, it was perfume. It was the smell he recalled that was in Rachel's room. It smelled like a flower, perhaps a rose. Whatever the odor, he liked it. He began reading:

'Dear Elijah,
Why haven't you been to see me? What are you trying to do, cause my heart to break from missing you so? I met your Uncle, your mother's brother. He seems like a good man and Father and Michael said he is a hard worker.

Just the other day, he was helping the servants till the soil. At first Father was upset by it, until Dale then explained he was just showing them how to do it the right way. He and Michael talk a lot. They spend time in father's library, looking up things that Michael has told him about. Our family is getting along so great. Except you and I, why aren't we? It's as if you loathe me.

I'll be leaving for school soon. I do hope to see you, some time before I go, which is just around the corner. There are some things I'd like to show you.

Your Friend Always, Rachel

P.S. It's about your Grandmother.'

Elijah read the letter a second time, before putting it with the other letter in the tin can. He repeated to himself LOATHE. He scratched his head L.OAT.HE., LOAT.HE, he couldn't understand what she meant by loathe. He wanted to ask his grandmother, but then she'd wonder where he had heard the word. He didn't want to tell her about Rachel's letter. He felt his grandmother would fuss at him. In Rachel's letter she mentioned something about his grandmother, what could that be? Whatever it was, he was he would find out that very night. He got up and went outside where it was cooler.

Walking along with Red he said, "Boy, sometimes I wish I was a dog like you and we'd just run off with no worries. Maybe chase a couple of rabbits and coons or just lay around in the sun like you do." Red gave Elijah a look as if he was telling him, he wished he was human.

"Let's go boy," they started out toward the pond, then Elijah ran back toward the house. He went around to the back porch and grabbed a bar of his Grandmother's homemade lye soap. He laughed, remembering the time Ester had put him in the wash tub on the back porch scrubbing his knees and elbows with the lye soap using corn shucks as a wash cloth. She scrubbed him cleaned. It was little memories like this of his grandmother that he cherished most.

He ran down to the pond, stripped off his clothes and dove in. He lathered up from head to toe, then swam around a while. After getting out, he jumped up and down to dry off some, then put his clothes back on.

Red lay nearby watching. Elijah had an idea. He grabbed Red and tossed him into the pond. Red paddled back to shore and shook himself off. Elijah grabbed him by the neck with one hand and started rubbing soap all over him with the other. After he got Red lathered up good, he scratched and scrubbed the dog with his fingernails. Red enjoyed it.

As he was scratching and scrubbing his rear end area, Red's leg began to kick and thump the ground. Elijah remembered his grandfather had said that was a flea bed, a place where dogs can't scratch, lick or bite. Elijah shoved him off into the water again then rinsed his hands. The dog got out of the water, shook and took off toward the house as if to say he had enough.

Elijah strolled back to the barn. He prepared a pipe of tobacco and had a smoke while waiting for darkness. Ester, Moses and John were gone to Ester's sister's house to help make preserves and shell some peas and beans. That was all the way in Laurinburg. Elijah could have gone along, but he wanted to finish his work. They would likely stay all night, especially if the men folk took to drinking corn liquor. He went inside feeling the fatigue of the day's work and hungry. He walked over to the stove, lifted the lid on the bread warmer and saw biscuits and salted ham. He took 2 biscuits and placed a slice of the ham between each. He poured himself a glass of water and enjoyed his food.

After eating he decided to go lie down. Sleep over took him within minutes of his head touching the pillow. He was later awakened by the sound of thunder and lightning. He walked over to his window, shut it and went around the house to make sure all the others were closed too.

As he stepped into the parlor, he lit the lamp. The bright lantern lit up the small room. He saw the huge family Bible and picked it up. Opening it the way his Grandmother did, he called out "Prophesy, prophesy, prophesy. Show me God."

The book opened to the last page of Ecclesiastes. The first words on chapter twelve caught his eye. "Remember now thy creator in thy days of thy youth, while the evil days came not, nor the years draw nigh. When thou shalt say I have no pleasure in them." He shut the book wondering what the saying meant. Did it mean he needed to love God while he was young or that if he would grow old he would find no pleasure? He even wondered if he was a seer like his Grandmother and he shouldn't be fooling around. "I'm sorry God," he said aloud.

He walked onto the porch to see if the rain had stopped. He went out in the yard and saw it was still misting rain.

He didn't want to wait any longer, so he decided now was as good a time as any to make his way over to the McCloud's house. He gathered a pocket full of corn and headed out. It felt like it was taking him an eternity to reach the McCloud's plantation as he walked through the tree line. He stopped before he entered the open area of the front lawn and driveway that led up to the porch. No lights were shinning inside the home. He walked quickly across the yard.

At the side of the porch, he pulled the corn from his pocket and was about to throw it, when he heard a voice whisper, "I see you." It was Rachel's voice from above.

He dropped the corn and walked over to the huge chimney and started his climb. He got about 5 feet off the ground, lost his balance and slipped backwards and fell on his back. The wet grass quickly soaked his clothing. He picked himself up and started wiping his hands on his pants' legs. As he ascended up the chimney again, he was careful to wipe his hands dry after every grip. His feet would slip easily, but he quickly gripped the stones holding tightly with his hands. Finally he made it to the rooftop. The slate roof was a challenge, but nothing could deter his determination to reach Rachel.

Rachel lit a lantern in her room. He stopped at the window ledge and sat there looking in. "Boo!" she called out from his left.

"Gal, you scared me, I've done 'bout broke my neck trying to make it up here," he whispered.

"Well come in. I've got you a towel to dry off and a towel for your feet."

Elijah swung his feet in with his boots on. "I see you chose to wear shoes tonight," she laughed.

"Yeah, it's wet outside, plus it's getting a little cooler these days, ain't wanting to catch a cold."

"Well, that is smart on your part, but you can go ahead and remove them now and come on in," she smiled.

He climbed on over the window sill and removed his boots, leaving them on the towel. He dried himself off a bit then walked over to the mirror to get a quick view of himself. He saw his hair sticking up in the back and quickly smoothed it down. Rachel was rummaging through her large trunk.

She took out a stack of old newspapers. She lay them on her bed then walked over and grabbed Elijah giving him a tight squeeze.

Elijah was taken aback by the sudden embrace. "You're wet," she said.

He said, "Yeah, I know, I slipped out yonder climbing the chimney."

"That reminds me, the first night you climbed it, Michael and father were in the library and heard you. Father thought it was bats inside the chimney. I told him I would burn some waste in the fireplace to get rid of them." She grabbed him again and held him tight. "Hug me back," she pleaded, "Elijah, I've missed you."

He awkwardly and slowly put his arms around her. He could smell the sweet fragrance of her hair. It smelled like peaches. "Your hair smells good," he whispered.

"It's my favorite shampoo from Georgia. Do you like it?" She asked.

He whispered "Um hum."

Rachel loved having him embrace her. Elijah glanced over at their image in the mirror and smiled. Inside, his heart was racing. He had never been held like this since his mother held him when he was a little boy. His mother would hold him especially close on nights he had nightmares. She would rock him back to sleep.

Rachel was the first girl who hugged him, other than a family member. Her body felt so soft to him. He was feeling somewhat uncomfortable. He tried to release her, but she held him tighter for a few seconds more. As she pulled away, she had tears in her eyes. "Elijah, I don't know what I've done to you. My heart has been aching every day, hoping to see you. But you never come. If I've done something to offend you, I'm sorry and hope you will find it in your heart to forgive me."

At that very moment his heart was breaking inside for this beautiful young lady standing before him. "Awe Rachel, you aint done nothing. I didn't know you're feeling like you wuz. You ain't done nothing. I just been running with Danny and my cousins, just doing boy stuff. And besides, I was kinda scared to come back cause of my Grandma and your Pa." He was looking for excuses to tell her why he hadn't returned. He couldn't tell her how he really felt. He felt she was too rich for him and she made him feel ashamed of himself.

All of a sudden, something came over him, none of that mattered to him now. She was in tears and he could see, she clearly cared deeply for him.

"I'll sneak up here some more now that I see you want me to come round. I don't know what you see in an old rusty tail thang like me, but hey, I think the world of you. It's just, I reckon I was chicken too."

"Well, I'm so happy you came." She spoke as she walked over to her bed where the papers were. "Let's see," she picked one up.

"I wanted to ask you what does loathe mean? That was the only word in the letter I couldn't understand."

She looked at him with sad eyes and said, "It means to dislike or despise or hate something."

"Well," said Elijah, "That's not right, cause I don't hate you or nothing else in this world. That's a word I don't like, so I guess you could say I loathe the word."

She looked at him, and understood just what a jewel he was. Elijah's feelings for her were anything but loathe. In fact, he knew deep inside, he would give his heart to her for a life time. Yet he also knew his heart keeps telling him 'no, you can't marry her.'

Rachel was flipping the pages searching for the newspaper article. "Come here," she said, showing him a page in the newspaper.

"What is it?" Elijah had seen the men from Gibson, Laurel Hill and Laurinburg looking at the newspapers as if they were sacred, like the Good Book.

"Father brought some newspapers back from his travels. This is what I wanted you to see. *'The Republican Party nominates Abraham Lincoln'*. Now listen, that man has a Bible name. You remember what your Grandmother said. She talked about my family holding people in bondage. Well, this man is against slavery and if he becomes president, he says he's going to end it. Now the folks around here are all upset about this. In almost two months the population will vote for our next president. Rumor has it, that If Lincoln wins, states with slaves are going to fight to keep them."

"If that's true, it's bad news, Elijah. I overheard Michael talking to Father about this. Father feels that if Lincoln wins, he'll set the blacks free. And the blacks will kill the white folks in the slave states. It's in these newspapers. Look there are arguments for and against abolishing slavery."

"I just can't imagine what would happen. The slaves running about like blood thirsty savages. I was in Gibson and the men in the barber shop were in an uproar about it. They said the black men would be hunting white women to rape and ravage. It's such a horrible thought.

I look at this house and I think of what a wonderful home it is for now. If something such as that were to take place, then I worry it would become a place of pure horror. I've never given slavery any thought until recently, when your grandmother spoke of it and now after I read these newspaper articles. It's frightening, I tell you. I grew up with servants surrounding me, never has one ever ill-treated me or my family that I know of. Father says it is mostly just talk. Breckinridge should be our next President, since he's our Vice President now."

Elijah sat there speechless. He wouldn't comment on things he knew nothing about and until then, slavery was something he hadn't given any thought to.

She realized he had grown quiet. "Hello, are you still in there?" she asked.

"Um, I was just thinkin' about what you wuz talking bout. I don't think you should worry too much Rachel. It's like you said, these black folks ya'll got round here ain't gonna hurt you."

"How can you be so sure about that? You never know Elijah. What if Father leaves or Michael isn't here and they decide to rise up and kill me?"

"Don't talk like that gal! You run and holler your throat out for me, and I'll come running with a shot gun and shoot somebody if they try to hurt you."

Rachel smiled, reaching out and touching his hand. "Elijah I do believe you would try to protect me. I could feel it in your arms when you embraced me. I felt strength in you. Remember the day I saw you at the bridge and you touched my hand? It was then I felt an unexplainable power emit from you. I know it may sound silly to you, but it's there."

She continued, "Your hands are calloused, but they are gentle too."

He interrupted, "I believe I got me another blister on my pinky today, a handlin' that plow flippin' the dirt in the field."

"Flipping dirt, why do you call it flipping?" asked Rachel.

"Well, you know, it's just turning the soil over, just the process."

To break the tense moment, he nervously started talking about farming life. He told her different things about how to cure meat, clean a pelt and all about life in the outdoors.

She smiled, and put her index finger up to his lips to quiet him. He felt her soft finger press against his mouth, "Shhh," she whispered. "Kiss me, Elijah."

Elijah took hold of her wrist and removed her finger from his face. His nerves were on end. He had never kissed a girl before, he was afraid of making a fool of himself. He wondered too, if that would be the fornication his Grandmother talked so much about.

"Look now, I got to be going," he said.

She pleaded, "No please, don't go." She looked him in the eyes, "Will you hold me once again even if you won't kiss me, please?"

Elijah held his arm's open, she stepped into him and felt his warm embrace. He wanted to kiss her so badly, but he didn't. Instead he reached for her shoulders and gently pushed her back. As she looked up, he tilted his head and kissed her on the forehead.

She giggled and touched the place where his lips touched her forehead. "I wanted you to kiss on my lips, silly boy."

"Well we ain't married and it just don't feel right. I want to respect you that's all."

She quickly stood on her tip toes and grabbed his cheek, turned his head to face her and gave him a kiss on his lips. He pulled away as if she had slapped him. "There now, we've kissed and I'm not ruined." She stood there with a devilish look on her face biting her bottom lip, as she twisted her upper body back and forth.

The sound of howling dogs interrupted the moment. "Them dogs?"

"Oh that's just our blood hounds." Elijah went to the window.

He turned, and said, "Look here, I need to go."

She went over as he was putting on his boots. "Elijah do you care for me?" she asked.

He looked at her, "Yeah, gal, I care 'bout you."

"What if someone tried to rape or kill me, what would you do?"

"I'd stop em." "But what if there's a bunch of them?" She asked again.

"Well, I'd still try and stop em, and if I couldn't, they'd have to kill me too. Anyway, your imagination has going wild tonight," he smiled. "Listen up, I near bout killed myself coming to see you tonight. So, if there was too many and I couldn't handle them, they'd have to kill me. 'Cause I'll die for you."

He scurried down the chimney to find Red waiting with his tail wagging.

"Hay, who's dat?" a voice called out. Elijah was caught. There stood James, with a lantern.

"What ya doin' here this time a night Masser Clark?" he asked.

"Hunting my dog," said Elijah.

"Well yo dog dun an woke them hounds up and ya needs to git from here fo Mr. Henry gits up and goes to shootin'." The old man looked up at the chimney and then back at Elijah, he smiled. "You needs to git on nows, you hear?"

"Yes sir Mr. James, I'm going sir." "Let's go Red", he called as he jogged away.

Chapter 14

Mother Land

Michael came home tired and weary. He had traveled for two days searching for a job in both Laurinburg and Rockingham. Nine different Law Firms had interviewed him, yet none offered him a job.

As he walked into the mansion, he was greeted by James. "Massa Michael, ya back soon today, I hopes ya dun got yas some work."

"Unfortunately James, today was no different than yesterday. The people treat me as if they are going to hire me, yet, they don't. Maybe my accent ruins my chances. If my credentials don't impress them, then I'm at a loss. I did have two gentlemen tell me they would have taken me on, until they learned I'm against slavery. This southern environment may not be for me. I guess I can always go to work for Zack Tate in his bank. In fact, I'll do just that tomorrow. I'll call on Zack for a job."

After a moment of silence, he declared "I'm parched James, I'd love something refreshing to drink. I feel dehydrated from all that dust."

James just said "Yess'um," and continued standing there.

Finally it dawned on Michael that James didn't comprehended what he meant. "Could you get me some orange juice, tea or something, please?"

"Yessa, Massa, with that James left for the kitchen. Mary appeared carrying a large glass of orange juice. "Here da juice ya wants, Massa Michael."

He took the glass from her and said, "Thanks. Come let's go to the library," he said to Mary. "You aren't busy right now are you?"

"I has to go helps Moo... I means Sarah prepare supper Massa."

"What were you going to say or who were you going to help before you changed it to Sarah. Who's this Moo?"

Mary looked around concerned. "I dun an said too much."

But Michael persisted, "Who is this Moo?"

So Mary decided it best if she confided in Michael. "It's Sarah, sometimes we calls Sarah Moola, it's her African name. I gots to go Massa."

She went quickly toward the kitchen and disappeared behind the door she had emerged from.

Michael walked upstairs to his room. Once inside, he sat at the desk and looked inside his brief case. He looked at his degree.

'Some good you are. A doctorate degree and still can't find employment', he thought to himself. He just couldn't understand the southern way. He carefully placed the framed document on a shelf for display along with a few other law books and his personal dictionary.

As he continued to rummage through his brief case, he brought out his most prized possession. He handled it ever so gently, as if it were a newborn baby in his hands. It was the necklace he had always cherished. It was very unusual, yet simple. The necklace appeared to be a primitive Native American arrow head with a black cross carved in its center and adorned with two cowrie shells and four small wooden beads on both sides of the arrow head. It was all aligned on an 18 inch piece of leather tied together with a knot.

When Michael was twelve years old, the orphanage Priest, Father Marcus Peterson gave him the necklace and told him that it was wrapped around his little ankle when he arrived at the orphanage. Father Peterson had told him he started to discard the necklace as some pagan instrument that perhaps had been used in a vile ritual, until he inspected it closer and saw the cross.

Father Peterson allowed Michael to keep the necklace, but forbade him to wear it in public. Michael had the Smithsonian Museum authenticate it in 1857. He was told by a historian that it was a common north to southeastern style shaped arrowhead, hundreds if not thousands of years old. The two shells come from the ocean and are used as currency for some tribes in the South Pacific and Africa.

Michael wore the necklace only twice since the age of twelve. He placed it around his neck on the day he entered college and then again on the day he left with his degree in hand.

For some odd reason, he felt compelled to put the necklace on this afternoon. He carefully pulled off his shirt, placed it around his neck and walked over to observe himself in the mirror. He then went to the window to feel the breeze. He began reminiscing as he touched the necklace. He often wondered where it came from and what it had to do with him. He thought perhaps, his Father or his Grandparents were Native American and they wanted him to know who he was. It was a mystery that had haunted him for years.

The sound of knocking came from his door. He walked over and opened it. There stood both Mary and Sarah.

Mary held out a pitcher of cool water while Sarah held a large silver tray filled with food. "Massa Michael, we looks for ya in da library but yas wuz gone, so we brung you sometin' to eat up chere. We knows yas worn out from da ride all day," said Mary.

Sarah stood looking at him. She took note of his bare chest and her eyes fell on the necklace. They opened wide and at that very moment she fell unconscious dropping the filled tray to the floor.

The noise brought Rachel out of her room. Michael quickly reached down and grabbed Sarah's head. Mary stood by in shock. Michael cupped her head in his hands. He knew it was a horrible fall. He could already see a lump forming on her forehead. He scooped her up in his arms and carried her back to her room.

Rachel pushed the door open and asked, "What happened?"

Michael carried Sarah over to her bed, and laid her down ever so gently. Mary was cleaning up the mess in the hall when Michael came out giving her directions to go and get a water bucket with cool water and some towels. Mary took the things she had gathered and immediately left with the tray. Michael reentered Sarah's room where she lay unconscious with Rachel holding her head. "What happened?" she asked Michael once again. "She fainted, maybe from the heat. It is overbearing today."

He was standing at the side of the bed looking at Sarah. She began stirring about and moaning. Mary appeared with the water and towels. She dipped a cloth, wrung it out and placed it on Sarah's head. Sarah tried sitting up.

"Lay back down Sarah, you've had an accident," said Rachel.

Sarah looked up at both Rachel and Michael. She started crying and buried her face into Mary's lap. "Bless da Lowd, bless da Lowd," she kept repeating.

Her crying was on the verge of wailing. "Dear God, what is wrong, Sarah?" Rachel asked. She moved over to the bedside and started rubbing Sarah's back. Sarah forced herself up and grabbed both Mary and Rachel and cried as she hugged them.

Michael at this point, was very uncomfortable. He didn't know what he could do. From the tone of Sarah's sobs, he knew something was horribly wrong. He walked over to the bed, and stroked her head and said gently, "Do you need a doctor?" "No, I's gonna bes good." She began sobbing again.

They couldn't understand everything she was telling them, but she kept repeating "I's gonna bes good." She jerked between sobs to catch her breath. She looked up at Michael, and then collapsed on the bed, sprawled out as if she was dead.

Michael went over and put his shirt back on and rushed down the stairs to get help. He asked James, where Henry was, and was told he was at the cotton gin. Michael ran to the gin yelling, "Uncle Henry, Uncle Henry!"

Henry called out, "Yes boy."

"Sarah fainted, you need to get a doctor. She seems to be delirious, I could go find a doctor, but I don't know where to locate one."

Without another word spoken, Henry took off toward the mansion. Michael was on his heels. Henry ran upstairs to Sarah's room. Sarah was sitting on the edge of the bed, pressing a handkerchief to her red swollen eyes. Rachel and Mary remained at her bedside.

"Sarah, are you in need of a doctor?"

She looked up at him and said, "I's alright now. I's alright, ya'll hear?" She got up and started to leave.

Rachel insisted, "Sarah you need to rest, please lay back down."

Mary was gathering up the water and towels. "I's help ya," said Sarah. As she started to gather up a towel.

Rachel said, "Sarah, lay down and rest, I'll not take no for an answer. Father please tell her."

Henry said, "Sarah it would be good for you to relax. If you've had a fainting spell, you need to lie down."

Sarah walked over to her bedroom door opening it and said, "Ya'll scoot on up outta chere," motioning for them to leave.

Rachel patted her arm and whispered "Get you some rest. I'll help out, don't you worry none. I'll bring you a bite to eat."

Henry was the last one to leave the room. He could sense more than meets the eye was going on. Sarah grabbed him by his arm, "Bless da Lowd, ya man ya."

She looked out to see if she was overheard, tears were welling back up in her eyes. "Lowd my baby's come home. Bless da Lowd." Henry left immediately.

He was distraught. How did she know? Who else knew? His head was spinning. This couldn't be. It had happened over twenty years ago. Henry had had an affair with Sarah.

It was only for a short while, but she had become pregnant. He had known Sarah since she was twelve, they had played together, it just happened. She and Henry had grown up together, they had become friends. It was only natural he turned his attention to her.

Henry's father had caught on, when he saw Sarah leaving Henry's room one night. He was furious that his son would do such a thing. He threatened to sell Sarah. Henry begged and pleaded with his father not to. In fact, he cried and promised if he didn't sell Sarah, he would find and marry a white woman. When he learned that Sarah was pregnant, Henry's father nearly died from a heart attack. Henry promised him, he would rid the McCloud's plantation of the bastard child.

Sarah was a field hand at that time. After a heavy down pour of rain, she had found an arrow head in the field. She was so excited and decided to make a necklace. She had taken two cowrie shells, shells that had been given to her by her father, before she was sold off to the McCloud's at a young age. Before she had given birth to the child, she gave the necklace and shells to James to put some beads on it. James was known in the area as a wood carver. He carved beads, canes, bracelets and all sorts of stuff. She had asked James to put 8 beads on it. She wanted to give the necklace to her child. She didn't know about the plan to take her baby from her when she gave birth. When it came time for her delivery, Henry's father arranged to take the child the moment it was born.

Henry was directed to take the infant to an orphanage in Massachusetts. His father knew the child had McCloud blood so he let it live. Henry was sent with James, who was his father's own personal servant at the time. The men and the baby left on the midnight train. They finally arrived at the orphanage after a long layover in a small town on the outskirts of Boston. Henry's father warned Henry to have James turn the baby over and claim he found the child.

Henry went into a nearby pub to drown his misery and heartache for what he was doing. He wondered what would happen to the baby.

Before James approached the orphanage, he secretly placed the necklace on the baby's ankle. The baby was resting peacefully. He knocked on the door and then ran away. He hid behind the building and saw an elderly white woman bend over and pick up the child. A little later, after downing several drinks, Henry went banging on the orphanage door and demanded the return of his son.

The Headmaster, Priest Marcus Peterson, refused and threatened to call authorities. He knew he could be arrested, so he calmed down and pulled out of his jacket pocket a money bag that held 1,000 dollars. This was a considerable amount of money at that time. He handed the money to Father Peterson and told him to care for his son. He told him the child's name was Michael Joseph McHeir. The priest accepted the money and blessed Henry. Henry did not mention the child was of African descent.

Sarah knew Henry had taken her son. She didn't speak to him again until his father died. Soon after his father's death, Henry moved her into the mansion. When Rachel's mother passed away, she cared for Rachel as if she were her own daughter.

"I'll take the meal up to Sarah," said Henry to Mary and Rachel.

"Father we have it, besides I want to serve her, she's served me for so many years, I want to do something for her now."

The ladies went on upstairs with the tray of food for Sarah. "Sarah, I came in to check on you, are you sure you don't need to see a doctor?"

"I's shor. I's good."

"Well you two leave Sarah to her meal," Henry ushered Mary and Rachel out of the room. "I'll come back and check on you and gather the tray for Mary," said Henry.

Henry needed to speak privately with Sarah. He was fully aware she had discovered Michael's true identity.

As Henry left the room, Sarah exclaimed, "My baby's come home." Without a doubt, he knew she knew. He wasn't sure of what the others knew. He thought perhaps James had told her. Then, he wondered to himself, how on earth would James have known. He decided he would pay him a visit out in the cabin.

James was sitting with his feet soaking in a tub of cold water. "Massa Henry, I says it sho is hot out today. Got's these olds foots a soakin', cools me down a bit."

"Yea, it is a warm one. James, I need to ask you a question. I hate to bring it up, but I've got to know."

"Did you tell Sarah I brought Michael back here?"

James looked at Henry with a wrinkled brow? "Sir? What ya means?"

"Michael, you know Michael, don't you?" "Yessa Massa, he's yo nephew."

Since James couldn't see too well, Henry guessed James didn't know Michael.

"James said, "That Delilah runs herself in here and say Sarah is hurt and sick. I's gonna sees bout her after I's soaks my foots."

"Well she's fine now, James. There's no need for you to worry yourself, you relax and keep soaking them feet. I'll go myself and check on her again." Henry patted his shoulder then left the cabin.

He walked around a bit, perplexed about the situation at hand. He went inside, walked up the stairs and peered into Sarah's room. As he shut the door, he walked over and gathered up the tray along with the plate and silverware. He held it in his hands and sat on the edge of the bed.

"Sarah, tell me what's going on? How did you come to know about Michael?"

She just looked at him with heartbroken eyes. Then she spoke. "Henry, I's knowed that child when ya'lls comes here. They's was somthin' insides me. Ya an me is that boys peoples. I's wondered and wondered when my po eyes seent him. That night's ya had us playing dem old cards. I's felts him. Today's I's saw that necklace around his neck and I knowed for sho, he wuz my baby. What I's wants to knows, is yas gone tell him?""

"Lord, listen Sarah. Please listen to me for a moment. You've had a shock, but listen to reason. Do you want me to destroy both his and Rachel's life? What would they think? If word would get out they could take everything our boy has worked for because he's got black blood in him. The reality is some of these white people around here would cast me out. It would be hard on all of us I'm afraid. This isn't something I have just given a little thought to. I've had twenty plus years to think about the ramification of the situation we now find ourselves in. You know what it's like being a slave. Is that what you want your son to be subjected to? Is this what you want for him? I know we haven't talked about this, simply because we didn't have to, it was all settled once and for all. And now, oh Sarah, please don't go there."

Sarah looked up at the ceiling and started crying. She felt so hopeless. Here she was a mother of a son who she has never held or could hold. She hated the world she was born into. Oh if only she had been born in the Mother Land as her father used to call Africa. "We gonna wait. But I knows dat's my child when I's seens that necklace round his neck. I's knows he's mine."

"What necklace?" Henry asked?

"Ya's 'member, that arrowhead, I's found in dem fields. The one yas put that cross on. I's ain't forgotten."

Henry remembered the cross. She had brought the arrow head to Henry wondering what it was. He explained it was for hunting and also told her that a warrior would use it to protect his loved ones. Sarah told him, she hoped to have many warriors one day and she would give the arrowhead to one of her children.

Henry asked Sarah, if he could add something to it that would help whoever wore it. He took the necklace and had delicately engraved a cross into it and painted it black. He presented it to her some time later on a strap of leather. She loved it. He told her that the wearer of the necklace would have the Lord on his side. Two strong symbols, the arrow for protection physically and the cross for the Lord's protection spiritually. She was very pleased.

At times, Henry would sneak into Sarah's cabin and read from the Bible to her and the others who lived with her. His father punished him severely when one night he discovered him in the act. He was told to never try to educate a servant. As long as they were uneducated they would have to depend on the white man. This was the key to slave ownership.

Chapter 15

Throw Rocks

It was a half-moon lit night as Elijah sat under the old elm tree at the end of the road waiting on Danny. "Where have you been Danny? I've been sitting here twenty minutes waiting on you."

"Ma was up with little Dale tending to him, he's got a cold or something. You know the weather's a changin' and all that brought it on, I reckon. Daddy says that changin' of the seasons causes sickness, all dem germs floating around. Dem germs try to run and hide, so they run up peoples noses. Plus little Dale got that bump on his lip. Old fever blister, I believe ma called it. She gives us all two spoonful's of castor oil. Had me shitting my guts out yesterday."

Elijah laughed, as they walked along talking. "It ain't funny that little rascal got sick and me and Dewey got to pay for it. Dewey had to run to the woods, 'cause I was in the outhouse. We need us a two seater like ya'll got. After we wuz done, he said he'd had to use some leaves to clean his old stinking tail. Said every time that he'd wipe himself off, he'd have the runs again. I knew what he meant, but I had cobs on hand, I know I used bout 5 myself. I thought I had to fart, but found out too late it was the squirts."

Danny hush, "I ain't wanting to hear no more bout you taking craps." Changing the subject, he asked "How's Pam doing?"

Danny stopped. "Lijah, I believe she's pregnant."

"What?" said Elijah. "She told me she's been sick a couple of mornings, throwing up and mess, then I told her I said you probably got that cold like little Dale. She told me no that her woman time didn't come like it supposed to." "Woman time?" said Elijah.

"Yeah, you know when they do that woman stuff, bleeding."

"Okay, okay," said Elijah.

"I didn't know what it was neither till she told me," said Danny.

"She goes on and tells me she feels like they's a little butterfly fluttering around in her belly. Well, any how I wonder 'bout it all day, so finally I tricked Ma into telling me some signs. I asked her don't she wants some more youngins and she tells me she'd love to have us boys a little sister. I gone ahead and ask her how's she know she was having us. She says she missed her moon. That's what she called her woman time.

She said that she felt like a worm was crawling around in her belly, when she was pregnant with me. She said it felt like a bee buzzing around with Dewey and a butterfly with little Dale. When she said that thing about that butterfly, Lord, I know. Pam's got a youngin inside her."

"Shoot don't act surprised, you put it there. Ole coon dog," said Elijah grinning.

"Elijah you don't understand cuz. One day her pa told me let's talk a spell. I follers him out to the smoke house. He goes in and cuts him a chunk of salted pork. He then cuts it in half and offers me a piece. I take it. He says Danny, I know yo daddy's a good man and all. He seems to care for you cause you look fit as a stud horse. He smiles and then gets all serious. Well, the minute you feel you want to take my gal, you need to ask her hand in marriage and I'll give it to you. Now you see this knife here I got boy, do you know what castrating a hog means? If you don't take care of my gal, now believe this, I'll do the same to you that I do to them hogs. I love my gals, cause they my blood, but it's up to a man to provide for his own, and I expect that from you."

I lied, I said "Mr. Jones me and Pam ain't like that."

Then the old fool puts that knife to my throat and says, "Boy don't you lie to me never again. That gal tells her ma everything and her ma tells me everything. So don't lie to me 'cause you'll start off on the wrong foot."

"Elijah, I thought he wuz gonna cut my head off, you see that little scratch right here?" Danny tilted his head and pointed to a place on his neck.

"Nah, it's too dark to see anything," said Elijah.

Danny continued, "Anyhow I got to go marry that gal or get myself castrated, his exact words, and Lord knows I ain't wanting that."

"Well, do what's right, marry the gal. Damn, you about to be a daddy and you younger than me."

"Hey you ain't but two months older than me." They continued talking a bit more, till they reached Rachel's dirt road.

As they got closer to the mansion, Elijah noticed it was all lit up. There were lights shining all throughout the house. There was no way he was going to visit tonight with the place all a glow. He didn't want to tell Danny he had been slipping up there in the dead of night so as to not be seen by anyone. "Well, I'll holler at you cousin," said Danny, as he turned to continue on to meet Pam.

"Hold on, I'll walk with you a piece farther," he said. Sounds like you're in a bind and need to talk. So I'm here for you"

Danny said, "Fool, what can you do?" They laughed and continued down the road.

Danny said, "I'm just gone tell him I got Pam pregnant and aim to marry her. Maybe they won't be no problem with him, seeing I got you with me. Hell, if he's wanting a problem and tries to cut me, you and me can whip him. Shoot, I forgot my pocket knife. Ain't you got a old tree brand pocket knife Elijah?"

Elijah stopped walking, "Hold on, hold on... I ain't going over there with you to jump on nobody, especially not that gal's pa. Are you foolish? Look he's done told you, he'd let you marry his youngin, so just ask him. If you gonna want to fight, then I'm turning around and heading back home."

"Aw come on Lijah, I ain't gonna start nothing. I was just shucking and jiving you cuz."

"Alright then Danny, I don't want no trouble."

They walked along in silence for a while. They were about to cross the bridge at Bayfield when they heard a man scream. "I's sorry."

They looked around and saw a fire flicker through the woods off to their right. They decided to head over in that direction to see what the commotion was. "Aw Lowd, please I's so sorry. What has I done for yous to do me such a ways?" Said the pleading voice.

"You shut your mouth nigra." Elijah recognized the voice. It was Samuel McDonald.

Elijah felt a chill run up his back. He stopped and knew they should turn around. He whispered to Danny, "Come on."

"Hold on Lijah, let's go take us a look and see."

"No Danny, that's Samuel McDonald down there, we need to mind our own business and get out of here. Come on," Elijah pleaded.

"I ain't scared, I'm gonna have me a look."

Elijah grabbed his cousin's arm and said, "Listen, your pa took that man's job and he aims to start trouble with us. They jumped my pa and Red, him and his boy and Allen Johnson."

"Hell, I ain't no chicken, look, me and you can take him."

A slashing and crack of a whip could be heard.

The miserable slave's voice groaned and cried out. "Why's you doing this Massa, I's sorry."

"Let me whip him some, Sam," another voice called out.

Elijah didn't know the other man's voice until Samuel said, "Allen you just hold your horses."

"Now nigra, you tell your Master, you run from him and I caught you. Yessa Massa, I's says anything you want me to."

Danny pulled away from Elijah and headed back in the direction of the commotion. Samuel and Allen had been kidnapping slaves and then taking them back to the plantation owners for a reward. The going price for females was $10 while the males were $15 to $20 depending on their size.

Elijah followed behind his cousin, calling out "Come back Danny." "I'm gonna leave you."

Elijah stopped but his cousin continued. Elijah went back and stood on the bridge waiting. He figured once Danny got his eyes full and saw what he wanted to see he'd run back. After a short while Elijah could still hear the sounds of torment, so he decided he'd go and find out what the holdup was. He had never seen a human being whipped before, and he dreaded the thought. He wanted to do something. He had an idea. He went to the edge of the river bed and began gathering up stones. Elijah then headed in the direction where he thought Danny might be. Danny was standing behind a cypress tree.

Elijah crept over. It startled him. "Shhh. Look a yonder Lijah. They got him tied to a tree with his shirt off." They could see his back was bleeding. Allen had the whip in his hand, while Samuel sat on a log drinking.

Elijah's heart broke and tears welled up in his eyes. He whispered to Danny, "We got to do something."

'What, they got guns?"

"How do you know?" asked Elijah.

Danny pointed to a tree and leaning against the tree was two rifles. "Plus, he's got one on his side yonder," pointing to Samuel.

"Look, I got me an idea; you go on back up the path toward the bridge. I got some rocks here, and I can chunk um in their direction. Here you throw some too. Wait til we get a little ways away from here, cause he might shoot at us."

"Come on cuz, that's smart thinking," said Danny.

Or dumb, Elijah thought. They turned and started up the pathway. After they neared the bridge, Elijah stopped. Let's throw um. They threw the rocks as hard as they could.

Throw Rocks

The rocks could be heard, striking tree limbs and branches. Elijah pulled more rocks from the river bed and handed them to Danny. They continue throwing handfuls of rocks several times.

Just then gun shots rang out. Samuel was cursing, "I'll kill you, whose there?" he shouted.

Samuel blasted two more gun shots. The boys turned to flee, when Danny cried out "I'm shot!"

Elijah turned as Danny fell into him. Elijah grabbed hold of him. "I hear you," yelled the voice from the woods. Two more shots were heard.

Elijah could hear lead bouncing off the bridge. "Where you hit?" he asked Danny. He looked down the path and saw a torch light coming toward them. He began tugging on Danny.

Danny started crying, "It's burning Lijah. God, it's burning."

Elijah dragged him a bit farther. His strength was giving out. "Just hold on Danny," he whispered. He took Danny underneath the bridge, "Just hold on. You gonna be alright," he kept whispering. "Where'd it hit you?"

"In my hip. It feels like a mule kicked me and broke it then someone stubbed a cigar out on me like I wuz an ash tray. Lord, God it's burning."

A light emerged from the trees. Elijah saw it was Samuel with a pistol in one of his hands and a torch in the other. Allen was holding both rifles and pointing toward the bridge.

Elijah knew they were in danger. "We got to hit the creek," he said. They sneaked over to the river's edge and eased in the water. The water was extremely cold and dark. "Let's go over to one of them support pillars," Elijah whispered to Danny.

Danny held on to Elijah "Don't let me go, please cuz, don't let go."

"I ain't gonna let go, but you choking me. Help me, use your hands and arms, they ain't shot is they?" Elijah said.

They floated across to a support column and hid behind it.

Sure enough the men walked onto the bridge. They kept shinning the light in the water. Elijah kept praying, "Oh God, don't let um look down." Both of their boot prints were visible. The men stopped, Samuel holstered his pistol and took the whiskey bottle from his pocket, pulled the cork out with his teeth then spit it into the river. He gulped down a swig.

"Hey old greedy hog, save me a swaller," said Allen.

Samuel passed the bottle over to him. He held the torch up. "Kill it boy and let's get back to our nigra.

Throw Rocks

Fars we know, whoever was throwing rocks is long gone. We ought to get us at least $20 from old man Morgan tomorrow for this nigra. Soon, we gonna hit McCloud, the son of a bitch. We'll git a couple of his."

Allen finished off the remainder of the bottle and slung it against the column post where Elijah and Danny were hiding. Glass struck Elijah in the top of his head. Both he and Danny ducked under the water holding their breath. After about a minute they came up for air and noticed the men had left. They could see the light heading in the direction of where the slave was.

They made their way over to the opposite bank. "Oh God, I'm crippled, cuz. It's gone to throbbing. I can feel my heart pounding. "I'm gonna die, Lijah," cried Danny.

"Tell Ma, Pa, Dewey, and little Dale, I love em." He grabbed Elijah's shirt and said, help take care of my baby. Make sure they name him after me when I'm dead and gone."

"Man shut up, here they come." Danny started sobbing. Elijah had to place his hand over his mouth. Once Samuel and Allen got up to the bridge, Allen dropped the man down on the bridge, and went to get their horses. They slung the man across one of the horse's back and rode off.

Elijah pulled Danny to the top of the bank. "Look here, Danny, can you put pressure on your other leg?"

"I don't know, but I'll try."

Elijah braced him, leaned up against the bridge and said, "Let's figure out where you been shot."

Danny leaned over the railing of the bridge and pointed to the area that hurt the worst. "This is it," he moaned.

Elijah touched it gently. "Yeah, he popped you a good un. I feel the skin torn." "Am I gonna die Lijah?" Elijah began probing a little more.

Danny squealed, "Stop cuz, you killing me."

"Ah hush! I believe I feel bone or a piece of lead. Take me to Pam's whimpered Danny. I'm bleeding to death, let me make it there Lord."

"Hush and come on," said Elijah. Elijah removed his shirt and wrapped it around his cousin's hips. "That ought to help some," he said.

The Jones house was pretty close. As they walked up to the house the Jones' beagle began baying. Pam's father came out onto the porch. "Who's out yonder?" he demanded. The old man had a shot gun aimed at the boys.

Throw Rocks

"It's me, Mr. Jones, Danny replied." "Boy, what in tarnation is the matter?" When they reached the porch, he could see that Danny was in trouble. A boy was behind Mr. Jones holding a lantern. "What happened to you Danny? Hand me that lantern Joshua," said Mr. Jones. He shined the light on the boys and noticed the blood stained shirt.

Elijah untied the shirt and they both inspected the wound. Elijah was able to see what he thought was bone was really a flattened piece of lead.

Pam appeared on the porch, "What's wrong Danny?"

Danny put on a tough face. "Got shot is all." He then turned to Elijah, "You gonna help me out or not?"

Mr. Jones said, "Ya'll hold on now, I need to get some whiskey to pour on that wound, infection can set in." He went into the house and came back with a bottle of whiskey. "Danny, you need you a swaller of this for ya operation?"

Elijah pulled his pocket knife out. "Pour some on this," he said to Mr. Jones.

"Hold it near the wound so when I pour it, we can clean the wound and the knife at the same time." Elijah decided not to argue, but did what he was told.

Danny grimaced and played the tough role in front of Pam. He was crying inside, but refused to let it show. "Go head Lijah, get it out of me." Elijah stuck the knife into the wound and pried the lead out. Danny passed out. Mr. Jones doused Danny's injury with whisky again. This brought Danny back around. Pam's father couldn't resist, "Looks like you done passed out on us old Danny boy."

"Nah, I just took a nap," he said smiling at Pam.

Elijah pressed his shirt into the wound making Danny whelp. "Hey you ain't got to be so rough on me cuz". "I just needed to stop the bleeding, Danny." Mr. Jones slapped Elijah on the back, "Yeah, you was just trying to help old Danny boy."

"Who shot you honey?" asked Pamela.

"I ain't for sho. I believe it was some coon hunters. Me and Lijah just walking past them woods and heard some shots. For I knew it, I was hit."

She reached over and touched him. "Goodness sakes Danny, you wet and Lijah wet too," she said touching Elijah's head.

"Git your hand off his head. You my women, not his," Danny said, feeling all courageous now. "We wet cause, go ahead and tell her Lijah."

145

"Well your man here went to hollering, his hip was a burning, so we went in the water to cool it off."

"Sure did," agreed Danny.

Mr. Jones came out the door with a long white tip match and some gun powder. "Turn on your side Danny Boy, and face the house."

Danny rolled over on his side exposing his wound. Mr. Jones poured the black gun powder on it then struck the match on the wooden porch boards and touched it to the gun powder causing a quick flash of flames.

Danny rolled off the porch and hit the dirt yelling, "Oh God, he's trying to kill me."

Mr. Jones and Elijah went and pulled Danny up. "Daddy, don't hurt him please," called out Pam.

"Hush gal, that was good for him, won't it Lijah?"

"Yes sir, I reckon." Elijah looked and saw the ring of black charred flesh where the bullet hole was.

"It stopped the bleeding for sure."

"Did it?" asked Pam.

Danny looked down at the wound and nodded his head, yep, "I believe it did."

"Hell, I learnt that when I wuz you boys age. Me and my cousins were hunting wild turkeys and one flew out from behind a bush. And Charles, my cousin, shot his brother trying to shoot that bird. Patrick hollered like a scalded dog. Uncle Wayne sealed up the hole with gun powder. Patrick's wounds healed up pretty fast. It was his pinky finger and it didn't work as good as it used to, but the rest seemed to work just fine. Danny's a tough old boy, ain't you Danny."

"Yes sir," said Danny with a painful smile.

Mr. Jones inquired, Now boys, just what happened?" The coon hunting story was repeated. "Well, we need to go down to the beach and find dim fellers." Nobody said a word, they just glared at one another.

"I guess we need to let the sheriff know and let em handle it," Pam said.

"Gal, what's the sheriff's gonna do if the boys can't tell the sheriff who shot him."

"See if you can walk Danny, try making a few steps," said Pam. Danny tried standing with Mr. Jones and Elijah on each side. They asked him to put some weight on his hip. "Just walk, said Elijah, we here in case you fall."

Danny took two steps and the pain was still there, but he gritted his teeth, and said: "To be honest it's hurting me something awful."

"Well let's get him back to the chair, you dun an got yourself a bone bruise, that's all," said Mr. Jones.

"What's a bone bruise?" asked Danny.

"That's where you get struck real hard and it hits your bone, you know like a blue eye. If it was broken or shattered, you'd still be laying on that ground crying like a baby. I'll give it to you son, you one tough old possum." He looked over at Pam and said, "Your honeys in a little bind gal." "Hush daddy, quit punning."

Elijah announced he wasn't as tough as Danny, and asked if Mr. Jones had a smoke. Mr. Jones replied, "Yeah boy, come on in." They made their way into the house, leaving Danny and Pam outside.

Danny said to Pam," I'm gonna keep my eyes on you and Elijah. I saw you rubbing his hair."

"Well, he got some pretty black hair," said Pam, and I was only checking it out, cause it was wet. Besides, you my baby's daddy. Ma done told me I was pregnant."

"What, you told your ma?" asked Danny.

"No she told me. She said she'd wait for you to see how yous gonna act. You know, if you wuz gonna marry me, 'fore she told Daddy."

"Well, that's what I come for, to ask your pa for your hand in marriage. I'm gonna git Lijah to be my best man. I love you gal."

Pam giggled and grabbed him and kissed him quickly looking back to see if her father was near.

Shortly after, Mr. Jones and Elijah emerged, laughing and puffing away. "Mr. Jones," said Danny, "I came by tonight to ask you if I can marry Pam."

"Stand up boy," demanded Mr. Jones.

Danny and Elijah felt they were in for a scuffle from the tone of his voice. "Stand up boy," he repeated. Danny stood and Mr. Jones walked over and gave him a bear hug, shaking him and laughing.

"Yeah sir, I'm gonna be a granddaddy and I got me a grown man to help me out around here.

Joshua and Paula came out on the porch. They had been listening to it all. Paula asked Danny, "Where's Dewey?"

Throw Rocks

Mr. Jones looked up at Paula and said "Gal, git yourself back in that house. Here's your sister fixing to have a baby and make me a grand pop and you romping around out here hunting for your man. Go on back in 'for I take a stick to you."

Paula stomped her feet and went back inside. Everyone but Paula was happy. Then Elijah remembered his sweetheart, she was probably waiting on him. He told everyone he had to go. Mr. Jones told Danny he could stay the night, and sleep on the floor in the Parlor. There is no way he was going to allow him and his daughter the privilege of sleeping together in his house until the preacher man said they could.

It was late when Elijah reached Rachel's driveway. He was tired from the earlier events. He remembered the battered slave and was sorry that he couldn't have done more than just throw rocks.

Chapter 16

Broken and Shattered

Elijah went over to the McCloud mansion on the day of Rachel's departure for college. As he knocked on the door, James opened with a smile. "Massa Elijah," he announced.

Elijah nodded at James and walked in. "Oh hello Elijah," called out Michael who was sitting on the couch in the parlor. "What can we do for you?"

Elijah answered, "Well Sir, "I would like to see Rachel, if that's possible?"

"Now young man, she's upstairs with Ms. Sarah getting ready to head out. Had you been 10 minutes later you would have missed her. In fact, her father is already out back getting the carriage ready to carry her over to Laurel Hill." Michael sensed a change in Elijah, "So you would like to perhaps say your good byes huh? Your Uncle must have informed you."

"Informed me about what?" asked Elijah.

"Well about Rachel's departing."

"No, she told me," said Elijah.

"That's strange, I haven't seen you around, when did you speak with Rachel?"

Elijah almost gave away their secret rendezvous. "Oh she told me a long time ago, she said she was going off to learn nursing or something like that."

"Well come and sit, she should be down shortly."

Elijah slowly walked over to a chair and was about to sit when Michael called out, "Come on over to the couch and let's get more acquainted."

As Elijah took his seat beside Michael, Michael quickly stated, "You smell like tobacco. You smoke?"

Elijah reluctantly answered with a nod. "I smoke ever now and then," trying to sound all grown up.

"How about cigars, nothing better to relax you than a good old smoke," said Michael?

"I ain't never tried em, I usually just make my own smoke."

"You just hold on young man, I'll be right back." Michael walked into the library.

James was standing nearby and said to Elijah, "Ya old dog ain't come round here no mo is he?" He was smiling at Elijah.

Elijah knew he was speaking of the night he had seen him climbing down the chimney. Elijah grinned and said, "I believe he's run up here a couple more times." They both were laughing when Michael walked out of the library holding two lit cigars; one in his mouth and the other one in between his fingers.

"What's this?" he asked, "A private joke?"

"No sir," said James. James brought over a large crystal ashtray and sat it down on the huge table in front of the couch. They both sat on the couch savoring the smoke.

"This cigar's a pretty good smoke, it taste good enough to chew like plug of backer."

Michael laughed. He knew about them southern gents and their spit toons. "Well, I've never really took up that habit, I personally find it disgusting. I've noticed gentlemen in pubs doing it. All that spitting is not my style."

Elijah asked, "Pubs? What's that?"

Michael gave him a questioning look. "A pub is a bar, a saloon, a place that serves ale. Folks go in and have themselves a drink or two. Instead of a jug, they serve the ale in a glass."

"That's interesting Mr. Michael."

"No, please call me Michael or Mike."

"Ok," replied Elijah, "But you can call me Lijah."

"That's a deal," said Michael. "Lijah do you attend school?"

"Nah, not till winter and sometimes I don't then. But I'm gonna go since Rachel's going off to college. Rachel is way smarter than me, but you, you're smarter than Rachel."

"Well Lijah, men must excel in academics as well as labor, we have to run this country. Now the ladies, they just need to look pretty for us gents."

Mary came into the room carrying a tray of tea. "Here's you goes Mr. Michael," she looked over at Elijah, "And I don't knows you, who's you?" she asked

Michael interjected "Stop being so forward, and let me introduce you."

Elijah looked at Mary, and said "I'm Lijah, now what's your name Ms. Lady?"

Michael said, "This is Mary, and thank you Mary for the refreshments."

Mary thought to herself, so this is the youngin that had caught Ms. Rachel's attention. Sarah told Mary everything about their first encounter with Elijah.

Mary said proudly, "Sarah done whopped up Ms. Rachel's favorite cake."

As if on command, Sarah appeared carrying a suit case, which she placed near the entrance. She looked at Mary, and then ushered her quickly away from Michael and Elijah. She stopped briefly to tell James to come with them.

Michael asked if Elijah would like some tea, but Elijah declined. "I don't like drinking or eating when I'm smoking."

"I concur with you on that note," Michael said.

Elijah thought for a second, a cur means a dog to him, so what was Michael saying? He wasn't about to ask, he guessed he had shown his ignorance enough for one day.

Henry walked through the front door and announced "We're all ready, let's roll. James, take the suit cases out to the carriage for me."

Henry caught sight of Elijah and was wondering what on earth he was doing there. "Hello, Mr. McCloud," Elijah called out.

Henry didn't have time to speak before Rachael emerged. As she strutted down the stairs, she called out, "I thought I heard voices." Her face was beaming.

But before she could say another word, she heard James scream in pain. "Aw my heads a hurting!"

Michael and Elijah hurried over to see what had happened. "James, what's wrong?" they asked. James had his hands covering his face. He peeped through his fingers toward the dining room door, hoping Sarah heard his signal.

The door slammed wide open and Mary led the way with a pitcher of lemonade and glasses on a tray. She held the door open for Sarah who was carrying a cake.

"Lookie yonder," said James.

He was pointing at Sarah and Mary. "Bless ya Rachel," He added.

151

"James, you had me frightened. I thought something was terribly wrong, but what a nice surprise, my favorite cake." Rachel walked over and hugged Sarah and Mary. Henry, Michael and Elijah had a good laugh with James. "That was a good one Mister James. You had us all fooled didn't he Mike?" "I say he had me duped." Michael answered.

"What's with this Mike," said Henry. "So you two have become friends?"

Michael said, "Well we have gotten to know each other a little bit better over these cigars of yours."

Henry didn't bother to comment. "Let's go and see Rachel off, shall we Elijah, after all, that is what you came for isn't it?"

Michael and Henry made their way over to the table, where Rachel sat enjoying her cake. It was yellow maple cake with chocolate and walnuts in the icing. Her eyes met Elijah's. "Hello Elijah, you must taste this cake, it's absolutely marvelous."

Sarah had already cut him a slice, "You's gonna loves this child. I's spent all morning a cookin' it." Then Sarah walked over and served Henry a piece, while Mary served Michael.

Pointing to Elijah, Rachel said, "Come sit next to me."

He couldn't help but feel Henry watching him cautiously. He sat there nervously eating his piece of cake. "This is good. Ms. Sarah you sure can cook."

Rachel said to him, "You need a fork, stop eating with your fingers. I don't know what I'm going to do with you." She then handed him a fork from the table but to her chagrin, he had finished off the cake. She asked Sarah to cut him another slice.

Sarah was about to bring it over to Elijah, when Rachel took the plate and dipped her finger in the icing. She wiped her finger across Elijah's mouth area. She giggled seeing he had a white mustache. "Gal," he protested, and began licking his upper lip. Rachel lost herself for a moment and forgot they were not alone. She leaned in and kissed him.

Henry jumped up and in a matter of fact tone demanding, "What the hell is the meaning of this? Rachel, you are to act like a lady in my house and not like some little tramp. You—young man, leave my house this instant, you have come here uninvited and have disrespected my household." Elijah stood and quickly wiped the remainder of icing from his lips. "Mr. McCloud, sir, I, I didn't mean no disrespect to you nor none of ya'll."

152

Henry's face was turning red. Michael walked quickly around to Henry's side of the table. "Uncle Henry calm down, it is nothing for you to get bent out of shape about. Rachel's just having a little fun, something to think about on her journey to school."

"You stay out of this Michael, it doesn't concern you. Young man, you get out of my house and off my property. How dare you come in here and make advances on my child. Not here, not anywhere, if I have a say so."

"Father, leave him be, Elijah is dear to me," cried out Rachel.

Henry's eyes widened, "Lilly, you can't mean what you're saying, he's nothing but a commoner, white trash."

"Hey," said Elijah, "Don't call me that Mr. McCloud."

"Please leave Lijah," said Michael. Michael sensed Elijah was getting angry.

Rachel pleaded with her father, "Please, don't do this to him. I kissed him, he did nothing wrong."

Elijah was walking to the front door when Rachel ran behind him, her shoes clapping across the floor. "Stop," she cried. He stopped and turned, Rachel took him by the arms, "Please wait, and let me speak to father."

"Leave!" Henry shouted.

Rachel turned and walked back to her Father. "Please let him stay until I'm to leave at least, this is my wish. Please Father."

Henry looked down at his sweet precious child, whom he loved more than anything in the world. He turned, "I'll be in my library, when you are ready to go. Then he must go!" Henry stormed off into the library slamming the door behind him.

Sadness was in the air. "Come back Elijah, come over here with me," she said softly.

Elijah's pride didn't want to listen to her pleas, but his heart overruled his mind and he walked over to her. "I apologize for the scene. It's all my fault, I caused my father's actions."

"You ain't got to apologize, I shouldn't a come." He felt his heart breaking.

"But you should have come and I'm so happy that you did. Our hearts are intertwined with each other," she said.

Michael realized there was more to this than meets the eye. His cousin Rachel was in love, as well as Elijah.

"You two go and sit and have yourselves some alone time. I'll go have another piece of this cake Sarah has cooked up."

The two moved off to the parlor, but they didn't take a seat. Elijah pulled a ring from his jacket and held it out to Rachel. "I know you got a lot of jewelry, and this ain't much, but it means the world to me, just like you mean the world to me. Maybe you can put it on a necklace and wear it to remember me. It was my Ma's ring, my Pa gave it to me and said for me to give it to the woman I love. And I don't know of anyone I love more than you Rachel."

Rachel began crying softly, she looked up at Elijah and said, "I'll put it on a necklace with my mother's ring. Those two rings will be ever so special to me. I'll never forget you." She kissed him lightly. "Let's go get us some more of that cake."

James said to Rachel. "Miss. Rachel, I gots ah present fo ya." He pulled a necklace from his pocket. It was on a leather strap, loaded down with his carved wooden beads and a wooden star hanging from it. "I's carved dis fo ya, Miss Rachel."

He held it out to her. Michael looked and noticed something very familiar about it. "Can I see that?" he asked, as he sat down his glass of lemonade.

Rachel passed the necklace over to him. She then hugged James and thanked him. "It's lovely James, what a wonderful thought."

Michael pulled the hidden necklace from around his neck and compared the details of each. It was the same as his necklace. They came from the same craftsman. He looked up into James' eyes. "What is the meaning of this James?" he asked. He carefully removed the necklace from around his neck and placed it into James' hand. "Did you make these beads for this necklace?"

As Henry stepped out of the library, he noticed Sarah's look of hopelessness and loss in her eyes. "Time's up we've got to go," said Henry, staring down at this pocket watch which was attached to a gold chain.

"I asked you a question," demanded Michael, "Did you make this?"

Henry looked up to see what Michael was talking about and saw the necklace. His face lost color. There hanging from the necklace was the cross he had scratched into the arrowhead. "What's going on here?" he demanded. He knew the enormity of his past deeds was about to come to a head, "Oh God don't let it be," he silently prayed.

"Uncle Henry, I have in my possession a necklace I've had since I was left at the orphanage. Father Peterson said on the day I arrived I had this necklace wrapped around my ankle. I have wondered where it came from since I was twelve years old. Now I see this necklace with the same type of beads James said he made Rachel."

"Let me see that." Henry spoke softly. He took the necklace and then asked Rachel to let him see the one she had. He examined both. "They look similar but, anyone could have designed the one you have in your possession, Michael."

"Bull Shit," screamed Michael.

"Michael, please don't speak to me in such a manner. You stop this nonsense and for heaven's sake, stop badgering James. He needs to take Rachel and me to Laurel Hill."

Michael looked at James and said, "So help you God, tell me, did you make these beads?"

"Come James," interrupted Henry.

"No you hold up James, answer my question." cried out Michael.

"I said stop it Michael. Leave him be."

"No, sir, yous stop it, you leaves my child be. I's ya ma Micheal and Misser Henry McCloud bes yas daddy. I'm sick of lies, sick of dis chere."

Sarah was crying. The entire room became quiet. If a pin dropped it would sound like thunder.

Michael looked down at the sorrow filled eyes of Sarah and said, "What did you just say? Please repeat yourself."

"I's ya ma and he's ya pa."

Henry looked at Sarah and said "How could you. How could you?"

Michael pulled a chair out and flopped down into it. His mouth hung open. He kept shaking his head, trying to comprehend what she had said.

Henry moved to the table and slapped Sarah. "God damn it woman, how could you?"

In a leap, Michael was up and drove his fist into Henry's chin, sending him to the floor. Rachel passed out, but before she reached the floor, Elijah caught her. He lifted her up and carried her over to the couch. Michael struck Henry again rendering him unconscious. He proceeded to land another blow, when Sarah screamed.

Mary yelled, "Please stop."

Broken and Shattered

James grabbed Michael trying to pull him off of Henry. Michael shoved James to the floor, Elijah ran over and grabbed Michael and held him in a tight vice like bear hug. "God Almighty" let me go, let me go!" Michael began crying. He struggled and both he and Elijah fell to the floor.

Finally Michael stopped struggling as his body shook in convulsions. "God, God, why?" he kept saying over and over.

Finally Sarah walked over and asked Elijah to turn him loose. "Turn my boy loose," she dropped to her knees, hugging Michael who laid his head against her bosom and began to wail. He cried like a baby, her baby.

Henry crawled over and wrapped his arms around them both and said "I'm sorry."

Rachel had come to and walked over and dropped to her knees and hugged them too. Mary was tending to James. Rachel, Sarah, Michael and Henry sobbed for at least five minutes. I love you and I'm sorry were the only words spoken while the tears continued to flow. Elijah stood silently by, watching. It was a heart breaking sight. He left the room knowing he was leaving behind a family that was in need of some healing. Their lives were broken and shattered.

Chapter 17

Death's Coming

A few days had passed since Elijah was at the McCloud plantation. He still felt the pain of knowing Rachel was gone. He would miss seeing her waiting by her window to be entertained by their late night meetings. He wished with all his heart that he was rich, so he could have asked for Rachel's hand in marriage. Unlike his cousin Danny who was marrying the sweetheart of his life, he had to go and fall in love with someone way out of his reach. Mr. McCloud had it right, he was poor white trash.

He was feeding the pigs, when Dale and Danny rode up. Dale on Eagle and Danny on Sour Weed, both carrying guns. Dale asked, "Boy where's ya daddy?"

"I believe him and Grandpa's gone to Gibson. What's wrong Uncle Dale?"

"I dun an heard what happened about that mess with you youngins and that damn Allen Johnson and Samuel McDonald. Go git you a gun and strap up. Dem son's of bitches gonna pay for shooting at you boys. You can ride double with Danny. We aim to straighten this out today."

Elijah carried the bucket into the barn. When he returned, he asked "Why don't you just go tell the sheriff?"

"I done that already, and they say Samuel and Allen denied it and they got them an alibi to back it up. So go git ya gun like I said."

"Hold up now," called a voice from the porch. "Dale, what in tarnation you tellin' Lijah to git a gun for?"

Dale went into the spill of how Danny had been shot, and how the law weren't going to do anything at all.

"Don't be trying to talk my youngin into gittin' no gun and seekin' vengeance on no one. Lijah you stay put," said Ester.

"But Ms. Ester, they shot my boy and if they'd shot Lijah you would of wanted somebody to pay for that, ain't that so?"

"Dale son, you right, you speak the truth. I'd want somebody to pay for shootin' Lijah. But I tell you, now let's put it into the Lord's hands. Vengeance is mine sayeth the Lord."

Death's Coming

Dale just gritted his teeth, "Ms. Ester you just don't understand, they'll take us for being weak, and they'll think they can get away with doing us any kind of way. Shoot, they could kill one of our youngins next time."

Ester looked off toward the orchard, and then she looked heavenwards. Silence fell. "Dale honey, I ask you now, don't go through with this mess. You live by them guns, you gonna die by them guns. You say men might kill our youngins next time, but the Lord done looked after them this time and I pray they won't be no next time. Look at that boy of yours, his face tells me he's worried. Dem boys use to shootin' birds, possums, coons, rabbits and squirrels. You asking them to arm themselves to shoot a human being. Thank God they ain't dead. But today, if you go off huntin' trouble, you may be the prey. Leave it in the Lord's hands. That boy there, done got a youngin on the way and he could git killed. Then his youngin be without a daddy, is that what you want? Them boys got their lives ahead of them and today, you could cause them to lose them."

Dale looked over at Danny. "What's that Ms. Ester talkin' bout, you got a youngin on the way?"

Danny looked at Elijah, then turned and looked at his father, "Yes sir."

"Why the tarnation haven't you told me and ya ma?"

"I ain't wantin you to be mad at me Pa."

"Mad, hell no son." Dale jumped from Eagles back and walked back to Sour Weed and told Danny to climb down. Danny didn't know what to expect next. Suddenly his father grabbed him and lifted him off the ground in a hug. Dale let out a yell, "I'm gonna be a granddaddy." Then he went over to the porch and climbed the steps, and gave Ester a hug and kissed her on the cheek. "I'm gonna be a granddaddy," he kept saying. She smiled and watched as the proud father got up and mounted his horse.

Dale turned to his son and said, "Youngin, no I mean man, let's get back to the house and tell your ma. I'm sorry bout that Ms. Ester and Lijah, but I loves my family and I ain't wantin' no body hurting em."

Danny was grinning from ear to ear as he turned the horse to follow his father back toward their home.

"Lord child, how come you ain't told your Grandma bout them fools shootin' at ya'll?"

Elijah looked at his grandmother with loving eyes, and said "Cause I don't want you to worry Grandma. I'm alright so I figured there was no need to tell you."

Death's Coming

"Lord, I would care even if you wuz locked up in that big vault safe up there in Laurel Hill in that old man Tate's Bank with soft pillows all around you. Come on in this house and let me fix you a bite of that pecan pie I just made."

"Boy, we gone get us some money today," said Moses to his son John. They had left home in the early morning hours to attend Darrell's cock fighting Derby. Darrell was known around the area as Darrell Bean, the cock fighting king. He was a man of men, standing 6'1" tall and weighing 250 lbs. He had yellow hay colored hair and a smile that would befriend anyone. His wife Patricia was a beauty. A Carolina queen if there ever was one. She had golden blond hair that touched her small waist. She wore the finest dresses around. They were a match made in heaven.

Every four years the Beans held a bird fighting derby on their property. People would come from different states to put their birds to the test. Folks from South Carolina, Tennessee, Virginia and Georgia would show up for the big event. Over 2,000 people gathered for the weekend activities. They would smoke some pigs and cook a lot of chicken, turkey and fried fish for the occasion. Folks would bring musical instruments such as banjos, harmonicas, guitars, rattles, bells, washboards or anything that would make a melodious sound to play for entertainment. Good eating, good friendship and good whiskey, but it was mostly the betting that attracted the masses.

Some came rich, but left poor, while some of the poor would leave with money in their pockets. You just had to bet on luck, take a chance and decide which bird to stand behind. Bets were the name of the game.

Moses walked with John past the wagons as if he was on a mission. "What ya lookin' for Pa?" John asked.

"I'm ah huntin' the sure thing son, I ain't come to give no money away."

They had walked passed hundreds of wagons filled with people, kids and chickens. He finally stopped at a wagon where four young men lounged around and an elderly man sat nearby under a tree, smoking a long stem pipe. The young men leaned against quilts that covered square boxes.

"Hey there Mister," said Moses to the elderly man.

The old man had copper skin and grayish blue eyes. "Hello yourself," came the reply.

"Ain't seen you round before," continued Moses. The old man continued puffing on his pipe then finally he said, "I seent you before.

Death's Coming

Up there at that Laurel Hill place. It was backer day, when all us farmers round here take it to Tate's warehouses and sell it to him." The four young men eyeballed Moses and John suspiciously.

One of the young men said "It's yur turn." The youngest boy with the darkest skin, took the quilt and began lifting it.

Moses caught sight of wired cages and heard a few cackling and clucking sounds. "You got some birds you putting in today?

"Well, I got a few and them boys got a mess they want to try," said the old man. "Where you from?" asked Moses.

"Mister, you sure ask a lot of questions," the old man said, while standing up and tapping out the charred tobacco from his pipe.

"Oh I'm sorry. I ain't mean nothin' by it. My name's Moses Clark and this is my son John."

"How do you do sir?" said John, as he stepped up and shook the old man's hand.

"My names Jess Oxendine, dem are my grand yougins. That bigun is Jimbo, then Phil, Sandy and Chad. They my knee girl's boys. I'm from Clio, South Carolina. They from Sneads Grove. I lived up here since I got married."

Moses and the old man shook hands. "I'm from McColl, South Carolina."

"I know where it's at. That makes you my home state brother. John looked the young men over and began shaking hands with them. Jimbo wore a yellow bandanna around his head. Phil had a big machete knife at this side, and Chad, the younger one, just wore a smile. Sandy was a loner and wasn't bothering with any of the others.

Moses and John were walking over to their horses, when they heard the Derby Crier announce, "Five minutes to fight'n time."

Everyone had been given a number when they entered the property. There were thirty different pits for the birds to do battle in. In addition, there were two larger pits that would hold the Bean's Brawl match, where no gaffs or steel spurs would be on the cocks. The last one standing for a twenty count would be declared the winner.

The fights lasted for hours. The longest and first pitting lasted for six hours and forty-three minutes. Bean's Brawl the announcer called out. Sandy, the quiet one pulled a chicken out of a cage and walked away.

Death's Coming

The announcer marched up and down the line announcing fights by numbers. The numbers went to four hundred fifty, which is how many birds were on hand for this year's event. The derby announcer called out bird seven and bird eighteen pit one.

"Look here, we gonna bet my earnings this year and live off yourn till reaping time," said Moses. "If we win we ain't got to worry, we gonna live good."

Chad took a pair of scales from the wagon. He then pulled the quilts from the cocks' cages. The Roosters tried to get at each other. The men quickly rushed in and separated the cages. Twelve roosters crowed and flapped their wings.

"Dems some mighty fine looking birds you got there Jess," said Moses.

"Awe four of ems mine and the rest is dem boys."

"Well we fixing to walk the pits and we gone be looking for ya'll," called out Moses.

Moses and John walked through the pit areas watching both men and fowl. The crowds were gathering. A gambler was calling out "50 cent bet on a Claret". People were calling out different breeds, "Toppies, Greys, McClearns". There were roosters of different breeds, color and size. Black, white, a few speckled and red spotted all graced the pit. Some had yellow legs, while others had shades of green and orange legs.

Cheers and yells were heard throughout the pits. There were clapping sounds from the cocks flapping and hitting one another with full force to drive the gaffs into their opponents. The sharpened steel gaffs were mounted on the birds spurs to ensure the fights wouldn't last too long. The war birds appeared as if they had small knives strapped to their legs with the leather strips. The birds fought savagely.

When Moses caught sight of one of the young men he had met, carrying a rooster toward a pit, he hurried over with John in tow. "Got 2 dollars on this bird right here," he said as he pointed to Jimbo's chicken. Jimbo was carrying the bird into the pit to enter the match.

A referee would oversee the fights in each pit. In the event a spur got hung in a bird, he would hold the other birds at bay. The bird handlers would then enter and tend their birds. The referee made sure the man whose bird's gaff was hung would not twist or push it deeper into the other bird to cause more damage. A tactic many used when no pit controllers were present.

Moses and John accumulated 20 dollars in bets before the birds were released. As soon as Jimbo released his chicken and stepped out of the pit, the other man's bird rushed in with spurs aimed for the bird's chest. In a second, Jimbo's bird ducked, the opponent's bird missed him. Before anyone knew what was happening, Jimbo's bird lunged up with spurs down and drove them deep into the other cock killing it within seconds.

Money passed hands and losers congratulated winners. Jimbo had won 16 dollars himself from the opposing chicken's owner. Sandy was there to congratulate his brother. "We done got two wins already."

Jimbo looked at his brother, "The brawl over?"

"No, but its gonna be and Hoppers gone take um out. Come on." They all went over to the huge pit. Birds were everywhere. They were pecking, leaping and trying to take flight. At least thirty birds lay on the dirt floor dead or near death. Around forty still battled on. Hopper, Jess' bird was in a corner on guard. No birds came near him, they were all in frenzy. Some birds double teamed other birds, while others would gang up on the wounded ones. It was a fight true to its name, a brawl, a free for all.

Jimbo carried his rooster back to the wagon. Phil was there fitting gaffs on another cock. He wrapped the leather, tied it off tight and then tested the spike to see if it had any loose play in it. It was snug, so he clipped the excess leather and set the bird in the wagon bed.

Chad weighed the rooster, six pounds. Old man Jess gathered the bird up and walked. His number was seventy-three. He went to the pit. Moses and John followed to place their bets.

"You gentlemen can put all your money on this en. I raised him or better yet, he raised himself."

"What ya mean by that Jess?" asked John.

"I'll tell ya later."

Another bird the same size as Jess' was matched to fight him. Birds were placed in the same category by their weight and height. Darrell required this, allowing for good and fair fighting between the cocks. No one wanted to see a seven pounder maul a four pounder. That took away from the sport. However, before the derby was over, un-weighted matched birds would have at it. The day wore on and the fights continued.

Once Jess had won his fight, he went back and retrieved another one of his birds that had been fitted by Phil and weighed by Chad.

His grandsons had prepared the chickens carefully for the battle. This particular bird was smaller. Jess called him weasel because he was quick and slick.

John and Moses were 200 dollars richer. John called out "I got 20 on this bird here, pointing to weasel."

"I'll take that damn bet," said a voice in the crowd.

John looked up and saw Samuel McDonald standing there. Allen Johnson and another man all were glaring at John. "You gonna take the bet or just stand there looking like the chicken?" said Samuel.

"Aw hell you ain't got 20 dollars," said Moses mockingly.

"I do too old man," Samuel took out an old money bag and shook the pouch that sounded as if it was full of coins.

"Well bring it on, buddy boy, let Jess hold it." Jess looked at Moses, "I got my own bets to cover." "Aw hell, here." Moses gave Jess a 20 dollar gold piece.

Moses yelled out, "Got 20 on Oxen's bird." "Hold on now," said Samuel, "I got mine, and I ain't gonna let the nigra hold it."

Jess cut his eyes over at Samuel. "I ain't no damn nigra, you son of a bitch. My peoples Cheraw Indians."

"Oh excuse me Chief, but I'm not a son of a bitch neither, you need to watch your mouth. If you was younger, I'd come over there and teach you some manners."

"Come try". "Screw you, your bird and your bets," said Samuel, "Come on let's go to another pit." He said to Allen as they left.

Jess's bird's number was called. He entered pit twenty-six against another opponent. The fight lasted forty-nine minutes. But Hopper was victorious. Moses and John were 40 dollars richer by now. They went back to the wagon, where Chad was still at the buck board tying a set of gaffs on another bird. Phillip was over at a line hanging chickens up by their feet. All of the chicken's heads were gone. John and Moses watched, as he would pick up a dead rooster, lop off his head with a machete, then hang him up. It looked as if he was hanging out clothes on a clothes line.

Sandy came back carrying the Brawl Champion. Darrell was with him. "This is the man," said Sandy, pointing to Jess. Darrell walked over and shook hands with Jess and congratulated him for his cock winning the Bean Brawl. He pulled money from his pocket and took out a 50 dollar gold piece and handed it over to Jess.

Jess gladly accepted it. "Hold on Mr. Oxendine, there's more." Darlene, a young blonde that was the spitting image of Darrell's wife, brought over a cake and pie for the winner. "These are yours too", said Darrell. "And there's more, if that woman of mine will come along." Patricia Bean walked up with a blue ribbon at least a foot long. It was made from dried silk.

She handed it to her husband, "Lord I didn't think I'd ever find that thing. I thought it was in my sewing basket. Then I remembered I had put it up on the top of the book shelf for safe keeping."

Darrell handed it over to Jess, but before he passed it over, he made a show.

"I do present you, Mr. Oxendine, with this blue ribbon award for winning our Bean Brawl. Congratulations sir."

Jess looked the ribbon over, while Chad placed the cake and pie on the back of the wagon. "This is some mighty fine sewing, a real pretty ribbon Miss Bean," said Jess.

"Thank you," replied Patricia.

Just then an announcer called off one of their rooster's number. "Take care of that Jimbo." Jimbo scooped up the bird and left to enter it into battle. After a moment of chit chat, the Beans left. Jess asked if Moses and John wanted some pie and cake. They helped themselves along with Phillip, Sandy and Chad. "You boys save Jimbo some, ya hear?"

Finally the Oxendine's 12th bird was carried to the pit, they all went to bet and watch. Thumper was the name of Sandy's bird. When his bird was released it tore into the other bird. Prior to the fight Phillip had bet Allen 10 dollars and Samuel 20. John, Moses and Jess didn't notice it because they were preoccupied with their bets. The fight lasted only fifteen minutes. Thumper had plunged his right gaff into the head of the opponent bird ending its life.

When Samuel and Allen saw the deadly blow, they turned to exit the area. "Hold on," shouted Phillip. He followed behind them. Chad saw his brother and followed him. Chad called out to Jimbo, and motioned for him to come along also.

A confrontation was about to get underway. Darrell and a few men appeared, "What seems to be the problem?" he asked.

"These two is tryin' to shit me out of my money. They bet me and lost and now they won't pay up."

"Is that true?" Darrell asked Samuel and Allen.

"Hell no, we ain't bet him, he's lying." Looking back into the crowd of people who gathered around, Darrell asked "Who witness the bet?"

Phillip thought for a second and asked his brothers did they hear him bet the two men, but both said no.

"You see he ain't got no proof Mr. Bean. He's just trying to get some quick coins from somebody," said Samuel.

Moses, John, Jess and Sandy had appeared at Phillip's back. Jess asked what's the problem? "Dem two fellers backed out of paying money they owe me for a bet."

Jess looked at Phillip. "You let this be boy, them two yonder ain't no good. They'll get theirs one day."

"Is that a threat, you old high yellow nigra?" said Allen.

"No, you can get it now." Phillip pulled out his machete that he had been using to cut the heads off the chickens. He glared at Allen, and said, "I'll cut your head off calling my granddaddy a nigra, you piece of trash."

Samuel pulled a pistol and aimed it at Phillip's head. "Ain't your granddaddy told you bout bringing a knife to a gun fight boy?"

Darrell stepped up. "Hey ya'll on my property, I demand respect." At that very moment twenty guns came out pointing at both Phillip and Samuel. Samuel saw the odds and decided it best to holster his gun. Phillip sheathed his two ft blade also. "I'm sorry Mr. Bean," said Phillip.

"Look son, how much did you bet, I'll cover half." Darrell pulled a stack of cash out and was ready to count off.

"Won't nothing but 30 dollars," said Phillip, "but I'm alright, I just learned a lesson."

Darrell pulled out 15 dollars and shoved it into Phillip's chest, "Here take it boy."

"As for you two, I believe ya'll need to leave now. You are no longer welcome here. Bo, Aaron and Doug show these men off my property."

The three men, each six feet plus tall, carried shot guns. They pointed them at Samuel and Allen and sent them off with an armed escort.

"Sorry bout that, ever year, there's some ignorant ass that comes around and gets out of line. Last time four years ago, some man got shot, another one was cut and fist fights broke out everywhere. We started to put them in a pit and bet on them," said Darrell with a laugh as he melted off in the crowd. Moses and John decided it was time for them to leave so they'd be home before dark.

They counted their money and were leaving 1,800 dollars richer. They rode by the Oxendine wagon and noticed they were loading it up with the cases and birds. The boys had placed the quilts back in place so the birds couldn't see each other and hurt themselves trying to attack.

Phillip dropped by the food tent and located the blond girl who brought the pie and cake over. He gave her the 15 dollars and told her to give it to her daddy and to tell him thanks, but no thanks. He told her, her daddy was a good man to cover half his bet, but since he didn't lose anything, Mr. Bean shouldn't lose any money either.

John and Moses stopped by the Oxendine farm for a brief visit. Jess told his grandsons to escort his new found friends' home. The boys armed themselves and were about to leave when Moses asked where he could get a set of scales he saw them using to weigh the roosters.

"I got it out of Lumberton," Jess said. "I need to weigh me some stuff so I don't get cheated, but it'll be some time 'for I can get over to Lumberton." said Moses.

"Can you weigh it out in a few hours?" Jess asked.

"Less than that," said Moses.

"Well then Chad, grab them scales and carry em with you and help Moses weigh out the stuff he's talking bout."

Chad climbed down off his horse and gathered up the scales and tied them off with a rope. John and Moses said their goodbyes. A couple hours later, they turned into the Clark's homestead. They had three hours of daylight left.

Red barked and carried on as if he was the meanest junk yard dog around. Elijah came out to see what was going on. Moses told him to open the barn door. Elijah quieted Red as he was sniffing around Sandy's horse. He could smell the chickens that Sandy had.

"Will he bite?" asked Sandy.

"Only if you make him mad," smiled Elijah. Elijah knew Red wouldn't hurt a flea, but he wasn't going to share that bit of info.

Moses yelled out, "You youngins git in here."

Already, he had brought out the whiskey jug and was celebrating. Elijah went in and shut the door behind him. He greeted the Oxendine boys who remembered him from the swimming hole at the bridge.

Sandy laid some dead chickens out on the barn floor.

Death's Coming

Phillip pulled out his machete and asked if Moses wanted him to chop some of the rooster's legs off. "They would be good eating," he claimed. Elijah was talking to Jimbo about his bow. At that moment, the barn door opened, "Where in tarnation have you and John been? Didn't tell me nothing 'bout your where 'bouts."

"Hold on now Ester, we got company."

Ester looked over at the young men Moses had brought home with him. He introduced the boys to her. She noticed Jimbo wearing a yellow headband, Phillip carrying a machete knife and Chad, who was setting up a pair of scales on a barrel lid. Moses pointed to Sandy and said "The one over there with the dead birds is Sandy."

Sandy called out "Hey there, Miss Lady."

Ester's eyes grew big and she turned pale as the blood drained from her face. She touched her bosom area, and call out "Oh dear God, please forgive me. Please dear Lord, God Almighty, she turned and hurried back to the house as fast as she could move. The gang looked at each other, wondering what in the world had gotten into her.

Moses passed it off as nothing, "She musta left something cooking." He handed the jug of whiskey over to John.

"Look Chad, first off, I want you to weigh some peaches for me. Lijah, you go git us a pencil and paper so I can keep track of the stuff I'm wantin' this youngin to weigh for me."

Elijah passed the bow back over to Jimbo and left. He went inside the house and quickly noticed there wasn't anything cooking. He went into his room and found a pencil and some paper. As he walked slowly back through the house he spotted his grandmother praying.

Once back outside, he saw Red with a dead rooster in his mouth, "Hey," he yelled as he walked over to the dog. Red grabbed the rooster and took off toward the pond. "You hard headed mutt," he called out.

"Your granddaddy wants you," yelled Sandy. "I gave your dog that. I hope it's alright."

Elijah looked off in the direction Red headed, and saw him pulling feathers trying to get to the meat. "I just hope he don't turn into a chicken killer, cause Grandpa will work him over. If he ever tries to get in that hen house, that'll be the last of him. Plus we got a rooster round here somewhere. "Oh you got a game rooster?" asked Sandy. Elijah just laughed. "Nah, he's just an old yard rooster."

Death's Coming

"A Plymouth Rock?" Elijah turned around and spotted Rock under a tree. "Yonder he is."

"Nah, he ain't no game cock from what I see," said Sandy. "Lijah," yelled Moses. Elijah went inside. After handing the pencil and paper over to his grandfather, he decided he best go back and check on his grandmother hoping she wasn't ill or something.

He found her inside the parlor rocking in the chair like she was galloping away on a horse. "Lord, my Father God, has the time come?" she spoke out loud.

Elijah sat on the bench and looked at her. She stopped rocking and turned to him, "Child I've seen it, the time is coming, bad things, this world has never seen. I saw the signs in them people out there in our barn. Who are they and where did they come from?" she asked. "I wish to the Almighty, I had never seent them. But it truly must be the Lord's will, for me to see such a sight today."

"What sight Grandma?" Elijah was getting nervous and afraid. He thought his Grandmother had lost her mind. He had heard that old folks lose their minds. The brain starts dying before the body does. Elijah kept hoping this wasn't the case with his beloved Grandmother.

She said, "I saw the signs of Revelation 6 with my own eyes. The Lord's prophecy has visited us today child. I have seen the four horsemen of the Apocalypse."

Elijah pleaded, "No Grandma, thems just people from Sneads Grove, they went swimming with us. Them ain't nobody special."

"Child you don't understand, them people wuz sent here to show me a sign. Some hard times filled with trials and tribulation is coming, you mark my word."

Elijah knew asking questions got answers. "Grandma how you figure them people's a sign?"

She opened up the Bible in her lap and started reading to Elijah, once she finished, she said, "Every one of dem men fit those descriptions. One of them had a yellow band around his head like a crown and he had a bow, which is the first horse. The other one had a big cutting knife like a sword in his hand. That darker skinned one, had a pair of scales and balances in his hand. And Lord that last one was holding dead chickens in his hands. Death, I tell you death and hell followed him. Do you here me? There's gonna be death a comin."

Chapter 18

A Crazy Dream

Elijah turned up his driveway as he walked along carrying a book his teacher had given him. The school never allowed subject books to be removed from classrooms. Yet, they would allow teachers to let some students carry a book home every now and then. He carried a book titled *'Uncle Tom's Cabin'.* He was asked to read it and then write an essay about it.

His reading skills had improved greatly since his last attended school. He had been promoted from the 5th grade to the 9th grade. He knew Rachel had been a big part of his improvement.

He missed her so much. Each time he walked pass the McCloud's driveway, he would look up between the pecan trees at the house, just hoping she'd appear at the window waving or running down the drive way to meet him. Yet, she never did, because she was gone. For how long, he didn't know.

Red began barking. He stopped when he realized it was Elijah. As he entered the house, everyone inside yelled, "Surprise!" The kitchen and dining area were full of family members. They all surrounded Elijah, patting him on the back "Happy Birthday, they called out!" He had forgotten his own birthday. Normally, the family didn't pay too much attention to holidays, not even birthdays, so he wondered what gives.

"Today, my boys a man." said John, the big sixteen. There was a cake on the table with the number 16 written with strawberry icing in the middle. Ester did it up good. It was a vanilla-strawberry mixed eight-layer cake, with each layer having its own icing. Strawberry on one layer and vanilla on the next. Crushed pecans were sprinkled all over it. There was a feast of chicken, biscuits, potato salad, fried sweet potato bread, fish, hush puppies, corn on the cob and other tasty foods.

A few presents wrapped in cloth and brown paper lay on a bench. "Now he's here! Ya'll said I can have a piece of that cake when he come," Little Dale announced.

A Crazy Dream

His mother Gloria spoke up, "Lord Lijah this youngin's dying for a piece of your cake. I had to cut his legs twice all ready with this switch." She waved the small branch in her hand.

"Well, let me get a knife and we can all have a piece" said Elijah.

Ester said, "Hold on a minute, Gloria, Pamela and me's done cooked up this meal and y'alls gonna eat some food first, 'for you go to putting that sweet junk in your bellies."

With that said, she reached for a plate and fixed Elijah the first helping. She passed it to him and kissed him on the cheek, "Happy birthday youngin, God bless you."

Elijah gave her a big smile, "Thank you Grandma." He took his plate and went to sit down on the bench where Danny and Dewey joined him. "We got you something," said Dewey, "the whole family, me, Little Dale, Danny, Pa and Ma."

Once Elijah finished his cake, he bashfully thanked everyone, and said, "I love all of ya'll for being good to me. I had forgotten it was my birthday, but now I won't forget this day."

"Oh, honey, it's time to open your presents," said Ester.

Elijah moved over to the bench and began opening the gifts in size order, smallest to largest. He was so excited as he picked up a 10 inch box, "That's from me and Gloria," said Dale.

"And me too," said Little Dale. Elijah opened the box. It was a pipe with tobacco leaves carved in the bowl. He went over and gave them a hug.

The next gift he thought felt like socks with something hard in it. He opened it to find a bundle of cured tobacco and a pocket knife; "It's from Dewey and me, plus Pamela," said Danny. "You can cut that backer for your pipe." He repeated his affection for each of them.

Another gift was a new pair of coveralls and a new Bible. "Child you know who gave that present to you," said his grandmother. The last was a pair of boots, socks and two shirts.

"That one comes from your grandpa." Moses grinned. "Look in one of dem boots boy." Elijah pulled out a silver round pocket watch, with the initials engraved on its cover piece E.J.C.

"Wow! Thanks Grandpa, I won't forget the time now. Gosh, I just can't believe it, thank ya'll so much."

He was almost in tears of joy till his Pa said, "Hold on son, you ain't opened my present yet."

Elijah looked around, "I ain't seen it, to open it."

John walked up and said come on. He led Elijah outside and everyone followed. "Go yonder to the barn and open the doors."

Elijah dashed over to the barn, hoping in his heart he had him a horse. He swung open the doors and there stood the most beautiful black horse he had ever seen. He had a mark on his forehead that looked like a diamond. The horse had a mouth full of hay. There were bales scattered all over the floor. It was if he had slung hay over to Joe and Jim. The mules were eating their share through the gaps in the gates on their stalls. "Hot damn it, you better go get him for I kill him said Moses, seeing the mess the horse had made along with his overturned jug of whiskey.

Both Elijah and Moses darted into the barn. Elijah pulled the horse out and Moses checked his liquor jug in hopes that none had spilled out. "Dale and John y'all come help me restack these bales of hay that damn horse done knocked over." He held the jug up and Dale and John knew it was celebrating time. They had a few sips before the other family members arrived.

Elijah told Danny to hold the horse's reins. He grabbed his father and picked him up. "Pa thank you, thank you!!"

"Son, you would have had a horse sooner, but I was having to save up enough to get us another place. Then it dawned on me this was your place. Plus, I didn't know if you want another one after your last one died. I seen Danny running around on Sour Weed with his gal, and I figured I'd get you one. His name is Black Jack. He's gentle and can fly like the wind. He almost out ran Eagle when me and your Uncle Dale tested him out. He's still young though. I'm sure you and him gonna become the best of buddies."

"I love him, Pa."

"Maybe now you can get yourself a girlfriend to ride with you. Have you met any in school?"

"Nah I'm alright," said Elijah.

"Well go on and enjoy yourself, it's your birthday."

Elijah quickly mounted the fifteen hand high horse, and rode him at a slow trot and then a gallop. He could feel the power in the animal. He kicked his heels, clicked his tongue and Black Jack bolted. The horse seemed to pick up speed with every step. Elijah was going at full speed when he pulled back on the reins. He was now nearing the McCloud's drive way.

He looked up and saw James sweeping off the huge steps. "James! Hey Mr. James," he yelled.

The elderly man looked around, "Out here Mr. James. Hello," called Elijah.

The old man waved his hand and stood watching Elijah. Elijah was tempted to ride up and speak to the old man, but he only waved and turned his new horse and headed back toward his home. He rode the horse for the remainder of the day. Once he returned home, all the guest were gone except Dale, who was drunk inside the barn with his Moses and John.

They talked about how the people of South Carolina hated that Abraham Lincoln had won the presidency. That son of a bitch didn't even get the popular vote," said Dale. "I heard McCloud talking about it the other day." Dale continued to tell them, "You know that man's been acting different since his gal and that nephew of his left. He's always wanting me to come in and sit down and have a drink with him. It is either me or that Vernon, the gin overseer, and a few of his boys. He just wants company. They's four white men who works for him and he treats us like family. Before his gal and that nephew of his left, he kept his distance, only business. But now, he wants us all to be his friends. That Michael was fine Yankee people, he was always kind to me. I miss him myself if the truth be told."

Elijah listened, and then curiosity got the better of him. "Where did Michael go?" he asked.

"McCloud said he couldn't find work, so he decided to go back to Boston."

Elijah wondered to himself, if learning that Henry McCloud was his father had anything to do with it. He hadn't told anyone about what he witnessed at the McCloud's mansion on the day of Rachel's departure. He didn't like gossiping, cause his grandmother always said, "It was the work of the devil, his way to cause discord among the brethren," as she put it.

His Grandfather said, "It was what women do and if a man did it, it meant he had them women ways and may be crazy in the brain."

So, he refused to mention the McCloud family woes to anyone. "Where am I gonna put Black Jack?" Elijah asked his father.

John looked around the barn, and saw all three stalls on the right were full, with the two mules and the milk cow, Milly. "Clean out that back stall over there on that side and put him in there."

Elijah walked over to look. It was full of winter rations and seed for planting next year's crops. "What am I gonna do with all this mess?" he asked.

"Just stick it up there in the loft, I reckon," said John. "Ah shucks me and your Grandpa can do it tomorrow while you at school."

Elijah thought about school, he wished now he hadn't started back, now that he had him a horse to ride. Then he remembered the book. "Well, I got myself some reading to do, I better get on it. Where can I put Black Jack now?"

"You go on in, we'll tie him off in here till tomorrow," said Moses. "We gonna make sure he don't eat up no more hay. Plus, you need you a job to help feed him."

Elijah looked over at Moses with sadness in his eyes. He knew he couldn't work a job and go to school too. And he thought about all the work in the fields that needed doing especially at planting time.

"Boy, I'm just punning you, you got a job right here on this farm, your Pa and me gonna make sure your hay eating horse is gonna get fed."

Elijah looked at all three men in their happy drunken state, which he'd much rather see as opposed to a brawling condition. Elijah said his goodbyes and told them he was going inside to try out his new pipe Dale had given him. "I'm gonna break it in, he said proudly."

Before leaving the barn, he scratched Black Jacks ear and patted him on the neck, "Night boy."

He noticed Ester had already gone to bed for the night. So, he washed up and emptied out the foot tub, then excitingly put his presents under the bed where most of his clothing was kept. He lay on his bed and started reading his book. As he read, he tried to visualize the characters as being people he was already familiar with. Uncle Tom, he pictured as being Mr. James, the McCloud's butler. Eva was his sweet dear Rachel. He continued reading and fell asleep with the book in his hands.

He was awakened shortly afterwards, by Moses. "Boy you trying to burn the house down?"

Elijah sat up and realized he had left the lantern burning. His grandfather blew out the flame and made his way back out of the room. "Go back to sleep, we all done burnt up now," he chuckled.

Elijah tore off a small piece of paper and placed it in his book for a marker, then faded off to sleep.

173

A Crazy Dream

He started dreaming about Black Jack, they were galloping across wide open spaces. He trotted over a hill and on the other side Elijah saw a multitude of men. They were all fighting one another. The men covered a span as far as the eye could see. He watched on for a while with awe and wonder. Suddenly a group of men came up and grabbed hold of Black Jack's bridle.

"Get your hands off my horse," Elijah yelled. He kicked his heels into Black Jack and the horse reared up and began kicking his hooves, striking the men and dashing away. The men began pursuing them on foot. Elijah was riding Black Jack at full speed, but the men were right on his tail. They were yelling, "Come back here boy, the President of the Union needs that horse."

Elijah kicked his heels even harder into Black Jack's ribs. Soon they were about to make some lead way against the crowd of men. As they raced along, Elijah was thrilled he had gotten away from the madness and rush of the battling horde. As he rode along, he saw a river. His heart began to sink, he would have to stop and the men would catch up to him and take his horse. He pulled back on Black Jack's reins and the horse sped up, going faster. Elijah began to fear Black Jack would cause them both to drown. He yelled out "Whoa, Whoa boy." As they neared the river's bank, Black Jack leaped into the air and flew clear across the three hundred yard wide river. Once on the other side, the horse stopped and Elijah climbed off his back. He was frightened, but a sense of calmness overcame him as he looked across the river to the other side. They were safe. The men couldn't get to them. The men were shaking their fist at him and yelling profanities. He looked toward the crowd and something flew over their heads. It crowed, as it flew and landed on the bank where he and Black Jack stood. It was a Rooster, it crowed again.

Elijah looked down and saw it was Rock, the family rooster. "Hey Rock, I didn't know you could fly." Rock looked up at him and spoke.

"You need to get on up honey." Elijah almost wet his pants, he looked at the bird and the bird was speaking in his Grandmother's voice.

He felt a hand on his shoulder, shaking him. He woke up to see Ester there at his bedside trying to wake him.

"Morning Grandma."

"Morning child, get on up, you gonna be late for ya schoolin'."

"I had a crazy dream, Grandma."

174

Chapter 19

Welcome Here

Winter came along with a notable change. Ms. Rebecca Dutch, Elijah's teacher, announced that South Carolina had seceded from the United States Union.

Elijah asked, "What does that mean, since I'm from South Carolina?"

This came as a surprise to his teacher. "My, I thought you were from Gibson and Scotland County in North Carolina."

"No ma'am, I live right across the border heading out to McColl in Marlboro County."

She asked him to come to the principal's quarters to discuss this matter. Soon afterwards, Elijah was notified he had to leave school for not being a resident of North Carolina. This took him aback. But Elijah took it in stride and thanked his teacher for her work and told his classmates farewell.

He climbed on Black Jack's back and headed home. He doesn't know why, but he dismounted Black Jack as they walked past the McCloud's driveway. He wondered if Rachel would ever come back home. It had been more than a year and no sign of her. He saw a couple of carriages out front and figured the mansion had company.

Once he arrived home, he found an empty house. He watered Black Jack and gave him some grain. As he went inside, he noticed the stove was still warm with red embers. He added a few pieces of wood to the fire, and saw the wood box was empty. He thought to himself, since he had been kicked out of school, he might as well start on his chores.

He went outside to the wood pile and began chopping away at the logs. He worked hard and before long, he had to come out of his coat. The crisp winter air felt good to inhale. While he was splitting the wood, Red came over to investigate Elijah's work. A wood chip flew over and struck him in the side. This spot just wasn't for him. He began walking away, then his ears perked up and he started barking.

Elijah looked over in the direction the dog was barking and saw the buggy coming up the driveway. He immediately dropped the axe and took off running toward the visitor. It was his Rachel. She quickly pulled back on the reins to halt the horse.

She looped the reins on the brake hitch and stood up to climb down. Elijah rushed over and pulled her from the buggy. "My sweet Rachel, God it's you gal."

"Why'd you leave me, why'd you leave me?" she kept repeating. He sat her down and held her in his warm embrace.

She cried, "I missed you so. I was miserable without you in my life. It took me a month to go to sleep like normal, because I wasn't able to talk with you. I hated that placed. Every day, I was reminded college had separated us. That dreadful place is no place for a lady or woman as they called me. The students were horrible to me. I've never missed anyone as much as I missed you. I saw a man on a horse riding down the road and I knew it was you. I saw that beautiful black hair and couldn't wait to see your face. I rushed downstairs and got into the buggy and rushed on over to you."

They kissed passionately. The kiss they had taught one another. Elijah pushed her back an arm's length. "Let me take a look at you gal. Lord it seems like you got more beautiful while you were away." He pulled her back in and hugged her again. "God, I ain't wantin' you to leave me ever again, please."

She pressed her hands against his chest and pushed him away. She looked in his face, "Elijah it wasn't my plan to leave that day, my father didn't want me to. But the shame I felt and the distrust was too overwhelming. Anyway, I didn't leave for another two days."

Elijah held her hand as they walked to her horse and pulled it near the well pump. Her horse drank out of Red's drinking bucket. The dog was eyeing the bucket suspiciously, but didn't bark or growl in protest. He saw his master so he felt safe. He lay down under the porch while keeping them in view.

"Look I got me a horse," he told her. He led her to the place where Black Jack was tied to the barn door handle.

"He's beautiful. He's got black hair just like yours," she said, while stroking the animal.

He began telling her about what he had been up to while she was away. "I went to school while you were gone. I ain't in the 5th grade any longer, I'm in the 9th grade," he proudly said. "I know it's because of you Rachel, you make me better. I don't care what Grandma or the others say.

You are good for me. But, I guess now it don't matter, I dun and got kicked out.

Teacher said, since I lived in South Carolina, I couldn't attend school there. I guess it's ok, but we buy everything from Gibson and Laurel Hill. We never run down to McColl to get nothing."

Rachel got quiet, she looked off toward the road. Elijah could sense something was wrong, so he asked "What's wrong Rachel?"

"Oh Elijah, it's my Father, he's just not the same. He's lost something and he's drinking as we speak." She turned and started walking toward her buggy where she stopped and stroked her horse. "Elijah, I believe he's going mad. Since the day I discovered Michael was my half-brother, my father has not been himself."

She then turned and looked at Elijah and said, "Why did you leave without telling me goodbye?" Elijah dropped his head searching for words. "Please tell me Elijah, how could you forsake me in my time of despair?"

Elijah recalled the Lord's words as he was being hung from that torture stake. 'Why has thou forsaken me?' he asked God. He found confidence in those words and he answered, "I didn't forsake you. You could have come to me. I felt so sorry for your whole family. All of you sitting on that floor crying. You made me cry. I had to git out of there, 'cause it had nothing to do with me. I felt bad for you and I was worried if I would have come over to talk to you, your father might have tried to fight with me or something. He'd already told me to leave. So I left, but I ain't never forsaken you. Plus I ain't told a living soul, 'bout what I seen and what I heard that day. It was ya'lls heartache not mine."

Rachel walked over to Elijah and gave him a hug. Thank you for not spreading the word of our dark secret. Yet that's behind us now. "Uncle Dale said Michael left."

"I liked him and I was hoping he could have been my friend. But now he's gone. I reckon I'm gonna have to climb that old chimney like an old cockroach or spider again," he grinned.

"Come on, let's have a seat." They both sat down on the pump table. Rachel seemed to calm down a bit. She said, "I haven't spoken to anyone about what happened that day either. I felt so betrayed. We all sat around like a group of lost children. We gathered ourselves together and tried to regain our composure. I went to my room and waited by the window for you. I wanted to be with you. I finally fell asleep crying my eyes out."

"I'm sorry," said Elijah.

"Oh don't be, it wasn't your fault. I had to face the fact of why a truth like that was hidden from me. At first I wondered how my father could have possibly slept with a servant. Then, I realized they grew up together forming a fondness for one another no doubt."

"I accepted it, after I saw your cousin and Delilah playing together. They being two innocent children, not seeing race or color, only a little girl and little boy, the human race. So, in my heart I forgave father, thanks to Little Dale. I felt so sad for Sarah. Here she was a woman who had given birth to a child she had to give up. Not only was it unlawful but on top of that, my grandfather adamantly disapproved. I heard Father pleading and telling Michael this."

"Michael wasn't so forgiving, I'm afraid. He demanded Sarah's freedom that very night, he made father sign the papers right there on the spot. I truly thought Michael was going to kill Father. Sarah kept pleading with him, and swore by God, Father had never been cruel to her and when he struck her that day, it was the first and only time. There she was, a slave with freedom. I cried, the day she left. I loved her like my own mother."

"Michael told me that I was his blood and family, and if I wanted to, I could come to Boston with them. I was more than welcome there. I think he loathes my Father."

"My father hugged Sarah and begged for forgiveness, but she told him there was nothing to forgive. She even thanked Father for saving Michael for so long. However, Michael didn't see it her way, he saw it as a betrayal filled with lies and evil doings perpetrated by my Father. I don't think he'll ever forgive him. I asked them to stay, but Sarah said freedom was just as good to her as it was to me."

"She had wanted her freedom and her baby had come back to give it to her. Once she was away and saw what freedom was about, Michael told her then she would see the evil Henry had committed against her. He claimed father had taken advantage of his mother."

"Sarah interrupted Michael, telling him they could have taken his life. That would have been the most evil. But Henry saved her son's life and all the evil was forgiven in her eyes.'"

"So my Father is a broken man. I don't think it's because of Sarah's leaving but because of Michael hating him and his total rejection of him.

He was willing to play the role as his Uncle, and was proud of him, even though his identity could never be known. Father cherished the time Michael was here. I later learned Father had paid for Michael's schooling and had donated money to the orphanage to give special care to him while they raised him with a Christian rearing."

"On that night when Sarah stood up and said 'The Bible says the truth will set you free.' I think all of us were set free." Rachel continued, "I know I was set free from thinking whites were superior to blacks. Love has no boundaries and loneliness calls on everyone at sometime in their life. I used to be lonely living out here away from people. Then David McDonald and his father came along. David was my friend."

"Then I met you that day, you were not a friend or an enemy. I saw you a few times in town with your parents. I even gave you a pretend name, 'Raven Hair,' she laughed. I used to imagine you as my boyfriend, you know like Romeo and Juliet. Once, my Father told me about a pirate, named Black Beard, who ruled the Atlantic Ocean. After that, I dreamed of you and me on a boat sailing and you were a pirate. I was so silly over you."

"My father told me to stay away from people like you and your family. He said you were on the same totem pole as the slaves. I told Sarah about you one day, father overheard me laughing and asked 'What was the reason for his little girl's laughter?' Sarah revealed the reason. He was furious, and told me to go to my room immediately." Father told me I was too precious to be tied to the lower class, but he used the other word."

"White trash?" asked Elijah.

She didn't say anything, but he knew. "He said men like you would never amount to anything. All they do is drink, fight and abuse their women and children. He said I was to never get caught up thinking about a commoner again. But, Elijah, I now know Father was wrong. Father has had his own skeletons pulled out of the closet, and you will never be one of them. I've never met a man as gentle, kind and hard working as you. You've been very respectful to me and I've never smelled alcohol on you. I don't imagine you drink?" She smiled. Then she commented, "You do take part in that tobacco stuff, which I must say, I find appalling."

"Hold on now, what's appalling mean?" he asked.

"It means shocking, horrible, awful, in other words nasty," she giggled.

"Sounds good to me, 'cause I got me a new pipe and it smokes pretty darn good," he answered with a grin.

"As I said, Father is wrong, if anything, it's the wealthy people who can be cruel and abusive. All of those male students at the college were from rich families. They thought I was a tramp or whore. They were very disrespectful to me when they saw I was not promiscuous."

"Now there you go again, what's promiscuous?"

"That means a loose hussy or floozy, someone they could have sexual relations with." Elijah wished he had left that word alone, he felt very uncomfortable talking about sex.

He blushed and looked away. "Here Red," he called his dog over to change the subject and began petting him.

"Well, it really feels good to let all that out. Just talking to you about it makes me feel good."

At that very moment, Danny and Pamela appeared riding around the house on Sour Weed. "Hey Lijah," said Danny.

"Hey, Danny and Pam, this here's Rachel, she's..."

"I know who she is, my daddy works for her daddy."

"Hey girl." said Danny.

"Hello to you," replied Rachel.

Danny slid off of Sour Weed's back and walked him over to Red's bucket to take a drink. Red let out a growl, "Hush boy," called out Elijah.

"Help me down," said Pam looking at Danny. Danny lowered her down. She walked over and held out her hand to Rachel. "Hello, that sure is a pretty dress you have on."

"Lord, look Danny, she's got rings on and a necklace around her neck." "Those are some beautiful rings too," said Pam. She placed a double emphasis on rings, reminding Danny he needed to get their wedding rings.

"Hello to you and thank you," said Rachel.

Rachel asked Pam how old she was and discovered they were born two days apart. Rachel was the oldest. They started carrying on about girl stuff and walked over to Rachel's buggy.

"When she come back?" asked Danny.

"I reckon today or yesterday. I ain't even asked her," replied Elijah.

Elijah asked, "Man why did you have to go and bring Pam with you?" Elijah felt embarrassed, because he hadn't had relations with Rachel or any girl. He was still a virgin and there he sat talking with his younger cousin, who was already married and had a child.

Welcome Here

"Why'd you have Rachel over here showing off them rings, making Pam badger me about getting ours?" Danny asked. He looked over at Elijah as if expecting an answer, but Elijah just looked at the buggy where the two girls were sitting. They were deep in conversation.

"She came here 'cause I love her."

"Well, there you go, I love Pam and brung her with me." They both laughed and slapped each other on the back.

Danny pulled out a plug of tobacco and bit off a wad. "Come on," said Elijah. They went inside and got his new pipe and some tobacco. "I want you to try making some tobacco that is flavored like strawberries, peaches and apple flavor."

"Hot damn boy, you's a genius. I ain't never thought about that. You gonna help make your cuz rich before it's all over with."

"I done carried an old man in Gibson some of my backer for him to sale in his store. He set the price, I told him, we'd split it 50/50. I went by the other day and he had sold five of em. three smoking and two chewing plugs. I been giving my money to the black smith, Mr. McDowell, he's making mine and Pam's rings. Said they ought to be ready by January. I gave him some silver coins to make em with. He charging me 12 bucks and I still owe him 2. I tied a string around Pam's finger to let him know her size. I tied it on her knuckle. He took my finger size while I was there. Them rings in the store start at 30 bucks and dem is the cheap ones. Some of dem rings were 500 bucks. Can you believe, 500 bucks for a ring?"

They both walked outside and noticed the buggy was gone. "Now wonder where they run off to?" asked Danny.

"Boy your gal's done drove off with my ole lady." They looked toward the McCloud plantation and saw the buggy going up the drive way between the pecan trees.

"Let's go see what they up to, come on," said Danny.

"I can't," said Lijah, Danny wasn't aware that Henry had forbid him on his property.

"What ya mean ya can't? Come on."

"Her daddy don't want me up there," he admitted.

"That's bullshit, Lijah. Come on, my daddy is up there now, we can go up there." Elijah thought for a few moments and just maybe by him having family in Henry's presence, he wouldn't say anything. "Alright, let's go." Elijah ran and untied Black Jack and Danny climbed on Sour Weed.

They headed out to the McCloud's home. Elijah reined Black Jack to a halt. Danny turned and looked back at Lijah, "Come on cuz, we'll kick old McCloud's ass if he says anything to you, come on."

"Nah Danny, that's Rachel's daddy and I ain't gonna disrespect him, on count of her. You run on up there and ask her if she gonna come back out."

"You sure?" asked Danny.

"I'm sure." he answered.

Danny ventured on up to the mansion. He went inside. After a few minutes, he came out, jumped on the back of Sour Weed and charged down the driveway to where Elijah and Black Jack were waiting. "Old McCloud said come on up. I ain't seen them gals, but he told me to come get you and bring you up."

"Are you telling the truth?"

"More serious than a coon that's fallen out of a tree in amongst some hungry hounds," Danny said.

"Well that's serious, I'd say," grinned Elijah.

He was so excited, he kicked Black Jack's ribs and the horse moved on up the dirt drive. When they were in sight of the front steps, Henry stepped out onto the porch. Elijah couldn't believe the once clean cut smooth faced man appeared shabby and fragile. He had a beard and mustache and his hair had grown out.

"Ah, Elijah, Elijah, Elijah, your kin folk tells me you want to speak to me."

Elijah looked at Danny knowing he had been tricked in coming up here by his own blood kin. Danny shrugged his shoulders and looked quite innocent.

"Well, yes sir," Elijah began. "I would like to talk sir." He came down off of Black Jack and tied the horse off. Danny followed suit.

The three entered the mansion. "You sit down and relax," he said to Danny. He then told Elijah to come with him. Henry walked into his library. Elijah was overwhelmed by all the books. There were ten times more books in this library than were in his school's library. He remembered peeking in the first time he had visited Rachel, but he just didn't know how fully stocked it was.

Henry sat behind his desk and pulled out a bottle of whiskey and drank from the bottle. "Care for a drink young man?"

"No sir, I don't drink," Elijah answered.

"That's a good thing. Now where were we, yes, Danny said you would like a word with me. Speak up, what's on your mind?"

"Mr. Henry," Elijah began, "I love your daughter, and I want you to know that. I wish you and me was acting better toward each other. I respect you and I'm sorry if you don't share the same respect for me. I wish I could do something to make you respect me. I ain't out to hurt you or your daughter."

"Enough said," Henry interrupted, "You say you love my daughter. Do you love her enough to sacrifice your life for her?" Henry pulled out a pistol from behind the desk and pointed it at Elijah.

Elijah started to get up and run, "Hold up there young man." Henry set the gun down on the desk. "You got to understand me. The last time I saw you, I was a proud man. Today, I'm broken down with no pride left. I disgraced myself before my daughter. I never wanted her to know I had slept with a slave. I used to tell her it was wrong for races to mix. It would kill me if my daughter was to lay down with a slave. It's not right that a white man should do it but it is definitely wrong for a white woman to do it. I've thought of you often ever since that day. I wondered if you'd slander me by telling everything that happened in our household. The next day I waited to see if your uncle acted different toward me. But he acted the same. He and I in fact, have a brotherly companionship today. I asked him had he heard anything from you concerning my daughter. He said no, and that he doesn't stick his nose in other people's concerns."

"I ain't told nobody bout ya'll, Mr. McCloud," said Elijah.

"That I can believe son, so I want to apologize for calling you white trash. I know now you care for my daughter a great deal. There's something good in you. Elijah I do want to respect you, and I want to always have your respect. But I, like all fathers, wonder what you can offer my daughter. How would you support her? How can you keep her up in the life style she has become accustomed to? This is the only life she's known. Look around, she doesn't know a hard days labor, she doesn't know how to cook, clean, wash clothes, make a bed or even beat out rugs. Think about it. She'd be a burden to you. If anything, you'd become her servant."

"I'd do it," said Elijah.

"Damn," said Henry "I believe you would."

"I'd go find me work, if we ever come to the point of marriage."

"Would you come over here and take over this place if I needed you?"

Elijah was taken aback from the question, but without hesitation, he said "I'll do whatever needs to be done, to make sure Rachel is taken care of sir and if that's coming here and leaving my family to be with Rachel, I'd do it. I'd do it 'cause the Bible says a man will leave his family to cling to his wife."

Henry loved the answer and he smiled. The thought of a son who would take over delighted him. It's not a daughter's husband, but a father's new son. All the while he had been thinking of losing his daughter to this young man, when he in fact was gaining a son. "Elijah, you may come courting my daughter." He grabbed the gun off his desk and pointed it at him again. "Tell me now, have you ever had relations with her?"

"No, no sir." Elijah was frightened and said, "I don't know no woman, I ain't never been with no woman. That's for married folks, fornication is wrong in God's eyes," said Elijah.

Henry sat the gun back down and said "Damn son, you sound like a preacher. But I do love that you know the Lord's word. That tells me you were raised in a good household." He walked over and shook Elijah's hand, which reminded him just how rough they are.

"It's good for you to be a hard worker and take care of my Lilly. Don't ever abuse her, or put your hands on my girl. If you stop loving her, you leave her and don't turn back. She is all I have left in this world, and why she still loves me, only God knows. Why she loves you? I want to know. So I'll give it time to play out. Elijah, you are once again welcome here.

Chapter 20

Protect Me

Elijah cherished the time he spent with Rachel during the winter months. This time of year the farm work was slower. He even had a chance to help out with the McCloud's seasonal hog killings. Henry paid him generously for his labors. Elijah drove his wagon loaded with meats to Laurel Hill for the Tates. He picked up needed supplies while he was there. Every penny Elijah received for his work, he stashed away. He wouldn't accept any paper currency for wages, only coins, silver or gold and a little copper.

One afternoon, he was home tilling the ground to set tobacco out for the early spring, when he heard someone yelling. He turned and saw Rachel walking across the field toward him. "The wars started," she yelled.

"The war about what?" he asked.

"The War Between the States, she excitedly explained. Father thought they'd wait until six other states would secede. But, South Carolina has started the war by firing on Ft. Sumter. It fell into the Confederate's possession two days ago and Virginia seceded today. We are in a war, the North versus the South, Elijah. Dear God, Elijah, Father says they are asking for one hundred thousand soldiers to defend the Confederacy. He told me they are asking for anybody from eighteen years and up. She began crying uncontrollably as she walked over to Elijah."

"Let me run this row out and come back, meet me back yonder pointing to the opposite end of the field."

She looked in that direction, then sat down. Elijah drove Joe and Jim at a quicker pace. You could hear him geahing and hawing at the mules to make them move faster. He finally decided that he had done enough plowing for the day.

When he reached Rachel, he told her, "I'll put these mules up and we can find out what's going on." He unhitched them from the plows at the barn, then watered and fed them. He rubbed the mules down, as he had on each day they were worked. They brayed a couple of times as if to thank him for the short work day. "Look, I don't know why you letting it bother you so much, ain't no war coming here, he told her."

"It is," she said, all the men around here, have been gathering up and reporting to the county court houses in Marlboro, Scotland and Richmond too. They're going to ship them off to the forts to fight. My father said, 'He was going to have to decide before long if he should report. If South Carolina needs help, he'll serve.' If he leaves, I've got no one to protect me here in that big house. I've read in the newspapers, it has something to do with a state having the right to rule itself, and there's a rumor about stopping people from holding slaves, outlawing it altogether."

Elijah moved over to the well pump to wash his face and hands. He dipped his head under the water, while still listening as Rachel continued. "My father wants you to come see him, that's why I came."

"I'll come, soon as I have a bite to eat." Rachel kissed him and he tried to take hold of her, but she pressed him back.

"You're wet, go get you something to eat and come. I'll see you then." She climbed back into her buggy and left. Elijah walked into the house.

His grandmother said, "I saw ya and ya darling out there, she won't let ya lone long enough to plow dem fields so ya can get some plantin' done, I see."

"Aw Grandma, she's upset. Said, we in a war."

"A war?" Ester asked with a worried tone in her voice. "Dear child, what kind a war?" She asked. "The North versus the South, the Union versus the Confederacy. They fighting over a state having the right to run their own business. I believe she said, somethin' about stopping slavery too."

"Lord, I knew it, I knew it." "That's just a rumor Grandma." Elijah busied himself preparing him a plate of pork chops, biscuits, potatoes and gravy. He offered up a prayer before he began eating.

His grandmother chimed in, "I knew it won't gonna be long after I seen dem four horsemen." Elijah kept chewing his food and remained silent.

A knock sounded at the back door. "Come on in," said Ester.

Danny stepped in with Dewey following. "We done gone to war Lijah," he said. He had a pistol stuck in his waist band, and a powder horn draped across his shoulder.

"What in tarnation is ya doin' rompin' up in here like you foolish youngin?"

"I'm sorry Ms. Ester, I wanted to let ya'll know we wuz at war."

"I guess ya goin' fightin' with that pistol you got?" She asked.

"If dem North people come round here I'll fight em," he said. "I ain't scared of em."

"Why don't you and that brother of yurn fight on out in the yard to wait on this youngin'. Can't ya see he's got him a mouthful, get on out of here talkin' bout fightin'. You need a Bible in that hand, 'stead of that ole pistol. Youngin, dem peoples got cannons that sound like thunder. Leave here with that foolish talk, I tell you." Danny was shamed. Dewey snickered, "Yes ma'am Ms. Ester." Danny turned and shoved Dewey in front of him, as they walked out the door.

"Ya see, already, peoples gone foolish. That youngin in here ready for war. I've seen cannons as big as you honey. They'd knock this house right off its foundation. Lord it's a sad day child. The Lord don't like ugly" she got up and went into the parlor.

After Elijah finished eating, he peeped in and saw his Grandmother reading the Bible. She looked up at him. "The Lord's all we really got now child, put your trust in him." She turned back and started searching the scriptures.

When he walked out, Danny was sitting under the chinaberry tree next to the barn. Danny looked up, "Cuz, that Grandma of yours is tough, ain't she? She lit into me like a dog on a cat."

"Well, she's just worried that's all. Rachel had done told me about the war starting."

"Yea, her daddy told Pa. I rode up there to take him some lunch; then Pa told me. So I went home and got my pistol and come over to tell you."

"I'm about to go see Mr. McCloud now," Elijah said as he was bridling Black Jack for his ride to the plantation. Danny decided to tag along riding Sour Weed. "What happened to Dewey?" questioned Elijah.

"I popped him up side his head 'cause he kept laughing about your Grandma blessing me out. He took off toward home whining. I know he's gonna tell Pa, but I ain't caring. Pa looks at me as a man now," Danny said grinning.

They climbed off their horses and approached the McCloud's door. Just before Elijah knocked, the door swung opened. There stood Rachel with a big smile. "Come in Elijah, Daddy's in the library."

Elijah entered the library and closed the door behind him. "Elijah our state has fired on Fort Sumter, which is a Union Fort.

187

Protect Me

They claim the Union President, Abraham Lincoln, ordered the Fort be restocked and prepared.

South Carolina took this as an act of war. If you ask me, the Federal Government has got their hands and noses in all the states' business. What are they doing with a Fort in our state anyway? That just goes to prove our State was right in seceding from the Union. We can govern our own affairs. Now, word has gone out that volunteer soldiers are few and far between. I may have to report for service before too long myself. I need to help defend our state. If the situation turns too bad every man may need to arm himself. Do you own a gun Elijah?"

"Well Sir, I sometimes use my Pa and Grandpa's guns," replied Elijah.

"I'll take that as a no," Henry added as he pulled two pistols out of his desk drawer and placed them on top. "This is a Colt Dragon, six shot, repeating revolver. It has an eight inch barrel. It's good for a little further distance shooting than this one, picking up another weapon. This is a Colt peace maker with a five and a half inch barrel."

He reached in and took out some ammunition and placed it on his desk alongside the guns. "I'm going to give you these guns. I've purchased me two brand new Colt revolvers. If I have to go and defend our great state, you must be able to protect my Lilly and keep her from harm."

"I can't take them Mr. McCloud, my Grandma would kill me." He explained.

Henry raised his eye brows and remarked, "Do you not remember telling me that you would protect my daughter?"

"You said you would sacrifice your life for her. So take these guns and protect my daughter and yourself as well."

Reluctantly, Elijah reached over and picked up the guns. He looked down the sights and aimed at a couple of novel bindings. He reached for the ammunition, as Mr. McCloud remarked, "Son, you may have to protect that grandmother of yours too."

He stuck the guns in his waist line and placed the ammunition in his pockets. "I almost forgot." He pulled a holster off the coat rack, "This is for the peace maker. It's a shoulder holster."

Elijah looked it over. Henry held it up "Here, stick your arm through this hole. It's like putting on a shirt. You can wear it buckled or loose."

Although Elijah felt awkward, Henry stated, "You look like a first rate soldier, ready to serve and protect.

188

The Confederacy needs young men like you. It's a shame you're not eighteen yet. Now, I'll tell you what. If I go away and come back in one piece, I want the peace maker back and you can keep the other one as a gift. Is that a deal?"

"Yes sir," answered Elijah.

"Rachel tells me you were working when I asked her to fetch you. If you need to go back to work, our business is done here."

"I already put the mules up for today. I can get back at it tomorrow."

"Well then, you can come with me and take a look and see what my chores are around this place. You probably think I'm just some wealthy plantation owner who sits on his ass all day drinking. I will admit, I do have some wealth and I do like to drink, but I don't sit on my ass all the time, just some of the time," he laughed.

They went outside and walked over to a storage barn. Elijah was amazed at the animals and the crops inside. Henry began telling him about his holdings. I have five hundred sixty-six acres. One hundred of it is pasture land with twenty-two cows, six calves, two bulls, four milk cows, twenty goats, eight sheep, ten horses and thirteen mules. I have dedicated acres to hogs, chickens, guineas and ducks. There's eight hundred chickens and at last count three hundred twenty-seven hogs and piglets. You see those store houses there, pointing to a large circular typed structure, those are my fodder houses. Over there is hay for the animals, there's tons of that stuff. Now the food is kept up there in the loft. I should have five hundred bushels of peas, four hundred bushels of butter beans, two hundred bushels of sweet potatoes and three hundred bushels of regular potatoes. We have a tremendous number of bushels of corn to feed the animals, servants and the household. There are bushels of apples, pears, and pecans too. Rachel tells me your folks have peaches, nothing better than a juicy peach on a hot summer day. We grew peaches and plums, but they became diseased and died. Over in our smoke house, we have at least one thousand pounds of smoked pork and bacon and a little beef."

As he continued to show Elijah around, James walked over to say hello. "Masser Elijah, how's you doin' today?"

"I'm alright Mr. James." "You looks as if you gettin' ready to go huntin' with dem guns a hangin' off ya."

189

"Well we are in war now, Mr. James and them people from up North may come to attack us, so I want to be ready," said Elijah.

"I got some knives I use if they tries to hurt me, said James."

"Excuse us James while I continue showing Elijah our stock and produce." "Yes sir Massa Henry," James replied.

Henry began telling Elijah what it takes to run his plantation. How it takes some planning and calculation to ensure all get fed and the crops get planted during planting season. Henry explained "I especially have to make sure our everyday needs are met. Now come back here with me. Let me show you my gin. That's the main source I make my money from." They walked toward the gin.

Elijah saw two tiny kids sitting against a wall. The little girl Delilah was standing over them with a switch. "I's gonna cut yo legs in half if yous two don't act right," she was saying as she held a stick in her hand shaking at them.

James calls out, "Hey nows, leave dem boys be child." Both twins got up and ran over to James and hugged his pants' legs. Delilah, said "Papa James, I s'pose to watch em why theys mammy's out in the fields. She's says she can't be leavin' dem wid you, cause you's a busy man workin' for Massa Henry."

Henry looked at the little girl and smiled. "You keep them out of mischief Delilah." "You keep them in line," he added

"Follow along Elijah," they moved on leaving James and the children behind.

"She's a tough one, ain't she Mr. McCloud?" asked Elijah. "I believe she's been whipping them children. Well, James will sort it out."

Henry showed Elijah his two cotton gins. This is where the seeds and hulls are separated and any other mess that may get hung up in the cotton is removed. I've got a crew of white men to come in and supervise on reaping days. They process the cotton and I sell it. I come by periodically to make sure all is well. A man has to have his wits about him to know what's needed to operate a production such as this."

Elijah was itching inside wondering if Henry was as cruel as the plantation owner in the book he read, '*Uncle Tom's Cabin*'. "Do you ever have to whip your slaves Mr. Henry?"

Henry gave him an odd look. "Why no, why would you ask me such a question?"

"I read a book called '*Uncle Tom's Cabin*' and the slave owner beat Tom to death."

"Come now, Elijah that book is hog wash. That woman is from Connecticut. She has never seen a plantation. It's a pack of lies on some accounts. I've heard of cases where slaves have been killed for uprising and revolts or even trying to escape. Some say that the author of that book was fed lies by slaves who had escaped. They complained they were abused and mistreated just to draw support from the Northerners. Rachel read the book once and asked me the very same question, about whipping the servants. I find it strange how both you and she would ask me that question. Anyway, to beat a man to death for nothing, I can't believe such and you shouldn't either. In fact, I fired Samuel for mistreating James."

At that moment, Vernon and Dale came up in a wagon. "Mr. McCloud," Vernon called out, "We've got the parts and supplies you needed.

"Excuse me Elijah," said Henry.

"Hey Lijah," Dale called out.

"Hey Uncle Dale, he answered back." Elijah walked over to the large oak tree and leaned against it. He pulled a pistol out and began observing it in more detail.

The twins ran up to him. "Masser, who's you? What they call you?"

"I'm Elijah, he answered, sticking the gun in plain view. "Now who might you two be?" mimicking their speech.

"I's Matthew, I's Mark," they spoke one right after the other.

Elijah knew who Delilah was. So he asked them, "What did you boys do to cause Delilah to threaten you with a switching?"

"She's whooped up on us cause we won't play like we's her babies. She says she's our mammy, when's our real mammy is workin'" they answered. "Well now, who's your real mama?" Elijah asked. "Her is Helen," the twins answered in unison.

"Well you need to play nice and don't be mean, she ain't you boys' mama, but she's' like your big sister, so you two be nice ok?"

"What's ya'lls doing botherin' Masser Elijah?" Delilah asked as she walked up still carrying the switch.

"They ain't bothering me, Delilah. I was telling them you were like their big sister and for them to be nice." "A big sister?" Delilah asked looking up to the heavens. "Hum. I's like that Masser Elijah, I's theys big sister. Comes on litter brothers, bye bye Masser Elijah," said Delilah.

"Bye, bye" called out the twins, giggling as they left.

Elijah watched as the little twins held a rope and Delilah ran and jumped it. "Higher" she said. They lifted it higher, and she ran and jumped over it again.

As Elijah passed the wagon, he saw a large grinding stone in the back of it. Dale, Vernon and Henry were carrying some wooden beams and metal to the barn. As they emerged from the barn, "Good we got some help," said Dale.

"Two of ya'll get on that side and me and Lijah will grab this side." Dale, Vernon, Henry and Elijah retrieved the stone off the wagon and placed it on the ground.

"Damn, it's a lot heavier than it looks. Let's roll it." said Henry. Dale and Vernon rolled the stone.

"What's that for?" asked Elijah.

"It's a milling stone. Instead of hauling the corn over to X-Way, we can mill it ourselves right here. The corn, wheat and barley can all be milled here."

A cry rang out. Elijah looked over and saw one of the twins on the ground crying. He walked over and picked up the child. "What's the matter little man?" "I's alright." Then he heard a slap, and the other twin started bawling. Delilah had struck him across his hand. "Hold on now, hold on," said Elijah. "Why you over there being mean to your little brothers?"

"I's ain't being mean, Matthew and me was a holding the rope letting Mark jump de rope and Matthew pulled it up on one side and makes Mark fall. So I's popped his hand, cause he knows he do wrong. Matthew rubbed his hand and looked at Delilah.

"Now look, ya'll need to be good to each other or I'm gonna ask Mr. James to do something with ya'll."

"I's sorry" said, Matthew to Mark.

"Well give him and your big sister a hug and ya'll quit being mean," said Elijah.

"I's sorry for popping you," said Delilah, as she hugged the little twins.

As Elijah was walking toward the mansion, he heard Rachel call. "I spotted you out there playing with the kids, aren't you a little old to be playing games?" she asked. "You need you some of your own children to play with" Rachel commented.

Elijah knew Danny and Pamela had given her that idea. "Come in, I want to show you something and I need your help."

Elijah followed her up to her room. She had a hammer and a chisel in her hand. I want you to pry a few boards loose from over there. I want a place for my jewelry box. And, you don't worry about nailing it back. If you'll just remove the nails, I'll be so thankful to you."

"What you want to hide it for?" Elijah asked.

"In case they come and attack us, that's why. I don't want them with my jewelry, especially our rings. It will be a secret hiding place. You never really know. I could be gone one day and a rebel could come in to our house and rob us."

Elijah did as she asked. He pried two boards loose in the floor against the back wall of her closet. He removed the nails and Rachel inspected it. She lifted the boards and saw a perfect compartment in which to place her silver jewelry box. Being so happy with the job Elijah did, she reached over and pecked him on the cheek.

"Thank you so much my love. I see father gave you his old pistols. He picked up a new set just yesterday while in Laurel Hill. They were crates full of rifles, a model 1861 I think that's what father called it. They were secretly brought down from Maryland. The men folk are getting ready for war Elijah. If father leaves, I need someone here. I need you. I want you to come be with me and protect me."

Chapter 21

Hurt and Ashamed

Almost a year had elapsed since the start of the war. South Carolina had taken over Fort Sumter. It was in April of 1862. Elijah, John and Moses were in the fields planting seeds. Elijah had trained Black Jack to pull a plow so all three men could work at tilling the dirt at the same time. All of a sudden a gunshot was heard in the distance.

"What the Devil," Moses dropped his plow and hurried toward his house.

"Watch these animals," John called out. There were more than seventy-eight armed men gathered around their home. Elijah was determined to see what was going on too, so he unhitched Black Jack and the mules and led them out of the field, leaving behind their plows.

As he approached the house, he heard Samuel McDonald. "Moses, the confederacy needs more men and there's a draft that came out this month. My boy David is signed up and it's only right that your grandson be a man too. I know he's 18 by now."

The gunshot had come from Ester. "You leave this land now, she yelled. Moses was trying to restrain her. My baby's 17 and he ain't fightin' no foolish war. Come here child," she called out to Elijah as he approached.

"Look here, said John, what's the cause for all these men coming up here, scaring my ma and talking 'bout signing my boy up for the military. He ain't old enough and that's that."

Elijah moved up onto the porch. He had not told his Grandmother that Henry had given him a pistol. He had hid it in the barn in the wall of Black Jack's stall.

"Look here now, one of you Clark men is gonna serve or we aim to have you hanged for treason against the Confederacy."

"I need to put the animals up," said Elijah as he hurried over to untie them and take them into the barn.

"Well dammit, said John, I'll go, but my boy stays." Samuel snapped back "We need both of you, and I know he's eighteen years old, he's been courting that McCloud hussy and she's near bout twenty herself. Now John, my son's down in Charleston as we speak and your boy should have his tail at the fort too. I believe you are lying just to protect that youngin."

"You just wait here a minute," Ester yelled.

Moses had taken the pistol from her. He followed her inside, thinking she was going to get another gun. He saw her enter the parlor and grabbed her Bible. "Ester, them men ain't wanting to hear no preaching, they aim to take John and Elijah to draft em."

"Moses, get out of my way," she pushed passed him and went outside onto the steps.

John was in Samuel's face, "You a damn liar, my boy's seventeen."

"Stop It! Stop it!" Ester yelled. She opened the Bible to the first page, which had the dates and births of all the generation which included Elijah's birth. 'Elijah John Clark, 1845, November the ninth, father Elijah John Clark and Mother Helen Kay Callahan. Bennettsville, South Carolina. She passed it over to Samuel. "Well, Miss Clark I do beg your apology."

Elijah had made his way from the barn and stood behind Samuel. Samuel said, "Well he's saved till November, if we still at war and the confederacy needs him, we gonna come git him."

"But you, John, you are an able body man, and we intend to conscript you, so let's go to Bennettsville and get you signed up in the military."

"Look, I change my mind, I thought it was me or my youngin, now you know my boy ain't old enough, I ain't going. That war ain't got nothing to do with me from what I hear it's over rich men, them plantation owners and such."

Samuel pulled a pistol out and aimed it at John's stomach. "You gonna get conscripted today or I'll leave you dead right here.

"Lord, Moses pleaded, please leave my boy be Samuel McDonald, we've got nothing to do with this devil's war."

At that moment, Elijah pointed his pistol at Samuel's temple. "You ain't taking my Pa nowhere. You leave here now, while you can. You dun an caused enough problems." Guns cocked and raised and pointed at Elijah.

Samuel smiled, "Put that gun down boy and no body's gonna get shot. Your daddy needs to do his service that's all."

"What?! Child put that gun away," Ester cried out.

"Grandma they gonna take my Pa from me." He started crying, and his hands trembled as he pressed the gun harder into Samuel's temple. Samuel knew then that the young man was serious.

"Listen to your Grandma, boy," Samuel demanded.

"NO! you listen! These men you brought here might shoot me down like a dog, but I'm gonna blow your head off first. Grandma, you and Grandpa be mindful so the bullet don't come out his head and hit ya'll. Go on in the house," said Elijah. "Samuel seems to think I'm a man, and today, I'm gonna show him what a man is made of."

"Baby, please don't, you ain't never disobeyed your Grandma, I beg you to please take that gun from Samuel's head."

"I can't Grandma, I can't let these people take my Pa, I'm done heard about the war. McCloud gets that paper up yonder, they's people dying, getting legs blown off and they marching into gun fire and just don't care. I let my Pa go, he's gonna die."

"Why, ain't you going to war Samuel? Why?" Elijah asked angrily. Samuel grew nervous. Cause – cause, I'm in the County Guard. All of us men are in it. We protect the county. When all the other men go off to war, we keep nigras from rising up and killing off white folks, such as your family and mine, son."

"Don't call me son. You ain't my daddy. Get that gun off my Pa now!"

Moses moved past Ester, and pointed his shot gun directly at Samuel's head. "Lord God Moses, please, what are you doing?" she asked.

"Get on in that house woman. NOW!" Moses yelled.

Ester bowed her head in defeat and turned and went inside holding on to her Bible.

Danny appeared around the corner. "Hey now," the County Guard turned pointing at him. He held his hands up and backed up around the corner of the house. He had Sour Weed tied off on the back porch rail. He climbed on him and darted off for home.

Moses started speaking up, "Now what's it gonna be, Samuel McDonald?" "You take your so called County Guard and leave our place. Cause ain't no Clark gonna go off with you today. I know come November, Lijah will be a man, but today, he's still a boy, John's boy and my grand boy. Right now you are trying to take my boy. Now if you take either one you'll ruin us. Our farm won't stand a chance. How come John can't be a part of ya'lls County Guard,"

"If I didn't know better, it seems like you got it in for a Clark. Well today we can end all that. I ain't seen these men you've brought here. Where ya'll from anyway?" They all took turns calling out the hometowns. Bennettsville, McColl, Masons Crossing, Barfields Landing.

"Well them's decent people from them places. What in God's name ya'll want to come up here terrorizing my family for? I got kin people in Barfields Landing. My mama was a Barfield." Nearly thirty of the men present were Barfields or related to them.

They lowered their guns off of Elijah. Moses took note of this. "Samuel that boy wants to kill you and if he shoots you I guess we all aim to die here today."

"Hold on Mr. Clark, I'm Douglas Barfield, and some of these are my brothers, some cousins, some married into my family. We ain't come here for no killing, especially, not our own family. You say your mama's a Barfield, what's her name?"

"Nancy," answered Moses.

"Well, I be, Nancy's my Grandma Judy's sister. Get them guns off my family, you hear?"

Douglas, a huge brute of a man, stepped near the porch where Moses was. "Now look Samuel, you told us these people weren't loyal to the Confederacy. You had us believing that boy with that gun up side your head was a draft dodger. Now we know it ain't so and you trying to take his daddy from him."

"Boy, where's your ma?" Douglas asked Elijah.

"She's dead." He answered. Sympathetic sighs could be heard from the Guardsmen.

"Well I believe we gonna leave that youngin and his daddy alone, cause he's all the people he's got."

"You ain't got a brother nor sister?" Who's that one that ran round the house a while ago?"

"No sir, I ain't got nobody, but my Grandma, Grandpa and my Pa. That feller that was around the house, he's my cousin."

"I got my gun on one, Lijah," a voice called out from underneath the house.

The crowd looked down and Danny was aiming at the man nearest him. "Go ahead and shoot that Samuel McDonald, kill him cuz," called out Danny.

"Now hold on young feller, I'm trying to talk here."

Danny pointed the gun at Douglas. "Well, I'll be damn, look at you, come on out from under there." Danny crawled out, still aiming his gun at Douglas. "Who are you young man?"

197

"Danny's my name." "Well young Danny before you crawled upon us, I was trying to calm this situation down. You just hold steady, don't shoot me, I'm trying to be a peacemaker. Mr. Clark and all ya'll, we're sorry to bother ya'll today. This is all a big misunderstanding. We are to protect not kill. Sam, go ahead and put your gun away. Samuel slid his gun in his holster and raised his hands up in a surrender fashion. Elijah you can take that gun away from Sam's head now, your daddy ain't leaving today."

"Why he can't be a County Guard?" Elijah echoed what his Grandpa asked earlier.

"Well, I don't see why he can't. I'm the Major of this County Military and I think your daddy will fit in just fine. Now if you remove that gun away from Samuel's head, we'll be on our way."

"Shoot him Lijah, remember cuz, he shot me and tried to shoot you."

"Lord youngin, hush, I'm gonna tell Dale to straighten you out," spoke Moses, who still had his gun pointed at Samuel too.

"Son, I believe Mr. Douglas Barfield. You can take the gun away from Sam's head." Only then did Elijah comply with his father's request.

Samuel rubbed his temple area and gave Elijah a disgruntled look, then turned and walked over and mounted his horse. "The rest of you mount up, we've got more plantations to check on," yelled Samuel.
"Put your gun up Danny," said Elijah. Danny still had his gun pointed at Douglas.

"Boy, how old are you?" asked Douglas. I'm seventeen, like my cousin. He's two months older than me. Well, let's see his Grandma says he's born in November, so come '63, you'll be eighteen too. Well, if we still fighting you need to sign up. The Confederacy could use you. Them their Yanks want to tell us how to live, so we seceded from um and we fighting to have our own government. Them Yankees spending our money building themselves big cities and industries with our hard earned tax dollars. We ain't even got city roads like them. All we got is dust and dirt paths, which is fine with me cause my horse ain't shoed. But still our tax money should go to help us."

"Some people's saying Abraham Lincoln's gonna free nigras," said Moses.

Douglas looked at him and remarked, "I heard that too, I don't know how, cause we winning the war. Since South Carolina took Fort Sumter, we beat um at Bull Run and up yonder in Wilson Creek, Missouri too.

They say the Yanks won at Shiloh earlier this month and the Pea Ridge battle in March. We've been whipping um in Pennsylvania and in Virginia. So that gives us an edge four to three so far. We gonna whip them Yanks, you'll see. Like I said, I'm sorry for the situation we caused, ya'll be sure to tell the Miss we apologize."

"John, come Monday you go to Bennettsville and sign up for the County Guard. I'll leave word for you, that is, if you want to. So long ya'll." As the Guard left, they went up to the McCloud's plantation.

"Boy, I thought you was gonna plug that old Samuel. I wished ya popped him, Lijah," Danny said.

"Youngin hush, we could of all been dead by now. Just be thankful." The men all went inside where Ester was in the parlor steadfast reading the Bible.

Elijah stepped to the doorway and said, "Grandma, I'm sorry I disobeyed you."

She acted as if she didn't hear a word he said. "I say, I'm sorry Grandma." She looked up at him with tear filed eyes. As she wiped the tears, Elijah walked over closer to her and said once again, "Grandma I am sorry, but they was gonna take my Pa away."

She stared at him as he went over and gently kissed her forehead, "I'm sorry Grandma." She still didn't speak, and he walked out feeling hurt and ashamed.

Before the year would end, four more battles would be fought with many smaller skirmishes along the way. The South won the Pennsylvania battle and Fredericksburg. Antietam was one of the worst days in the war. Many fell, it was like a draw between both sides, but it was at great cost. It was estimated over four thousand Americans died on that battlefield. Thousands of lives lost, sons, uncles, fathers, brothers, nephews and friends. They all died. Many wondered if Davis and Lincoln felt hurt and ashamed for asking such a sacrifice.

Chapter 22

Too Tard

It was November, Elijah and his family knew the dreadful moment had arrived. It was time for him to sign up for the draft. South Carolina placed him with the County Guards. Little did Elijah know Henry McCloud had paid 800 dollars to get him in the County Guard. Elijah rode with the Guard making rounds once a week around the County's plantations and homesteads. Their job was to ensure peace was still held. Rumor had it, Lincoln would declare all slaves free in the Southern Confederacy and if the slaves were fit enough, they could help fight with the North. On occasion when the County Guard, whose number now exceeded one hundred men, showed up the slaves were excited to see them. They thought it was the army freeing them. It was then that Elijah realized the seriousness of the situation and just how much danger Rachel and her father could be facing.

He spoke to Rachel about it on December 31st the day before the Emancipation Proclamation would come into effect. "Have you seen any of your daddy's slaves looking mad or mean toward you as if they wanted to rebel?" "No, she replied."

"I asked Uncle Dale. He said no also. I sometimes wish ya'll didn't have these people as slaves, Rachel. That President's done give um a reason to rise up and fight against ya'll."

"They wouldn't do such a thing. We care for them. Why would they? We feed them, clothe them, provide cabins for them and they have jobs. That's all a person really lives for Elijah," she stated.

"No Rachel, sweet heart it's more than that. They ain't free. Freedom means life and living it. They just like ya'lls animals, gal. They like hogs, dogs, or mules. That's what they are, mules. You give em what they need to survive, just like your animals, but freedom is what makes a human live. Being free to go fishing, hunting, to school and church. And being able to go to the store to buy things, to own things. There are so many things they can't do. Things that mean something in life. Can they marry? Can they have children of their own choice? No. I heard a plantation owner in Gibson talking about these people like breeding stock. Talking about how he'll run contests on em. He said, he lets em play tug of war to see who's the strongest. Then he dunks em under water to see who can hold their breath the longest. He'll know if they have stamina and can work longer.

Too Tard

He said he did the females too. That way he would breed them together, to make a better stock of slave. I've heard my Grandpa say that some of the slave owners would fight slaves against one another. One plantation owner would get his biggest and meanest slave to fight against another plantation owner's toughest slave. They would fight like game cocks. That is sad, Rachel. If I had to live a life like that I might want to fight or kill somebody to be free. Tomorrow's the first and ain't no telling what's gonna happen. If the South loses the war, they might make white people slaves. Look how many men they have compared to us."

"Please Elijah, please be quiet for me. You are driving me insane with all this slave revolt talk. I too wish father didn't have slaves. I don't know why he keeps them now that the cotton barn is full of cotton. He can't have it shipped away, railroads have been destroyed, and ports are blocked off. It's truly maddening Elijah. I wish so much that you would take me away from all of this. Marry me Elijah, marry me and take me away. Or better yet, I'll take you away. My brother Michael used to write me at least once every month. I haven't heard from him in three months. Even Sarah has written me, although she has the hand writing of a child, it's still legible. She is happy, so yes, I know the slaves would love to be free. You and I could travel to the North states. I know Michael could find employment for you. Take me away."

"Gal, I can't take you away, I ain't got nothing. I can't even afford us an outhouse to live in."

Rachel giggled, "You silly man. No, I could provide for us until you became established. We can take Pamela and Danny away with us. You and Danny could work on his tobacco products and we all could become rich in those Northern States."

"Hush, I wish it was easy as that."

James knocked on the library door. "Come in."

James stepped in, "I's thoughts Massa Henry was in here. They's somebody coming up the way, Miss Rachel."

"Thank you James." Rachel got up, went out into the parlor and looked out the window. She saw about thirty men gathered outside.

Henry walked out onto the porch to confront Samuel. "What's the meaning of this McDonald?" "Henry, we've come to protect your house from rebellious nigras. There's a proclamation that goes in effect tomorrow and me and these fine men have come to ensure white folks safety."

201

"Well you can take your men and move along, for I see no disturbance or rebellion here."

"Now, you see that ya'll," Samuel spoke to the crowd of men who held torches and rifles. "Because this man is a big plantation owner and holds more than 20 nigra slaves and doesn't have to serve in the Confederacy, he thinks he's some kind of king or something."

"No, it's not that Samuel. My place is at peace and we don't need trouble stirred up here, so if you would be on your way, it would be much appreciated."

"We will be on our way, when we check your nigras quarters and make sure you have em all. I recollect you had around twenty-seven of dem. Let's go boys, their cabin's out back." Samuel led the armed men toward the back of the mansion.

"Stop!" shouted Henry.

"What you gonna do, call the sheriff, Henry? Today or much rather, tonight we are the damn law. Let's go." The men headed in the direction of James' cabin. Henry rushed out behind him. Samuel opened the door.

"Samuel don't come on my property with your bullshit. He grabbed the door handle, remove yourself off of my property now."

"Listen McCloud, I have sworn to protect the citizens of Marlboro County and the state of South Carolina from any enemy domestic or foreign. You need to stand down or you will be arrested for delaying the military from carrying out their sworn duties. We need to know your slaves ain't in revolt or tryin' to rebel against the County or the state of South Carolina. All's we gonna do, is search and conduct a count. So step back or get taken down."

Henry could smell alcohol on Samuel's breath, and knew a drunken man was hard to deal with.

Elijah stepped out armed with his rifle and pistol. "Mr. McDonald," he called out.

"Well look here, Old Clark."

"Where's the rest of the militia, the County Guards?" "I only see around twenty-seven of you."

"Well you make twenty-eight, so follow orders."

Samuel was the Sergeant and Elijah knew he had sworn to protect and preserve the freedoms of South Carolina. He knew he had to obey a superior officer.

If he disobeyed an order during times of war, it would be an act of treason. He didn't want to be shot under court martial. He looked over at Henry, "I'll help, Sergeant McDonald, please go back inside."

As he glanced toward the mansion, Rachel was standing in the back door. "She needs you sir."

Henry smiled at Elijah, "Thank you Elijah, you keep the peace."

"I'm here to do just that," he answered.

Samuel pulled open James's door all the way, "Where's this wooly nigra, at?" he shouted out to Henry who was walking toward the house.

"He's inside our home," Henry answered.

"Well I need to see him now."

"Rachel, please fetch James," Henry instructed his daughter.

She turned to obey and saw James standing beside her. Samuel walked over to the back porch. "James, show your face," he yelled.

James stepped to the back porch doorway. "I's here, right here.

"If you try to rebel, I'll kill you on the spot, you hear nigra?" "Ya'lls God Abraham Lincoln has said you all are free, but not tomorrow or anytime soon. They gonna have to win this war to be able to free you, if then. Now if you were to go ahead and kill that damn Henry McCloud who loves you people, I won't mind," he said laughing.

"That's enough Mr. McDonald, are you counting?" asked Elijah.

The officers went inside and tossed James belongings around and flipped his bed over. They found his carving knives and brought them out. "These were found in his possession, Sergeant."

"Say what do we have here? You planning on something?" Samuel then walked over to where Henry was standing at the bottom of the steps.

"Those are my knives," said Henry. "I allowed James to use them for wood carving, so if you please, hand them over to me," said Henry.

"Hold up now, I may have to confiscate these," smirked Samuel.

"Listen, you cannot come in here and deprive me of none of my property. I know the law. If you try to leave here with any of my property, you have stolen it. You have taken it without consent and you'll be arrested for it."

Samuel thought for a second, he remembered something about protecting a person and their property, so he passed the knives over to Henry. "You need to keep dem out of nigra's hands, 'for you find it in your back, McCloud," he said.

Too Tard

"Well, let's get going boys, they are more heads to be counted."

All slaves were finally accounted for except one to Samuel's recollection. At first, Henry grew worried. Rachel then reminded him that Sarah was no longer with them. She left with Michael.

"Michael?" Samuel asked. "Oh yeah, that old uppity Yankee you had with you the day you fired me. I remember. Old Yankee boy didn't like our southern hospitality, huh?"

"Mr. Samuel, you have counted our servants, now we do wish for you to leave," Rachel said.

"Well, I'll be damn if it ain't the queen of the McCloud plantation giving out orders again. Well little miss, I'm a Sergeant in the military and you can't order me anywhere. It's called Marshall Law for your information. You watch your tongue to me."

"Sergeant, are we finished here sir?" said Elijah steaming inside.

Samuel saw the anger in his eyes. He knew the Clark youth showed heart when he was with seventy-eight men. He didn't want to test him with the few he had now.

"Clark, while on leave you are still bound by duty. Maybe you should ride with us tonight." "Major Barfield has excused me until 12 o'clock tomorrow, and he is to come and retrieve me then Sir. I'll be idle until then. You have a nice night Sir." He saluted Samuel.

"That's right, you better give me respect, boy," said Samuel with venom in his voice. "Let's go men."

The loose assortment of half drunken military men left with no incident other than disturbing the residents of McCloud's plantation. Afterwards, Henry commended Elijah for his conduct. "You handled yourself like a real soldier out there. I'm really proud of you. I take it Samuel doesn't like you son," Henry stated.

"He ain't liked me since you fired him. Plus he's got more reason to hate me now since his son's in Charleston and I got to be in the County Guard."

"I sure appreciate you helping me, said Elijah." Henry played the surprise role and the innocent act." "You appreciate me for what?"

"For going to Bennettsville and getting me on the County Guard, that's what," replied Elijah.

"Where on earth did you ever get that idea from?" asked Henry. "Well, my Grandpa and Pa went to speak to the magistrate and recruiter.

205

They told them a Mr. McCloud had already taken care of that and I would be assigned to the County Guard."

Henry replied sheepishly, "Well that girl of mine was not going to rest until I did something. Besides, I like having you around. Your family needs you around too, to help out with the farm. It was the least I could do."

"Well I need to be getting back home, but I'll be back tomorrow to check on things and make sure everything is ok."

Elijah got up and Rachel followed him out on the porch. The moon was shining brightly overhead. "Why don't you come see me like Roachman?" she asked.

"Roachman? What on earth are you talking about?"

"You know silly, you could climb up the chimney like you use to, even though father allows you to court me now. I miss our late night talks. You were brave out there tonight. That old Samuel, I hate that man, he is so repulsive to me. What do you say? Will you come crawling to me Roachman?"

"Hey, I don't like that name, how come I can't be like a fly man? They crawl. Or even a spider man, they crawl too." Oh no, I hate both spiders and flies, they are disgusting creatures, a roach is bearable."

She kissed him, "Are you going to come see me, my Roachman?"

"I swear gal, I ain't wanting you calling me Roachman."

"Do you remember the book I told you about '*Romeo and Juliet*'?" Rachel giggled. He would holler at her through a window. I can be your Juliet and you can be my Romeo? I'll ask tonight where art thou Romeo?"

"Now it sounds like you using words out the Bible, saying thou. Look, I ain't got to report for duty till 12 tomorrow, so I can sleep a little late. I might crawl up to your window, but if I don't, I was just too tard. He kissed her and left.

Chapter 23

This Dreadful War

"It's not looking good for us," Elijah said to Henry as they sat in the library.

"What do you mean son?" he asked. "I hear we lost the battle of Chattanooga, another hit to the Confederacy. Now them Yankees can march into North Carolina, South Carolina and Georgia if they want to. That Sherman and his army got hundreds of thousands of soldiers. We should have never seceded. Over the last few months they've been riots in both Alabama and Virginia over bread. And now the Confederate's dollar is worth a measly 8 cents. We are ruined, I tell you."

"As many times as I've traveled to the Northern states and saw their industrial might, I should have known we couldn't contend with them. All we got down here is a bunch of barns and gins full of damn cotton. I've sent eight of my hardest working hands to help build defenses in Georgia. That's the price I gave to keep you and I here. Elijah these are some hard days. Thirty-five more days and it will be 1864, what on earth will come on us then."

He walked around to his bar and poured a shot of whiskey. He couldn't receive imported spirits. He had to result to purchasing corn liquor from an old man, Mr. Norton, in Old Hundred. He took a swig of the whiskey and grimaced while stating, "She's got a double whammy both a bite and a kick. Elijah I'm ready to give it all up and retire. I'm sick of this life. I'm sick of plantations, slaves, the war, the Confederacy and the Union. This business of the North and the South has tired me out. I just want to call it quits and relax and enjoy the rest of my life. Maybe fish, hunt and enjoy the company of a woman, whenever I get the urge. I think it's time to settle down. I never thought I'd have a change of heart about my daughter. To me, no man was good enough. Hell, I found ever reason under the sky as why I'd reject a man from marrying my daughter. Too rich, too poor, too middle class, every scenario you can come up with was there. I even judged them as too short or too tall. You see I would sit here in this library, just imagining what I would tell some young man, talking to myself, pretending to have conversations with various suitors who would want my girl's hand in marriage." Henry poured himself another drink.

Elijah packed his pipe, puffed and sat listening attentively. "I see my daughter go crazy over Pamela's little girl and I know she wants some children of her own. Lately, I've found myself wanting grand babies surrounding me in my old age. I can hear their little voices now, Grandpa this, and Grandpa that. I'd only want to love them."

Henry's eyes grew sad as he looked up at the ceiling. Then in a flash, he was back to normal. "Have you made out with my girl Elijah?"

Elijah was embarrassed by the sudden personal question. But he stood erect and looked him straight in the eye. "No sir, I've never defiled your daughter by committing fornication with her and I never will." Elijah then thought to himself, 'He would be so disappointed if he only knew how often his daughter had tried to seduce him.'

Henry looked Elijah in his eyes in return and said "I believe you son, and that maybe the sole reason I'd give you my daughter's hand in marriage. Because, I believe you are an honest man. Something inside me tells me you would be a good husband and a good father, a real family man. I'd be proud for you to be my son-in-law. I want you to take over this plantation. You hear me?"

"Mr. Henry I wouldn't want to keep nobody in slavery. So I couldn't do that."

Henry burst out laughing. "Hell Elijah, those people are free. I'll go out right now and tell them all they are free. Come on let's go."

Henry stood up and walked out of the library. There he found in the parlor, Pamela, Rachel and Molly Lynn, Danny and Pamela's daughter. Molly Lynn was going on four years of age and very spoiled, thanks to Rachel's kindness. Rachel gave the little girl, dresses and even jewelry, she played house with her, pretending to be her mom at times.

"Hey little Molly," Henry called out.

"Hello Uncle Henwee," she spoke.

"You ladies keeping warm in here?" he added.

Molly answered, with a serious look on her face, "Fire hot, fire hot, it will burn ya."

Henry called to Elijah to come. It being a Sunday and the winter so near, no work was being done except their own personal work. They were in the process of cooking a hog. All the whole slave community was gathered at the feast. Harmonica's chimed, hands clapped and flutes blew. There were four women sitting around four cooking pots.

This Dreadful War

Two women were cooking pork skins and making lard, while the other two were boiling chitlins, pig's feet, pig ears and hog jowls. The smell was awful. "You know how to cook chitlins Mr. Henry?" Elijah asked. "You boil the shit out of them. You get it? Chitlins being pig intestines."

"Oh Yes, I get it," said Henry. "And you can smell the shit being boiled out of them now."

Henry walked up to James, "James you are free to leave whenever you feel like it. And you being the Patriarch around here you tell everyone else they are free also. Now come Elijah, let's go back in, shall we? I'm cold." "That's all? That all you got to do, I thought you had to write some papers or something," asked Elijah.

"Well, I never thought of that, I'll check it out, but right now, it's chilly out here and I need another drink."

Once inside, they made their way back into his library. Little Molly ran up to Elijah calling out "Cousin, cousin, when you gonna marry Auntie Rachel, so she can give me somebody to play wid. I want a little cousin."

Elijah reached down and picked up the little girl. "Now who sent you in here to ask me that?"

"Nobody Lijah, I see you and Auntie Rachel kissin' but you don't got no youngins. Mommy says youngins come from kissin'," grinned Molly.

"Well, you go and tell Auntie Rachel when the times right, we will give you some cousins. Until then, you go play with her and your ma."

He tickled her ribs, she giggled and yelled "Stop, stop it cousin Lijah, that tickles me."

He sat her down and she ran back over to her mother and Rachel.

When Elijah entered the library, Henry was already indulging in another shot of liquor. "Ah, that hits the spot." He remarked.

"I'm going to be a white liquor drinker by the time this war is over. I use to enjoy me a shot of brown whiskey, now this old corn is growing on me. Seems like it's got more umph in it than old brown does."

"So have you made up your mind? Rachel is dead set you are the man for her. Now, I can't stay young forever, and I'm losing both my good looks and my hair. I'll soon retire from this business. What I need to know from you, is when you aim to ask me for my child's hand in marriage?"

Elijah thought for a moment while Henry poured another shot into his glass. "Mr. Henry, I wanted to save up enough money to afford a house and things for Rachel before I ever put that question to her."

"Hell Elijah, you have this home, what more could you ask for? Look, I'll not bullshit you, so don't bullshit me. I wanted Michael to take over this place. But that is shot to hell now. It will be Rachel's when I die. It's hers now. I signed it over the day this God forsaking war began. I thought I would have to serve until I learned any plantation owner who holds twenty or more slaves was exempt."

"Yes, I remember you took the peace maker back from me," said Elijah. "I'll tell you what, Mr. Henry, I will ask your daughter's hand in marriage when this war is over. Only then, can I help take care of her. Cause right now I'm running here and there with the County Guard. And any minute, the Yankees might attack us. Didn't you say they could enter our state or North Carolina or Georgia from Chattanooga?" "Yes I did. Now dammit, here you go taking us back to the miserable thought of this dreadful war."

Chapter 24

A Good and Pure Love

The war raged on. Sherman conquered Georgia, which included the cities of Atlanta, Augusta, Macon and others all the way down to Savannah. After Georgia, he marched his men through South Carolina and destroyed Columbia.

The people of South Carolina were terrified, as they learned Sherman and his soldiers had burned many houses, mills, cotton gins, courthouses and even churches. The Army claimed the churches were burnt by mistake. The soldiers robbed throughout the regions and the small communities in their path. They took anything of value, including livestock and food. They called it foraging, but the people who fell victim called it robbery.

The Confederate Military put up a good fight in each skirmish, but nothing stopped the madness and marching of the soldiers. Newspapers reported destruction stretching two hundred fifty miles long and forty miles wide in Georgia alone. The rebel forces were no match for Sherman's sixty thousand men and the thousands more slaves who joined in to help with labor projects for the Union army.

The path of destruction was headed North at a rapid pace of twelve to fifteen miles a day. Danny had been conscripted to hold down a fort near Charleston. He later deserted and made it back home in February of '65, two months after the fall of Savannah.   David, Samuel's boy was conscripted to aid in the protection of Columbia. He was killed in battle. Samuel didn't learn of it until April.

Later that year Sergeant Samuel and six of his men approached the McCloud's mansion, hell bent on vengeance. It was said troops were on their way toward Bennettsville. He came before the Union troops. He hated them, they had killed his son. He wanted to make more people pay. Several of his men had shot and killed nine blacks while riding across the land randomly shooting.

Elijah sat with Rachel in the parlor when he heard a distant gunshot. He could hear the men yelling, "The Yankees are here."

Behind them were three thousand infantry men scavenging the country side. The army force was passing through Bennettsville, SC.

Foragers searched out the land for food and plantations that would be in support of the army.

Elijah looked out and saw Samuel in the darkness with his men. Elijah marched out onto the porch with Rachel in tow. Samuel began yelling "The Yankees are coming! They gonna kill all nigras and plantation owners. They've killed my boy."

James roused the other servants up and told them to prepare to hide, for he didn't know what evil Samuel was up to. He sent Delilah and the twins to play hide and seek within the cotton bales inside the gin. The children were frightened at first, because of the darkness, so Mary went with them.

James took his knives out and stuck the longest one inside his waist line. He was prepared to die before he would allow Samuel to abuse him again. Elijah looked out and saw what appeared to be thousands of lights lighting up the dirt road coming from McColl. They were at Dale's house. "I got to go Rachel."

Henry quickly stepped out onto the porch demanding to know what Samuel was up to tonight. He was ready to put a stop to it. He held two pistols in his hands.

"Them damn Yankees is killed my boy, Henry and they coming, look yonder," he pointed down the dirt road.

Henry saw the thousands of torches, "My goodness, it's an army."

Elijah had already jumped on the back of his horse and hurried his way toward his home to inform his family. After he made his family aware of what was happening, he scurried over to his Uncle Dale's home, which was already swarming with Yankee soldiers.

Molly was crying, as Pamela stood rocking her. All the family was out in the yard with guns pointed directly at them as the army questioned them.

"Do you people stand loyal to the rebellion of the Confederated States? Do you fight for the Confederacy?"

"We don't care nothing about the Confederacy," answered Dale.

Danny was hiding in the woods thinking, it was confederate soldiers hunting him down.

"We never have cared, we don't own no damn slaves, you people leave us be," said Dale. "Now that's what I like to hear and hope to believe sir," said the officer. "Now to prove your loyalty to the Union, we need that fine horse, the mule and those hogs you've got out there."

The men were leading Eagle out. "Now wait a damn minute," Dale said, as he started to move toward the man who led the horse. At least two hundred guns cocked and aimed at Dale.

He realized these people would kill him and they may even rape his wife and daughter-in-law.

Elijah decided not to ride directly into the army. He saw others move off to the Clark homestead and went back. He moved through the orchard groves out of sight in the darkness.

"Now, our Commander, General Sherman, gave strict orders not to bother those who show no resistance and hostility, they were to be spared. Are you Sir trying to deny the Union the assistance of what we need?" We will let you keep your chickens. That is if you are helping us. Now if you aren't being helpful, you are being rebellious and hostile. So therefore you are with the Confederacy."

Dale was cornered. "Sir, take what you need, just leave my family something please. Take the horse, hogs and whatever else you need," he repeated.

"Don't worry. Before the sun goes down tomorrow a whole division will be through here. There are I'd say three thousand two hundred of us foragers. Sherman's Army is anywhere from sixty thousand to eighty thousand, it depends on how many Negros latch on to us. You know they are good for helping us find their Master's food stocks. They are also a hell of a labor source. He turned to his men, and said "Go ahead and get your bellies full, for in two days the rats and rodents will have to bring their own provisions to eat."

The men laughed, as they carried off butchered pigs, and the four that were in the pin. They slung them over Eagles' back.

Elijah made his way back and watched as they ransacked the barn killing some chickens. They seized everything. Elijah wanted so much to speak out against them. He was in a losing situation. He stayed out of sight as he watched them leave Dale's home. He counted his kin on the porch; he noticed everyone was there, except Danny. They may have him as a prisoner, he thought. After seeing the last torch move away, he rode Black Jack around the outer perimeter of the field and then to the house. He saw Dale and Dewey along with Little Dale ringing chicken's necks out in the coop.

He rode up, "Uncle Dale, Lord, that's an army indeed, I ain't never seen that many."

"That you Lijah?" asked Little Dale.

"Yeah, it's me," he rode up closer to the chicken coop. It was only a quarter moon, yet with the aid of the stars, there was enough light to see through the darkness.

"That bastard, said they was sixty to eighty thousand more behind him Lijah," said Dale.

"We needed that meat. They took off with our hogs, our cured meat, bushels of taters, beans and all. And they took Eagle. I wanted to get my gun and shoot em, but they took that too."

"Hell, Uncle Dale, you done right, you got to live for the family. Look up yonder at that burning, cried out Little Dale." All the men looked to the direction Little Dale pointed. Elijah saw the cotton gin ablaze at the McCloud plantation.

Samuel said "Look here, Henry, they coming, you can't let em have your cotton, Set it on fire, burn it, and don't let them have it."

"Are you insane, there's tens of thousands of dollars worth of cotton in that gin," said Henry.

"You side with them, they gonna get it. Didn't you read how that son of a bitch Sherman captured thirty-eight thousand bales of cotton down in Savannah, when that coward Hardee ran off instead of fighting? I say, you can't let em have it and damn if I'm gonna let em. Let's go," said Samuel to the other men. They galloped off toward the back.

Rachel stood looking off in a distance toward the Clark's farm. She saw the torches as the men were making their way down the road toward their plantation. "Father the Yankee army is descending upon us, they are coming for us."

Henry looked back and went to his daughter's side. "Lord, Samuel is a mad man. He aims to burn our cotton gin. I must stop him."

Rachel grabbed her father's arm, "No father, let him be, for those Yankees will take it for their own gain. We own slaves. They'll punish us, father don't leave me."

"Let's go men," Samuel threw a torch into the gin's doorway and up onto the platform. The fire caught quickly. "Burn you, son of a bitch, burn."

213

Inside the barn off to the side, Samuel saw what appeared to be a shadow, move. He called to one of the men, "Justin, bring that torch."

James came out from the side of the building and plunged his knife into Samuel's heart and buried it deep.

Samuel grabbed at James's hands, he fumbled. "You nigra, damn you" blood spewed out of his mouth. His eyes bulged in his head as he was holding onto James' hands in a death grip.

Justin pulled his pistol firing at James, striking him in the side of his head. Both Samuel and James dropped to the ground side by side. Justin ran over to where the men lay. "He's killed Sam, boys," the other men ran over. The flames from the burning building lit up the night, their red blood poured from their bodies and mingled onto the ground.

Just then a woman's voiced screamed, "My chil."

The men turned holding guns on her. When she stepped around the corner, "They killed James," said the lady after seeing his lifeless form on the ground. "Save my girl and de boys I's beg you please," she begged the white men. "They's in the gin, please Massers, I begs ya, please don't let my Delilah die, please."

A couple of strong young black men ran around the corner from the place they had been hiding out at. They saw James down and charged at Justin who fired off another shot into one of the men's head.

Before long the area was covered with thirteen slaves who all had pitchforks, hoes and buckets, anything they could get their hands on, to attack the men. Mary tried to get into the gin, but the blaze burning in the doorway was too hot. She screamed for Delilah but got no answer.

Elijah was riding up to the McCloud's mansion when he heard the gun shots. He had seen Rachel and her father going inside so he continued in the direction of the gun shot sounds. As he neared the gin, he rushed over and saw a mob of black slaves fighting and chasing the white men. Then he heard Mary's screams and pleas for her child. He rushed over and pulled her away from the burning blaze.

"No Lawd, let me die, my chil's burnt up, Lawd let me die."

"Where is she, Mary?" Elijah screamed.

"Lawd's she and dem boys is burnt up in that buildin'."

Elijah looked and saw the fire consuming the center portion of the far back wall. He cupped his hands to his mouth and yelled out "Delilah?"

Again, he cupped his hands this time to his ears hoping to hear her answer over the roar of the flames. He heard a faint scream and some coughing. He recalled a horse trough on the other side of the gin. He darted off to it hoping it was full of water. He saw it was enough for what he wanted. He quickly climbed into the trough and covered himself with water. He splashed it all over his head and then made his way back to the side. Smoke was bellowing out like clouds. He dove through the open window space. Once inside, the heat was torturous. The smoke was blinding. He covered his mouth with his shirt.

"Delilah," he yelled.

He heard her plea, "Help me, please Masser Lijah." He strained to see, but his eyes kept watering causing his vision to blur. Finally, he squatted down, he saw her; she was in between the bales of cotton. He rushed over and grabbed hold of her and went and made his way to the window. He sat her down and began climbing out.

"Matthew and Mark, days in der, Masser Lijah, said Delilah."

"What?" said Elijah, not believing his ears. "Where are they Delilah?" "I didn't see them," he yelled.

"They play hide and seek from me."

"You go get away from here, go!" He screamed at the child to get away from the window. Elijah crouched. He turned and got on his knees, the building was almost fully ablaze. He yelled, "Mark, Matthew! Mark, Matthew!" He called out again, but didn't hear a response. As he crawled around, a rafter fell off to his left exploding as the ceiling was collapsing near the front entrance section. He continued crawling and calling out, "Matthew, Mark, please answer."

He started praying, "God, please don't let this hurt a child. Please let me find the boys, God Almighty, in the name of your son Jesus I pray, please, please."

He kept crawling, he then spotted both of them huddled up in a corner as if they were asleep, he crawled over and saw vomit beside one's head, the other was convulsing.

He grabbed one up in one arm and grabbed hold of the other by his shirt. He had held on to the both of them as he headed for the window. The flames were engulfing the place, he felt his lungs were about to explode.

The area around the window was quickly disintegrating. He moved faster and finally made it to the window.

He took one child and jumped to the ground with him and laid him down in the soil, then went back and got the other child and took him to safety. After placing them both away from the flames, he stood up taking deep breaths. He began puking and coughing. He gathered both boys up and headed to the mansion. The place was swarming with Yankee soldiers.

They were stabbing hogs with bayonets. Rachel and Mary were sitting on the ground in the yard. Rachel was trying to comfort Mary who was delirious and sobbing uncontrollably.

"Where's Delilah?" Hearing him call her daughter's name, Mary raised her head up. She saw Elijah holding the twins.

"What choo mean where's my Delilah? Lawd yous saved de boys," she went and fell on them crying. "I got Delilah out too, where is she? I told her to get away from the burning building."

Rachel jumped up and grabbed Elijah. "Lord, I thought you were dead. I heard those gunshots and went to see what had occurred and found poor James dead and Mary hysterical." She hugged him and kissed him.

"Get your damn hands off me," Henry yelled as he walked around back. "I expect no less from you scoundrels, thieves and degenerates. I know what you've done in Georgia. Darling Lilly, we are being robbed by the Union Army. Men who are to be respected and carry themselves as military men are acting like nothing more than an army of bandits and outlaws."

"Sir, you've got no room to speak now. In fact its people like you who got us in this war. It's like this, you rich people started it and the poor people are doing your dirty fighting. You've earned your living off the Negro slave labor. Now had you dare shot at us with those guns we confiscated from you, we would have been obliged to kill you. And no telling what would have happened to your women folk."

"Already you set fire to that cotton gin, thinking you'd stop us from achieving success and being able to forage. So now we've got to make do with what we can find from that nice big home you've got here. I'm from Ohio and only the wealthiest have huge homes like yours. So don't go whining to me."

"Young lady?" "Yes," said Rachel.

"Not you, the negro woman with those two boys. You and those boys are free to go. You are no longer a slave. So you are free. Mary looked at the officer who was speaking," "Where's I gonna go? Dis is the only place I got. I lives here.

A Good and Pure Love

I gots no place Massa Henry and Miss Rachel is been good to me. Massa Henry done told us we's free. "Where is James," asked Henry. "They's killed him, Masser," said Mary.

Henry marched over to the gin. He saw both James and Samuel dead, two white men, and three black men all dead. A woman was also deceased from what appeared to be gunshot wounds.

As the roof of the gin came crashing down, it startled Henry who ran backwards and placed his face in his hands to avoid the sparks and smoke.

"I said I took Delilah from the building, Mary." Elijah again explained.

As the soldiers continued their pillaging, they went into the salves' cabins to rob them. There they found a little girl crying. Taking her to the main house, one soldier asked, "Whose child is this? We found her in an old shack; she was hunkered down in a corner."

Mary saw Delilah. She grabbed the twins and ran to Delilah. She threw her arms around all the children and cried. Rachel was in tears, as Elijah looked on. He pulled away from her.

"I got to go check on my family, Rachel." He looked around for Black Jack and then saw two soldiers pulling at his reins. He ran over and reached for him. "He's my horse, turn him loose."

One soldier stepped back. The other soldier yelled, "Stand down, you damn rebel, this is Union property now." He pushed Elijah back and two more ran up with bayonets pointed at him.

"Release that horse's reins," A Yankee soldier by the name of Chester demanded. "That horse is property of the Union States now."

"Wait a minute, ya'll took everything we got, you ain't takin' my horse." Elijah protested. He began struggling with the soldier who would not let loose of the reins. The solder swung his fist at Elijah, but Elijah dodged the oncoming blow. Elijah kicked the man square in his chest, the soldier stumbled backwards. Elijah then took hold of the reins. At this point, Black Jack was becoming excited.

"Calm down boy," Elijah spoke consolingly in his ear. He was then struck in the back of the head with the butt of a rifle, he heard Rachel's screams.

"No stop," as another gun butt smashed into the side of Elijah's face, sending him into total darkness. They hit him three additional times, before Rachel reached him. She kneeled down screaming and then laid her body over his limp body. The soldiers stopped and backed away.

A Sergeant came to investigate the disturbance. "What is going on here?" he demanded. One soldier stepped forward and began shouting; he had hold of that horse's reins, pointing to Black Jack.

"This damn rebel here tried to prevent us from seizing this horse for the Union cause, Sergeant." "Shoot the traitor." The soldiers aimed their guns both at Rachel and Elijah, who was groggily awakening from the blow that had left him momentarily unconscious.

Elijah screamed out, "No please, please no."

"Hold on soldiers, you do not assault a female. Stand down." The Sergeant moved over to Rachel. "Miss, remove yourself from that traitor."

"You tried to abuse and strike him," said Rachel from the ground. The Sergeant reached down for her. "No," she yelled back, "Don't touch me. I don't want you putting your hands on me."

"Gentlemen pick up that rebel."Soldiers moved in grabbing Elijah, hauling him to his feet. Elijah was still unsteady.

Rachel stood, clinging to him pleading, "Leave him be please, I beg you."

The Sergeant moved up and slapped Elijah across the face. His arms were restrained by two other soldiers. They struggled with him, and then pulled out his revolver and pointed it toward Elijah's head. "I order you to stop rebel, or I'll blow your brains out." Elijah stopped struggling after hearing the threat.

"Now miss, you back away from our prisoner, like I asked." "No please, I beg you."

Henry walked up, "My Lilly, are you alright, have these ruffians molested you?" He went to his daughter's side. The Sergeant then turned the revolver on him. Other soldiers followed suit and pointed their rifles at Henry.

"Sir, I advise you to take this woman and get her away from our prisoner. Before, we detain her and have her arrested for obstruction of military duties."

"Rachel, come please," Henry said. She looked at Elijah and touched his swollen cheek. She kissed him and then moved to her father's waiting arms. "Please, I beg you have mercy on him," she pleaded.

The Sergeant began questioning Elijah, "You sir, you are of the age to be a Confederate soldier. Did you take up arms against the Union States in this rebellion?"

"I don't understand what you mean. I ain't got no gun on me, so no, I ain't took up guns against ya'll. If I did, I would of shot as many of ya'll as I could when I seen ya'll comin'. Ya'll done robbed us."

"My question is, have you entered into the army of the rebellious Confederate States, to oppose the Union?"

"No, he answered, I was in the County Guard." The Sergeant's eye brows rose upward. "And what does this County Guard do? Were you all armed men, given orders to fight the Union Army?"

Elijah looked to the heavens to try and remember his pledge and what he was told to do. He knew at a point what he said, could have them all killed. "Mr. I tell you this. I was a part of men who wasn't soldiers fighting against ya'll North States people. We were to protect the white people of this county from slaves who might rise up, since all the white men had gone off to fight ya'll. People around here were scared. So I was picked to do that duty."

The Sergeant thought for a second. He saw the reasoning in the young man's words. "So you telling me, at no time, were you going to fight against the Union in this rebellion?"

Elijah looked at him. He knew in his heart the County Guard could not stand up to this army of over three thousand men. "Sir I love life. I ain't wanting to die. For me to stand against ya'll, I ain't got no reason or neither was the County Guard big enough. There was only around fifty of us. And we only wanted to protect white people from being killed by slaves."

Henry spoke up, "Sir the young man is telling you the truth. He was assigned to help protect the white populace from any slave revolt. To protect little young white children from getting their brains bashed in by vicious slaves and to keep white women from being raped. That was his commitment."

The Sergeant began scrutinizing the actions of Elijah to determine if he was a real threat and a rebel. "You men release him." "Hey, wait." A soldier then walked over and kicked Elijah in his groin area. Elijah fell down on one knee.

"Stop it," cried Henry and Rachel.

"Soldier stand down, I say," the Sergeant moved over and shoved the soldier. "That's enough abuse."

Elijah stood up and glared at the soldier. "What about my horse?" asked Elijah.

"Young man, I suggest you drop it, because the way I see it, if you continue to protest, you are in rebellion. But if you allow your animal to be donated to the cause, you will show you are not against us, but for us."

"Let it go, Elijah," said Henry.

"Yes Sir," replied Elijah. Rachel moved over toward Elijah. He looked at her with pity in his eyes, "I'm so sorry for this. I wish we had left here before this night, but right now I've got to go check on my family," he told her.

Elijah hugged her and told Mr. McCloud, how sorry he was at what had happened.

As he got to the Clark's homestead, he found his grandmother alone in the parlor praying. Moses and John were out in the barn appraising the loss and what they would need to recover.

"Come to me child" Ester spoke. Elijah walked in. "Lord honey, I've set here and prayed since I saw those God forsaken blue suited devils come on our land. I prayed you were safe. Now, I thank the Almighty you are okay. They've come here like a thief in the night and treated us worse than animals."

"They took Black Jack from me, Grandma," he said blinking back the tears.

She looked at him and saw the blood around his neck and collar, "Lord, child you bleeding. Did they abuse you?"

"They beat me up Grandma. I was gonna make um let me keep my horse, but they was too many of them. They took all of Dale's stuff but left some of his chickens. He said they gonna be more soldiers coming through here by tomorrow. So, if there's anything left, we need to hide it."

"Lord, I can't think of nothing," she said as she looked around in a daze. "Child, I know they've just had themselves a good time up there at them McCloud's place. Have you checked on your sweet heart?" she asked.

"She's okay. They robbed them pretty good too. She stopped them soldiers from beating me somethin' awful. Somethin' worst woulda happened, if she and her pa hadn't stepped in."

"Well bless her heart, they is somethin' strong about that child, even though she ain't spoke to me since I had that talk with her. But Lord knows you've done enough talkin' to her for us all. I know you been a slippin' out at night to go see her." Elijah felt embarrassed. Then he said, "Grandma, I love her and I'm gonna marry her when this is all over. She ain't no rich gal no more, she's poor just like all of us."

"That's the truth child," said Ester. "Honey, you're a man now and you do what you must. You got my blessing and I hope you and her have a long time and love together. I know you love her. And I now know she loves you too. So you do what's right. I don't believe you fornicated with her and that's good. You spose to wait till you get married cause then you belong to her and she belongs to you. Now that ain't so with whores and whore mongers. They are lost. But two innocents is a good and pure love, a love that will last through eternity."

Elijah hated it when she talked that talk to him. "I'm tired Grandma, I'm gonna go lay down." He kissed her cheek and told her goodnight, then went into his room which was in a total disarray. His mattress was on the floor. He didn't bother to pick it up, he just laid down and fell off to sleep

Chapter 25

Old Hound Dog

Elijah awoke to the sound of Rock crowing. He was sore all over, especially his head. It was pounding. Just then he heard a gunshot and quickly got out of bed. He went outside to investigate. The yard was full of soldiers. He looked and as far as his eyes could see there were thousands upon thousands of men moving in all directions. They were clustered in groups around cooking fires. The men had stripped some of the fencing and sides of the barn. Wagons lined the road for over a mile. He could see cannons being carried by horses, oxen and mules. Soldiers were laughing and talking as they rode along.

It didn't take him long to discover what the gun shot blast was from. A soldier walked by with Rock dangling upside down, dead in his hands. He shouted over to a group of men who were around a fire.

"Boys I've got us a Plymouth Rock for breakfast. I had to kill him, he's one of them traitors coming way down here. You know Massachusetts is a long way from here."

Elijah looked over at the well pump where a group of men were filling their buckets with water for their canteens. He went over and asked, "Can I have some water ya'll?"

The men turned and gave him a look. Realizing he was not one of them, they shrugged and continued filling their buckets. Elijah was furious inside. He thought of going out and getting his pistol and ending it. He would kill as many as he could, before they could finish him off. After waiting a few moments, the men moved away with their buckets, so Elijah washed his face and soaked his head. He then took a drink, "Ahhh." He nervously looked around for his family. Where were they? He walked around the house but didn't see them. He started over to Dale's house and discovered Red lying dead on the dirt road. The dog had multiple stab wounds in his face and stomach area. Elijah dropped to the ground and wept. His heart and soul was broken as he saw Red's lifeless body. This was his faithful and loyal companion laying there. He had been at his side since he was a puppy. A friend he knew and loved for twelve long years. There he lay with white hair all around his muzzle. Old and dead. Elijah picked up his dog and carried him out to the barn. He looked around for a shovel.

Old Hound Dog

All the tools were gone except a broken hoe head. He gathered it up and went to digging a hole near the porch next to his dog's favorite place. He dug four feet deep and two feet wide. As he laid the dog into the cool ground and began covering it up, he said a little prayer. "God, I don't know if you let dogs in Paradise. But if they's somehow you will let me in, will you let my dog come in too please?" He patted down the dirt and stuck the hoe head it in. He found a rock and scratched "Ole Red" on the flat side of it.

He realized he was thirsty, thirstier than usual. It was because of his loss of blood. Elijah thought it could be because life had become a living hell. Yes indeed he was in a place of torment.

As he made his way over to Dale's house, he found his Grandmother and all of his family sitting around eating chicken. They had killed all nine of the remaining chickens for themselves, so the soldiers would not take the food from their mouths. Little Dale had crawled under the house with his food.

"Want some chicken, cousin Lijah" Little Molly asked as she stood in the doorway.

Danny looked as if he had been starved to death. He was so much skinnier than Elijah had remembered.

"Hey cuz," said Danny. "Come on in and git ya a bite. It's all we got." Uncle John said they took all ya'll had too." Elijah moved in and ate what was offered.

Danny said, "Boy, it's a good thing ya'll got that orchard over yonder at ya'lls house. We ain't gonna starve to death, we'll eat dem apples, pears, and peaches."

"I'm glad we got at least some crops in the ground," added Moses.

"The Lord finds a way to provide for his own," added Ester.

"Praise the Lord on that Ms. Ester," Gloria said.

"Pray the Lord," little Molly chimed in. Everyone laughed at the precious little blue eyed angel in their mist.

"Me and you ought to go plunder from them bastards," said Danny.

"Watch your mouth son, said Dale."

"Well me and Lijah ought to go get us some vengeance on them soldiers. Hadn't we Lijah?'"

Elijah looked at his favorite cousin and said "Danny, brother, I'm tired of this war. I'm tired of fighting.

Old Hound Dog

I ain't threw but one kick and that was 'cause they took my horse. His look saddened as he told them, they killed my buddy Red. I buried him at the house."

"James, the old black house butler, Samuel and a few more is dead. Samuel's son's dead. Shoot, they even killed our rooster, Rock. They took all our stuff. But they ain't took our lives and if we go attack them, that's what they gonna end up doing, taking our lives. Now God knows I wanted to get me a gun and commence to killing a crowd. And I was a hair from doing it, when I seen my dog dead."

John said, "They killed him last night as he ran at em and bit one. Ole Red died fighting," he added. "Let's just leave well enough alone and let them soldiers leave here. We shouldn't hold em up. I want to see em gone."

"Yeah, I reckon so," Danny said. "But if you want to, I got a rifle and a pistol back yonder in dem woods hind the house."

"Nah, we need them guns to help feed our family cuz," said Elijah. "Let's not waste a good bullet on them Yankees."

"You right, they ain't worth a bullet," said Danny. He reached and took a swallow of water.

It took a full four hours for all the wagons of men and animals to pass the Callahan's home. Elijah made his way up to the McCloud's house. The place was full of blue coats. Elijah saw Rachel near the doorway and called out to her.

She jumped up and rushed over to him. "She kissed him and tenderly touched his bruised face. She spoke in a whisper. "They've taken everything my father has, but I still have my jewelry box. I saw it this morning. I had to run an ugly Yankee out of my room. He stole my candy, the sorry no gooder. Anyway, I locked my door and went to the hiding spot and there it was. So you and I are okay. Sweetheart, do you hear me?"

Elijah was somewhat comforted to know his mother's ring was still in safekeeping. "You are smart, I'm glad you had me do that."

"Elijah, there you are, please come here a moment will you?" asked Henry.

Henry was standing at the entrance to his library, "Elijah, this is a General in the army. He is accusing me of torching my cotton gin. Rachel and I have repeatedly told him it was done by Samuel and his men. Which he and two others are now dead. He tells me a child will lie for her father."

The General looked at Elijah, "And who may you be young man?"

"I'm Elijah John Clark, Sir."

"Are you in rebellion also?" he asked.

"No sir, in fact, I gave up my horse to the Union Sir," said Elijah.

"That's well, for we do not tolerate rebels and others who show hostility. Now I've been told the only army in this area was a County Guard, who was organized to protect white people from slaves revolts were you part of that?" asked the General.

"Yes sir."

"It's a good thing. I'm not down here to free slaves or to play the Negro advocate. I have been sent to crush any resistance to the cause. I've been a military man for over twenty-five years. I hate a coward, for a coward is a man of no honor. I've tried to keep a tight rein on my soldiers under my command. I issued a field order for the districts and neighborhoods to ensure those who cooperate with the army will not have their property destroyed. But bush whackers have tried to stop our objectives. I gave word to my army commanders to be relentless in destroying the enemy and to forage liberally on any hostile people. Let me remind you, South Carolina was the first to start this rebellion, when they seceded. This state deserves the punishment she gets, and as I've said, I hate a coward. I believe Mr. McCloud tried to hide behind his fair daughter. I also believe he had the cotton gin set on fire so it would not fall into our possession. So I feel he has cheated the Union out of a contribution he could have made. My infantry have made up for some of that loss by taking his possessions. In doing so, it will ease the punishment that is to be dealt."

The General stood up and started making his way out of the library. "Clear this house of all human occupants," he commanded. He then made his way to the front porch and looked around. "It's a lovely place you have here Mr. McCloud." Rachel, Elijah and Henry followed out behind him. The General continued on down the huge steps. He placed his hat on his scruffy hair and receding hairline.

"Now Mr. McCloud, I pronounce you guilty of setting fire to that cotton gin and by doing so, you have deprived these slaves of, excuse me, these free Negros of some retribution." Once out in the yard away from the home, the General turned and looked back at the mansion shaking his head. "Yes sir, Mr. McCloud you and your family grew wealthy off of slave labor. Many soldiers have said it's a rich man's war and a poor man's fight. Well, before this is all over and done with, I want you to walk in a poor man's shoes.

I wish I could say a slave shoes, but they very rarely have shoes, thanks to people such as you."

"Now hold on," said Henry, "I don't and haven't ever abused my servants, they all got shoes, if the need is there."

The General looked at Henry and smiled, then continued, "Listen, there's three white men buried back near your burnt down gin and four Negros. I think you not only burned it but tried to murder the slaves so we wouldn't find out the truth."

"That's a lie," said Rachel. "Samuel burned it, and I told you so."

"Well, little lady, all the witnesses seem to be dead? How about you there?"

"It's Clark," said Elijah.

"Oh yes, forgive me Mr. Clark, did you see this? Did you see Samuel's men start a fire?"

"I can't say I did, but they said they was going to and away they went."

"Stop, enough of your testimony. You said, you could not say, in your beginning words, so I'm afraid there's no concrete evidence."

He then turned to the slaves. "You all are free to go. If you are to travel with my army, do not hinder our march. You can carry your own provisions. The Lieutenant walked over and began explaining the situation to them. The General turned around again and said, "Now Mr. McCloud, you could be held prisoner right now, but that's too good for you, I don't need you eating up our provisions since the armies are in need of them. So I will leave you here with a reminder that you never will forget. Tell your grandchildren what happens when one becomes a traitor against the ones who feed, clothe and have given them their freedom. Yes, that's right, your freedom, freedom of a Union, Freedom of the United States of America."

"The house is clear Sir," shouted a soldier. With that, the General gave a command. "Burn it to the ground!"

At once the soldiers began throwing the lanterns into windows and open doors. The flames began to roar, as the oil splattered and splashed.

"No," screamed Rachel, as she ran to the front door about to enter when one of the soldiers grabbed her and pulled her back.

Elijah stepped up and took her into his arms lifting her from her feet and pulling her away from the blazing house. "Please Rachel, calm down, the jewelry will just melt and we can search through it and get it back.

Old Hound Dog

"Move out," the General yelled, as he climbed onto his horse. Most of the soldiers mounted their horses, but several stood around the house to prevent anyone from trying to enter. Of all the slaves only five stayed with the McClouds. Mary, Delilah, the twins, Mark and Matthew and their mother, Helen. They felt they had no other place to go. The flames grew intense. Even the soldiers backed away. The entire first floor of the mansion was engulfed in flames. Glass was heard breaking. Sobbing franticly, Rachel buried her face in Elijah's chest. Henry just sat on the grass and looked on as if he was in a horrid Armageddon.

"Elijah, our rings are in there. Our wedding rings. My grandfather's ring I gave you and your mother's ring you gave me."

When the soldiers finally departed, Elijah turned to Rachel and told her "I'm going to get your box." He ran to the chimney and began climbing just as he had done so many times to reach Rachel's room. Once he got to Rachel's window, he climbed inside. The walls were being consumed by the raging flames. He grabbed the spread from Rachel's bed and began beating back the flames near her closet door. As he entered the closet, flames were bursting forth from the floor. Clothes were on fire. The smoke began choking him. His eyes watered. He tossed the large comforter on the floor to try and extinguish the flames that were bursting through.

He threw the boards aside that covered the jewelry box. Flames were all around the box. There was no time to think, he reached in and grabbed it. The box was red hot. His skin fried. He could smell the burnt flesh odor. He barely felt the pain, because of his thick calloused hands. He realized his hands were stuck to the metal. He rushed over to the window and yelled I got it. He held it up. Rachel began jumping up and down waving her hands yelling for him to come down. He had to free his hands. The flames were consuming her room. He ripped the flesh from his hands, freeing them so he would be able to climb. He flung the jewelry box out toward her. She went over to pick it up and immediately felt the heat the box was still emitting.

After tossing the box, he heard the floor break and felt it move beneath him. He reached for the window, but fell backwards into the open space where the second floor had collapsed in. As he dropped he knew it was the end. In a flash, he felt the intense burning combustion. Then he saw a light, a light which was brighter than the flames themselves. In the light was Rachel's face, a face of an angel.

Old Hound Dog

Outside Rachel looked over and ran to see if her love was crawling down the chimney. But there was no Roachman, no Flyman, no Spiderman, and no Romeo. She looked up fearing the worst. She began screaming as the roof caved in. The whole top floor then exploded in flames and collapsed.

When its destructive force struck bottom, a huge fire filled whirl wind twisted from the wreckage and shot skyward. The sight blazed up into the heavens like a flamed tornado and disappeared as quickly as it appeared.

Delilah looked and pointed "Did you sees dat fire go to heaven?"

Mary saw it and so did Rachel and Henry. The house continued to burn hot for another six hours.

Rachel lay in the grass staring up into the heavens and holding the box next to her body.

Henry was aimlessly poking around at spots where the smoke still puffed. The twins had sticks doing the same. Delilah Helen and Mary sat cracking pecans, the last remnants of food they could find. They cracked two full pails.

Danny and Pamela were the first kin folk of Elijah's to arrive on the scene.

"Rachel, where's Lijah?" Danny cried out.

She turned her head ever so slowly and looked at him with swollen eyes and tear stained cheeks. Her eyes were blood shot from all the crying. She broke out sobbing again and gave out a wrenching cry, "He's gone, he's gone, Danny. He died in the house. He burned up, God, he burned up."

Pamela moved closer to her as she wept. She put her arms around her and hugged her friend gently. Pamela began weeping with Rachel.

Danny looked to the sky. "No, No, Please don't tell me that, no, no God, no please no. How did it happen? Did them Yankees kill him and throw my cousin in the fire, he asked. Did they? Please tell me."

"Rachel began telling him, "No, he went into the burning house to get my jewelry box out of the fire. He never made it out. I saw him when he tossed it down to me and it hit the ground. I went over to retrieve it and when I looked up, he was gone."

"A damn jewelry box? He risked his life to git a jewelry box? " He ran into that burnin' fire for a box," he kept repeating. Danny was beyond himself searching for answers.

"Yes, his mother's ring and my mother's ring are in it.

Old Hound Dog

We were going to let the place burn down and retrieve the melted jewelry later, but he did not want to lose his mother's ring which he gave to me for marriage," she quickly explained.

"Ain't that romantic?" said Pamela.

"Romantic my ass, my cuz done killed himself over some damn rings."

Danny walked to the pecan tree kicking it, swearing and then began sobbing. After a good cry, he said to Rachel, "Rachel, I'm sorry. That was pretty nice of Old Hound Dog. I was his Old Coon Dog cousin and I called him Old Hound Dog. He moved over to the girls, as he wept."

Pamela got up and went to comfort him. "God, that's bad. It's gonna kill Uncle John, Mr. Moses and Ms. Ester. Lord that old woman and man might die when they learn what happened to Elijah. God I can't believe it."

"You Old Hound Dog, why'd you run off and leave me?" Danny asked while looking up at the sky.

"Look at this," said Rachel. She showed them Elijah's handprints that had been burned into the jewelry box. The lid had Elijah's thumb prints, the sides had an impression of his palm and the bottom displayed his eight remaining finger prints.

Afterwards

Everyone helped and searched through McCloud's burned mansion, removing all the charred wood, metals, glass, tile and stone, but never found a trace of Elijah's remains. Ester continued long after others gave up. She searched for many months. One day she finally stopped. When asked why, she said she had a dream that her grandbaby came to see her on a chariot of fire and told her he was alright.

Moses passed away in 1876. Ester followed exactly one year later on the same day. John found her body propped up against his father's tombstone. She had flowers in her hands.

Dale felt really bad for John and asked Danny and Pamela to move in with him for a while. John gave Danny half of his tobacco crop and Danny started up a small tobacco company that specialized in pipe and chewing tobacco. He named his pipe blend "Elijah's Enjoyment".

Henry had a fortune in Tate's bank. When Tate learned that the Union soldiers were headed to Laurel Hill, he had the majority of the bank's money placed in Richmond's Lake. The lake was near a machine shop that produced gun parts for the Confederates.

After Sherman's army passed through, he recovered the money and gave Henry about seventy-five percent of his original deposit, claiming the Union Soldiers had stole the rest.

Henry built a small three bedroom brick home in front of the mansion about one hundred yards closer to the road. He lived there alone until he died.

Henry gave Mary, Delilah, Helen, Mark and Matthew the money he had set aside for James. They used it to move to Gibson, where Delilah grew up to be one of the first teachers at Fredrick Douglas School for African Americans. Matthew and Mark both became preachers. They organized two churches for blacks, a Methodist Church in Gibson and a Baptist Church in Laurel Hill.

Rachel went north and wasn't seen in the area again until the end of World War II. She came back to the plantation site with her great grandson. Rachel felt it was important to show the young man where she and his great grandfather grew up. As the two of them walked a freshly plowed field, an adjacent land owner yelled, "Hey there, you're trespassing." The two kept walking. The neighbor marched across the field following them.

Afterwards

When he caught up to them, he said, "You people are trespassing on Willard Gibson's property. You need to go now."

"Well, Sir, my grandmother claims she lived here during the days of the Civil War," the young man replied. The man was curious and asked Rachel, "You say you use to live here?"

She looked at him and said "Yes, my father had a mansion that sat right there." Both men looked in the direction she pointed. Weeds, vines and all types of trees covered the area. The old woman continued walking with her cane tapping it until it struck something hard. "Come, wipe me off a seat Elijah," she said. The young man rushed over to his great grandmother's side and discovered a huge set of stone steps. He removed the foliage that obscured the foundation and the remains of the burned down house. The old woman looked up at her offspring, "This was the McCloud Plantation."

"Wow," said the neighbor. "I've lived here for thirty years and didn't know this place was here."

"Yeah, I wanted to forget about it myself until that horrible World War started up and reminded me of it all over again."

"Good grief ma'am, how old are you?" He asked.

"I'm 102 years old Mister," she answered.

"I am Rachel Ann Clark and this is my great grandson, Elijah John Clark. He's my favorite. He's got his great grandfather's name and his beautiful black hair too."

Rachel then asked, "Who did you say this land belonged to?" "Willard Gibson," the man answered.

"Well, the land I'm walking on is my land. I've paid taxes on this property for eighty years. When my father gave me half of his fortune, I left this place. I hate it for what it took from me. But deep in my heart, I also love this place for what it gave me."

Just before Sherman's men came through, Elijah and Rachel had secretly married each other. They put their cherished rings on each other's fingers and pledged their love to one another. They recited their vows while placing their hands on the Bible. It was on that night that Rachel finally succeeded in seducing Elijah and they promised God they would love each other forever. Before Elijah left Rachel's room, they put their rings back into the jewelry box and returned the box to its hiding place in the closet for safe keeping.

Afterwards

Within days after the mansion's destruction, Rachel, who did not know she was carrying Elijah's baby, moved to Boston with her brother Michael. She gave birth to a son whom she named Elijah Henry Clark. Her son was the grandfather of the young man who traveled with her.

Revisiting the site where she lost the love of her life proved to be too hard on Rachel. It was later that very night, Rachel too passed away. She was at the home of Danny and Pamela's daughter, Molly, when she died in her sleep.

Meet the Author

Joseph Sheppard is of Native American and Anglo American descent. He grew up in Scotland County, North Carolina where General Sherman's Army marched through on their return route up North.

Joseph has a wide range of interests. His hobbies include painting, sculpting, drawing and Native American Arts and Crafts. He has a strong belief in a Creator. His passion for the arts, life, family, friends, animals, and especially the earth has helped shape his value system.

His love of music, sports and storytelling is portrayed throughout his writings. He has written more than thirty manuscripts in many different genres making him a unique and amazing writer.

33744102R00141

Made in the USA
Middletown, DE
28 July 2016